PATERNOSTER

AN EDEN GREY MYSTERY

KIM FLEET

PATERNOSTER

AN EDEN GREY MYSTERY

The
Mystery
Press

To Mike,
for everything

Original cover photograph © iStockphoto

This is a work of fiction. Any similarity with real persons,
organisations or events is entirely coincidental.

First published 2015

The Mystery Press is an imprint of The History Press
The Mill, Brimscombe Port
Stroud, Gloucestershire, GL5 2QG
www.thehistorypress.co.uk

British Library Cataloguing in Publication Data.
A catalogue record for this book is available from the British Library.

ISBN 978 0 7509 6368 8

Typesetting and origination by The History Press
Printed in Great Britain

PROLOGUE

Thursday, 1 November 2012

01:19 hours

The warehouse was gloomy, haunted by shadows and strange splashes as unseen objects bumped against the dock. Fog slunk in off the Thames and picked at Jackie's bones. She tugged her jacket tighter, the ends of her fingers numb with cold. Impatient, she rasped her thumb against her index finger. Her cuticles were nibbled to rags.

Soon it would all be over. She dreamed of sleeping in her own bed at last, desperate to scram from the hostel she'd called home for too long. Her own toasty bed and a good meal. Steak and chips and a creamy pepper sauce. She'd been starving herself for months, creating the jutting collarbone, pallid skin and skinny arse of a heroin addict. It'd worked: they all thought she was shooting up. She sighed loudly.

'Give it a rest, Jackie,' growled one of the men. A thick bull's neck, his bald head jutting forwards. Known to his friends as Dave the Nutter.

Jackie flicked two fingers at him. 'Piss off, Dave.'

'Bitch,' Nutter muttered.

'Why can't we have more lights?' A chewed-string bit of man-boy, sitting on a packing case. A book of wordsearch puzzles lay in his lap. In one hand he clutched a blue inhaler. Nineteen, with the mental age of a pork pie.

'So's you can do your puzzles?' Nutter said, cracking his knuckles. Each finger was freighted with a sovereign ring.

'Wha's wrong wi' that?' Chewed-string boy said, his Scots accent plaintive.

'Little Jimmy wants his colouring book.'

'Don't call me that.'

'Come over here, Jimmy,' Jackie said, 'sit with me.'

He dragged the crate over. 'Thanks, Jackie.'

'Don't annoy Nutter, eh?' Last thing she wanted was him going off on one his tantrums. Could cost her the whole operation.

She ran her hand over her head: her scalp prickled. She'd shaved her head on one side, with a long piece hanging down beside the other cheek. When this was over, she'd shave the lot off and grow her hair back again. Well fed, a proper hairstyle: she'd be a different woman. Just a few hours left to go.

'When's the lorry coming, Hammond?' she said, quietly.

Hammond stepped into the light. Tall, with fair hair, his dark suit bespoke, his jaw professionally barbered. Good looking, the sort of man you could take home to meet your mum, if you didn't care where his money came from. Hammond had charm in spades when he wanted.

'Got a date, have you, Jackie?' he said, smoothly. 'Somewhere you'd rather be?'

Jackie cast a glance round the warehouse. 'Nowhere I'd rather be, Boss. Just getting cold, s'all.'

God, she'd be glad to see the back of the gang. She hadn't had a break from them for ages. All that leave was piling up and she was going to take it. A holiday somewhere hot; sandy beaches; a stack of paperbacks to dive into. She could be there in a few days, soaking up the sun and letting the past two years melt away.

They fell silent again. Far off, a police siren howled and receded. Closer, there was a splash of water. And coming closer still, an engine.

'Put the lights on,' Hammond ordered. 'No fuck-ups this time. Remember what happened to the Russian.'

Dave the Nutter yanked the handle and the warehouse flooded with light. They blinked at the sudden brightness, and turned towards the wide doors. A lorry chugged outside.

'Let them in, Jackie,' Hammond said.

Jackie heaved one door open, then the other. Outside, the night was inky black. The lorry extinguished its lights and rolled past her into the warehouse. She slid the doors closed behind it as Hammond, Dave the Nutter and Little Jimmy sprang to open the back.

The driver jumped down from the cab and helped them unload case after case, stacking them in a pile at the back of the warehouse. Jackie cranked open the cases and checked the contents, hefting out weapons and weighing them in her hands. As she lifted the lids on the crates, she gave a verbal audit.

'Semi-automatic, twelve cases of twenty. Handguns one hundred. Ground assault anti-aircraft four.' She paused. 'Hey, weren't there supposed to be six of these?'

The driver shrugged and swore. 'Our supplier couldn't get them,' he said in a thick Eastern European accent. 'He sends more Russian automatics instead. Plus some grenades, with his compliments.'

Hammond gave a short, mirthless laugh. 'So that's how he trades with me, is it?' He approached the driver and grabbed his chin. 'Then you give him this, with my compliments.' A knife slashed across the driver's face. He fell back, clutching his cheek, blood pouring between his fingers, screaming a torrent of abuse.

Jackie lurched forwards, remembered herself, and halted, her heart banging. Let it soon be over.

'Yes, yes, but none of us speaks monkey here,' Hammond said mildly, wiping the blade on the driver's coat. 'You tell him he double-crosses me again, and I'll do to him what I did to the Russian. Understand?'

The driver's eyes widened in fear. 'I understand,' he said. 'The Russian. I know. I tell him, my Boss. I make him understand.' He gulped and glanced round the warehouse. His eyes rested on Jackie.

Hammond saw the direction of his gaze. 'You like that, eh? You want some?'

'I mean no disrespect, she is yours,' the driver said, backing away, his hand pressed to his face.

Hammond laughed. 'Yes, she is. But you can do me a favour. I have a problem.'

Dave the Nutter straightened and glanced at Hammond. 'Boss?'

'One of my little team has got above themselves,' Hammond said. 'Thought they could double-cross me.'

Nutter swallowed. 'What you talking about?'

'Someone's been a little piggy and gone squealing to the police about our business venture.'

Little Jimmy was on his feet. 'It wasn't me! I swear it wasn't me.'

'Shut up, Jimmy. I know my little piggy, and there'll be no more roast beef for her, though she may go wee wee wee all the way home.'

The gang stilled.

'She?' Little Jimmy said.

Hammond clapped once, twice, three times. 'He gets it. Give him a chocolate watch.' He stopped in front of Jackie. 'How long have you been with me?'

She met his eyes, fighting down panic. 'Couple of years?'

'A couple of years.' Hammond turned away. 'In it together, I thought, but it seems I was wrong.' He whipped round and struck her across the face with the back of his hand. Her head snapped back and she staggered. 'Take her,' he ordered.

The men hesitated.

'Take her!' Hammond shouted. 'She's going on a little journey.'

Nutter sprang forwards and pinned Jackie's hands behind her back. The truck driver dragged a rope from one of the crates and bound her arms to her sides.

'You've got it wrong, Boss,' she said, kicking as the rope looped her body. 'I'd never cheat on you.'

'Very convincing, Jackie, but I know better.' He advanced on her. 'You won't have long, but I'd like you to have something to remember me by.'

The knife flashed as he swung it to and fro in front of her eyes. She tracked its arc, left to right and back again, and trembled with fear. He suspended the knife in front of her a moment longer, then slowly sliced across her arms, high up on the biceps. A slice across each thigh. Blood soaked through her jeans, and ran down her arms to her palms.

'Boss, you've got this wrong, truly,' she said, wildly. She struggled against the ropes as the blade flashed again.

'I don't think so, Jackie,' Hammond said, and plunged the knife into her stomach. Her knees buckled and she fell Her face ground against the cement floor as she writhed in pain, each breath agony.

'She'll last a little while before she bleeds to death,' Hammond said. 'Long enough for her to repent of her actions.' He motioned to Nutter. 'Put her in the truck. Our friend here is going to repay the favour he owes me.'

The driver started to say something, then stopped. Drops of blood fell from his face on to the floor. Her blood joined his, her life pumping out.

'You take her away from here, somewhere quiet, and toss her into the river,' Hammond said. 'And don't make a mess of it. Understand?'

The driver muttered something she couldn't make out. Her ears rang with her own heartbeat. She heard the cab door open and the engine start. Nutter dragged her across the floor,

Her hair was grown out into a crop by the time she was called to trial. She'd long ago left the hospital and been transferred to a safe house, guarded by a different set of policemen. She itched to be free of them, to start her life again. Eating proper meals and sleeping a solid eight hours a night had transformed her. Gone were her pallor and the bruises round her eyes. Gone, too, the stick arms and legs. Slowly she'd built up her muscles again, lifting cans of soup until she was strong enough to get to a gym. The policemen came jogging with her. It was safest to go at night, and that winter they pounded the streets in nobody-town where nobody knew her, and slowly she became herself again. Whoever she was, now.

When she walked into court, she was in a dark trouser suit and high heels, her chin tilted up. She met John Hammond's eyes as she took the stand and swore to tell the truth. When the judge told her she could sit to give her evidence, she did so, her shoulders held back and her thumb rasping against her fingers. John Hammond and Dave the Nutter occupied the dock just yards away. Their barristers sat in line like boys waiting to be called into the headmaster. Their strategy seemed to be to pour the blame on to the others and to paint their clients as misguided innocents.

She drew deep breaths every time she answered a question. Her training held firm. Even when she was asked to repeat what had happened that night, how she'd been cut, who did what to her. Even when Hammond's barrister rose to his feet, twitched his gown, stared at her over the top of his spectacles and commenced his interrogation with, 'You infiltrated the gang?'

'Yes.'

'And you took drugs?'

'Yes.'

'That was part of your …' he waved his hand as though searching for a word. '… Cover?'

'Yes.'

'You were an addict?'

'No.'

'No? But you took heroin?'

'When I had to.'

'When you had to. I see. And you'd taken heroin before this alleged incident took place?'

'Yes.'

'Could your drug taking have affected your perception? How sure are you that you saw what you claimed to see? Or was it all a product of your febrile imagination?'

Jackie sucked in a deep breath. 'I wasn't under the influence of any drug when I was attacked.'

'Yet tests done on your blood and hair indicate that you had taken drugs.'

'Not recently. But during my time with the gang, yes, I took drugs to show I was one of them.'

'Did you ever see John Hammond take drugs?'

'No.'

'No?' The barrister peeped again over his glasses and play-acted astonishment. 'Then why did you take drugs, when the gang's leader did not?'

'The others in the gang, the subservient ones, did so. I did the same. It meant I could go unchallenged for two years.'

'Yet you were challenged, weren't you?' A flap of a piece of paper. It could have been a shopping list, it was just a prop. 'They found you out. I put it to you that it was your incompetence that precipitated that incident.'

'No.'

'You got too comfortable with your role in the gang, and you broke the rules, didn't you?'

'I did what I thought was necessary.'

'Your own training manual doesn't say anything about taking drugs in order to pass as a gang member. Had you taken drugs before?'

Her armpits were swampy. 'At university. Once or twice.'

'Once or twice at university.' His voice dropped. 'No one condones what happened to you. But I put it to you that your methods were unorthodox. You went native and jeopardised a long running operation.' He pointed at her across the courtroom. 'You were not authorised to take the actions you took, were you?'

'Objection, my lord. Bullying the witness.' The prosecution barrister woke up and made a desultory attempt to get things back on track. They had enough evidence to convict. Hammond's barrister was doing what he was paid for, having a go, and trying to take her down with him. She was finished.

The judge released her at the end of the cross-examination, and she crept from the courtroom, humiliated.

Her heels clattered down the hallway and she shoved through a wooden door into the Ladies. Her face was ghostly in the purplish light: years before, the first time she'd attended court, she'd queried it and been informed that the light prevented drug takers from finding a vein. The cisterns were bolted shut, too. No hiding packages in there.

Jackie jumped when the door banged behind her.

'You OK?' Her boss, Miranda Tyson, kicked open the door to each stall, checking for eavesdroppers. 'You had a rough ride in there. Tosser.'

'He's doing his job,' Jackie said, running a bowl of cold water and splashing her face. She dabbed it dry with a paper towel and said frankly, 'I'm finished, aren't I?'

'No.' Miranda hitched her bum against a basin. Her nails were painted navy and a huge tiger's eye ring dominated her middle finger. 'When do you want to come back to work?'

'Undercover?'

Miranda shook her head. 'You're outed, sweetie.' As Jackie started to protest, she said, 'It's not the drugs. I understand all that. Been there myself.'

'I never injected. Smoked, yes. I could control that.'

'I know. But you've taken a pounding, and two years under-cover is enough for now. Try something new. There's plenty to get your teeth into.' She leaned into Jackie and said in a tempt-ing, sing-song voice, 'Mobile phone cash transaction fraud.'

Jackie wrinkled her nose.

'Hey, don't diss it. International transactions, links to terror-ism. Could be a scoop.'

Jackie tossed the paper towel into the bin.

Miranda studied her. 'I could arrange a secondment, if you like. Five expressed an interest.'

'Five?' MI5, the Security Service. 'Agent running?'

'No. But casework. You'd be good. They've asked for you to design some training for their rookies, too.'

'What about Six?'

'You don't want to work for those wankers,' Miranda said. 'They all think they're James Bond, comparing willies all day long.' She paused, 'You'd have a bigger willy than any of them. They wouldn't like it.'

'I'll think about it.'

'You coming back in? Watch the rest of the trial?'

'Maybe.'

'Shame you missed the first day,' Miranda said. 'James Little gave evidence while you were holed up in the witness room.'

'Little Jimmy?' Jackie cast her mind to the skinny Scot with his love of puzzle books. 'I heard he pleaded guilty.'

He'd already been sentenced; was already serving time in some Victorian monstrosity that retained its hanging shed.

'He did. He also testified against the gang.'

'Hell.' Her guts crunched at the thought of how much cour-age that must've taken.

'Spilled the beans about it all. What the gang was up to, where the guns were headed, the whole lot.' Miranda scrutinised herself in the mirror and smoothed her fingertip along a wrinkle beside her eye. 'And how he sneaked out of that warehouse and called the police. Told them what Hammond had planned for you. Even gave them the number plate. It's down to him they found you so quickly.'

'What?' Jackie felt a stone in her stomach.

Miranda turned to face her. 'Little Jimmy saved your life.'

Jackie couldn't face the courtroom again that day. She wandered the London streets, dazed, barely aware of the hustle on the pavements and stink of hot bodies on the Tube. The Thames flowed by, brown and unperturbed, deprived of her corpse but sated with others. She turned her back on it and headed into the city, and lost herself in the litter and lights and crocodiles of European school kids sporting identical backpacks.

She lurked at the back of the court to hear the summing up, and was there when the jury returned guilty verdicts against both defendants. Dave the Nutter was sentenced to twelve years. He jabbed his arms through the bars of the dock and swore at the judge, threatening to kill him. The judge didn't bat an eyelid, just intoned, 'Take him down,' with a yawn.

Dave the Nutter's invective echoed behind him as the prison guards yanked him down the steps to the cells.

John Hammond was expressionless as the judge sentenced him to life imprisonment. He lifted his head and his gaze scoured the packed courtroom as Nutter's footsteps receded. Jackie cowered down in her seat. Hammond's eyes locked on hers, and he drew his finger across his throat.

Then they led him away and she started to breathe again.

CHAPTER
ONE

Monday, 23 February 2015

08:16 hours

The target house was on the opposite side of the street. A red-brick semi, in a part of Cheltenham where all the roads were named after poets. Wide, tree-studded pavements surged with mothers, kids and pushchairs on the school run.

Eden Grey lowered the car window. Chill air gusted into the car, carrying the children's babble on its wings. She waited for a cohort to rumble past, then lifted the camera to the open window, adjusted the focus, and rattled off a series of shots. A white van was parked outside the target house, the logo of its former owner a spectre looming over its new identity: Wilde About Gardens. A website and mobile phone number were written in green swirling text underneath a drawing of a tree and flower. Eden closed in on the website and mobile number, and the shutter snapped.

A woman came into view, herding along three children on scooters. Eden shoved her camera under a newspaper and adjusted the car's heater until they were out of sight.

'Come on,' she muttered. 'Time for work.'

As if he'd heard her, a man came out of the target house. He was in his early fifties and had a flat bottom and saggy jeans like the back end of an elephant. A Christmas pudding bobble hat was tugged down over thick grey hair. A woman in a quilted dressing gown appeared in the doorway behind him, planted a standard eight-pound pressure kiss on his lips, then waved as he clambered into the van and drove away.

Eden gave him a few seconds' headstart, then slipped in the clutch and followed.

She almost lost him at the junction. He hurtled out in front of a bus coming from the right, and a BMW from the left. The BMW driver made the international hand signal for 'wanker' and flashed his lights. The van tore up the road with a belch of blue smoke from the exhaust.

Eden waited at the junction, tracking the van with her eyes, drumming her fingers on the steering wheel. She'd lose him at this rate. If only one of these cars would let her out. She sighed with a pang for the glory days, hurtling round the streets with the lights flashing and the siren blaring, the comforting heft of a gun tucked in her side.

Someone let her out and she hit the accelerator. The van had turned left into a housing estate, a maze of identical houses. Damn! She could waste the morning trawling round trying to hunt him down in there. Her heart sank at the prospect of another morning lurking outside the target's house; all the windows in the street had Neighbourhood Watch stickers.

Her luck was in. Rounding a corner, she caught sight of the van. Surging ahead, she followed it through the warren until it drew up outside a large detached house. She slowed and drove past, parked up at the end of the street, slung her camera round her neck, and walked back, keeping the target in view.

Christmas pudding man had the back of the van open and was lugging out bags of compost.

'Bad back, is it, sunshine?' Eden said to herself. Ducking behind a car, she raised the camera and took thirty shots of him hauling out compost. Inching closer, she scouted round for a good viewpoint, somewhere she wouldn't be seen. There was a house ahead, curtains and blinds closed, no cars in the driveway. A good bet the owners were out. Perfect. She clipped up the street and ducked behind the gate. From there, she had an excellent view of the van and the target.

She kept the camera trained on him as he heaved ceramic pots and paving slabs from the back of the van, recording every move. He wasn't the sort of scumbag that used to be her prey – the pimps, drug dealers, gun runners and general forgers of misery – that was over now. Now it was insurance frauds and cheating husbands. Eden sighed. You can't go back, she reminded herself. Jackie's dead, remember? But the weight of Jackie's ghost pressed on her shoulders.

A woman with a toddler turned the corner ahead of her, their voices high on the fresh February air. The little girl had on a red duffel coat and pink shoes, and was clutching her mother's hand, chattering.

'That's right, Molly,' the woman said.

Molly. Eden's head snapped round. Molly. Her heart clenched. The girl was too young to be her, and she had blond hair. She'd always imagined Molly with dark hair, but the name snagged her, and familiar grief started to simmer deep in her mind.

She shrank back as the woman and child drew level. Her eyes met the girl's; she smiled, and Molly smiled back.

It happened in an instant. A cry of 'pussy cat!', a flash of a red coat, brakes squealing. 'Molly!'

Then Eden was across the road, her arms snatching up the girl, and the two of them landed heavily on the pavement.

Eden sat up, wincing. 'You all right, sweetheart?'

'I've bumped my head!' Molly cried.

'Let me see. Oh dear, you have got a bump. I'm sorry, sweetie.'

'There was a cat,' Molly said, tears brimming in her eyes. Eden glanced round. An ugly orange cat perched on a wall nearby, licking its tail.

'Molly! Are you hurt?' Molly's mother ran across the road and gathered her into her arms. She stroked the blond locks back from her head, examining the bump. She turned to Eden, 'Are you OK? How did you … thank God … thank you.'

Eden scrambled to her feet, testing herself for injuries. Luckily the camera was on a neck strap and had been shielded by her body as she landed. She unwound it from her neck and inspected it, relieved to find it wasn't broken. She couldn't afford a new camera. The car was due its MOT soon and she was already praying it would pass, knowing in her heart it wouldn't.

The driver of the car and Chris Wilde hurried across.

'She all right?' the driver asked. 'I nearly died when she ran out like that.' He turned to Eden. 'Where the hell did you come from?'

'She was hiding,' Molly said. 'She's taking photos.'

Chris Wilde rounded on her. 'What are you doing here?'

'I'm a private detective,' she said, trying to remain calm. 'I'm collecting evidence for a client.'

'What sort of evidence?'

'It's confidential.'

'We'll see about that.' Wilde snatched the camera from her hands and flicked through the photos she'd taken. Shit, she was outed now. The camera had days' worth of evidence.

Chris Wilde's face blossomed red. 'They're all of me,' he said. 'Hundreds of photos of me.'

'Give it back.'

'That's my house, and my van,' he said. Furious, he barked, 'What the fuck are you up to?'

'Give it back. I won't tell you again.' Each word was a rattle of bullets.

He snorted in her face and held the camera above his head. 'I could smash this right now.'

Eden took a step back and sized him up. He had four inches and maybe five stone in weight on her. Then again, she had twenty years on him, and she ran six miles three times a week. Wilde was still sweating and puffing from the effort of unloading his van.

In one movement she leapt and grabbed his wrist, twisting and ducking as she brought his arm round and high up behind his back, his hand bent backwards. She bent it back an inch further, feeling the tension flex. One tap on his elbow and his arm would snap.

Wilde screamed, 'Let go of me, bitch!'

She prised the camera from his hand and let him go. He stumbled back, rubbing his arm. 'Fucking lunatic.'

She looked down at Molly. 'You OK now, sweetheart? You're a brave girl.'

Eden turned and stalked back to her car, clutching the camera to her chest, aware they were watching her every step. She slid into the driver's seat and started the engine, thumping the steering wheel as she drove away. The operation was blown.

08:57 hours

Christ knew what she'd tell the client. There was no way she could report to him in this state. Her jeans were torn, her head thumped and her wrist was swelling up. She headed home: an art deco flat in a block near the centre of Cheltenham. The block was dun coloured with curving balconies; a swathe of lawn puddled round the block, guarded by stately cedars. She'd lived there for two years and loved its wide windows and aura of more sophisticated times, half expecting a glimpse of a flapper sipping a cocktail and twirling a rope of pearls each time she let herself in. Her flat was on the second floor. She trudged up the stairs, aching as though she'd been beaten up. She'd fallen hard on her shoulder when she dived across the road.

She paused outside her door, listening. There was no one in the corridor, the only sound the distant thrum of a radio on

been converted from residential dwellings, their once elegant front gardens concreted over and clotted with executive cars.

At the reception desk, she asked for Paul Nelson's PA, and was told to wait. A man in a suit strolled past her, clutching a coffee carton. As he drew level, he nodded hello, then his gaze dropped to her legs, and her short kilt riding on her thighs. She uncrossed and recrossed her legs, smirking when he spilled hot coffee over his fingers.

'Eden?' Janice, Paul's PA, stood before her: short and sturdy, in an immaculate trouser suit and with a wayward lilac streak in her white hair that indicated she had a wild side, you just weren't going to witness it during working hours. 'Sorry to keep you waiting.'

'Only just got here,' Eden said, and followed Janice to the lift up to Paul's office. Janice swung the door wide and ushered Eden inside. As always, Eden was struck by the size of the room. She could fit most of her flat in its square footage. It was tricked out in beige and cream with flashes of cinnamon, so tasteful she imagined he'd seen a picture in a magazine and had simply said, 'I'll have that.'

Despite the modern décor, Paul's desk was antique mahogany – huge, dark and imposing – the sort of desk where peace treaties are signed. His laptop lay open on the desk, alongside a silver pen tray that held a fountain pen and a silver propelling pencil.

Paul, in grey suit trousers and red braces, rose as she entered and came round from behind his desk to shake her hand. He had an athletic build, and sandy hair that was just starting to recede in two scoops from his forehead. In his early fifties, he was still a good-looking man, with an air of authority about him that wasn't entirely down to the massive desk and executive chair.

'Eden, great to see you again. Take a seat.' He motioned her to a seat opposite him then turned to his PA. 'Could we have some coffee, please, Janice?'

Paul was the president of a development firm that specialised in converting historic buildings to new uses. The shell would be retained, in some cases just the façade held up by hydraulics while the remainder was demolished and rebuilt. It preserved the ambience of an area, kept the beauty of the old and installed the convenience of the new, he had explained to her when she first met him. The best of both worlds. She'd seen one of his projects: a wall, the face of a building, like a film set, with nothing behind it.

Paul resumed his seat behind his desk. Though impeccably groomed, his skin was greyish at the temples and there were blue smudges beneath his eyes.

'You've got something for me?' he asked. She caught him frowning as he looked at the bruise on her face, a shadow lurking beneath the makeup, but he was too polite to mention it.

Eden slid the folder across the desk to him. He picked it up and shook out the thumb drive.

'All the photographs I took are on there,' Eden explained.

Paul leafed through the report, skim-reading it. He put it down when Janice came in with the coffee: an elegant silver coffee pot, white cups and saucers edged in gold. Eden suppressed a sigh. If only she had more clients like Paul. Once this was done, business was going to be slack with just surveillance on a cheating spouse on her books. That wouldn't keep her in chocolate hobnobs.

'So, what have we got here?' Paul said.

'It appears that Chris Wilde is running a gardening business,' Eden said. 'I saw him lifting compost and pots out of a van. He's got a logo on the van, with his name, and a website. I checked the website: he claims he handles all sorts of garden work, from building patios to erecting garden sheds, plus general maintenance and landscaping.'

Paul snorted.

'There are a number of client testimonials dating back about four years,' she continued. 'It could be that he's been running it as a sideline. However, I ran a financial check on his business and he's been bringing in reasonable money through it for the past six months.' She paused to sip her coffee. 'I'm sorry, Paul. It looks like he's faking the bad back.'

'Not your problem.'

'It's pretty horrible when you find out someone's lying to you, though.'

'He's worked here for eight years,' Paul said. 'I'll give him a chance to explain, obviously, but between us I doubt he'll still be on the payroll this time next week.'

Eden paused. 'There was a problem when I was collecting evidence this morning. Wilde saw me, and he knows that I've been taking photos of him.' She briefly explained about the child running into the road. 'Wilde probably realises the game is up. If you're thinking of taking action to protect your interests, I recommend you act sooner rather than later.'

'What do you mean?'

'If Wilde hands in his notice now, while he's still on sick leave, he'll be entitled to his pension. If you sack him for faking a bad back, he'll lose his pension.'

Paul whistled. 'That's why I hire you, Eden, you've got a devious mind. You've probably just saved me thousands. I'll see Chris Wilde today, if possible.'

'I'm sorry about the stuff up,' Eden said, 'and sorry it's forced your hand.'

Paul waved her apologies away. 'Probably best in the long run.'

Eden drew an envelope out of her bag and handed it to him. 'The invoice, I'm afraid.'

Paul smiled. 'No problem. I'll get that paid straight away. I know what cashflow's like in a small business. Was there myself once.'

'Thanks.' Eden rose to leave.

'Have you got a minute?' Paul said.

'Sure.' She sat back down again, pleased to see him refill the cups. Janice's coffee was excellent: strong and not too bitter.

'I wondered if I could ask you to do some work for me personally, not for the firm.'

'Of course. What is it?'

'I was divorced seven years ago,' he said. 'Zoe, my wife, took the house, Tessa and Holly, my two daughters, and a good chunk of my money. It was a bad time to lose a sizeable amount of money, but I paid her off rather than let her have a percentage of my business.'

Eden nodded. 'More of a clean break.'

'Exactly. It was tough, as you can imagine, but I've built myself back up again, got back on my feet.'

Eden smiled to encourage him to continue. Sometimes clients just needed to get their story out of the way before they could get to what it was they wanted her to do. They crafted a tale for themselves that had to be told in a certain order, and had to be heard before they could move on.

'Anyway, Zoe has seen that the business is holding on. In fact, between us, I think it might be about to do much better.' He smiled a wolfish smile.

'Oh yes, got a big contract coming your way?'

'Going to a meeting about it later today, in fact.'

'Great. And your ex-wife ...?'

'She keeps asking me for more money. I pay maintenance for the girls, but she says it's not enough. She thinks I'm paying myself huge bonuses and she wants a slice of it.' He rearranged the pens on his desk. 'I've heard that she's got a new man in her life, and I wonder if he's behind her asking for more money. I want to know how much of the maintenance I pay for the girls actually gets spent on them.'

'You want an idea of her income and outgoings?'

'Is that possible?'

'I can see where she works, where she shops, what kind of life-style she has, run a credit check to see what she's got on her cards.'

'That would be very helpful. It wasn't an amicable divorce at all, and she's been sending me some pretty unpleasant messages. I wish we could just sit down like civilised people and discuss it.'

'Keep all her messages, emails, letters, and make a note of all phone conversations,' Eden advised. 'She'll have to go to court to change the maintenance agreement, and you'll be better off if you show you've tried to be reasonable and she's been abusive.'

'I don't mind paying for the girls,' Paul said. 'I pay their school fees, ballet classes, horse riding, and I've got funds for each of them in case they want to go to university.'

'Sounds like you're doing everything you can,' Eden said. 'As always, no promises. I can only report what I find and I won't make the facts fit the picture you want to paint. OK?'

'Wouldn't have it any other way,' Paul said. 'Talking of pictures. You've got a good eye, haven't you?'

'Well, I'm observant, if that's what you mean.'

Paul rose and went to a filing cabinet and selected a framed photograph from the cluster on the top. All of the photos there were of two blond teenaged girls, sometimes posing with Paul, often together, arms linked, beaming into the camera. He carried the photo back to the desk and handed it to Eden.

A pretty girl aged about thirteen, her straight hair lying across her shoulders, beamed out from the photo with a smile that testi-fied to the leaps and bounds British dentistry had made in the past twenty years. Self-conscious about her crooked teeth, despite the hated braces she had endured as a child, Eden felt a pang of envy.

'Lovely girl,' she said.

'My younger daughter, Holly, taken a couple of years ago,' Paul said. 'It's what she's standing in front of that's intriguing me.'

In the background was a painting. A country scene with a thatched cottage, a tan millpond and white ducks. Eden peered at it.

'Not really my thing,' she said. 'What is it?'

'It's a Constable. It hung in the foyer at my daughters' school, Cheltenham Park.' Eden's eyebrow twitched. Cheltenham Park was one of the most exclusive, and expensive, public schools in the country. Apart from the fees, which were eye-watering, the school offered a menu of extracurricular activities, from sailing to rock climbing, at a premium. When his daughters went to university, Paul would find the fees a doddle and his pockets considerably heavier.

He continued, 'The painting was stolen about eighteen months ago.'

'I think I read about that. So?'

'I'm quite interested in art, and I've been doing some classes in art appreciation,' Paul said, looking faintly embarrassed. 'Look at this.'

He fetched a book from a shelf: a hefty tome on the history of art. Flipping it open, Paul pointed to a small photograph. 'I know it's a different painting, but this Constable here seems different to the Constable hanging in the school.'

'Painted at different times?' Eden hazarded. She peered at both photographs, unable to see any difference. Both dull, brown, idealised pastoral scenes with a wash of golden sunlight. Not a combine harvester or GM crop to be seen.

Paul shrugged. 'The school's picture doesn't seem quite right. Clumsier, somehow. See this duck here.'

She squinted. 'That yellow blob?'

'Exactly. See the duck in this painting.' He pointed to the book. That was definitely a duck. 'I saw the school's painting about fifteen years ago: it had been lent to an exhibition at the art gallery. I stood in front of it for about twenty minutes, mesmerised. It had a quality about it that just made me want to gaze and gaze.'

'And this one doesn't?'

'I walked past it dozens of times when the girls started at the school, and I never stopped to look once.'

'What's your point?'

'It seems wrong, that's all.' Paul snapped the book shut. 'I'm getting ahead of myself,' he said, making a self-deprecating grimace. 'Think I'm some sort of art expert after two terms of classes. Thanks for indulging me.'

'Sorry not to be more help.'

'Not at all.'

'If you could give me some details about your wife, I'll get cracking and see what I can turn up,' Eden said.

Paul scribbled on a sheet of paper and handed it over. 'There. No rush, just be interested to see what you come up with.'

'I'll give a preliminary report in two weeks. Is that OK?'

They shook hands and Janice materialised to show her to the lift. As the door closed behind her, Eden turned back and saw Paul, elbows on the desk, his head in his hands.

14:08 hours

Eden left Eagle Tower and headed into town to pick up some stationery. As she clipped down the Promenade, a tall figure emerged from the Municipal Offices and strode along the street just ahead of her. Her heart jumped at the sight of him. Aidan. Handsome, intelligent, and still hers, even after ten months. He stopped at the coffee cart by the war memorial and foraged in his pocket for change. She waved, and ducked through the traffic to join him. Today he'd swapped his usual garb of jeans and sweater for a black suit and grey dress shirt, a dark tie with a subtle silver thread through it fastened in a fat knot at his throat.

'Hello, gorgeous,' she said, kissing him. 'What are you doing all dressed up? Been up in court?'

'Ha ha,' Aidan said, giving her a tight hug. 'Been to a funding meeting. Had to look the part. Looks like the Cultural Heritage Unit will live to fight another day.'

She slipped her hand into his and he squeezed her fingers.

'You look good in a suit. I like this executive side to you.'

'They've teased me all morning at work.'

She could imagine Aidan's colleagues' response. The Cultural Heritage Unit was formed of archaeologists who sparred to wear the grubbiest, most hideous sweater they could find. The front runner was currently an orange and lime green stripe with an appliquéd polar bear. Its owner, Trev, maintained it was unbeatable. Rather to Eden's relief, Aidan had eschewed the competition. But then, he was the oddball in the bunch: he washed his jeans. Often.

'You want a coffee?' Aidan asked. A breeze lifted his hair.

'No thanks, full up to the gills already,' Eden said. 'You heading to your office? I'll walk you back.'

Aidan took the foam cup of coffee and they headed down the Promenade, weaving through shoppers and past the buskers, to where it joined the High Street. Aidan's office was tucked down a side street, a Georgian building with delicate wrought-iron balconies. The Cultural Heritage Unit oversaw archaeological digs, and advised on preservation and protection of heritage in Cheltenham.

His phone rang just as they reached the front door.

'Aidan Fox. Yes, just about to go in. Ah. OK, give me time to grab my boots and I'll be right there. Don't let anyone else near until I've had a look.'

He snapped the phone off. 'Interesting.'

Eden raised an eyebrow at him.

'They're digging foundations for a new building at Cheltenham Park School,' he explained, 'and they've just unearthed part of a skeleton. That was the police. Want to come?'

CHAPTER
TWO

Monday, 23 February 2015

14:19 hours

Silly question. She followed Aidan into the Cultural Heritage Unit, peppering him with questions.

'What have they found? Are they sure it's human? Have they got forensics in?'

'A few bones, possibly limbs, judging by the length,' Aidan said. 'Forensics have had a look and want an archaeologist in to give an initial opinion. They find it embarrassing to call out the pathologist to a dead dog.'

'Someone say bones?' Trev hove into view, a stained mug clamped in his paw. He greeted Eden with, 'All right, my lover?'

'I'm just going to get changed and head out,' Aidan said. He pushed open the door to his office and stripped off his jacket and tie, then closed the door.

'What's going on, Eden?' Trev asked.

'They've found some bones on a building site. Not sure what they are yet,' she said. 'The police just called Aidan.'

'Bones, lovely.' Trev's face lit up. He barged open the door, and they were treated to the spectacle of Aidan in his boxer shorts. Trev wolf-whistled.

'Trev! Do you mind! I'm trying to get changed here.'

'S'alright. Eden says it's a building site. Dug up a dead 'un.'

'A dead 'un?' Mandy – unnaturally red hair in plaits hanging beside her face – scurried over.

'You know, I'd rather have some privacy,' Aidan grumbled.

'I've seen it all before,' Mandy said.

'Not mine you haven't.' Aidan shut the door in their faces. They shouted through to him until he emerged, clad in jeans and a sweater, and carrying a pair of steel toe-capped boots. 'Right,' he said. 'I'm going to do an initial assessment. If, and I mean if, there is anything interesting, I'll call you and let you know who and what I need. I don't want you all getting over-excited and charging down there in a pack. Got it?'

'Yes, Aidan.'

'Yes, Aidan.'

Fat chance of that, Eden thought. She'd socialised with the team on many occasions, and was both impressed and disturbed by the joy they extracted from digging up the long dead.

'Come on, Eden.'

'See you later,' she called to Trev and Mandy.

'Eden! Make sure he calls us in!' Trev stage whispered to her, 'You know how to get round him. Grumpy git.'

'I heard that.' Aidan grabbed a toolbox from the store cupboard and lugged it out to the car park.

Aidan's car was an eight-year-old black Audi. A bundle of pens bound with an elastic band was stowed in the cup holder between the seats, and the shelf beneath the glovebox held copies of *Britain's Best Churches* and *Britain's Best Buildings*. The side pocket was lined with maps in alphabetical order. When he fired up the ignition, the car filled with Monteverdi. Eden reached for the volume control and was still fastening her seat belt as Aidan reversed out of the parking space. He was as excited about the skeleton as Trev.

'Lucky they saw that bone,' he said. 'Those diggers aren't the most subtle of machines. When they got in the hole they found more, thought they could be human, and called the police. If they *are* human, it can hold up the development. Some builders just pretend they didn't see anything. The police want me to guestimate how long the skeletons have been down there.'

'It's funny,' Eden said. 'I was just talking about Cheltenham Park School today.'

'Oh?'

'Client has two daughters there.'

'Must be loaded.'

'Yes, I suspect he is.' And troubled, she thought, recalling Paul slumped over his desk and the fatigue etched on his face.

They drove away from the town centre and along elegant boulevards edged with Regency villas, the pavements punctuated by trees topped with lollipops of mistletoe. The school was set in extensive grounds, the main building itself just visible from the road, peeking out behind a screen of cedars. As they approached, up a snaking driveway flanked with sycamores, she saw a substantial Georgian building in pale amber stone, with a red-brick extension of a much later date, and surrounded by satellite buildings cataloguing building fashions of the past century.

'I had no idea it was that big,' she commented as they drove up the driveway. 'When did it become a school?'

Aidan glanced at the school building. 'Around 1920, I think.'

'And it was a private house until then?'

Aidan shook his head. 'Don't know. I'd have to do some digging.'

Formal gardens were laid out to one side of the original house. Beyond the satellite buildings stretched playing fields, and beyond them, a small rise was capped with a round domed building sporting impressive columns.

It must have been a glorious sight for any prospective parents visiting the school: the place reeked of privilege. Today, though, the scene was disturbed by a large yellow digger and a billboard

advertising new facilities at the school. *Peterman Developments,*
Eden read, *creating school facilities of the future.* She glanced at the
artist's impression of the new science block and gymnasium:
gleaming glass and metal constructions like a spaceship butting
up against the main house.

The ground was churned into deep ruts by the construction
traffic, and a huge excavated square already formed the foundations for the new gym. The hole for the science block was only
partly dug, however, and all the machinery was still.

Aidan parked the car and removed his shoes, pulling on the
battered pair of steel-capped work boots. He grabbed a hard
hat and high-viz jacket from the boot of his car, hefted out the
toolbox, and made his way towards the construction site. Eden
hurried after him, her boots slipping on the grass.

The builders clustered together by the silent machinery,
muttering to each other in a language close enough to Russian
that she could understand it.

'You son-of-a-whore, you should have turned a blind eye.'

'What will happen to us now?'

'Who's in charge here?' Aidan asked one of the builders.
The man shrugged and pointed towards the school. 'No, who's
in charge of the site? Foreman?'

The builders glanced uneasily at each other and hung their heads.

Eden tried, her Russian creaking after a long hibernation.
'Кто отвечает здесь?' *Who is in charge here?*

The men refused even to look at her. She tried again. 'Где скелет?'
Where is skeleton?

Avoiding eye contact, the youngest pointed, and muttered,
'Не моя вина.' *Not my fault.*

She was at Aidan's shoulder as he walked towards the trench,
where a policeman was unfurling blue and white crime scene tape.

'Dr Aidan Fox,' Aidan introduced himself. 'Cultural Heritage
Unit. You called me.'

The policeman nodded, then peered past Aidan at Eden, taking in her short kilt and electric blue leather jacket. 'Who's that?'

'She's with me.'

The policeman waved to another man, standing well back and smoking a cigarette as though his life depended on it. 'Archaeology's here!' he called. To Aidan he explained, 'That's Detective Inspector Ritter.'

Ritter was a rat-faced man with dirty blond hair, greasy at the roots. He cast an anguished look at his cigarette, sucked a last, forceful drag, then tossed it on the ground and smudged it out with his toe. He stumped over and shook hands with Aidan, giving Eden a good ignoring.

They stood behind the police tape and peeped into the trench. Eden felt the chill breeze nipping at her fingertips and dug her hands in her pockets. It had been a long time since she was sent on a forensic procedures course, and she dredged her mind for protocols and crime scene management procedures.

Aidan nodded at the trench. 'Who found the skeleton?'

'Haven't established exactly what happened,' the detective said. 'The foreman is the only one who speaks any English.'

'At all?'

Ritter shrugged. 'The only one who seems to understand. Bloody EU.'

While Aidan shucked on a set of white crime scene overalls, Eden craned to see into the trench. In the claggy soil she could just make out bands of different coloured soil. At the bottom of the trench was something she initially identified as a hollow stick. Her assessment changed as her eyes followed the line of the trench and picked out other sticks, one with the smooth double bulb of a hip joint.

Aidan climbed into the trench, carefully avoiding the protruding bones. For a long time, he simply stood and looked, mapping one square of the trench before moving on to scrutinise another.

Itching with impatience, Eden called, 'So? Human or dog?'

With a small trowel, Aidan scraped away the soil clinging to the rounded hump of a rock poking out of the cut. He worked away until it was fully exposed, then gently eased it out of the mud and held it up. 'This one was never called Fido.'

It was a human skull.

Ritter groaned. 'Shit! How long's it been there?'

'Your first question should be how many,' Aidan said.

'What the …?'

Eden's pulse quickened as he pointed to a brown hump at the far end of the trench.

'Another cranium, so at least two people,' he said, drily. 'Unless this was a burial ground for circus freaks.'

'Wouldn't surprise me,' Ritter muttered. 'OK, how many?'

Aidan straightened. 'Can you pass me a tape measure from my kit?' he asked Eden.

It was slotted in place in the lid. All his tools were clean and neatly placed in the toolbox, not thrown in any old how covered in muck. She leaned over the trench to hand it to him. Just his head and shoulders poked out of the trench, his head swaddled in white plastic like a snowman. One by one, he measured the long bones.

'Only two at the moment,' he said. 'We've got two skulls, and the thigh bones are of two lengths.'

'Is this a burial ground?' she asked.

'Doubt it,' he said. 'The bones are all over the place, suggesting there was no coffin. And they're not oriented the same way. It looks as though they were slung in unceremoniously.' He caught Ritter's eye. 'Means this isn't a conventional burial.'

'Suspicious circumstances,' Eden said, her mind quickening. This was more like it. Better than trawling for adulterers all day.

'Bloody hell,' Ritter said. 'How old are they?'

'I'd have to do some carbon dating to know for sure, but the discolouration on the bones suggests they've been in the ground a long time.'

'Ancient?'

Aidan crouched down and bent his face to the earth and sniffed where he'd removed the bones. 'I'd say over a hundred years old,' he said.

'You can tell that by the smell?' Eden asked, horrified and fascinated in equal measure.

'An old burial only smells of earth,' Aidan said. 'And these bones are crumbly. I'll have to run other tests, but I wouldn't start panicking about a serial killer just yet.'

He clambered out of the trench.

'We'll treat this as a crime scene until you've got all the bones out and can confirm it's a historical burial,' Ritter said. 'Make sure everyone suits up and photograph and measure as you go. Treat it as forensic, not archaeology. OK?'

'Sure,' Aidan said. 'I'll get a team in to lift the bones and go through the spoil heap.' He grimaced at the pile of soil the digger had hacked out.

'Rather you than me, mate. It all looks the same.'

'Could be more bones in there.' Aidan drew his mobile out of his pocket and called his team. The call made, he turned back to Ritter. 'I'll leave you to deal with the builders.'

'Thanks,' Ritter groaned. He pulled a cigarette out of the packet with his lips and patted his pocket for a lighter. Approaching the builders, he spoke to them in exaggerated English. 'Where is foreman? Boss, where? I speak to Boss man.'

Eden considered going to help him. Her fragmented Russian would surely be more use than his staccato bursts and gesticulation. Then again, Ritter had ignored her since she turned up. Let him work it out himself.

Aidan sent Eden to the car for his camera and to get herself a crime scene suit. She bagged up at the car, wriggling her kilt down inside the suit. She'd forgotten the feel of the suits, the rustling at every twitch, and the smell sent her spiralling back through the past. Last time she'd worn one she was attending the aftermath of a shoot-out between rival drug lords. Brains and intestines sprayed over the walls of a lock-up garage. A gang of white-suited colleagues, like survivors from a pandemic, moved about the scene, photographing, swabbing, measuring, and maintaining a constant, lurid banter, the rowdy camaraderie of violent death. Later, they'd mobbed the pub close to the Unit, sinking pint after pint, joshing each other and making up jokes about the corpses until the horror was washed away. Happy days.

Eden blinked away the memory. She missed the comradeship the most. The teasing, the nicknames, the un-PC jokes. But here at least there was a crime scene, and good old Aidan had smuggled her into it. She rootled in the car for the camera and slung it round her neck. As she returned to the trench, she found a smartly dressed woman in her forties trying to duck under the crime scene tape.

'Who's in charge here?' the woman demanded, a severe black bob skimming her jaw.

'And you are?' Eden said.

'Mrs Mortimer. Rosalind Mortimer, the headmistress. Who are you?'

From within the trench, Aidan called, 'I'm the archaeologist. My team are on their way.'

'What's going on?'

'Talk to the police, Mrs Mortimer.' He turned to Eden. 'That lump is definitely a skull.'

'A what?' Rosalind Mortimer paled and staggered away a few steps.

Eden took her arm and led her back towards the school. She didn't like people fainting or being sick at crime scenes. It created a lot of paperwork. 'Are you all right?'

'Just a shock. He said skull, didn't he?' Mrs Mortimer said. 'Do you know what's happened?'

'The builders have unearthed a couple of bodies,' Eden said, watching Rosalind Mortimer's face closely. Mrs Mortimer's hand went to her throat. Her nails were well manicured and painted in pale peach varnish. She had a silk scarf in a fussy pattern looped around her neck, making her look older than she was.

'Bodies? Who?'

'They're skeletons,' Eden said. 'Who told you the police were here?'

'I was away from school at a meeting. When I came in, my secretary said there was a disturbance and the police were here.' Rosalind paused for breath. 'I never imagined it was a murder.'

The word hung on the air for a moment before Eden said, 'Who said anything about murder?'

Rosalind coloured. 'You said … and the police … and the skeletons.' Rosalind pressed her hand to her eyes and visibly tried to compose herself. 'I'm sorry. You must think I'm hysterical. It was a nasty surprise, being told the police were here. I imagined terrible things. The girls …' Her gaze swept the school buildings.

Eden caught sight of the billboard with the artist's impression of the new science block and gymnasium. She nodded at it. 'Big project,' she said.

'We desperately need new facilities. The parents have such expectations,' Rosalind said. 'We're lucky we can still offer boarding. Many have had to give that up.'

'Why?'

'It simply isn't financially viable any more.'

'I thought you'd have to build something that was more in keeping with the main building,' Eden said. 'Georgian, isn't it? Is it listed?'

'It is, as a matter of fact,' Rosalind said, icily. 'But this isn't a museum. We have to move with the times.'

Eden ignored the hint and carried on. 'My aunt had a grade two listed house and she had to get planning permission to change the colour of the railings outside.'

'Really.' They'd reached the main entrance: a colonnaded portico of cream marble. 'I must get on. Goodness knows what I'll tell the governors. Hopefully the building work won't be held up too long. We've got a tight schedule. We need that new science block to be opened by September.'

Eden whistled. 'That's pushing it.'

Rosalind gave her a frosty smile and clipped up the steps into the school. Her calves were well developed, her ankles skinny, and she was wearing seamed stockings. Eden watched her go. Fussy scarf and naughty librarian hosiery: there was an enigma.

When Eden returned to the trench, Aidan was positioning measuring sticks against the edge of the dig so that the photographs would give an indication of scale. He moved cautiously, photographing the protruding bones from all angles.

'We'll keep on photographing as we take this layer back,' he said to Eden. 'Make sure it's all recorded. It looks like an old burial to me, but I don't want to get to the bottom and find a digital watch, then realise we've destroyed a crime scene.'

Eden made a rueful face. At least they weren't skidding in blood, or dodging a rookie cop's vomit. Compared to the crime scenes she'd attended, this was pristine.

'You're pretty handy with a camera, aren't you?' Aidan asked.

She thought of that morning's work with a telephoto lens. Scumbags from all angles. 'I know my way round a camera.'

'You busy?' Aidan asked. 'Or have you got a couple of hours spare?'

'Sure.' It was either this or skulking in her car outside a house for a cheating husband. Random skeletons won hands down.

'I'll tell you what to shoot,' Aidan said. 'It means when my gang gets here we can concentrate on getting the skeletons out.'

'Definitely your turf, not mine,' Eden said.

She had just started photographing, to Aidan's barked instructions, when Mandy, Trev and Andy arrived, bagged in white and looking deliriously happy.

41

'We've got two skeletons, possibly more,' Aidan told them. 'The digger has cut through them and there might be bones in the spoil heap.' He pointed his trowel at the heap of claggy earth stacked beside the trench. 'There's not enough room for all of us in the trench, so Andy you can help me take this back in here; Mandy, can you record the site and finds; and Trev, riddle your way through that lot.'

Trev swore and pulled a long-suffering face but set to with a riddle and soon struck pay dirt with some finger bones, which cheered him up and he tackled the task with much more gusto from then on.

They worked hard until the light started to dim, painstakingly removing bones, cataloguing and storing them in cardboard boxes lined with bubble wrap. Aidan and Andy scraped back the soil from the skulls, then left them *in situ* while they worked out the orientation of the skeletons. The scratch of trowels was soothing, Eden thought, crouching to photograph a section of rib cage that Andy had unearthed.

A few minutes later, Andy said, 'Aidan?'

'Uh-huh?'

'Have a look at this.'

Aidan straightened. Andy sat back on his heels, the rib cage in front of him, a pick-up sticks of thin bones. He pointed his trowel. 'What do you reckon?'

Aidan squinted at the ribs and sucked in a breath. 'Looks like we might have a cause of death,' he said. He called to Eden, 'Photos needed here!'

She scrambled over, and narrowed the lens in to where he pointed. He inched the tip of his trowel into the bones and lifted out a small object. He rubbed it clean with his glove and held it up to the light. It was a metal point. 'Looks to me like the tip of a blade.'

She raised her eyes to his. His face was serious. 'Better phone our friends at the nick,' he said.

CHAPTER
THREE

London, March 1795

Rachel Lovett flung down her fork and rang the little bell on the table. A maid answered, a chewed-up and spat-out girl who trembled when Rachel nodded at the breakfast remains and ordered her to clear the dishes.

The girl bobbed a curtsey and set about clattering the china into a wobbly pile.

'When you've finished that, Kitty, come and help me dress,' Rachel said.

'Yes, miss.'

Rachel swept out of the parlour and into her bedroom. Heavy drapes adorned the windows and tumbled to the floor, and the bed was festooned with pink silk swags and hangings. Her sheets were rumpled: the remains of a poor night's sleep. Not the first these past weeks.

Pouring hot water into a bowl, she turned a bar of scented soap over in her hands and lathered herself clean. The soap was French, the very best, a present from Darby. The whole room was a present from Darby. Her eyes made a swift inventory: the tangle of dresses a knotted rainbow on the divan; the shifts of lace and satin tumbling out of drawers; the candles everywhere. Wax, not tallow. The big gilt-looking glass that flooded the room with light.

The face that confronted her in the glass was heart shaped with pert tendencies, a small mouth that could soothe and caress when it wanted, or screech like a docker's whore when it chose. A bosom not rounded but there was enough there to push upwards and create two plump pale delights.

And it was all Darby's. The Honourable Darby Roach, her lover. Who had been growing absent over the past few weeks. A missed appointment; a blank look in his eye; problems poking the fire. Not that the shit had been near her for five days. And a man who shuns his mistress for five days must have another cat in the bag.

Rachel hissed at her own reflection, just as Kitty crawled into the room and set about picking up dresses and folding them away, gathering up stockings and chemises as fine as spiders' webs.

'How old do you think I look, Kitty?' Rachel asked.

Kitty cast her an anguished glance. Calculation chased over her features; the girl never could dissemble, no matter how Rachel instructed her.

She sighed. 'It doesn't matter, Kitty. Come, my finest today, I think.'

'Mr Roach calling?'

'He'd better,' Rachel said. Further conversation was impossible, as Kitty had her knee in her back and was straining on the stay's laces like a thoroughbred given its head in the Derby.

Two hours later, Rachel was draped in a lilac silk gown and her hair was curled and arranged in loops about her head. Each wrist held five bracelets, a slave bangle throttled her plump forearm, and her bodice glittered with trinkets. Her face was powdered, rouged and painted. She was ready.

She draped herself over the sofa in the drawing room, arranging herself on the cushions in a series of artful poses. None of them was comfortable enough to sustain for longer than a few minutes, so she picked up a novel, curled her feet underneath her, and threatened to strangle Kitty if she showed in Mr Roach without warning her mistress first.

So the morning passed.

And the afternoon.

At three o'clock, when no carriage had stopped at her door and Kitty had still failed to creep into the room to hiss, 'Mr Roach, miss,' Rachel sprang from the couch, threw her novel across the room and shouted for Kitty.

'Get my pelisse and gloves and my shoes,' she said. 'The new ones. And my bonnet. And put on your spencer and bonnet, too.'

'Miss?'

'I'm going out.'

'What about Mr Roach, miss? What if he calls?'

'Then he can leave his card like everyone else,' Rachel said, coolly. 'He has chosen not to call for the past few days.' Five days. Five days and no message from him. A worm of uncertainty crawled in her stomach. He couldn't have, could he?

'He might be ill, miss.'

'Then he should have sent a note.'

'He might have been called to the country. His father's place.'

Rachel fixed her with a stare. 'Bonnet, gloves, and pelisse, Kitty.'

'Yes, miss.' Kitty fled and was heard clumping about in the bedroom, flinging open closets and drawers in search of outdoor clothing.

'Come on, girl!' Rachel snapped her fingers and walked to the looking glass. Let him come. Let him come now, and find her gone. Let him worry that she had found another lover and was bestowing her affections elsewhere. Marylebone was not so fashionable that she couldn't trade up as plenty had done before her. Yet the worry wouldn't be banished, and for once she was glad to see Kitty's pale sweaty face as the girl hurried back into the room.

Moments later, mistress and maid sailed out of the house. Rachel kept her head upright, staring straight ahead of her, but out of the corners of her eyes she searched the street, desperate to hear a carriage drawing to a halt behind her. Or even the clip of gentleman's boot on the pavement and a cry of 'Miss Rachel! A moment!'

Nothing. They reached the end of the street uncalled, unstopped, and as Rachel feared, unwanted.

Time to show Darby Roach that she wasn't a girl to be trifled with.

Kitty trailing two paces behind her, Rachel flounced into shop after shop, each one more luxurious, more extravagant, and more obsequious than the last. And quite right, too. She had the command of Darby Roach's patronage, and he was heir to a substantial fortune. While she entertained no hopes of marrying into that fortune, she could at least maintain a household that many an honest woman would envy.

'Miss Lovett, good day.' The haberdasher dipped a low bow to her and ushered her to a chair. 'What might I show you today?'

'Stockings,' Rachel said.

'I have some new ones in the latest colours. A delicate peach and a very striking green.'

'Let's start with those.'

He scurried about, fetching stockings from drawers and laying them out for her inspection. If her aunt could see her now! She was a long way from the tiny Northamptonshire village where she grew up as Ann Sharp. The first nine years with her parents, then when they died, with her mother's sister, who taught her how to keep the pigs and how to hack the head off a flapping chicken. That home lasted three years, until Ann started to bloom, and her aunt's eyes narrowed every time her uncle's gaze fastened upon her. There was no place for her, then, and her aunt introduced her to Mrs Dukes, explaining that she was to go to London and learn manners and go into service.

'Yes, we'll soon have you in service,' Mrs Dukes said, licking her lips as she looked Ann up and down. Her aunt and Mrs Dukes exchanged a look and her aunt nodded. Mrs Dukes pressed five pounds into her aunt's hand and bundled Ann into the stage-coach and took her to London, where her tutelage began.

Pretty manners, dancing, dressing her hair in the most fetching style, learning how to make gentlemen feel special. All these arts she accomplished easily. Too easily, for just a few weeks after arriving at Mrs Dukes's establishment near Covent Garden, that staunch businesswoman had sold Ann's maiden-head to a corpulent judge for twenty guineas.

She sold it again once the soreness subsided. And again. And again. Then she inspected the merchandise and decided that even her sales patter couldn't talk up that battered plateau. Ann Sharp was dropped from the catalogue, and Rachel Lovett was launched in her place. An instant success with the customers.

And so her new life began. Well fed, well dressed, and well loved by some of Mrs Dukes's customers. And then Darby Roach swaggered in with a group of his friends, chose Rachel from the girls posed around the room, and promptly fell in love with her.

He wasn't her first favourite, but he was the most persistent. After a few months of sharing her favours, he declared he would have her as his own. He paid Mrs Dukes for the loss of custom, and installed Rachel in a house in Marylebone. She was just eighteen then.

Now she had been Darby's mistress for just a year, and already his visits to her were starting to wane.

'Make hay while the sun shines,' Rachel muttered to herself, as the shopkeeper spread before her a selection of new shawls that had just been imported from India.

'No one has these yet, miss,' he said, running the fabric through his fingers. 'You would set the fashion.'

The shawls were beautiful: large enough to drape her whole body and caress the length of her arms, and soft as rose petals. One was embroidered with peacock feathers in vibrant sapphire and emerald; another glowed in dusky amber and peach hues. Yet another, of finest wool, was a pale dove colour.

'Yes, thank you,' Rachel said.

'Which one, miss?'

'All of them,' she said, airily.

The shopkeeper hid his reaction with a bow. Not so Kitty, who gasped, 'But miss, *all* of them!'

'Mr Roach is a devoted man,' Rachel said.

'I'll charge it to his account,' the shopkeeper said, and ordered the shop boy to wrap the scarves and stockings Rachel had selected. The boy handed the parcels to Kitty, who was already burdened.

'I could deliver those for you, miss.'

'No, I'll take them,' she said. Once she had the goods in her hands, they were hers. No shop boy was going to show them off to his sweetheart, and exchange a feel of the new shawls for a tussle with a whey-faced scrag.

'Good day, Miss Lovett.' The shopkeeper held the door wide for her and bowed as she strutted past.

Rachel favoured him with a nod of her head, and snapped, 'Come along, Kitty. Do try to keep up!'

When she and Kitty arrived home, laden down with shawls, a new bonnet, and stockings in all the latest colours, Darby was waiting for them. He sprang to his feet as she marched into the drawing room.

'Rachel!' he cried. 'Thank goodness you're back!'

'Good day, Darby,' she said, coolly, pulling off her gloves finger by finger. She glanced at him again. His face was pale as pudding and dark crescents underscored his eyes. He paced the room, clenching and unclenching his fists. 'Darby? What is it?'

She drew in a deep breath, preparing to hear him say he'd found another mistress, that he was tired of her and casting her off. Well, she'd see about that.

'You've got to leave. Today.'

'I will not.'

'You don't understand; you've got no choice.'

Rachel planted herself on a sofa and crossed her arms, her lips set.

'Rachel, I've made the most terrible mess of everything.'

'Really?' When she found out who this girl was, she'd claw her eyes.

'I've been gaming, that's why I haven't visited you. The card game lasted days. I was winning, then my luck changed.' He swallowed. 'I borrowed to stay in the game. I knew my luck would change again, but it didn't. I lost and kept on losing.'

'And you kept on borrowing?'

He nodded. 'It finished this morning, very early.' He raised a haggard face to her. 'It finished, and I'm finished.'

'How much?'

'Twenty thousand pounds.'

'Darby!'

'I'm ruined. I can't pay. I was forced to see my father and confess. He's agreed to cover the gambling debts as a matter of honour, but I have to give up my London house, this house, everything.'

'Even me?'

'Especially you. You're an expense I can no longer afford.' His gaze raked the room and he let out a short, mirthless laugh. 'The word's round London already. None of this is paid for, the furniture, your dresses, the paintings, nothing. They'll be here to strip the house and take it all back soon.'

A stone fell in Rachel's chest. 'All of it?'

'Every stick and handkerchief.'

'But you must have paid for something!'

'No. My name is my bond. The shopkeepers all knew they'd get paid eventually. Now they know they won't.' He ran a shaking hand over his face. 'Everything I owned is being sold anyway, to try to clear my debt.'

'But you said your father was paying that?'

'He'll pay what remains after I've sold everything I have. Even my horse, Rachel. I love my horse.'

That cracked her. She rose and slapped him hard across the face. Darby reeled and crashed on to the sofa.

'Rachel, I wish ...'

She never heard what he wished, for at that moment, hammering shook the front door, the force vibrating through the house.

'They've come,' Darby said, his face white.

'Don't let them in,' Rachel cried, as the front door opened and boots were heard on the stairs. A thickset man in a long brown coat shoved a bill at Darby.

'You're expecting us, Mr Roach?' he said. 'Here to reclaim goods unpaid for. Off you go, lads.'

The lads – two swarthy brutes – grabbed the sofa and tipped Darby on to the floor, then hefted it out of the room.

'You can't just take my furniture,' Rachel cried, squaring up to him.

'Yes, I can miss. None of this is paid for. Now out of the way, I need to roll up that carpet.'

More men came, with bits of paper they thrust at Darby. One went through her closet, snatching her gowns, underclothes, shoes. Another unhitched the looking glass from the wall and carted it away. The ornaments were wrapped in paper and stacked on a cart. Her jewellery box was plundered and the contents stuffed into pockets. A receipt for the goods taken was made out and handed to Darby.

He slumped on the bare floorboards, his head in his hands, as more and more tradespeople arrived to claim what was rightfully theirs, terrified they'd miss out on the loot. Rachel wept as the house was dismantled around her. Her delicate chairs were lumped outside and swung on to a cart, and carried off to grace someone else's house. Some other Marylebone whore, her star rising, decorating her love nest with the best of everything. To think she'd dreamed of trading up to Westminster. Now she'd sell her soul to keep her smart little house and Darby.

'Do something, Darby,' she cried, as they dismantled her bed. Their bed, where they'd lain entwined and he'd sworn he'd never let her go, ever.

'Do what?' he said.

'Stop them!'

'I can't,' he said, shaking his head.

'But where am I to go?'

'I don't know.'

'You said you'd protect me. I have no lodgings, no money, only the clothes I stand up in.'

He fixed her with a look she didn't like. 'You'll find a new favourite soon enough,' he said. 'Go back to Mrs Dukes.'

'Go back to …' She couldn't. How the other girls would crow. High and mighty Rachel Lovett, who'd snagged herself a wealthy lover and now was above common whoring, back to the seraglio and submitting to anyone who paid a few guineas for her favours.

Kitty inched into the room. 'Miss, they're saying they're taking everything, miss, and I haven't been paid this quarter's wages.'

Rachel turned to Darby. He shrugged and looked away.

Hand on her hips, she addressed Kitty loud enough that everyone in the house could hear clearly. 'Well, Kitty, it seems our master, Mr Darby Roach, cares nothing. He's advised me to be a common whore. No doubt he'd counsel you to do the same.'

At that Kitty burst into tears and fled the house.

'Off you go, miss,' a large self-important-looking man announced. 'The lease has been sold.'

'But where ...' She pleaded with her eyes to Darby. He ignored her, just dragged himself up from the floor and dusted off his breeches. He bowed to her. 'Good day, Miss Lovett,' he said, and strode from the room.

'Darby!' she called after him, but the self-important man had her arm in his grip, and was hustling her downstairs and out on to the street with a well-practised shove in the back. She sprawled on the pavement. Two women stopped to watch, and a boy laughed.

'Damn you, Darby Roach,' she cursed under her breath.

They hadn't stripped her body, these men who stripped her house and closets. Maybe they forgot, or maybe it was the dangerous glint in her eye that urged caution. Whatever the reason, it meant she had bangles on each wrist, her brooches, her clothes and her rings. Luckily she wore a ring on each finger, so with one pawned she could afford cheap lodgings in Covent Garden and work out what to do next.

Going back to Mrs Dukes was impossible. She'd rather starve. She'd rather rent her petticoats and hump in alleys than turn up there.

Fortunately she had her education to fall back on, and before the day was out she'd thieved and fenced two pocket watches and a walking cane. Sidling along the street on the lookout for another mark, she heard her name called.

'Rachel! It *is* you!'

She turned. A girl swayed towards her, dressed in the voluptuous costume of a Haymarket courtesan: bosom pushed so high it was abed with her nostrils; rouge, paint and patches all over her face; and vibrant silk skirts.

'Jenny,' Rachel said. She had known her at Mrs Dukes's. Jenny must be what, at least twenty-six now. Old. Raddled. 'What are you doing here?'

'This is my patch,' Jenny leered. She looked Rachel up and down. 'More to the point, what are you doing here? I heard you'd got a rich cully and was above it all.'

She pressed so close that Rachel could smell spirits on Jenny's breath and the sweet rot of the pox.

'You heard right,' Rachel said, smoothing the line of her dress so that Jenny could see her calfskin gloves.

'And there was I thinking you was in a rented dress and stealing my trade.'

'Oh no, I couldn't work round here,' Rachel said, glancing about at the riff-raff. 'I'm used to the quality. And you?'

Jenny stamped her foot in vexation. Giving it away for a guinea a time. And getting more than she bargained for from the look of that sore on her cheek.

'Can't stand here talking all day,' Jenny said. She snatched her skirts about her and swayed down the street. A barrow boy pitched an orange at her, and she bit into it, skin and all.

Pissed old whore. That's what happens when you get old and your looks have faded, thought Rachel. Not that Jenny had much in the way of manners and arts, despite Mrs Dukes's best efforts to teach her. No wonder she was tossed out. But the same wasn't going to happen to her. She had youth and good looks, and she valued herself too highly to stalk the inns at the Haymarket prowling for a gin-pickled prick. No, Westminster was where she belonged, and to Westminster she would go.

The money lasted until the end of the week, then Rachel took herself to Westminster, hawking for a likely keeper. An MP or a lawyer would be a fat catch. They had money even if they didn't have lineage. As she'd found, lineage came at a cost. No one who was behoven to papa, that's what she wanted.

The shops in Westminster were smart; the haberdashers' windows hung with the most tantalising bonnets and shawls. She stood before a fanned display of gloves in a shop window for a long moment, her breath fogging the pane, before she ventured inside. The shopkeeper sized her up immediately.

'I've been asked to choose a present,' she said. 'My brother will come and pay for it, if it can be set aside.'

'Of course, miss. Your brother is?'

'Mr Harvey Humbold.' She'd almost said 'the Honourable' and pulled herself back in time. Evidently she guessed right, that the shopkeeper knew every honourable and peer in town, and assumed Mr Harvey Humbold was new money, for he simply turned the name round on his tongue a few times and asked what she would like.

She asked to see the gloves, and he set about arranging them on the counter. She slipped her fingers into a pair of very tight, elbow-length saffron kid gloves. Divinely soft, and how delicate her hands appeared. The colour was exquisite: the latest thing.

'Hm,' she said, turning her hand to and fro and squinting at it. 'I'm not sure. Maybe something not quite so bright.'

More gloves were fetched. She fingered them, bit her lip as she considered the colour, and asked if there was anything with more buttons, fewer buttons, a brighter blue, a softer pink, sending the shopkeeper scurrying to every box and drawer he had in the shop. When she'd almost exhausted his stock, she said, 'And maybe some in plain white cotton,' and he headed into the room at the back of the shop.

As soon as his back was turned, she scooped up three pairs of gloves that were lying on the counter and shoved them in her pocket. Still wearing the divine saffron gloves, she hurried from the shop. She was part-way down the street when she began to run, then heard a cry of 'Stop, thief!' behind her.

She grabbed the hem of her gown and held it high, pelting down the street, round corners and up alleyways as she hadn't done since she was a girl, chasing the chickens to come and be executed. Her chest heaving, she dashed into an open doorway and hid behind the door. The thief-taker galloped past. She peeped out through the crack in the door, making sure no one else was in pursuit.

Her breath came hard and fast and her heart hammered against her ribs. She flopped back against the wall, her fist pressed into her side, and fought to breathe.

'Hello, my dear.' A voice spoke out of the shadows.

Rachel whipped round. 'Who is it?' she whispered.

'Only me, dear.' The woman stepped into the light. A brightly painted bawd with a brown hairpiece pinned to grey tresses, her mouth a scarlet slash, her front teeth brown stumps. 'What have you been up to, then?'

'A misunderstanding, that's all.' Rachel made to leave, and the woman's hand shot out and gripped her wrist.

'I know your type,' she said. 'Want me to hand you over to the thief-taker?'

Rachel's heart dropped. The gloves were still on her: if she was handed to the courts they'd surely find her guilty, and that meant transportation, or death. 'No.'

'You got a place?'

'Yes, I have a keeper,' she said, affecting superiority.

'Nah you don't. That's the only gown you've got, my girl.' The woman sucked her stumps. 'Come with me.'

Rachel struggled, but the woman had hold of her wrist, and looked like she wouldn't think twice about screaming for help. She allowed herself to be hustled upstairs, where she was shown into a large room lined with sofas, draped with silk and reeking of perfume. Each sofa held at least two girls in a state of undress – reclining in erotic poses for the entertainment of two university fellows sniggering beside them.

Rachel's eyes swept the room, pricing the furniture, the hangings, the clothes the girls almost wore. Not expensive, not cheap. Definitely a step down from Mrs Dukes's place.

The two boys selected the girls they wanted and the four of them scuffled out of the room.

'Won't be long,' the woman sniffed. 'The amount they've had to drink.' She turned to Rachel and smiled, 'They're the best kind: easy come, easy go, move on to the next bilk.'

'Who are you?' Rachel asked.

'Mrs Bedwin. And you?'

'Rachel Lovett.' Rachel tilted her nose up.

'Rachel Lovett? I've heard of you. Wasn't you Darby Roach's piece?'

'I was.'

'Lost all his money? Stripped his house they did. Betting is he'll blow his brains out before long.'

Rachel shuddered.

Mrs Bedwin grinned. 'You are down on your luck, my girl. Keeper's lost his money, likely kill 'isself soon, thrown out on the street and the thief-taker after you. Thinking you'll join Darby Roach in heaven?' She laughed until she wheezed. 'Nah, you're mine now. I know too much about you.' She snapped her fingers at one of the girls, who broke out of her artistic pose. 'Celia, take Miss Lovett and show her a room. Get her changed and back here. Going to be a busy day, I can feel it in me water.'

As Celia led Rachel out of the room, she heard a clatter of boots on the stairs. Young men, from the noise. Behind her, she overheard Mrs Bedwin's whispered instructions to the posing nymphs, 'Empty their pockets, girls. Wine's two guineas a bottle now. Remember not to tell them till after. Get to it, girls!'

Though her establishment was not as high-class as Mrs Dukes's, Mrs Bedwin was an astute businesswoman constantly on the lookout for new opportunities. The gentlemen who frequented the house found girls who were plump, cheerful and willing to please. Want a chop? Sally will fetch it for you, sir. Only five shillings. Thirsty, sir? We have the finest wine for you, only two guineas a bottle. Every peccadillo, every taste, every craving was catered for at Mrs Bedwin's. If a client had a particular secret urge that her girls couldn't satisfy, she bought a girl who could and added the speciality to the menu of delights she laid out for the customers.

Several times a day a sedan chair pulled up outside and a message came that they were to collect Miss Susan, or Miss Hart, or Miss Roseanne, a black former slave who was a particular favourite. These girls climbed inside and were carried off to the bagnios and the gentleman who had requested them specially. It wasn't long before the sedan chair started to call for Miss Rachel.

Mrs Bedwin had the magistrate in her pocket, and the house was never raided. She supplied girls for parties, transported them to some of the highest houses in London, and was said to have once bedded the Prince of Wales himself.

'Keep your eyes on the prize, girls,' she told them. 'And don't go soft on me. There's no room for sentiment in business.'

After Rachel had been at Mrs Bedwin's for five months, Mrs Bedwin closed and bolted the front door behind the last gentleman to leave, and called the girls together in the seraglio.

'I have good news, girls. We're moving on.'

'Leaving here?' Roseanne cried.

'Yes, dear. Going to a fine new place, mixing with the cream of society. A place where even royalty can be found.'

She paused, and her gaze raked the room. 'Girls, we're going to Cheltenham.'

CHAPTER
FOUR

Monday, 5 November 2012

16:48 hours

The name shadowed him to prison. Little Jimmy. His real name was James Little, but people always called him Little Jimmy, even at primary school, even his mam's boyfriends. When he stumbled out of the prison van, the screws cacked themselves laughing when they saw him, with his pale skin and pigeon chest, his permanent sniff and asthma.

'Little by name, little by nature,' the screw who searched him said.

Jimmy said nothing. People always laughed. Even Hammond had smirked.

That first meeting with Hammond haunted him. He lay in the narrow metal bed in the narrow cell, with its smell of farts and sounds of men jacking off, and watched the grey light seeping through a high window. Like drowning in dishwater. The rough blanket scratched his chin. Spots freckled his throat and there was a dab of blood on the sheet where one had spurted. He was afraid to close his eyes, because then the dreams would come.

A year ago his conviction sheet listed shoplifting, a few taking without consents, theft and a public order offence.

No biggies. And then he met Dave the Nutter. Not met. Their paths crossed. Jimmy was in McDonald's nicking a woman's bag from the back of her chair while she shovelled soggy fries into a kid's gob. He slid the bag from the chair and shoved it up his jumper, then strolled from the store. Soon as he was out, he legged it. Down the High Street and round the corner, up the alley near the Indian takeaway, over the bins and smack into Dave the Nutter.

'Watch where you're going,' Dave said. He clocked he was running, clocked he was up to no good, and clocked the bulge in his jumper. 'What we got here?'

'Nothing,' Jimmy stammered.

'We'll see about that.' Dave thrust a paw down his jumper and yanked out the bag. He raised his eyebrows at Jimmy. 'Little thief, are you?'

'No, it's my sister's,' he stammered.

Dave the Nutter had hold of his arm. He was a heavyset man with a shiny bald head and air of pent-up aggression. If he held him any longer, Jimmy thought he'd piss himself. Dave was looking at him and breathing heavily through his mouth, weighing something up. Jimmy prayed he wasn't a bum bandit. Not here, on the bins amongst the garlic sauce and cat piss.

'I've got a proposition for you, my lad,' Dave the Nutter said. 'You can come along with me, or I'll call the police.'

'Go where with you?'

'See my boss.'

Jimmy nodded. There might be a chance to run. Besides, if he called the police he'd definitely be sent down for nicking the bag and he'd get bummed anyway.

Dave the Nutter dragged him off to see Hammond. 'Thought he might be useful, Boss.'

Hammond sized him up, nodding, running his tongue over his teeth. 'What's your name?'

The voice was smooth and posh. Not what he expected.

'James Little. Jimmy.'

Hammond laughed so hard Jimmy got a flash of his fillings. 'You're Scotch, eh?'

'Yeah.'

'Little Jimmy. What d'you say, Dave?'

Dave chuckled. 'No one's going to think a squirt like him works for you, Boss.'

'I think you might be right.' Hammond circled him. 'Right, Little Jimmy, you work for me now. You do what I say, and I'll see you're all right.'

Hammond sent him on errands. Jimmy slipped unnoticed into places where Hammond, with his big personality and swanky clothes, couldn't go. Dave the Nutter was sarky to him and pushed him around. Jackie was all right, though. She made him a cup of tea when he came in out the cold. Asked him how his mam was. Didn't make fun of his puzzle books.

She still called him Little Jimmy, though.

Thursday, 5 February 2015

10:00 hours

The prison gate slammed shut behind him. He stood on the street, the wind whistling up the road, and chips of ice in the rain. He was wearing the suit he wore in court when he was sentenced and had his bus fare in his pocket. He supposed he ought to go to his mam's.

As he trudged up the road to the bus stop, a car drew alongside. The passenger window descended.

'You Little Jimmy?'

'Yeah.'

'Get in.'

He hesitated.

'I'm not telling you again. Get in.'

He opened the rear door and got in. The car reeked of cigarettes and the upholstery was tacky. The air was all fugged up with smoke and he fondled the blue asthma inhaler in his pocket.

The car set off across London. He didn't know where they were taking him. The two men up front – the driver and the bloke in the passenger seat – never spoke. They just smoked. Cigarette after cigarette. Lighting the next with the smouldering stub of the one just finished.

The car stopped in a street of terraced houses. Some of them were boarded up and graffitied over. Metal gates barred the front doors. Pakistani kids in flowery dresses played in the road, talking scribble to each other. A woman shielded in black from head to toe pushed an old pram along the pavement.

The men got out of the car and dragged him from the back, hustling him into a house and slamming the door. It was gloomy inside: all the windows were either boarded over or masked by curtains. They shoved him through the front room and into the back. A kitchen led off it – orange chipboard units with the doors hanging off. A tap at a drunken angle hanging from the wall. No sink.

There was a wooden chair in the back room. One of those with a shelf for prayer books. They pressed him into it and bound his hands behind him with plastic cable ties.

'Delivery!' The man from the passenger seat shouted, and the two men left the house. A few seconds later he heard a car start up and drive away.

Footsteps on wooden boards. Someone came down the staircase in the corner of the room. It was a boxed-in staircase and Jimmy couldn't see who it was until he was at the bottom. A lean, hungry-looking man, his neck, head and face garlanded with tattoos.

As he clumped on to the last step, he grinned at Jimmy. His teeth had all been removed and replaced with steel fangs.

'Hello, Jimmy,' he said. 'I hear you've been a naughty boy.'

'No, no I haven't,' Jimmy said, struggling against the ties. It only ratcheted them tighter.

'I heard you grassed someone up. Blabbed to the filth and got in the way of a very important operation.' Fang Face licked his lips. He had a stud in his tongue. 'You've made some very important men very angry indeed.'

The knife was in his mouth before he knew it. The cold steel sharp against his lips. Fang Face pressed hard, and the corners of Jimmy's mouth stretched and split, until his mouth spread the width of his face. Jimmy tried to spit out blood. It dribbled down his chin and dropped on to his shirt.

'Blabbermouth,' Fang Face said, and set about some DIY facial reconstruction.

The copper was a rookie and hadn't seen this kind of thing before. All he knew was Mrs Unpronounceable Name at number twenty-two was jabbering on about an empty house in her street. Her English was shit, and her ten-year-old son was translating for her. In the end, he gave up and promised to check it out. Probably squatters. Not his business but anything to stop her mithering.

Number twenty was a sorry piece. Windows boarded up, hideous curtains mouldering upstairs. Could be a crack den. Maybe that's what she heard. He tried the door. Stuck. Damp probably. Didn't seem to be locked. Better check it out. He thumped his shoulder against it and the door opened.

Kids gathered on the pavement. This was a new diversion. He fixed them with his sternest look and ordered them to go home. They ignored him.

He stepped into the house. Flowery wallpaper that was a crime on its own. He felt a crunch beneath his boots. A syringe? No, a blue inhaler. The plastic case all smashed up.

And there was a smell. What was it? Sweet and unpleasant, it caught at the back of his throat. Pressing the back of his hand to his nose, he inched further into the house.

The back room held just a wooden chair, the sort you find in church halls. It was tipped over on its side, a brown stain underneath it. Beyond was a scabby kitchen. Empty.

A boxed-in staircase in the corner of the back room. The copper called upstairs, the hairs on his neck prickling. Something wasn't right here. Step by step he went up the stairs, his sturdy police boots rapping.

'Hello?' he called, his voice high and nervous. Pull yourself together, he scolded himself. You're supposed to be a police officer, for God's sake. Maybe he should radio for back-up? And say what? He'd got a nasty feeling on this one? They'd never let him live it down when it was only a sodden tramp or a feral cat.

Top of the stairs. Two doors leading off. The smell was worse here. He tried to breathe through his mouth. Front room more hideous wallpaper. Back room bare floors, bare walls, and the festering remains of Jimmy Little.

about his appearance was an attempt to keep his wife's interest, perk up a stale marriage, even at the cost of having someone drilling into his scalp.

The new call wasn't a number she recognised. She pressed connect, praying it was a new client. Now she'd got rid of Mrs Townsend, there was no more work on her books.

'Is that Eden Grey?' a woman's voice asked.

'Yes. Who's speaking?'

'This is Staff Nurse Watson. I'm calling from Cheltenham General Hospital. Paul Nelson was admitted earlier today.'

'Paul? What's wrong with him?'

'We're not sure, we're still running tests, but he's asked to see you.'

'Me?'

'You're down as his next of kin,' the voice said. While Eden was still digesting this news, the woman added, 'Come as soon as you can. Mr Nelson's condition is serious.'

She was directed to the intensive care unit where Nurse Gail Watson buzzed her in and ordered her to sanitise her hands with gel.

'What happened to him?' Eden asked, as she was led down a corridor.

'We're still trying to find out. It looks like an extreme attack of gastritis.'

'Vomiting and diarrhoea?'

'Yes, but his heart is racing and he's had convulsions.'

'Poor Paul,' Eden said.

'Are you his partner?' Gail Watson gave her a look of sympathy and briefly touched her arm. Eden went cold.

'Has anyone called his ex-wife, or his daughters?' she asked.

Gail shook her head. 'He asked for you. Said he didn't want his daughters to see him like this.'

The nurse showed her into a small room at the side of the ward. Paul lay with tubes attached to his arms and a heart monitor threading an irregular green line.

'He's been slipping in and out of consciousness,' she whispered. 'But sit and talk to him. It might help.'

She left, soles squeaking, and Eden dragged an orange plastic chair over to the bed. Paul looked like hell. His skin was slack and white, and the bruises beneath his eyes bled into his cheeks.

'Paul?' she whispered. 'Paul, it's Eden Grey. They said you asked for me.'

She squeezed his hand as it lay on the sheet, and his eyelids flickered. His hand was dry, the fingertips icy. She chafed them, trying to rub warmth into him.

'Paul, can you hear me?'

The monitor traced another line. Another blip. The readings changed; changed again.

'Do you need anything?'

No response. She patted his hand. 'I'm here, Paul. I'll just wait here until you wake up.'

The hospital was stiflingly hot. She stood and slipped off her leather jacket, hanging it over the back of the chair. Paul's hospital notes were in a clipboard at the end of the bed. She flicked through them, reading his symptoms and the tests the doctors were running, the medication he'd been given. Observations every fifteen minutes: blood pressure, temperature, pulse rate all over the place.

The chair squealed as she sat down and Paul's eyes flickered open.

'Sorry, didn't mean to wake you,' she whispered, shocked at how he looked now he was awake.

'Eden,' he croaked. His fingers trembled on the sheet. She grasped his hand and squeezed it.

'I'm here. You asked for me. Do you want me to tell your wife what's happened?'

'No, not yet.' He struggled to sit, failed, and flopped back down again. 'Need you to find something out.'

'All of that can wait until you're better.'

'No.' His face contorted as a spasm ripped through his body. 'This. Deliberate.'

The world rocked and stilled. 'What?'

'Tried to kill me.'

Cold washed over her. 'Who? Who, Paul?'

Paul gargled and his body jerked. Eden hurtled to the door and shouted, 'Somebody help!'

She stood back helplessly as nurses charged into the room, holding Paul down as they injected him with something to stop the seizure. His feet drummed on the mattress and his spine bowed as the convulsions racked him. A terrible strangling noise gurgled in his throat. At last the fit passed, and he slumped against the bed.

'He should sleep now,' the nurse said.

Eden kept vigil by the bedside, fiddling with the beans on her bracelet. She'd bought it from a New Age market stall years ago. Her first music festival; mud, pot and beer. She'd gone wandering round the stalls, the tarot readings and henna hand painting, and stopped to watch a long-bearded man playing the didgeridoo. Next to him was a stall selling bead necklaces and bracelets, dream catchers and incense sticks. She'd bought this bracelet and a matching necklace, which had snapped its string and scattered the beans in the mud only the second time she wore it. Idly she wondered if strange bean trees sprouted now in the field where her tent had stood.

The hours ticked by as she watched Paul's chest rise and fall. The windows darkened and in the panes she saw an echo of herself, a small figure huddled by the bedside of a man she barely knew.

Around eleven o'clock, Paul's eyes opened and fixed on her hands. A shadow passed across his face. 'Paternoster,' he breathed, then closed his eyes again.

He didn't open his eyes. The nurse who came to take his obs warned that he'd gone into a coma and told Eden to prepare herself.

A few hours later, Paul Nelson died.

'I'm so sorry for your loss.' The nurse handed her a plastic bag. Paul's clothes, shoes, wallet, keys. 'These are his things.'

'I'm not sure I'm the right person …'

'He named you as next of kin.'

'But …' Eden bit her lip. *This. Deliberate. Tried to kill me.* 'Where do I collect the death certificate?'

The nurse squirmed. 'It won't be available for some time, I'm afraid. There'll have to be a post-mortem.'

Eden's gaze held hers, her mind whirring. Of course there'd be a post-mortem.

'It's usual when we're not sure of the cause of death,' the nurse added, quickly. She squeezed Eden's arm. 'Take care.'

As she squeaked off down the corridor, Eden stared at the plastic bag in her hands. *This. Deliberate.* A plan formed in her mind. She'd have to tell Paul's ex-wife, but right now it was three in the morning and there was no point waking the woman up and getting Paul's daughters upset. Besides, what did Paul mean? What was he trying to tell her in those final moments? Maybe a few hours' headstart was a blessing.

She went home. Normally her heart lifted at the sight of its clean lines and geometric windows, but today, in the dark hours, it seemed impersonal and grim. Her apartment was cold. The central heating had gone off hours before, and when she switched on the living-room light, the room looked abandoned and unfamiliar, like a stage set. Eden put a match to the gas fire and sat cross-legged in front of it, her palm wrapped around a cup of tea, and upended the plastic bag over the rug.

She went through the clothes first, quickly stuffing Paul's socks and underpants back in the bag. Thank goodness he was a fastidious man. His shirt was plain white, expensive, tailored, fastened with cufflinks. The cufflinks were still in the sleeves: plain heavy gold studs. A pair of grey wool suit trousers, expensive, well-tailored. The pockets held only a folded white handkerchief that smelled of cologne.

The suit jacket was next: also grey wool, with a silk lining of vibrant orange. The front pockets were empty; the inside pocket held a slim diary. She skimmed through it then set it aside to study.

A smartphone, his wallet and his keys. She switched on the phone. The screen bloomed into life, requesting a password. She switched it off and put it on top of the diary: she could work out the password later. His wallet held a hundred pounds in notes; and there was a debit card, three credit cards, some photos of his daughters, a supermarket points card which she found vaguely touching, a condom, and an unfilled prescription for antidepressants dated two weeks previously.

No wallet clutter. Interesting. She'd expected to find colleagues' business cards, old till receipts, scribbled phone numbers, appointment cards for the dentist or optician, but there was none of that. Years ago, doing her undercover training, Eden had learned how much could be gleaned about a person from the scraps of paper in their wallets; that a simple bus ticket could make or break a cover story. Now, she wanted Paul's receipts so she could reconstruct his movements and establish a pattern of life. They weren't in his wallet – maybe he decanted them at home at the end of each day.

She weighed the keys in her hands. This might be her only chance. As soon as it was a reasonable hour she'd have to ring

Paul's ex and let her take over. Paul's ex. The woman he'd hired her to follow, check out her spending habits and work out whether she was duping him. *Tried to kill me.*

Suddenly she was on her feet, grabbing her coat and car keys, ramming her camera in her backpack, and thundering down the stairs with Paul's keys in her hand. He'd turned to her when he knew he was dying, he'd asked her to find out who had done this. Tracking down scumbags – it's what she did best. She'd do it for him. She was back in the game.

Paul's flat was in an impressive modern block near a super-market. Executive apartments, gated entry, and an underground car park. She tried several keys before the gate opened, then a few more tries to get into the building. Inside, the atrium was of polished pale marble with a central circular water feature surrounded by Australian tree ferns lit from below by ghostly blue lights.

A lift carried her to the penthouse. As she ascended, she took a pair of latex gloves out of her backpack and slipped them on. If Paul's death *was* deliberate, his flat could be a crime scene, and the police wouldn't let her near it. She wouldn't leave any trace that she had ever been there, but she was claiming first dibs on searching the place.

She got the apartment key right first time. The door was heavy, opening with a moneyed swish over a thick, oatmeal carpet. Doors led off from a large entrance hall which con-tained a coat rack holding a black macintosh and two golfing umbrellas, and a small table with three unopened letters on it. The letters were postmarked the day before, two were circulars, the other possibly a credit card statement. As she replaced them, she noticed that the table was remarkably dust-free.

Moving down the hall, Eden tried each door in turn, get-ting her bearings. The living room was huge, glassed on two sides and looking out over the town and to the hills beyond.

Duck-egg silk curtains were drawn back from the windows, giving over the full expanse of window to the view. Two large, cream leather sofas faced each other across an expanse of carpet. One wall held a plasma TV, another held a Hockney print. Not bad to come home to.

Starting with the hall, she photographed the whole apartment. As soon as the news was out about Paul's death, this place would swarm with family and friends. She wanted an accurate record of how it looked when no one even knew he was sick; a record that wasn't subject to the vagaries and mendacities of human memory.

Then she searched the place, starting with the desk in Paul's study, methodically emptying each drawer and replacing the contents in order. Paul was scrupulously neat, and the flat was tidy and clean. Lines from recent vacuuming striped the carpet. Everything was filed and sorted. Bank statements (overdrawn), credit cards (maxed out), utility bills (red reminders). No wonder Paul was worried his ex might try to screw him for more maintenance. No company accounts: they must be at the office, but from the state of his personal finances, his business couldn't be doing as well as he'd hoped. Was that why he'd seemed haggard when she saw him in his office? She lifted the camera and photographed each bank and credit card statement, mentally totting up the figures as she went. Paul owed thousands.

Eden lowered the camera as an icy shiver ran over her skin. *This. Deliberate.* Had it all been too much for him? She recalled the prescription in his wallet. Antidepressants. He wouldn't be the first person to commit suicide over financial pressures.

In the bathroom cabinet she found a packet of antidepressants, partly taken, a different brand to the prescription. The last pill was taken on Sunday. She slid the information leaflet out of the packet and pocketed it. At the back of the cabinet was a bottle of sleeping pills. She tipped them into her palm: twelve left.

The label on the bottle showed that there had been thirty when it was filled, about four months previously. She scribbled down the name of the sleeping pill and shoved the bottle back in the cupboard.

Cotton buds, aspirin, a box of condoms. She opened the box and counted how many remained: he'd used four. No tampons, extra toothbrush or feminine clutter in the bathroom. She tipped the bathroom bin on to the floor and riffled through the contents. An empty shower gel bottle. Cardboard tubes from loo rolls. An old Elastoplast. She shovelled it all back in and went into the bedroom.

The bedside table held a biography of Mrs Thatcher, a pile of receipts and loose coins. She gathered up the receipts and glanced through them. Cash withdrawals, business lunches, a bottle of expensive wine. Underneath it all was a membership card, *Elegant Introductions* with a photograph of two champagne glasses touching. A handwritten date showed Paul had been a member for the past seven months. There was a website and an email address. Eden focused the camera and photographed both sides.

She had just upended the washing basket when she heard the front door opening. She froze, straining her ears. The door clunked shut again, and there was a clink of keys. Hurriedly she stuffed the laundry back in the basket and cast around for somewhere to hide. A walk-in wardrobe to the side of the room. She slipped between the suits and pressed herself against the back wall.

Paul's cleaner? It was only half past six in the morning. A girlfriend? Ditto. Eden held her breath. The suits prickled against her cheek. She didn't fancy her chances explaining her presence in Paul's flat to whoever it was, never mind the photos she'd taken, nor the fact she had a set of his keys. Too late she remembered she'd left her backpack in the sitting room.

Papers rustling, and drawers opening and closing in the living room and study. The drawers banged shut. Whoever it was wasn't expecting to be disturbed. Someone who knew that Paul wasn't going to be home. But who knew that he was dead, apart from her?

Eden shrank further against the wall as the bedroom door opened. She daren't peek round the suits to see who it was, but she stifled her breath and listened hard. The bedside table drawers opening and closing. A frustrated slam. Footsteps advanced on the bathroom, then hesitated, turned away. Eden turned to marble as the footsteps receded and shortly afterwards the front door banged and was relocked shut.

She staggered out of the wardrobe, gasping for breath, her heart thudding. For a moment, she leaned against the wardrobe while black spots danced in her vision. When she'd steadied herself, she crept round the flat, peering into each room. The flat was empty. The desk drawer was left partly ajar in the study. Eden yanked it open. The pile of papers had been rearranged. She'd left the credit card bundle on top, now the bank statements were at the top.

And there was something else. A sensation in the room. She walked round, her senses at hyper-alert, nailing it down. A smell. Deodorant or body spray. Quite strong, freshly applied. An amateur, then. Someone who wasn't used to searching houses without being detected. And there was something else. The pristine table top in the entrance hall was smudged with fingerprints. Someone was either careless, or simply didn't care. The thought didn't comfort her.

Checking she'd left nothing behind, Eden inched open the front door, closed and locked it, snapped off her latex gloves, then slunk from the building.

CHAPTER
SIX

Wednesday, 25 February 2015

07:20 hours

The hair across the doorway was still there. So was the one she'd planted across the window latch. Eden breathed a deep sigh and her shoulders slumped. Suddenly she was dog tired. Her eyes were gritty and her mouth felt foul. Hours slumped in a plastic chair at the hospital hadn't done her back and neck any favours: her spine was a Jenga tower after a few turns by drunk students. A long hot bath and a few hours' sleep were screaming out to her, but first there was Paul's ex-wife to deal with. She needed to be informed of Paul's death and Eden had no idea what her phone number was.

A quick search of the phone directory and a call to enquiries revealed the number was ex-directory. She riffled through the pages of Paul's diary: the number wasn't written in there. He knew it by heart, why should it be? So that left the phone. The number was undoubtedly saved in his contacts, in the phone that was password protected.

It was years since her training, and she dredged up the basics for how to access a password protected device from a memory that was faded and tattered with fatigue. Start with the most obvious solution first. Most people had so many passwords to remember that they simply wrote them all down in a place that was easy to find. The back pages of Paul's diary yielded a few passwords, but they were too long for a phone. A couple of four-digit pin numbers – careless. There were also some random number and letter configurations that probably granted access to his bank accounts.

But there was nothing that would get her into the phone. She bounced it against her chin while she thought. It must be an easy password, then, not a combination of letters and numbers, and it must be a word that Paul wouldn't forget.

She switched on the phone and tried his surname: Nelson. Password incorrect. Damn, too easy. Another two goes before she was locked out of the phone altogether and she'd have to seek out a little scrote to break in for her. Her fingers hovered over the keys. It wouldn't be Zoe, his ex's name. What were his daughters called again? Her tired mind ferreted out a snatch of her meeting with Paul two days ago. Tessa and Holly. That was it.

She typed in Tessa. Password incorrect. One more go left. As she typed in Holly, she worked out which scrote she'd likely find waiting outside the magistrates' court that morning. Just as she'd realised gloomily she could count on Stinky Mick appearing in court, the screen fired up and an array of icons tiled the display. Bingo. Who said parents didn't have favourites.

The phone immediately started beeping with incoming text messages. She scrolled down the list, scanning for anything interesting. They could wait, his ex couldn't. Any longer and the delay would look suspicious, which, of course, it was.

Zoe Nelson. Mobile and two landline numbers. She dialled the first landline from her own phone. It went to an answering machine stating the office was closed. Eden didn't wait for the message to finish. She hung up and dialled the other number. It rang five times before a harassed voice answered, 'Yes?'

'Zoe Nelson?'

'Yes. Who is this?'

'My name's Eden Grey. I'm afraid I'm ringing with some bad news about your husband, Paul.'

'Paul? He's my ex-husband.'

Eden waited a beat, kicking herself. She should have gone to the house, imparted the news face to face, seen the woman's reaction. 'I'm very sorry, Mrs Nelson, but Paul died in the early hours of this morning.'

'Paul? Died? What are you talking about?'

Eden stood and paced to the window. There were beads of rain on the glass, a mucky cloud hanging over the hills looming beyond the town. 'He was taken ill yesterday and went to hospital. He died there this morning.'

'But I ...' Zoe pulled herself up short. Whatever she was about to say, she changed it to, 'What did he die of?'

'It was a serious stomach disorder.'

'Are you calling from the hospital? Are you one of the staff?'

'No, I'm ...'

'Are you that woman he was seeing?'

'No, I'm a friend. I was with him when he died.'

'Hang on a minute, why didn't you call me earlier?' Eden noted the change in tone. 'I should have been notified as soon as he was taken ill.'

A shift from making sure Eden knew Paul was her ex. Now she was claiming territorial rights over his corpse. Eden bit the inside of her cheek. 'Paul didn't want you or your daughters to be upset. He particularly didn't want the girls to see him so distressed.'

A sob the other end. 'I only spoke to him the other day. I can't believe he's dead.'

Eden softened her voice. 'When did you last see him?'

'Yesterday, no Monday. It was Monday.' Zoe's voice came out as a small squeak. 'I can't believe he's gone. The girls are going to be devastated.'

A cup of tea. Bed. A few hours' sleep. Eden stripped off her clothes. They reeked of hospital – detergent and floor polish – a smell that summoned bad memories for her. She stuffed her clothes straight in the washing machine and set it going, unwilling to have the stink in the washing basket even for a moment.

She lay in the cool sheets and tightened and relaxed each muscle in turn. She'd need a hot bath when she awoke, her skin smelled stale and sour, but now she was going to sleep. Her mind whirred for a few moments and then gave up the fight. She turned on to her side and slept.

'Mummy?'

'Molly? Is that you?'

'Of course it's me, Mummy. I've come to wake you up. Sleepyhead.'

Eden ran her hand through her hair. It felt lank, as though she'd been on a long train journey. 'Mummy's tired, Molly. Why don't you come in and snuggle for a minute?'

The little girl tugged back the covers and slipped into the bed beside her. Eden wrapped her arms round her and pressed her cheek against Molly's soft hair with its scent of apples and sunshine.

'There, that's nice, isn't it?'

Molly wriggled. 'Mummy? Mummy?'

'Yes, Molly?' Sleepiness overcame her.

'Mummy, hold me! I'm slipping!'

She reached for the girl. So tired.

'Mummy!' She lunged for her. Their hands connected, slipped, and Molly plummeted, screaming. Eden awoke with a cry.

Two hours. She'd only slept for two hours. With a groan, Eden flopped back on the pillows. More than six years she'd been having these dreams, following Molly as she grew up and got steadily older. Had she lived. The dreams always ended the same way, with Molly falling out of reach, away from her grasp and the safety of her arms. Just as she had done in real life.

Sleep was impossible now. Once the dream had delivered its salvo she knew she'd have no peace, however hard her head ached or her mind yearned for repose. Eden threw back the covers and clambered out of bed, her back nipping. She set the taps running in the bath, pouring in lavender and bergamot bath soak and fluffing it into bubbles. While the bathroom filled with steam, she fetched a clean towel from the linen cupboard: it smelled biscuity from the tumble drier.

The thing Eden liked most about her flat was its bath, large enough that she could lie full length. Inching her numb body into the water, she slipped down until her head was submerged. The water blocked out noise and she was alone with her thoughts. A hot soak was just what she needed to scrub away all the grot and despair, and work out what to do next. Piece by piece she examined what she knew.

Paul was taken ill. He died. He told her his death was deliberate. Hours after he died, someone searched his flat.

On Monday, when she'd seen him, he mentioned that he was hoping that his business would pick up. He also asked her to investigate his ex-wife, suspicious that she was spending the money he sent for his daughters. The ex was also demanding more money from him, and he was refusing to pay. Was that a motive to kill him?

Paul had serious financial difficulties: that much was obvious from his bank and credit card statements, and the stack of unpaid bills. The antidepressants and sleeping tablets suggested he'd been under stress for a few months at least. Had he borrowed money from a loan shark and found himself unable to pay? Who else did he owe money to? And was it enough to get him killed?

There was another possibility, one she didn't like at all. Maybe Paul tried to kill himself. Divorced, separated from his daughters, business struggling, money problems: he wouldn't be the first man to crack and end it all. She knew that male suicide typically was a big, no-going-back affair: a shotgun, hanging, jumping from a tall building. Paul could have jumped from the top of his office block or his apartment block, though his tidy approach to life suggested this messy death, its trauma for others, would be abhorrent to him. An overdose was cleaner, if that's what he did. But if he had taken something and changed his mind, why not tell the hospital staff what he'd taken, when he was admitted?

There was something else that bothered her. Paul was neat: his flat was clean and tidy, his financial records were filed and ordered. So where was the suicide note? He didn't seem the sort of man to leave his daughters without explaining why. He loved them; he wasn't cruel enough to sentence them to the rest of their lives with that question burning in their hearts.

Eden rose out of the bath water, shampooed her hair, and dunked down under the water again. Perhaps Paul was worried that his insurance wouldn't pay out on suicide. Then why tell her it was deliberate? Why go to the hospital at all if he was set on ending his life?

This. Deliberate. Tried to kill me. Not *tried to kill myself.* She swallowed, a horrible feeling crawling in her stomach. Murder. Who would want to kill him? His ex-wife, possibly hoping for more money or even just complete control over their two daughters. Then there was Chris Wilde, the employee with the fake bad back: Paul said he would give him an opportunity to explain himself. Had Paul seen him and how did the confrontation go? A jilted lover? A business rival?

Eden sat up and pulled out the plug. The water was too cool now to enjoy wallowing. As she stepped out of the bath, her mobile rang.

'Hello, skiver.'

'Hi, Judy.' Eden tugged her towel closer about her and shuffled her feet into slippers. 'I missed Zumba, didn't I?'

She'd met Judy at Zumba classes shortly after she'd moved to Cheltenham and they'd soon become friends. Now they had a routine of going to the pub for a drink and a gossip after the class. In the turmoil at the hospital, it had completely slipped her mind.

'Are you all right?' Judy asked. Tall and statuesque, she had a voice to match, her vocal chords serviced by being mother to three lively boys and working as a teacher.

'Yes, I'm fine. Sorry, it was a bit of a night.'

'A likely story. You knew she was going to be a right sadist, didn't you? She made us do those bum-toning exercises for about two hundred years.'

Eden giggled. Judy's fake exasperation always cheered her. For a moment, the shock of the past hours ebbed away. 'It's good for you. Think how pleased Marcus will be with your new-found bottom.'

'Marcus!' Judy groaned. 'Because my so-called friend – that's you by the way – didn't show up, I had to go home right at the end of the class instead of going to the pub and drinking wine and mainlining crisps until I'd put all the calories back on. I get home, and all the children are still up, not bathed, not in their pyjamas, and overexcited because he was teaching them how to wrestle.'

Eden laughed. 'You decided to have three children, you only have yourself to blame.'

Judy tutted. 'I didn't choose to have three boys. Have you any idea how many socks and underpants are welded to my carpets?'

'Thousands, I imagine.' Eden always loved the cosy chaos of Judy's house, and she liked Marcus, Judy's husband, a kind, gentle man who was completely overshadowed by Judy's huge personality.

'Let this be a warning to you,' Judy continued, 'one mucky weekend in Venice and next thing you know it's Calpol at all hours and boobs down to your knees.' She paused for breath. 'What were you up to, anyway? Snuggled up to that gorgeous Aidan, I bet, you lucky sod.'

'Jealousy is a very unattractive quality,' Eden said, teasing. 'I was at the hospital. No, I'm OK, but a client of mine was taken ill and he asked for me.'

Judy's tone changed to concern. 'Oh dear, Eden. Is he all right?'

'No; he died. I was with him when he died.'

'How awful! What happened?'

'They're not sure at the moment.' *This. Deliberate. Tried to kill me* echoed in her mind.

'Do you need me to do anything?' Judy asked.

Eden was touched. Judy's life was hectic with work and three young children to look after, but the offer to help and comfort, should Eden need her, was genuine. 'I'm OK, thanks, Judy, but how about we catch up later this week?'

'Sounds good. Take care, loves, bye!'

Eden hung up, thinking. Without a cause of death, she couldn't tell when Paul was given whatever it was that killed him. She could, however, focus on opportunity and motive. She'd track Paul's movements from when she saw him on Monday.

Janice scrunched up her tissue and reached for another. 'I can't believe it,' she said, again. 'I'm sorry, what must you think of me? It's just, he was a lovely man to work for, you know?'

'I know,' Eden said. She handed Janice a fresh tissue. The older woman took it and gave a hearty blow, her hands trembling. She was in her usual elegant trouser suit, this time in a pale jersey that flowed about her stout frame. Her eyelashes were coated with navy mascara, now clumped with tears.

They were in Paul Nelson's office, side by side on the black leather sofa at the far end of the room, the door closed to prying, inquisitive eyes. A spare suit and shirt hung on the back of the office door. On Paul's desk, all the pens were lined up beside the blotter and the computer was switched off. A model for a new development was set out on a table pushed against one wall.

The best way to find out what a man's life was really like, Eden thought, was to speak to the person who knew him best: his PA. A PA ran his diary, his life; was simultaneously confessor, confidante and guard dog. Janice had been Paul's PA for over ten years. If she didn't know every detail of his life, no one else did.

'Janice,' Eden started, 'are you up to answering some questions about Paul?'

Janice sniffed and drew back her shoulders. 'Of course. Anything I can do to help.'

'Take me through Monday. What he did, who he saw.'

'Let me get his diary.' Janice disappeared into her office and returned with a large diary. Post-it notes flapped from the pages. 'Here we are. Monday. He met with the architect at ten, to go over the designs for a new development. There was a planning meeting about them that evening and I think he wanted to check he had all the facts at his fingertips. He was like that, meticulous.'

'He came across that way,' Eden said.

'He had lunch at his desk, quite early, before twelve. He asked me to pop out and buy him a sandwich.' She blinked a few times. 'That was unusual; he wasn't the sort of boss who gets his PA to pick up his dry cleaning and buy his wife a birthday present. I've known some who think you're at their beck and call.'

'But he asked you to get his lunch that day?'

'Yes, he said he had to make some calls. He seemed a bit preoccupied, now I think about it.' Janice consulted the diary again. 'One o'clock, you saw him. Then he was at his desk until nearly five, when he left.'

'Where did he go?'

Janice folded her hands on top of the diary. 'I think he went to see Chris Wilde. He made a comment when I took in his coffee at three. Something about Chris treating him like a fool and he'd see about that. A spur-of-the-moment decision.'

'And after that?'

'There was the planning meeting at seven. After that, I don't know. He came in at the usual time yesterday, but he looked ill.'

'What happened yesterday morning, Janice?'

Janice sighed and another tear escaped and ran down her cheek. She brushed it away with her hand. 'Paul came in at eight as normal, and said he wasn't feeling too well. He looked poorly: his face was grey and he was sweating, but he said he had work to do.'

She paused to blot her face. Eden smiled to encourage her to continue.

'When I came in at ten with his coffee I could see he was very ill,' Janice said. 'I rang the doctor for him and he spoke to him over the phone. The doctor told Paul to go to casualty. I ran him down there, even though it's not far, he was just too poorly to walk and I didn't want him to go on his own. We got him checked in and I left him with the doctor.' Janice reached for the tissue box. 'I wish I'd stayed.' She swallowed. 'He rang me to let me know he'd been admitted. He sounded terrible, in awful pain. That's the last time I spoke to him.'

'What time was that?'

'About two, I think.'

'Did Paul leave the office at any time between eight and when you ran him to the hospital just after ten?'

'No, apart from to go to the bathroom.'

'And did anyone come to see him, go into his office at all?'

'Chris Wilde. He saw Paul for about five minutes not long after he got to work.'

'Chris Wilde? Didn't you say Paul saw him the evening before? Monday evening?'

Janice turned to her. 'He said he was going to see him, but I don't know if he did. Maybe Chris was out.'

'What did Chris come here for?'

'I don't know. There were raised voices, but I couldn't hear what they were saying.'

'And after Chris Wilde had gone, did Paul say what it was about?'

Janice shook her head.

'Did Paul have a lot on his mind?' Eden asked. 'Was he stressed or worried about anything in particular?'

Janice gave a short, humourless laugh. 'He runs this business, I should think that's enough to give anyone sleepless nights.' She caught the expression on Eden's face and her voice dropped. 'Why? What are you saying?'

Eden chose her words carefully. 'Just before he died, Paul told me that what was making him sick was deliberate.'

Janice squeezed her hands together. 'I don't believe it. He wouldn't kill himself, not Paul. Is that what he meant?'

Eden didn't answer, just left the silence to hang there, and waited for Janice to fill it.

'Yes, but … the girls … he wouldn't do that to them. Not even if he was desperately unhappy.'

That's what Eden suspected, too, which left her original interpretation, the only meaning she'd put on Paul's words until she'd searched his flat and seen he was up to his eyeballs in debt.

'Did Paul have any enemies?' She threw out the question casually.

'Paul?' Janice turned round astonished eyes on her. 'No! You know what he was like. His ex-wife, Zoe, she was always after more money. There were a few dozen solicitors' letters flying back and forth, I can tell you. But enemies? Not Paul.'

Another thought occurred to her. 'Did Paul have a cleaner? For his flat?'

Janice gave her a quizzical look. 'I don't see how that …' She sighed. 'Yes, he did. He asked me once if I thought he ought to buy her a birthday present. I told her it depended on whether she scrubbed behind the taps. He laughed at that.'

'Do you happen to know which days she cleaned for him?'

'Mondays.'

'You're sure?'

Janice shrugged.

'Did the cleaner have a key to let herself in?'

A shake of the head. 'No idea. Why? What's that got to do with anything?'

Eden changed tack. 'When I was here, Paul showed me a photo. There was something in it that puzzled him. Do you mind if I borrow it?'

She went to the filing cabinet and found the photo Paul had shown her, of a blond girl in the school hall, in front of a painting that had piqued Paul's curiosity. Probably nothing, but worth checking out.

'I don't mind. Make sure you give it to his daughter when you're finished, though,' Janice said. She glanced up sharply. 'You think someone killed him, don't you?'

This. Deliberate. Tried to kill me. Janice was too shrewd to be taken in by airy demurrals. 'Yes, I do.'

Janice stared her fiercely in the eyes. 'Find who did it, Eden. For Paul.'

The council offices were a line of elegant townhouses with white stonework and delicate ironwork overlooking the war memorial and the farmers' market. Eden went up the stone steps into the building and asked for directions. A winding staircase led to the second floor, where a glass door was stencilled 'Planning'.

'Can I help you?'

'I'd like to speak to someone about Monday's planning meeting, please.'

'What about it?' The woman looked her up and down without obvious interest.

'It's about a planning application.'

The woman pressed a button on her phone and summoned a colleague. 'Donna's coming,' she informed Eden, as though she'd know automatically who Donna was.

Eden nodded and loitered in the lobby, reading the notices pinned to the wall until Donna arrived.

Donna was in her mid-forties, with chubby knees and an overdone hairstyle. Her black and red patterned skirt was too short and too tight and a red blouse gaped as it strained across her bust, betraying a snatch of red lacy bra. She flushed as she bustled up.

'I'm Donna Small. You've got a question about a planning application?' she asked.

'I've got a query about Monday's meeting.'

'You'd better come to my office.'

Eden followed her across the offices into a small cubicle that held a computer, desk and chair. The edges of the monitor were tiled with post-it notes and the desk was cluttered with framed photos. A large black Mulberry bag occupied the only other chair in the cubicle. Donna hurried to move it so Eden could sit down.

'Greg isn't here at the moment,' Donna started, 'but I may be able to help you.'

'Greg?'

'Greg Barker, the head of planning. I'm his PA.' Donna frowned. 'You did say you'd got a query about a planning application?'

'It's more a question about Monday's meeting,' Eden said, leaning back in the chair and crossing her legs. 'Can you tell me who was there?'

The pause button between Donna's eyes deepened; the question evidently wasn't what she was expecting. Her words tumbled over themselves as she answered. 'The planning committee, as usual, and anyone who'd been asked to attend to discuss their application.'

'Were you at the meeting?'

'I take the minutes.' A moment's hesitation. 'Are you a journalist?'

'Is it possible to have a copy of the attendance list and the minutes?'

'Not until they've been approved at the next meeting.' Donna sounded affronted, as though it was the rudest question she'd ever been asked. 'Look, what is it you want to know?'

Eden cut to the chase. 'Was Paul Nelson at the meeting?'

'Paul Nelson? Why?'

'I just want to know if he was there, and how his planning application went.' Donna raised her eyebrows. 'You do know Paul Nelson?'

Donna's eyes swivelled sideways. 'Not really. I know who he is.'

Eden said nothing for a few seconds, watching Donna fiddling with her computer mouse, making a couple of clicks, her back half-turned to her, letting Eden know how important she was. Donna's fingernails splayed out at the end, like shovels, and she wore them long. They clacked against the computer mouse. She had an expensive manicure, the sort that needs redoing every couple of weeks. She wore a sapphire ring on the middle finger of her right hand, and an emerald ring on the index finger of her left hand, but no wedding ring.

When Donna stopped fussing and turned back to her, Eden asked, 'What time was the meeting?'

'It always starts at seven,' Donna said. 'Look, what's this about?'

'Paul Nelson died this morning. I'm trying to find out what happened to him.'

Donna paled. 'Paul?' She blinked rapidly several times, then stared down at her hands for some time. When she spoke, it was a croak. 'Dead?'

Eden nodded. 'I'm afraid so,' she said, gently.

Another croak. 'How?'

Eden shrugged. 'We're not sure at the moment, that's why I'm trying to trace his movements.'

Donna's head shot up again. 'Are you the police?'

'I'm investigating Paul Nelson's death.' Eden leaned forward, her forearms resting on her knees. She looked Donna in the eyes and said, smoothly, 'Tell me about the meeting.'

'What do you want to know?'

'Was Paul Nelson there?'

A nod of the head.

'Did you speak to him?'

'No, not really ... that is, just normal things. You know?'

'How did he seem?'

Donna shrugged. 'Just as usual. Just ... Paul.'

'What about his planning application? He was there because he had an application that was being discussed. What was it for?'

'Erm, something about a development in Cheltenham. A Regency building he was going to convert. He wanted to dig below the foundations to create an extra floor.'

'Was his application approved?'

'I don't know. I can't say.' Flustered now, Donna was rearranging papers and muddling them up again.

'You took the minutes.'

'Yes, but ...' Donna swallowed. 'I think it would be better if you spoke to Greg about all this. He's the one to tell you, not me.'

'Tell me what?'

'Tell you anything.'

Exhausted from only two hours' sleep, and cranky that Donna had clammed up and refused to say anything until she saw Greg, Eden wasn't in the mood for games. Donna told her Greg would be back at two, but it was after three before he rocked up. Donna peeped out at her from the safety of her cubicle from time to time, her eyes wary, but she didn't speak to Eden again.

Greg Barker was in his early forties with sandy hair and an incipient bald patch, and nourishing a gut that was starting to overspill his waistband. He bundled into the department trailing a scent of cold air and a garlicky lunch. As he came in, Donna scrambled to her feet and started to call, 'Greg, there's someone here to see you.'

Before Donna could reach him, Eden rose from her seat and thrust out her hand.

'Greg Barker? I'm Eden Grey, I'd like to speak to you about Paul Nelson.'

'Paul Nelson?'

'In private, please.'

Greg raised his eyebrows but didn't argue. Not many people did when Eden used that tone, she'd found. He led her to his office, pausing on the way to demand Donna make him a large black coffee. Donna glanced up at Eden, a pleading look in her eyes, but for what, Eden wasn't sure. Don't dob me in to my boss? Don't let him know what I told you? Not that she'd said much.

Greg parked himself in an executive leather chair behind a desk that was too small, and leaned back with one foot resting on his knee. He was wearing superhero socks, a different superhero for each day. Today was Batman.

'Now, how can I help you, Miss …?'

'Grey. Were you at the planning meeting on Monday?'

'Of course, I'm head of planning.' A smirk rippled across his face as he announced this.

'Was Paul Nelson there?'

'Yes.'

'How well do you know Paul?'

'I've crossed swords with him over planning applications in the past, yes.' Greg grinned a wolfish grin.

'And his current planning application – was it approved?'

'That's between the committee and Paul, Miss Grey.'

Eden fixed him with a stare. Greg tipped back in his chair, rocking gently. Smug, comfortable, arrogant. Time to shake him up a bit. 'You'll have difficulty communicating with Mr Nelson from now on, unless you have a medium on your staff.'

A moment's confusion while he processed what she'd just said. 'What?' The chair thumped back down.

'Paul Nelson's dead. He died this morning.'

'What was it? A heart attack?'

'The doctors aren't sure how he died,' Eden said. 'I'm investigating the circumstances surrounding his death. The outcome of the planning meeting may be relevant.'

Greg bounced forwards in his seat. 'Yes, of course. Anything I can do to help.' He rang Donna and ordered her to print out a copy of the minutes. 'He didn't ... do anything silly, did he?'

'What makes you think that?'

'I mean, I know the building business isn't going well, and we all have our troubles, and you know, sometimes everything can get on top of you ...' He stumbled to a halt. 'Where's Donna with that coffee? Gone to Colombia for it?'

He picked up his phone and pressed a button, and told Donna to hurry up with the coffee. 'And have you got any paracetamol I can borrow?'

Donna appeared moments later with a mug of coffee and a packet of painkillers. Her hands trembled as she put them in front of Greg, and a drop of coffee slopped on to the desk. A look passed between her and Greg as she left; a look Eden couldn't interpret.

Greg punched two tablets out of their silver coffins and popped them in his mouth, swallowing them with a slug of coffee. They didn't go down easily, and he choked. Eden was reminded of her gran, who always crushed tablets up and hid the powder in a spoonful of jam, and she felt a pang for simpler times.

'How was Paul on Monday evening?' Eden asked, when Greg had thumped his chest and managed to get the painkillers to go down.

'Fine, I think. We didn't talk for long, just a few pleasantries before and after the meeting.'

'And his application?'

Greg inhaled noisily through his nose. 'It was rejected, I'm afraid. God, I feel awful now. If I'd known he was in that state of mind, well, you never think, do you?'

'How did Paul react when his application was turned down?'

Greg puffed out his cheeks. 'He seemed to take it on the chin. But then, maybe he went home and it all was a bit much. I remember thinking when he arrived at the meeting that he seemed a bit quiet.'

'He seemed depressed before the meeting?'

Greg shrugged. 'Not depressed, exactly, but as though he had a lot on his mind.' He raised his eyes to hers. 'That's what I thought – a man with a lot on his mind.'

'You said you spoke at the end of the meeting,' Eden said. 'Did he say where he was going then?'

'No, I presumed he was going home.'

'And that was the last time you saw him, or spoke to him?'

Greg's eyes bored into hers. 'That's right. Last time I saw him was when the meeting ended.'

Chris Wilde, he of the Christmas pudding bobble hat, was at home when she called round. His glistening hair and the whiff of deodorant betrayed that he'd not long got out of the shower. He stared at her for a moment before speaking, his brow furrowed.

'You're that nosy detective, aren't you? Taking pictures of me the other day.'

'That's me.'

'What do you want now?'

'To talk about Paul Nelson. You work for him?'

Chris Wilde pulled a face. 'Not any more, thanks to you.'

'What happened?'

'What's it got to do with you? You got paid to follow me, then I presume it was you who told Paul you thought I was on the take.'

'When did you last see Paul?'

Chris rasped the stubble down the side of his face. 'He came round here on Monday.'

She could imagine why. She herself had warned that if Chris Wilde put in his resignation before Paul sacked him, he could try to claim pension benefits.

'What did he want?'

'That's my business.'

'Paul Nelson's dead,' she said, bluntly, keen to see his reaction.

Chris slumped against the doorframe as the colour drained from his face. 'Was it a car accident?'

'No,' she said. 'You said he was here on Monday. What time?'

'Six. No, half five. He rang and asked to see me.'

'How long was he here for?'

'Not long: the wife was getting dinner ready and Paul said he was going to a meeting afterwards.'

'And?'

'And?'

'What did you and Paul talk about?'

Chris's eyes darkened. 'He accused me of lying about my bad back. I told him I was going to resign. He just laughed at me. I lost my temper and threw him out of the house.'

She'd seen his temper in action, grabbing her camera from her and threatening to hurl it to the ground. She wondered what he'd said or done to Paul. Had he hit him? Tried to kill him?

'Lost your temper?'

'Don't you start getting ideas. It's my house. I don't have to put up with him accusing me like that. I didn't kill him, if that's what you're thinking.'

'Who said anything about killing?' she said, as a red stain spread up Chris's neck and face.

CHAPTER
SEVEN

Tuesday, 24 February 2015

17:10 hours

There were a few bones missing from each of the skeletons. Little fingers, some ribs, a toe or two. They were laid out on plastic sheets on top of a gurney, the pieces of the skulls at the top, and the rest of the bones articulated below.

Aidan cast a professional eye over the skeletons and turned to the forensic anthropologist the police had called in to examine the remains. Lisa Greene: petite, thirty-five, with reddish hair in a pixie crop that lent her an elfin look; famous for her extensive repertoire of filthy songs and respected for her uncompromising approach to life and disregard for people she regarded as tossers.

'Old?' he asked, twitching his head at the skeletons.

'Old,' she replied. 'My report will put the age of the remains at over a hundred years. They're really crumbly so I wouldn't be surprised if they're two hundred years old, but I'd need carbon dating to confirm it.'

'Will the police pay for that?'

She laughed, a throaty growl that betrayed a dedicated cigarette habit. 'Not a hope.'

'We found the tip of a blade when we dug out the rib cage,'

Aidan said. 'I thought there were a couple of nicks on the ribs. What do you reckon?'

She selected one of the ribs. 'This one. Yes, there's a pre-mortem wound here. No sign of healing at all. Looks like the knife snapped when he was stabbed. A bugger, eh?' She looked across at the other gurney. 'There's nothing on the other skeleton, the woman, to indicate how she died.'

'We can probably rule out natural causes,' Aidan said drily. 'Considering how they were buried.'

Lisa snapped off her latex gloves. 'Can't say. There's nothing on her bones, that's all I can say. And all I can tell the police.'

'I don't think they'll be worried, seeing as the deaths were over a century ago. I doubt they'll be doing a re-enactment on *Crimewatch*.'

'No. Still.' She reached behind her neck to unfasten the straps on her green scrubs. 'Here, give me a hand with this, will you? I've got it knotted.'

Aidan picked the knot free, aware that his breath was tickling the down on her skin. There was a mole on the back of her neck; a tender place for lovers to kiss. A place familiar to him in memory. Suddenly he thought of Eden, and wondered if she'd come for dinner with him that evening.

'How old were they, when they died?' he asked.

'The woman was young, only just out of her teens, I'd guess. Her early life was tough: malnutrition when she was a child.' Lisa pulled a packet of mints out of her pocket and popped one in her mouth. It clattered against her teeth as she talked. 'And she'd got syphilis. There are a few places where you can see it pocking the bones. Must've been sexually active very young as it takes a while to develop to that stage.'

'Not congenital?'

'The teeth look normal.' She held up the skull to show him. 'With congenital syphilis, you tend to see peg teeth. She was very young when she contracted it.'

'Married young?'

'You dear innocent boy,' Lisa said, patting his face. 'More likely she was a prozzy. She'd been infected and re-infected several times over.'

Aidan glanced at the bones laid out on the gurney. 'Did she die of syphilis?'

'Weren't you listening? I can't find a cause of death on the skeleton. But probably no, she didn't die of syphilis, it wasn't advanced enough. Yet.'

'And the bloke?'

'The bloke, as you call this weedy specimen of manhood, was a short-arsed, pigeon-chested piece of piss. About five feet four, age mid-twenties. What he did to get a knife in the ribs I can't guess. He wouldn't have been able to fight his way out of a wet paper bag. Still, it takes all sorts.' She drew in a breath. 'Dinner?'

It was a moment before he realised she was asking him. 'You want me to pay?'

'Yes, you cheapskate bastard.' Lisa grinned. 'I promise I'll be more charming if you let me have a starter and a pudding.'

Aidan abandoned thoughts of calling Eden and springing a surprise midweek date on her. 'OK. But only if you come and look at where the skeletons were found first.'

'Why?'

'I'm intrigued, that's all.' He locked the lab door behind them and they clattered up the metal stairs to the ground floor of the Cultural Heritage Unit. 'I wondered if there might be any more under there.'

Lisa clomped over the turf to the excavation. A yellow digger stood silently by, like a frozen giant insect. At their feet the trench lay abandoned, its mud sides smooth and gleaming with rain.

'Clay soil?' Lisa asked.

'Uh-huh.'

'Sod, isn't it? I dug a hundred out of clay once. Nearly killed me.' She bent to the trench and he couldn't see her eyes. She'd worked on a war crimes excavation, and Aidan suspected the remembrance hurt her. She fiddled with the soil for no apparent reason. Collecting herself, he thought. He could read her as well – better – than he could when they were post-graduates together.

Lisa straightened and cast a professional eye over the school grounds. 'Could be more. Are they going to widen the trench?'

'It's all on hold until the police get your report.'

'Your team didn't find any extra bones so there could be just the two bodies. What was this place in the past?'

'A private house.'

'When did it become a school?'

Aidan shrugged. 'Why?'

'It's unlikely that the skeletons were buried when this was a school. Teachers are good at spotting when someone's been buried in the middle of the tennis pitch.'

'Court.'

She flashed a wicked smile. 'You never did know when I was winding you up.' Flicking her attention back to the trench, she said, 'If this was a garden before, it's quite easy to dump a couple of corpses in the shrubbery.'

'Not that easy, Lisa. Someone would notice.'

She looked him in the eye for a moment. 'You reckon? People go missing all the time. Even with our Big Brother, *you are on CCTV* culture you can get rid of an inconvenient corpse if you need to. Think about those serial killers who bury people a few inches beneath the soil in their back gardens. None of the neighbours suspected a thing.' She glanced again at the school grounds, at the looming amber building and the green swathes of rugby and hockey pitches and shuddered. 'Come on. Dinner.

This place is giving me the creeps. All those young people with their dreams and hormones.'

She tucked her hand into his elbow and bumped along beside him as they made their way back to his car. He held his arm stiffly, counting the paces until they were back at the car and he could shake her off.

As he started the engine, Lisa broke off blowing on her hands to ask, 'Why are you grubbing up these skeletons, anyway? I thought you were management now.'

He grinned ruefully and trundled the car over the mud-ridged driveway. The headmistress would go mental when she saw the mess the diggers had made. It looked more like a farm track than the elegant entry to an elite school.

'I miss being down a hole,' Aidan admitted. 'It's nice not having to scratch out bits of pottery in all weathers, but when something comes up I like to have a look.' He turned towards the town centre. 'And I've always had a soft spot for bones.'

'I remember.' Lisa smiled at him. She popped another peppermint in her mouth and clacked it round her teeth a few circuits before saying, casually, 'We could grab a takeaway and go back to your place, if you like.'

Aidan didn't answer immediately, but stared ahead through the windscreen and faked irritation at a youth dawdling across the street, texting on a mobile phone. He parked the car in a space behind the ladies' college.

'We're here now,' he said, and saw the shadow of disappointment flicker across her face. 'You still like Italian, don't you? You'll love this place.'

It was too early in the week and too early in the evening for the restaurant to be full. Aidan wasn't sure if he preferred it that way. An empty restaurant was less intimate than a busy one with its press of warm bodies, exhaled wine and shared secrets. Yet this table near the window felt exposed. He reminded himself he was only having dinner with a colleague; a respectful thing to do. They both knew that was a lie.

'A bottle of house red,' Lisa said, when the waiter came for their order.

'I'm driving,' Aidan said.

'That's OK. I'm not.' She spoke in Italian to the waiter, who clamped her hand in his and chatted back to her effusively, something that sounded flirty. Lisa lapped it up. She'd been the same that summer they were on a dig together in Italy. Hot studs panting after her everywhere she went. They couldn't get enough of this sunburnt rose with her dirty laugh and naughty eyes. He'd spent three months lousy with jealousy, his fists constantly balled, just in case. It didn't change a thing.

'Aidan? What're you having?'

He snapped back to the present and cast his eye down the menu, ordering the duck special.

Lisa took a slug of wine and studied him across the table. 'So why aren't you married, Aidan? You're well over thirty now.'

'So are you.'

'Yes, but I'm different.'

He tore open the paper wrapping on a breadstick. 'I thought you were going to marry that journalist. What was his name?'

'Luka, and that's ancient history. There've been a couple of contenders since then. Anyway, don't change the subject.' She topped up his glass. 'You're not bad looking; sensible job; quite good in bed.' She raised an eyebrow at him, making him strangely ashamed. 'I'm surprised some woman hasn't dragged you up the aisle a long time ago.' She swallowed a mouthful of wine. 'So?'

He shrugged. Lisa's pupils were huge in the dim restaurant and her skin was flushed from the wine. Beneath that pixie exterior was a passionate, intelligent woman. A description that could fit Eden, he supposed. Except.

'There is a woman, actually,' he said.

'That's great.' Lisa sat back in her chair. He glanced at her and looked away, knew she was regrouping and deciding on her new strategy; he wasn't sure how he felt about it. 'Tell me all.'

'We've been going out for a while. She's lovely. It's great. That's it.' He wished he hadn't said anything, wished he could suck all the words back in again. Too late, now, Lisa was in for the kill.

'What's she called?'

'Eden.' Saying her name, offering it to Lisa, felt like betrayal. Ridiculous.

'Eden?' He hated the quizzical way she said Eden's name. 'That's … unusual. Eden and Aidan. There's quite a ring to it, don't you think?'

'I've never thought about it.'

'Eden and Aidan.' Lisa's voice took on a sing-song quality. She snuffled a laugh. 'Eden and Aidan, sitting in a tree. K … I … S … S …'

'Your antipasta, *signorina*.' The waiter materialised with a plate of artichoke hearts which he swished in front of Lisa.

By the time she'd finished fluttering her eyelashes at the waiter and flirting in Italian, she'd moved on from Eden's name. 'What does she do?' Lisa asked, spearing an artichoke and popping it in her mouth. A slick of oil glazed her bottom lip.

'She's a private investigator.'

Lisa leaned forward, her eyes sparkling. 'A private dick? That's … well! Does she carry a gun?'

'No.' Did she? For all he knew Eden toted a pistol in that leather messenger bag she used as a handbag.

'What else?'

'What else what?'

'Tell me about her.' Lisa brushed her fingers over the back of his hand. He slid his hand away, off the table. 'Siblings? Where did she grow up? Where did she go to uni? How did she become a private eye?'

'No siblings, I don't think. Not sure where she grew up. Uni in London.' Had Eden said London? He wasn't sure. And why did she become a private investigator? It'd been a while before he even found out what she did for a living. Research, she'd said, for the first six months they'd known each other, until eventually she'd come clean. And she'd made it quite clear any further questions were unwelcome.

'Right.' Lisa had her face in neutral. He knew that look: it meant she was thinking a lot and was holding back. Trying to be polite. 'As long as she makes you happy.'

'Here's our pasta,' Aidan said, relieved, as the waiter approached again. There was the ritual of putting down the plates, the appearance of a block of parmesan and a grater, the wielding of an unfeasibly large pepper mill, then at last *buon appetito* and they were released to savour their meal.

'Serious?'

Aidan didn't understand what she meant. His fork hesitated, hovering above his plate as he frowned at her.

'You and Eden?' Lisa said. 'Is it serious?'

'Probably.'

The tide went out quickly on the wine bottle. He had one glass. After the pasta, Lisa put away a tiramisu, to the evident delight of the waiter, who brought them coffee for free. She ordered a limoncello to accompany it. When a pile of notes lay on top of the bill, Lisa yanked her coat from the back of her chair.

'Where's your place?' she said.

'I've got a flat in a Regency house.'

'Nice. Let's go, then.'

'Aren't you going back to Oxford?'

'Tomorrow morning. Got to write my report first.'

She turned and called goodbye to the smitten waiter, then they went out on to the Promenade. The wind cut down the street and the pavement was splattered with pigeon droppings. Tree roots had lifted some of the paving slabs. Lisa tripped on them and caught his sleeve. He disentangled himself, ramming his hands in his coat pockets.

'Still allergic to being touched,' Lisa said, lightly, but there was an edge of steel underneath her words.

He didn't answer, but walked further apart from her and was relieved the car was merely a step away.

He drove the short distance to his flat and parked in the only free space outside: always available because the ground dipped and formed a permanent puddle. Lisa crowded behind him, shivering as he found his key and opened the front door. Her boots clattered on the stone staircase as they toiled up to his flat.

'This is me,' he said, cracking open the door.

Inside it was clean and sparse. The sofa was a biscuit colour, well made and long enough for him to lie full stretch along it. A couple of scarlet cushions perched at each end, finely plumped and set at the same angle. The bookshelves, set into the alcoves either side of the fireplace, were crowded with books, arranged according to colour. A shelf of blue spines, one of old orange Penguins, a line of black paperbacks. Classic novels, mathematics, code breaking, Greek myths, architecture, poetry.

He watched her looking at the eclectic mix, at the old red Bakelite radio on the mantlepiece, at the perfect symmetry of the room.

'Cup of tea?' he asked.

'Sure.' Lisa wandered to the window and peered out at the mellow stone Regency buildings curving opposite. 'This is lovely.'

'I like it.'

'The Cultural Heritage Unit is obviously paying you well.'

He didn't answer, just placed a tray with teapot, cups, saucers and a jug of milk on the table. 'I can't remember if you take sugar,' he said.

Lisa shook her head. 'Or milk. Got used to having it black when I was abroad.'

The war crimes case. She'd been determined to take it, even though it took her away from him; even though it signalled the end of their relationship. A long time ago now. Ten years.

He poured a cup of tea and carried it over to her, and stood beside her while she sipped her tea and gazed out at the church tower lit up against the night sky.

When he turned to say something, she kissed him. Suddenly, yet not unexpectedly. The scent of her skin was so familiar it was like coming home. The perfume on her hair sent him spiralling back through the years. She broke away to put down her cup, then gently put her arms about his neck and brought his lips down to hers. She tasted of wine and chocolate and the ghost of cigarettes. So easy to fall back in love with her.

Aidan pulled away, picked up the cup and saucer from the carpet and carried them into his kitchen. The toaster wasn't quite parallel to the wall and he moved it back into place. A line of herbs, a present from Eden, sat on the windowsill. He plucked off a couple of leaves and crushed them in his fingers, releasing the scent of thyme.

'I'll walk you to your hotel,' he said, coming back into the sitting room.

The county archives in Gloucester had a box of materials on the Cheltenham Park School. Aidan bagged a table in the corner of the study room and took everything out piece by piece, placing it in front of him like a giant jigsaw. Photographs of rows of pupils with serious expressions and nineteen-thirties haircuts. The school during the Second World War, the hockey pitches dug up for vegetables and Anderson shelters. A plan of the house when it was built; designs for the pleasure gardens and the Temple of Venus in the grounds. Account books: page after page of scrawly faded writing. At some point the books had been exposed to water – ink slipped across the pages in a slick, the words obliterated for ever.

Aidan peered into the background of the school photos. The formal gardens – clipped hedges and geometric paths – were there, in the swathe of land between the building and the Temple of Venus. The skeletons were found there, in the formal gardens, close to the original building, an area that had hardly been touched in the past two hundred years, not even by war, until now, the diggers had grubbed it all up for foundations for a gymnasium and science block. Progress.

Aidan ground the heels of his hands into his eyes. It had been a mistake to walk Lisa back to her hotel last night. He should have phoned her a taxi, waved her off and escaped, instead. He groaned. Instead of walking her along frost-sparkled pavements to her hotel, agreeing to have a drink at the bar, talking over old times. Staying too late; drinking too much; chewing over the past and raking it all up again. And then she'd leaned forwards, her eyes dark and huge, and looking more than ever like a sprite from another world, and asked him something so startling at first he assumed he'd misheard her. When clarification proved he hadn't misheard, he recoiled, left in a hurry. And to make it worse, he realised he'd left his scarf in her room, handing her an excuse to be back in touch with him.

He groaned again, reaping a disapproving look from a dedicated genealogist occupying a study carrel opposite. It was a right fucking mess.

Aidan shuffled the papers around the desk until they formed a new pattern. In front of him were the plans for the building that was now the school: a massive Georgian residence of mellow stone, the Temple of Venus in the line of sight of the formal rooms on the first floor. A dotted line joined the house to the temple. He squinted at the diagram, struggling to make out the writing. What was that? It cut right across the formal gardens. Suddenly the pattern cleared. Pushing back his chair, he went outside, lurking by the fire escape to make a phone call.

'Trev? Aidan. Can you and Mandy get a geophys survey of the school site? I think I've found something interesting. I'll tell you where to focus.'

He sweet-talked the archivist into making copies of the diagrams for him. When she returned with the sheets, she also offered a leather-bound book which she carried in gloved hands.

'This is a diary, written in Cheltenham in the 1790s, when the house was built,' she said, handing him a pair of white cotton gloves. 'It was originally called Greville House. Could be some mention of it in here, if you're interested.'

'Sure, I'll have a look.' Any excuse to delve into the past, he thought, relishing the familiar tremor of expectation as he handled the book and wondered what treasures it contained. Details of what people had for dinner, gossip about their neighbours, complaints about tradesmen: it all fascinated him. He could spare another hour in the archives to browse through this. And by the time he got back to the office, Lisa should be safely on her way to Oxford and it'd be another ten years before he saw her again. Hopefully.

Ezekiel Proudfoot, the diary's author, was concerned with three topics: marrying off his daughters, the quality of the sermons he heard in church each Sunday, and his bowel movements. The last, it appeared, were not eased by the reputed health properties of Cheltenham waters, no matter how many gallons of the sulphuric brew he downed at the town spas.

Aidan settled in his chair for an hour's entertainment in Ezekiel's company. His descriptions of Georgian Cheltenham were diverting, and the acerbic comments about worthy Cheltenham personalities could have come straight from a contemporary gossip magazine. But what made Aidan sit up and reach for his notebook were the remarks Ezekiel made about one Mr Ellison:

Mr Ellison occupies the finest house in Cheltenham, Greville House, the largest villa in the whole district. It is a mixed honour to be invited there, though Mrs Proudfoot insists we should go. She, good innocent woman, thinks only of viewing the rooms and furnishings, perusing the pleasure gardens that have recently been planted, and of deciding which ideas she shall copy in our own much more humble home, at great calamity to my pocket, no doubt. But it is not the expense of new tables and curtains and paths that stays my hand. It is the reputation Mr Ellison is unhappy to own in Cheltenham, the rumours of the company he keeps and of a secret society that meets in his own home, in Greville House!

I am not one for idle gossip, as any who knows me will testify, but when I hear from our own parson that Greville House is linked in infamy with the Hellfire Club, then it becomes a place where I cannot let my dear wife and daughters pass a minute. No matter how grand the wallpapers nor how piteously they cry to be allowed to go.

It is rumoured that there is a society, the so-called Paternoster Club, that meets in Greville House, attended by many a fine gentleman and many a woman of low morals. Alas, even here in Cheltenham we have such women. Actresses, and worse. I cannot divine the purpose of the club, only that it is closed to any who are not of sufficient means, and any who are not of appropriate temperament. By which is meant, I infer, debauched, depraved, corrupt and dissolute.

No, I told Mrs Proudfoot firmly. We shall not accept the invitation to go to Greville House to see the rooms and gardens and the Temple of Venus now it is all finished. We shall stay at home, and count our blessings.

She was not cheered by this.

Lisa was outside his office, sucking deeply on a cigarette, when Aidan got back to Cheltenham.

'Thought you'd be back in Oxford by now,' he said, kicking himself for sounding churlish.

If she noticed, she didn't react. She ground the cigarette out with her heel and kicked the stub into the gutter. 'I've finished my report but thought we could add in whatever you got from the archives, and anything else the team have turned up.'

'Not your job to do this, surely?' They both knew it wasn't. Go in, look at the bones, make a pronouncement, go home, write a report. That was how it worked.

'I know, but it's nice to be working together again. It's been far too long. We don't see enough of each other.'

She held the door open for him, and they went into the office together.

'Ah, you're back,' Trev greeted him, a tea-stained mug clamped in his nicotine-stained mitt. Aidan experienced a rare sensation: being pleased to see Trev.

'Everyone in the meeting room?' Aidan asked.

'Just grabbing a cup of tea. Mandy's found a packet of biscuits!' Trev sloped off to the meeting room, evidently happy with life.

Aidan followed him, aware of Lisa close on his shoulder. Mandy and Andy were already in the meeting room, in deep discussion over a printout spread in front of them. Today Mandy's hair was an even more virulent shade of red than normal, making her skin jaundiced. She wore a silver ring on each finger, each set with a different semi-precious stone. Andy was young, strong and tattooed, his blond hair gelled into a quiff. Andy, Mandy and Trev. They sounded like children's TV presenters. Looked like it too, in their bright, stripy sweaters. Aidan sighed, seeing his team through Lisa's eyes.

Mandy and Trev were seasoned archaeologists who'd worked at the Cultural Heritage Unit for years. He'd inherited them when he took up the post of director. Andy was fresh out of university, hardworking and enthusiastic, and surprisingly tolerant of Trev's habit of referring to him as the YTS boy.

Lisa took a seat next to Mandy. She glanced at Aidan and announced in a stage whisper, 'Cute, isn't he?'

'Who? *Aidan?*' Mandy asked, her eyes round with disbelief.

'All right, my lover?' Trev said, huffing into the chair on Lisa's other side. He was a galumphing bear of a man in his forties, his hair a grizzled halo. A frowsty, stale wool odour hung over him like a miasma.

'I'm fine, thanks,' she said, quirking an eyebrow at Aidan as if to say 'quaint staff you've got here'. Aidan ignored her, drawing a black notebook from his coat pocket. It was fastened with an elastic band, and had a fountain pen clipped to the top. The notebook was expensive, an indulgence: Eden had bought him a stash of them for Christmas. Seeing it now brought a faint twinge of guilt.

Aidan cleared his throat to mark the start of the meeting. 'So,' he said, declining the biscuit packet as it circulated. How long had those biscuits been around? They looked prehistoric. 'Did you excavate those with the skeletons?'

'They're all right if you dunk them,' Andy said, bobbing his biscuit enthusiastically, until – predictably – it broke off in his mug.

'Amateur,' Trev said, shaking his head in mock dismay at the youth of today.

'All right, everyone,' Aidan said, trying to pull the meeting to order. 'On Monday we excavated two skeletons from the grounds of the Park School. Lisa,' he turned to her, 'you examined them. Can you tell everyone what you found?'

She ran through her findings with economy: a male and a female skeleton, over a century old and possibly much older. No evidence to indicate how the female, aged late teens, died, but the male had a cut mark on his ribs suggesting he was stabbed.

'We found an object in the ribcage when we excavated,' Aidan said. 'Andy, you cleaned it up and x-rayed it. What did you find?'

'Metal tip, probably from a knife,' Andy said. 'Probably snapped off in the body.'

'Can you date the knife?'

'I'd estimate a couple of hundred years.' His mouth drooped as he announced this, evidently hoping for something much more interesting and preferably Anglo-Saxon.

'It could have been an old knife used in the attack,' Lisa said. 'The knife isn't necessarily contemporary with the skeleton.'

'An antique knife used to stab a Victorian man,' Aidan said, drily. Lisa loved playing devil's advocate but he wasn't in the mood for outlandish speculation, especially not from her. He caught the hot flash of anger that crossed her face.

'And no sign of how the female died?' Trev asked.

'No.' Lisa tapped her pen on her notebook.

'I've done some research into the area, to see whether we should expect more human remains,' Aidan said, 'and I found something interesting in the archives. The school was originally called Greville House, and a local diarist heard rumours that it held meetings of the Hellfire Club there.'

'Wow,' Mandy said, spraying jammy dodger crumbs.

Andy smirked and made a lubricious face at Trev.

'Orgies, in Cheltenham?' Trev laughed, rubbing his hands together. 'Must be something in the water.'

'The diarist didn't specify exactly what went on there, just that he wasn't going anywhere near the place, and neither were his wife and daughter.'

Everyone laughed. The biscuits made another circuit of the room.

'But I did find something relevant,' Aidan said, as they settled down. 'There was a plan of the original house and drawings of the grounds. It looked like there was a tunnel that led from the house to the Temple of Venus.' He turned to Mandy. 'What did the geophys turn up?'

Mandy unfurled a huge sheet of paper, marked with dark patches. She used the end of her pen to show patterns under the soil.

'We surveyed the whole site that they're going to build on,' she explained, 'apart from the bit where they've already put new foundations. If there were skeletons under there, they've been minced to dust by now.'

'Any evidence of other burials in the geophys?' Lisa asked.

Mandy shook her head. 'Nothing conclusive. A few little patches of anomalies, but they could be anything. The ground has been disturbed for some school buildings already – they could be related to that.'

'We didn't do the whole site,' Trev added. 'It would take days to cover the whole thing.'

'However,' Mandy said, her eyes alight. 'You can see here there's a fainter patch in a straight line from the school to the Temple of Venus.' Her pen traced the route. 'Something hollow and man-made, and it's quite a size.'

'Could be talking about me,' Trev quipped. Aidan ignored him.

'The tunnel is still there?' Aidan said.

'Looks like it.'

CHAPTER
EIGHT

Cheltenham, August 1795

It was a long, rattling journey to Cheltenham. Rachel stared out of the coach window at the countryside and yearned for the harsh bounce of light on the Thames, haggling with pedlars, and the scramble of London life. She was going backwards. Back to where she came from – to soft mud and country towns, to people who spoke slowly as if there was no hurry in the world.

Now her dreams of snagging a rich lover and being set up in a house in Westminster were risible. No one in Cheltenham would set her up in a house. They wouldn't cart her back to London, not when they probably already had a mistress there. And anyway, who takes the spa waters and hopes to fall in love? Only honest women; not her sort of people. She was nothing but a holiday whore.

Her spirits sparked as they clattered into Cheltenham itself. At least there were houses here, and a long road of shops. They dined and rested the first night at the Plough on the High Street, the next day taking occupancy of their new home. They were to reside in Coffee House Lane, squashed between a malt house and the theatre. It was an old house, with sloping floors and beams low enough to crack the heads of the unwary, and with doors that either stuck and needed a kick to open, or else swung wide as though a ghost were announcing himself.

It was well furnished, though: the Cheltenham tradesmen eager for the rub of Mrs Bedwin's money and none too pernickety about the source of the revenue. She'd brought ten girls with her, including Rachel and Roseanne, whose black skin was certain to be a novelty in provincial Cheltenham. The girls ran from room to room, clucking with approval, as Mrs Bedwin stood in the hallway and calculated her profits.

They opened for business that afternoon. Gentlemen taking the waters for gout, nerves and skin complaints shuffled into the opulent room that served as the seraglio and gawked to think they weren't in London. A painted frieze around the room advertised the delights on offer – a nervous gentleman had just to point and it would be his. And what delights! Mrs Bedwin was no bucolic bawd: her board of fare was the same as in the city, outlandish and foreign enough to ensure there was soon a brisk trade.

'Get in first, girls, that's my motto,' she sang, as the bell rang and another gentleman was shown upstairs. 'The best brothel in Cheltenham. All tastes catered for. Front, back or sideways, we aim to please.'

Rachel shared a bed with Emma Trulove, a sallow-faced girl of seventeen who was known to be amusing to ladies. Mrs Bedwin had brought her from London with the others, and each night she and Rachel hunkered under the covers and sketched their futures.

'I shall find myself a rich husband who adores me and who allows me as many gowns and gloves and bonnets as I wish,' Rachel said, her fair hair tangling with Emma's auburn tresses on the pillow. 'And I shall have a little dog who sits in my lap and feeds off a saucer, and a bird in a cage to sing to me while I lie on my sofa.'

Emma sighed. 'I'll have a rich, handsome husband, but he'll be quite old, maybe even forty, and he won't be interested in bed so I can take as many young lovers as I like.'

'Men?' Rachel asked, slyly.

'Some of them,' Emma giggled, 'it's as well to have variety.'

They tugged the blankets up to their mouths to smother their sniggers.

'But what do you do?' Rachel said, rising on her elbow so she could look down at Emma's face. 'With a woman, I mean?'

'All sorts of things.'

'But there's nothing to go anywhere!'

'Oh there is,' Emma said, pinching Rachel playfully. 'Anyway, you'll see for yourself soon enough.'

'What do you mean?' Suddenly Rachel went cold. Servicing the men was one thing, but surely Mrs Bedwin wasn't going to sell her to a woman? She'd never live down the shame. Rachel Lovett, with her legendary maidenhead, a plaything of fat rich ladies? She'd rather die. 'I'm not a … Mrs Bedwin wouldn't … would she?'

Emma laughed. 'No, silly. But Mrs Bedwin's been asked to take some of us to a party, and she told me there was a woman who particularly wanted to meet me.'

Relief flooded through her. 'So, am I to go to this party, too?'

Emma nodded. She snuggled down under the covers for a moment, and then asked, 'What hold has Mrs Bedwin on you, Rachel?'

'What do you mean?'

'You could've left her place in London, but you didn't. And now you let her bring you here, when you obviously hate it.'

'I don't hate it.' Rachel sighed. That wasn't true. She did hate Cheltenham. The initial pleasure at seeing the town had soon waned. The water running down the middle of the streets and the stepping stones to cross from the butcher to the grocer. The local women in their drab dresses; the fine women with their haughty expressions. She was a long way from the hustle and grime of London, and she missed it with an ache that penetrated deep into her soul. And right now, she feared she'd end her days in dull, genteel Cheltenham.

'Rachel?'

Rachel puffed out her cheeks. 'Don't tell anyone.'

'Course not.'

'I thieved some gloves and Mrs Bedwin knows about it. I've got to keep her sweet or she'll sell me to the thief-taker.'

Emma gave a low whistle. 'Would she really sell you?'

'If I crossed her, or if it was to her advantage. You know what she's like.'

'At least the thief-taker won't find you here.'

That much was true, at least. She was safe in Cheltenham. May as well sit it out until she was well and truly forgotten. If she went back to London now, it could be Australia for the rest of her life, or dangling on the end of a rope with the crowd yanking on her ankles.

Yes, she was safe in Cheltenham.

'Best gowns, girls, and plenty of rouge!' Mrs Bedwin stood, flustered, her hairpiece awry, as girls scurried about with armfuls of silk and petticoats. 'And make sure you all washes your downstairses,' she added, with a grimace at Daphne, who was notoriously slatternish.

The girls lined up in front of her: Daphne, Emma, Roseanne and Rachel, each in a gaudy dress of magenta or lime or marigold; bosoms pushed high; faces transformed by paint and powder. Mrs Bedwin paraded up and down the line, tweaking a ribbon here, smudging a triangle of rouge there until she was satisfied.

'Do me proud, girls,' she exhorted them, as they all clambered into the carriage waiting outside. Squashed in together, their skirts a tangled flowerbed, the five of them were driven through the streets of Cheltenham to the outskirts of the burgeoning town and through a set of high iron gates, up a long driveway lined with weedy saplings, until the carriage came to a halt outside a huge amber portico.

'This is it, girls,' Mrs Bedwin breathed. 'This is where we makes our fortunes, doing what we knows best. Eh, girls?'

Her cheeks were flushed beyond the reaches of rouge, and Rachel realised with a start that Mrs Bedwin was nervous. She glanced again at the imposing house.

'Where are we?'

'Greville House,' said Mrs Bedwin with a gasp, as if the mere name were explanation enough.

Emma pulled a face at Rachel and tugged her up the wide stone steps and into a magnificent two-storey atrium. Rachel barely had time to marvel at her surroundings before she and the other girls were hustled upstairs and into a grand salon furnished with plush sofas and drapes of gold. Tables were burdened with baskets of fruit and flowers. Double doors, the height of the ceiling, stood closed at the far end of the room.

'Now, girls, get ready,' Mrs Bedwin said. 'Daphne, you're to lie here.'

'On the table?'

'That's it. Quick smart.'

Daphne hoisted up her skirts and clambered on to the table and lay down. Mrs Bedwin flew across the room and smacked the girl's thighs.

'Not like that, you fool! Get your clothes off first. No one wants a plate of ribbons and lace.'

'Plate?' Daphne said.

Mrs Bedwin tutted and started undoing Daphne's gown, her lips working constantly with instructions, imprecations and curses on all the girls. Roseanne was to strike a pose; Rachel was to drape herself enticingly on one of the sofas; Emma to mirror her; and Daphne was to be eaten alive.

She lay naked and squirming as Mrs Bedwin bustled about, placing oysters along her collarbones and draping grapes over her ears. Sliced pineapple lay from her chin to her groin. Cherries festooned her legs, miniature pies balanced on her arms, sweet puddings decorated her thighs. After she'd giggled so hard one of the puddings fell on to the carpet, and been rewarded with a pinch, Daphne lay subdued and submitted to being covered from head to toe in tasty morsels. By the time Mrs Bedwin had finished, only her face was bare.

'Just in time,' Mrs Bedwin breathed, as she placed the final oyster. Speaking sharply to Daphne, she said, 'Now you lie still, my girl. You hear me?'

Daphne's silence was evidently taken as assent, as Mrs Bedwin clapped her gaze round the other girls, then nodded at the servant standing nearby. He swung the double doors wide, and announced, 'Supper is served.'

There were four men and one woman. Well-dressed but no aristocrats, Rachel's finely tuned eye for detail informed her. New money. On the up. Still. A guinea's a guinea. They swept into the room, their eyes raking from sofa to sofa, from girl to girl, before resting on Daphne, lying as still as death on the table.

Mrs Bedwin dropped a deep curtsey. 'Mr Ellison,' she said.

'Mrs Bedwin, and your young ladies, I see.'

'Only my finest for you, sir, and your friends.'

Mr Ellison was tall and had a thin, flat face with a Roman nose. His friends were in their early thirties, sporting gay waistcoats and silly grins. The woman was in her fifties, and had a mouth that was more used to scolding than kissing.

Mrs Bedwin bowed herself out of the way, and watched proceedings from the small chair at the side of the room, as the friends selected a girl each and hoisted her on to his lap, while Mr Ellison selected the choicest morsels from Daphne's spread. Her eyes were huge as his face dipped to her collarbone, his lips snatching up an oyster. He tipped back his head and guzzled it down, then turned his attention to the pies and cherries.

I'm glad it's not me, Rachel thought, as she caught Daphne stiffen as Mr Ellison's teeth nipped her flesh.

'You're a table,' Mrs Bedwin had told her. 'And tables don't move, don't giggle and don't flinch. Got it?'

Rachel realised the gentleman who was fondling her breast was taking very little interest in it. His hand was clammy and his breath stale, huffing down the side of her neck, but like her, his eyes were fixed on Daphne.

Mr Ellison stood up from Daphne's spread. 'Hungry?' he said to Roseanne's paramour. He galloped up to the table and was soon gobbling away, mouth slobbering, his saliva juicing along Daphne's increasingly exposed body. Rachel twisted her head away from the sight.

The men took it in turns to eat from Daphne's body. When her gentleman got up to eat, Rachel found herself in slobber mouth's arms. His rubbery lips worked over her neck and down the front of her gown, sluicing her with the salty fishy smell of oysters. She found herself thinking of the pigs on her uncle's farm, and of the pig killer who came each year to split their bellies open and catch the blood in a bucket ready to be made into puddings.

The woman took her turn, too, nibbling at Daphne's instep as though shy, then suddenly plunging into the pineapple that covered Daphne's groin. Mr Ellison laughed as one of the men groaned.

'Too slow, my friend. Mrs Hardcastle has beaten you to the prize.'

When all the food was either eaten or trodden into the floor, Mr Ellison helped Daphne down from the table. Rachel disentangled herself from a pair of arms, thinking the evening was done, but it was just beginning.

Mr Ellison led the dance with Emma, and was soon joined by Roseanne and Rubberlips, and then by Rachel and a short, fair-haired man. In the manner of dances, partners twirled and moved on a step, and a new partner followed. The dance became raucous and drunken, a tangle of skirts and bosoms, sweating palms and avaricious lips. As the heat rose, Rachel realised that Mr Ellison and Daphne had disappeared. She twisted her head to scout round the room, but there was no sign of them, only Mrs Bedwin at the far end, licking her finger as she counted banknotes.

Daphne wasn't in the carriage that took them back to Coffee House Lane, either. They slumped against each other as the carriage rattled them back in the early hours of the morning, and Mrs Bedwin tucked them up in bed and ordered them to sleep as long as they wished in the morning.

'But where's Daphne?' Rachel asked, though her eyelids were drooping with fatigue.

'Never you mind,' Mrs Bedwin replied, and blew out the candle.

Daphne returned late the next day, and Mrs Bedwin immediately set about drawing her a bath in front of the fire, and called for hot wine and sweet cakes to restore her. Rachel was allowed in to sponge Daphne's back and wash her long dark hair. The girl was exhausted.

'Where did you go? Why didn't you come back with us?' Rachel hissed.

Daphne turned black-rimmed eyes on her. Checking Mrs Bedwin was out of earshot, she whispered, 'I went through the tunnels. To a place you won't believe.'

CHAPTER
NINE

Wednesday, 25 February 2015

17:30 hours

Eden stopped short when she arrived back at her office. BITCH was painted in red across the door.

'Who done that, Eden?' Tony, who ran the sandwich shop just along from her, was locking up. Balding, he over-compensated with a thin ponytail like a liquorice strap. 'Unhappy client?'

'I hope not.' She clipped along the walkway to him. 'Hey, Tony, do you know when it was done? I haven't been in my office since yesterday afternoon.'

He shrugged. 'Last night, I think.' He rattled his keys into his pockets. 'It was there when I opened up this morning. Bloody vandals.'

'Yeah.' She sighed and went back to her office, calling goodbye as Tony headed off down the stairs. She'd been called some names over the years, but somehow this single word, scrawled on her door, unsettled her much more. The letters dripped red, like a Hollywood vampire caught mid-suck. Not a great advert for her business.

Inside, she switched on the electric heater, which filled the office with the smell of scorched dust, and made a pot of coffee. There were no messages waiting for her on the answering machine. Normally that would make her heart sink, but today she felt a spurt of relief: it gave her time to devote to finding out what happened to Paul. She recalled the dry scratch of his hand in hers as he lay dying. It was she he'd turned to; she'd see it through to the end.

Taking out her notes from her interviews with Janice, Greg Barker and Chris Wilde, she constructed a timeline of Paul's movements from Monday morning until he died early that morning. Information, source of information, assessment of the reliability of the source, alternative interpretations. Her old training made the process subconscious. With no clue what had killed him, every detail was relevant. There was a gap between seeing Chris Wilde and attending the planning meeting, and nothing to suggest where he went after the meeting ended. She bit the skin at the side of her thumb for a moment, then her tired brain recalled the photographs she'd taken in Paul's flat.

They were quickly downloaded to her laptop, and she zoomed in on the close-ups of every receipt piled on his bedside table, noting the time, date and place of each one. There was nothing later than five in the evening on Monday: petrol bought at a garage near Chris Wilde's house. A full tank, by the looks of it, another hint that Paul wasn't thinking of killing himself any time soon. There were no receipts for dinner or groceries to show what he did after the planning meeting, or suggest what time he got home.

Eden flipped through the photos once more. There, a membership card for a singles club, Elegant Introductions, with a phone number in discreet italics on the back of the card. Eden picked up her phone and rang it.

'Elegant Introductions,' a female voice answered, the product of an exclusive boarding school.

'Good afternoon, my name is Eden Grey. I wondered if you could tell me more about your singles club.'

A well-bred tut. 'We're not a singles club; we're an exclusive introduction agency.'

'How does it work?'

'We meet once a week, for dinner, cocktails, wine tasting. We organise theatre visits to Stratford and sailing weekends in the summer.'

'Did you have a meeting on Monday night?'

'No. We meet on Wednesdays.'

'So there's one tonight?'

'Yes. If you'd like to come along to see if it's for you, we charge forty pounds for guests. Then if you want to join, it's fifteen hundred pounds for the year. Very reasonable.'

Eden bit back a choke. The price tag was guaranteed to sift out the time wasters and the chronically short of cash. She asked, 'Does that include the activities?'

The woman gave a short laugh. 'Good heavens, no. Activities are extra.'

'Will *you* be there tonight?'

'I'm there at every meeting, to greet everyone personally.' The woman sounded affronted.

Good, Eden thought, you'll know exactly how many times Paul Nelson attended.

She hung up, thinking. She could talk to the men there – that would be easy – she'd be fresh meat and they'd come flocking, but the women were different. She imagined Elegant Introductions was oversubscribed with women who wouldn't take kindly to a newcomer, and biological clocks chime loudly. She needed a sop to throw to the women, and she knew just the man. She dialled again.

'Hello, it's me. How are your bones?'

'What? I'm fine.' Aidan sounded stressed.

'I meant the skeletons you dug up, silly.'

'Oh those, yes. Well, they're still dead.'

'Pleased to hear it.' There were voices in the background. A call of, 'What're you having, Aidan?'

'Are you still at work?' she asked.

'No, we're all in the pub.'

'An all nighter?'

'Not necessarily, though don't tell Trev that.' She laughed: she'd joined the team for their Christmas party and had been impressed by their stamina. They could out-drink the drugs squad any day. A pause, then Aidan continued, 'What're you up to this weekend?'

'A walk in the Malverns if it's not raining,' she said. 'Fancy it? Actually, I was wondering if you're free tonight? Doesn't matter if you're not.' She crossed her fingers, willing him to say yes.

'No, no that's fine. What time?' His voice was eager. Maybe Trev was doing his impressions again.

'I'll come to your place about eight. I need to brief you before we go out.'

'Where are we going?'

'Singles club. Sorry, an exclusive introduction agency.' She copied the woman's snooty voice.

'Are you trying to tell me something?' There was a catch in his voice.

'I need your help with a case,' Eden said. 'It might be fun. You might get to trade me in for a newer model. You in?'

'All right, see you at eight.'

If only she had a photograph of Paul to show people. Sometimes people recognised a face but didn't know the name. She scoured the photos she'd taken in Paul's flat that morning: surely he had a picture of himself with his daughters somewhere? There it was: on the wall in the sitting room. Eden blew up the picture and cut out the image of Paul. It was grainy but you could tell it was him. It would have to do.

As she locked her office, a thought niggled away in the back of her mind. Who was it who let themselves into Paul's flat shortly after he'd died, and searched it? Someone who knew he wouldn't be there? The thought sent cold needles across her scalp. There was no evidence – yet – of foul play in Paul's death, but there were some coincidences she just didn't like.

Didn't like at all.

Aidan. Intelligent, difficult, independent, clever. Probably the cleverest man she'd ever met. A true polymath, it never ceased to amaze her the random facts he had at his fingertips. They'd met at a talk on dowsing, part of a series on 'More Things in Heaven and Earth' which had covered mediumship, astral projection, past lives and indigenous shamans. She'd gone to the weekly talks with her friend Judy from Zumba class, joined in the debate, and stayed for a drink and a gossip afterwards. She'd seen Aidan sitting towards the side of the room, his long legs crossed, scribbling in a notebook. Their eyes had met a couple of times.

Judy nudged her. 'He's a bit of all right.'

'Who?'

'Who?' Judy rolled her eyes. 'That bloke over there, the phwoar one, the only decent man in the room, who keeps on looking at you, that's who.'

She looked again. Yes, he was attractive, but she was off men. It was just too complicated to get involved when your whole existence only began a year before. Thirty-four years of backstory was a lot to keep in your head.

Judy had pulled out of the talk on dowsing at the last minute.

'So sorry, Eden,' she'd huffed down the phone. 'Small Child started vomiting an hour ago and doesn't show any inclination to stop.'

'Poor thing, and poor you,' Eden said. 'Can I help?'

'Only if you can teach husbands not to panic at the sight of sick, human or animal. I'm praying the cat doesn't join in out of sympathy.' Judy paused for breath. 'What is it with men and cat sick? Why is it only women who can clean up sick? Perhaps they should cover that mystery at one of the weekly seminars.'

'I'll suggest it to the organisers,' Eden said. 'You could be a guest speaker.'

'Get the bowl!' Judy suddenly shrieked. 'Oh God! Sorry, Eden, he's off again. Got to go. Bye!'

So Eden went alone to the talk and found herself in the seat next to Aidan.

'Where's your friend today?' he'd asked her.

'Sick child woes, I'm afraid,' she said. 'What about you? Are you here on your own?'

'No, I'm talking to you.' He nodded at her empty cup. 'Want to go mad and have another hot chocolate?'

'Why not? Let's live dangerously,' she said. 'No cream, but I'll have an extra marshmallow, please.'

'Coming up.'

They introduced themselves when he came back from the bar with their drinks.

'Eden, that's unusual,' he said. 'Are your parents called Adam and Eve?'

'Nothing so interesting,' Eden replied. 'I'm afraid they were just hippies who lumbered me with this name.'

'You were pretty lucky to get away with Eden, then.'

She laughed. 'Yes, it could have been much worse. Rainbow, or Dolphin.'

'And your kids?' he asked, his eyes meeting hers.

She held his gaze. 'I don't have any children, or a husband, or a boyfriend right now.'

'Good,' he said, 'I'd like to change that.'

The meeting was called to order and the speaker was introduced. As they clapped a welcome, Aidan and Eden glanced at each other, smiled, and looked away. She barely heard a word of the talk.

19:49 hours

Aidan was wearing a black suit and a pale blue shirt and looked very eligible. The women at Elegant Introductions were in for a thrill. He kissed her as she came into his flat. He smelled of lemon shower gel and crisp aftershave.

'You're looking good,' he said.

She'd pinned her hair up into a chignon and made up her face carefully to create the impression of a single business-woman. She wore a knee-length green dress with a fitted bodice and flared skirt, and black kitten heels, finishing it all off with a spritz of musky perfume.

'Where are we going?' Aidan asked.

'It's a singles club in Montpellier, exclusive clientele. Forty quid to get in, I'm afraid, but get a receipt and my business will reimburse you.'

'And we're going there, why?'

Eden tucked a stray strand of hair behind her ear. 'A client of mine was a member. He died early this morning. The circum-stances are suspicious, but I've nothing conclusive yet, so I'm doing some digging, see what turns up.'

'Suspicious how?'

'He told me that it was deliberate, that someone tried to kill him, but he didn't tell me who.'

Aidan whistled. 'Did he say anything else?'

'No. Yes, just before he died, he said "Paternoster".' She pulled a face. 'Mean anything?'

'Paternoster? It's Latin, means "Our Father", as in the Lord's prayer. Was he a Catholic?'

'I don't know.'

'Maybe he realised he was about to die and started to recite it.'

'In Latin?'

Aidan shrugged. 'Some people prefer it in Latin. I do.'

Eden studied him. 'I didn't know you were a Catholic.'

'I'm not any more. I'm very, very lapsed.' He took her hand and swung it gently. 'What do you want me to do at this singles thing?'

'Just hang around with the women, chat to them. Ask about Paul Nelson if you can – say you played cricket together a few years ago or something, and he told you about the club. Just see what they say.'

'Proper detective work, eh?' he grinned. 'Do I get to roll over the bonnet of a car?'

'Only if you really want to.'

The doorbell sounded. They both turned to look at the door.

'Are you expecting someone?' Eden asked.

'I'll get rid of them.' Aidan went into the hall and came back followed by a petite woman, chuntering away to him.

'Eden, this is Lisa. Lisa, Eden. Lisa's been examining the bones that turned up at the Park School.'

'Nice to meet you, Eden, I've heard a lot about you.' Wide-set blue eyes fixed unblinking on Eden.

'Nice to meet you, too.' Eden's skin prickled and she was glad she was wearing her posh dress and had her best face on.

'You off out? Both of you all dressed up. Gorgeous as ever!' Lisa flicked a piece of imaginary fluff from Aidan's jacket.

'I thought you'd gone back to Oxford,' he said.

'Tomorrow morning. But if any more bones turn up, I'll be back. Always nice to see you. It's been ages.'

'Did you pop round for anything in particular?' Aidan said.

Lisa tapped her head and pulled a droll face that didn't fool Eden for an instant. 'Silly me, forgot why I came. I brought your scarf back. You left it in my hotel room last night.'

She dug in her coat pocket and magicked out his scarf.

'Thanks,' Aidan said, coolly. 'You didn't have to come round specially.'

'No trouble. Anyway, better let you two get off,' Lisa said. 'Good to meet you, Eden. Bye, Aidan, will see you soon.'

Aidan showed her out.

'That was Lisa,' he said, when he returned.

'So I gathered.'

'She's …' He stopped whatever he was about to say. 'Shall we go?'

Eden fastened her coat and followed him down the stairs. They walked to Montpellier where Eden pointed out the venue for Elegant Introductions.

'You go in first, and I'll come in later,' she said.

'No, you go first,' Aidan said. 'I don't want you hanging around outside. It's dark, and a woman was attacked in the town centre the other week.'

She was touched by his concern, and tempted to remind him she could take care of herself. It was a kind thought, though, so she crossed the road, her heels clacking, and went into the club.

Elegant Introductions was held in the first-floor function suite of an upmarket wine bar. A woman with blond hair styled to within an inch of its life greeted her at the door and introduced herself as Velma Purefoy. Her nails were so long they scraped Eden's palm when they shook hands.

'Lovely to meet you, Eden,' Velma said. 'There's a cloakroom on the right for your coat, then go straight in. We'll have a few games to mix everyone up in a little while.'

Aidan wouldn't like games, she thought, guiltily. He'd hate all that false jollity. Still, he'd agreed to help her with this assignment. She collected a ticket at the cloakroom and went into the bar.

There were about fifty people there, surprisingly almost equal proportions of men and women. The women were possibly slightly younger than the men, averaging age forty to their fifty, and there was evidence of a booming trade in cosmetic surgery amongst Cheltenham women. The men wore suits in various shades of grey, with brightly coloured open-necked shirts. One chap – rotund, bald, camp, with a candy-striped shirt and outsize pink bow tie – patently belonged in a different sort of club altogether. Despite that, he had a coterie of women around him, giggling helplessly as he regaled them with stories.

Eden ordered a sparkling mineral water with ice and a slice of lime so it looked like vodka. She could drink if she had to, but her days of partying hard and maintaining her cover were long gone. Simpler to keep a clear head and remember why she was here.

As she leaned on the bar, she felt her scalp crawling. Turning slowly, as though taking in the room, she caught sight of Donna Small, Greg Barker's PA. Donna glanced away but Eden was certain she'd been staring at her. Only that morning Donna had denied knowing Paul Nelson; now it seemed they were members of the same exclusive singles club.

Time to find out more. As she left the bar, Aidan walked in. He nodded and smiled at her as if he was just being courteous. She smiled back, glazing her eyes slightly, and went to find Velma Purefoy.

'Mrs Purefoy?'

'Velma, please.' She was licking her fingers and counting out twenty-pound notes. 'Two hundred and forty. There.' She glanced up. 'Do you want to join?'

'Not just yet. Tell me, does a Paul Nelson come here?'

'I shouldn't really talk about my clients, you know.'

'But if I'm about to become a member?' She watched Velma calculating the cost of discretion against a new member's joining fee. Hard cash won.

'I suppose it wouldn't hurt to tell you Paul's a member.'

'Does he come here regularly?'

'Paul? Yes, pretty regularly. Sometimes he has work trips, you know. Not everyone can come every week.'

'When was the last time he was here?'

A shadow crossed Velma's face and she closed up. 'Now let me think. Paul, Paul. When did I last see him? No, sorry, I can't remember. So many faces!' she laughed brightly, but Eden wasn't taken in. 'Why are you asking, anyway?' Velma demanded.

'I'm a business associate,' Eden said. 'He mentioned Elegant Introductions, that's why I came.'

'Oh, well, that's all right then,' said Velma. She glanced down at her cash box and started counting again.

Back inside, Donna cradled a large glass of white wine at the bar. She was wearing a tight-fitting red dress with a low scooped neckline and red satin high heels with bows on the front. A jewelled evening bag hung from her shoulder, blue gemstones flashing. Eden sidled up to her.

'Hello, again,' she said.

'What are you doing here?' Donna said.

'Small world, isn't it. Is this your first time?'

'No, I've been a member for a while.' Donna flushed

'Did you know Paul was a member here, too?'

'Paul?'

'Paul Nelson. The man I was asking you about earlier today. The man who died.'

'I didn't know him.' Donna snatched up her glass. 'Excuse me.'

Eden caught Aidan's eye and stared hard after Donna. He gave the merest nod to show he'd got the message, peeled himself away, and went to introduce himself.

'You asking about Paul Nelson?' the barman said, coming over to refill a dish of olives on the bar. He was wearing a short-sleeved shirt and tattoos embroidered his arms from wrist to bicep.

'You know him?'

'Course I do. He's a regular here.'

'And Donna Small, the woman I was just talking to?'

The barman picked up a glass and started polishing it. 'Her! She's been coming here for years. Can't be good for the self-esteem, can it?'

'How d'you mean?' Eden asked.

'Coming to a singles club for years.' He gave a low whistle and Eden instantly liked him.

'Doesn't she get lucky, then?'

'Bit of a bunny boiler, that one, if you ask me,' the barman said. 'She meets a guy, they're going out, then suddenly she's back here and it's black looks and bitter feelings.'

'She can pull them in, then?'

The barman laughed. 'Yeah, she can pull them in all right, it's landing them, cooking them and eating them that's the problem.' He bent across the bar and in a low voice said, 'That Paul Nelson you were asking about. She went out with him for a while. I don't know what happened, if she got clingy or jealous, you know how these middle-aged women get. Anyway, it all went very nasty.'

'What happened?'

'She hated him, and she didn't care who knew it. They do these games where everyone has to talk to everyone else in the room.' He rolled his eyes to show what he felt about such shenanigans. 'She got paired with him a few weeks back and refused to speak to him. Turned her back on him and let him just stand there like a prat.'

'Not very nice.'

'Then last time he was in here …'

Eden pronged an olive with a cocktail stick. 'When was that?'

'Last week. Paul was here at the bar, chatting to me about cars. He's got a Spider, y'know? Beautiful thing. Anyway, Donna comes up and when I went to pour Paul's drink, she says to me, "Put arsenic in that for him".'

'Arsenic?'

'That's what she said. Slip arsenic in his drink for me.' He nodded for emphasis. 'And the look on her face, she meant it all right.'

CHAPTER

TEN

Thursday, 26 February 2015

06:26 hours

Aidan was already up when Eden stirred. She liked to leave her curtains open so the morning sun could filter in and rouse her gently, but this morning the window was as grey as thousand-wash knickers. Raining again.

She shuffled out of bed and pulled on her dressing gown. Tying the belt, she padded into her living room, where Aidan was settled on the settee with a mug of coffee and the TV news.

She plopped a kiss on to the top of his head. 'Morning.'

'Sorry if I woke you. I've got an early start.'

'That's all right.'

'You sleep OK?'

'Fine.' A lie. She'd dreamed of Molly again, and awoke feeling sick and depressed. 'Is there any more coffee?'

'There's a pot full. It's still hot, I've only just made it.'

As she yawned her way towards the kitchen, the phone rang. Half six! Who was ringing at this time?

'Leave it. It's too early,' she called from the kitchen. 'The answering machine will pick it up.'

She was pouring a mug of coffee when the answering machine clicked in and delivered her curt message. *This is*

Eden Grey. Leave a message and I'll call you back. Then a voice she hadn't heard for a long time sounded in her flat.

'Hi, it's Miranda. I'm calling to let you know Little Jimmy has been found dead. He was killed about two weeks ago.' A pause. 'Look, I don't want to frighten you, but Hammond's hallmark was on the body. So you take care. Bye.'

Eden stared unseeing at the coffee pot, only realising what she was doing when scalding coffee dripped on to her foot. Little Jimmy dead. Hammond's hallmark. Jesus, what a way to die.

'Eden?' Aidan appeared in the kitchen doorway. His face was white with shock. 'What the hell was that about? Who was it?'

She shrugged and set about cleaning up the spilt coffee. 'No idea. Wrong number?'

'Wrong number? It was about someone being killed, for goodness sake! You'd better call the police.'

'The police already know.'

Aidan blinked at her.

'The message said a body had been found. Someone will have told the police.' She lifted her coffee mug, realised her hand was trembling, and put it back down again. She forced her voice into normality. 'Nothing to do with me, anyway.'

Aidan dragged his fingers through his dark hair, glancing from her to the answering machine.

'Top up?' Eden said, pointing at the coffee pot.

'Erm, OK.'

He fetched his mug and she refilled it, then grabbed her coffee and headed to the bathroom, calling over her shoulder, 'I'll have the first shower, if that's OK. I can dry my hair while you're having yours. Help yourself to toast and cereal.'

She locked the bathroom door and sat on the toilet shuddering. Little Jimmy dead. Hammond's hallmarks on his body. She knew those hallmarks all too well. Her stomach clenched and she puked into the hand basin, running the cold tap full pelt to cover up the noise. Hot coffee and stomach acid scorched the back of her throat. She heaved and heaved until she brought up bile. She tipped the rest of her coffee down the sink after it.

She yanked the shower up hot and scrubbed so hard her skin reddened. A shot of cold water refreshed her. She'd call Miranda when she got to her office, find out what was what. No need to panic just yet. After all, she'd been safe so far.

Aidan shot her a funny look as he passed her and took his turn in the shower. Maybe he'd heard her retching, but if so, he didn't ask. She made herself eat breakfast, forcing down each mouthful, consoled by the comforting sound of another human being in the flat with her. Someone she could rely on.

Aidan reappeared with wet hair, wearing his clothes from the night before. 'I'd better go,' he said. 'I've got to go home and change and then head out to the Park School.'

He was desperate to quiz her about the answering machine message, she could tell. Time to divert him.

'Who was that Lisa who popped round to your place yesterday?' she said, carelessly, stacking their breakfast dishes in the sink. 'The one with your scarf?'

Aidan tensed and Eden realised she'd miscalculated. Uneasily, she waited for him to answer.

'She's an ex-girlfriend from university,' he said.

'Right.'

'She asked me something.' Eden nibbled the skin around her thumbnail as she waited for him to go on. He was so obviously uncomfortable that she knew this wasn't going to be a good conversation. Eventually he blurted out, 'She wants a baby. And she wants me to be its father.'

Eden flopped back against the kitchen workbench, unable to speak. She stared at him in disbelief.

'I know. She's crazy. I told her about us, but she asked anyway.'

'And what did you say?'

He shrugged. 'I said I'd think about it.'

'You … what?' She was stunned.

'Look, we'll talk about it later.'

'There's nothing to talk about. Either you want to have a baby with her or you don't. It's quite simple.'

'We'll talk later.' He kissed her cheek and let himself out of the flat.

A baby. Aidan having a baby with someone else. Her instincts bristled. What else did this Lisa want from Aidan? And what did he want from her?

Before she left the flat, she went through her usual routine more carefully than ever, checking each window was closed and locked, placing a hair across each window and doorframe, pulling out the drawers a fraction. She let herself out, locked the door, and strung a hair across the doorway. She scouted out the hallway and car park, making sure no one was watching the building. Before unlocking her car, she ducked down and examined the chassis and wheel arches for bombs.

All OK. She got into the car and engaged central locking, sealing herself inside. She sat for a while, steadying her breathing, before she turned the key in the ignition and drove away.

Aidan kicked himself all the way from Eden's flat to his own. It had come out all wrong, that nonsense about Lisa wanting a baby. He crawled with shame every time he thought about it. After they'd had dinner together in the Italian restaurant on Tuesday night, he'd walked Lisa back to her hotel. It was a chilly evening and she'd taken his arm and huddled close to him, sucking his body heat like a thermal vampire. At her hotel, he'd made to turn away, but she'd invited him in for a drink and a chat about old times, and like an idiot, he'd agreed. Maybe he was still reeling from the kiss in his flat; or maybe there was a part of him that was tempted to start everything up again with her, even though he knew it was sheer folly.

She'd raided the mini bar in her room, cracking the caps off two whiskies and pouring them into tumblers. He tried to refuse, but Lisa held his gaze and pushed the glass towards him.

'Go on, it won't kill you,' she said. 'Help you sleep. Medicinal, almost.'

So he'd drunk the whisky and they'd talked: talked far too much about the past, their relationship. They'd been together for a year at university, both of them doctoral students. He remembered the anguish of being with her: so beautiful, and yet so independent and free he never really felt that she was his. Lisa had replenished their glasses and fixed her huge eyes on him and told him she regretted losing him.

'You had ambitions,' he said, aware that he was flattered and discomfited equally.

'The war graves. Yes.' She sloshed another miniature into her glass. A bit overshot the rim and landed on her fingers. She licked it off. 'But I paid the price. Now here I am, single, lonely and childless.'

He didn't answer.

She continued. 'I keep on doing the sums. I'm thirty-five now. If I find a great bloke this minute, it'll be about a year before I know he's the one. Get married – that's another year to sort that out. That makes me thirty-seven. A couple of years getting used to being married: thirty-nine. Even if I get pregnant straight away, I'll be forty when I have a baby. Geriatric.' She glanced across at him. 'So, I've decided the best thing to do is cut out some of the stages.' She was slurring now. 'Forget about the handsome man and the tulle. What the fuck is tulle, anyway? Prob'ly something I don't need but brides are expected to have. Anyway, forget all of that shit, and just have the baby.'

'Sperm donor?' he said.

'Exactly. But not off the internet. Could be anyone. Someone in prison spending all day wanking for all I know. No, I don't want that. I want to know who the father is. Someone good looking and kind and clever.' She faced him. 'Someone like you, in fact. What d'you reckon? Will you give me a baby?'

He'd stared at her, stunned and shocked, afraid she'd simply lunge at him and seduce him and that would be her impregnated. Ta da!

'I've got Eden,' he'd stammered. Like the presence of a girl-friend would stop Lisa when she'd set her mind on something, or someone.

'Oh yes, Eden, the private dick,' Lisa said. 'I don't have to keep you forever, if you don't want, just until there's a baby. Soon as I'm up the duff, you can go scurrying back.'

Aidan winced. He didn't dare ask about the logistics. Even if he agreed to her mad plan. Which he didn't. But he presumed she had it all worked out, the mechanics of the thing, and that embarrassed him more than anything.

She read his mind. 'You worrying about how?' she asked. 'We could use a turkey baster, but I'd prefer the traditional method.' She walked her fingers up his arm to his shoulder and tickled his ear. 'Too gorgeous.'

Heaving himself to his feet, he'd said, 'I'll think about it,' and left, swiftly.

Now he'd blurted it out to Eden. The look of hurt in her eyes when he'd told her, not that Lisa had asked, he couldn't help that, but that he hadn't firmly said no at the time. He'd just grabbed his coat and scarpered; that's how he'd left his scarf behind, giving Lisa the perfect opportunity for causing more trouble.

Damn her! Why couldn't she just piss off back to Oxford and leave him alone, instead of coming here churning things up.

How well do you know Eden? That question kept haunting him. Damn Lisa for exploiting the chink in his armour. It's what she excelled at: finding the Achilles' heel and working it. Even after all this time, he didn't know Eden that well. It was as if she only existed from the day he met her. She never talked about anything from her past.

The phone message that morning creeped him out. What the hell was that about? Some man dead, hallmarks on the body, Eden needed to take care. What did that mean? More than the message, Eden's breezy assertion that it was a wrong number and there was no need to panic frightened him. She'd changed the subject but he'd seen the look on her face when the answering machine clicked on. She knew the caller, he was certain of it. And now she was afraid.

His mind full of doubts and recriminations, Aidan changed into his work clothes and drove to the Park School. He dragged on steel-capped boots and headed towards the excavation. It was raining, a fine mist that penetrated and soaked without you realising. He'd called in to speak to the site manager the day before to warn him about the tunnels, and that there were some anomalies in the geophys that could be more human remains. They agreed to halt the building work while Aidan's team excavated the anomalies, and while further geophys confirmed the tunnels wouldn't be underneath the foundations of the new sports hall.

'You don't want the whole thing to give way,' Aidan had said to the site manager.

The site manager looked as though he couldn't care less, time was money, but agreed that hauling a JCB out of a Georgian tunnel wasn't going to be good for business, and allowed the team until the end of the week to clear the site archaeologically.

Aidan strode over to the excavation, relishing the thought of a day in the fresh air, despite the rain, scraping back the soil and recording finds. He stopped dead when he reached the trench.

At the bottom, where they'd unearthed the skeletons, a woman lay crumpled, face down in the mud. Her short red dress strained across her rump. She was wearing one red satin high-heeled shoe; its twin lay on its side in the earth, the bow on the front caked with mud. 'Oh God,' he breathed. He jumped into the trench and inched towards her. 'Hello? Can you hear me?'

No movement. He was beside her now, looking down, praying she would groan and ease herself up out of the mud.

Nothing.

He grasped the woman's shoulders and turned her over. Two glassy eyes stared at him. He staggered back with a cry and crashed into the side of the trench. For a moment, he gaped at her, gasping and fighting to keep control. Short, hard breaths escaped through his mouth. The woman had fallen back on to her face when he let her go. He wanted to turn her over, to give her some dignity, but he couldn't touch her again. One glimpse of those dead eyes was enough.

His hands fumbled for his phone. He dialled the police, gave details in abrupt, disjointed sentences and hung up. He fought to control his breathing. Black dots filled his vision, and he doubled over to stop himself passing out. He sucked in cool, rainy air until the panic subsided, then called Eden.

None of the other units were stirring when Eden arrived at her office at just past seven. The building creaked as she entered, and she was thankful that the overhead strip light dispelled some of the gloom. She locked the door behind her and made a coffee to steady her nerves before picking up the phone and dialling. Five rings. Six. A pulse jerked in her throat as she counted.

Just as she was about to hang up, a woman's voice said, 'Hello?'

'Miranda? I got your message.' Her throat was so dry her voice came out as a scratch.

'Who is this?' The voice, tetchy and familiar, spun her back across the years to her rookie days and meeting Miranda for the first time. The ballsy, no-nonsense woman she'd resented at first, then come to rely on.

Eden said, 'You left me a message about Little Jimmy.'

Silence for a beat, then, 'Christ. You shouldn't have called me. How are you?'

'Surviving. Tell me what happened.'

'He came out of prison and disappeared. Didn't check in with his probation officer, no surprise there. Then someone reported a funny smell from an empty house in nowhere-ville, and it was him. What was left of him, poor bastard.'

'Hammond?'

A click and a deep breath: Miranda lighting a cigarette. 'He's still inside, but he has plenty of people on the outside. We only know about five per cent of them, tops. Jimmy was kept safe in prison, by them, not us. We took our eye off the ball, then soon as he was out, that's it.' Another deep inhalation. 'Hammond's patient, I'll give him that.'

Eden clutched the phone tighter, her palm slick with sweat. 'Revenge is a dish best served cold,' she said, hardly able to force the words out between her teeth. Her throat kept spasming as if she was going to be sick.

'He got his revenge all right. Arrogant prick left his hallmark on the body. Bragging that it was him, but he's inside so we can't finger him for it.'

'Any evidence?'

'Pure as a wipe-clean wimple. A pro.'

'Thanks.' Eden swallowed, her throat clicking. 'Just needed to know. You know.'

'Look,' Miranda said, hurriedly, 'you take care of yourself.'

'I always do.'

A laugh. 'We both know that's not true.'

Eden smiled ruefully. A long time ago, now, she reminded herself. A different life. 'How are … Mum and Dad?' she asked, suddenly afraid.

Miranda sighed. 'I don't know, and I can't find out for you. You know the rules.'

'I know,' Eden rubbed her eyes and said, softly, 'Thanks, Miranda,' and hung up before Miranda could say anything else.

Her pulse was just returning to normal when Aidan called. She almost didn't answer, assuming he was calling to talk about his announcement that some other woman wanted to have his child. Molly's dark eyes swam before her and her heart tightened. Squashing down a surge of grief, she picked up her phone.

'Hello Aidan.'

'You know that woman you told me to talk to yesterday?'

Her mind chased its tail for a moment. So much had happened, she didn't know who he meant.

'At the singles club,' Aidan added. 'Donna something.'

'Donna Small?'

'She's dead in the bottom of my trench.'

The traffic was light and Eden had an easy journey across town to the Park School. Aidan ran towards her as she bumped over the muddy verge and clambered out of the car. He waved at the blue lights flashing at the building site.

'They told me to get out of the way,' he said. 'They're going to interview me later. Do I need a lawyer for that?'

'Did you kill her?'

'No.'

'Then you probably don't need a lawyer. Not yet, anyway.' She paused, a thought occurring to her. 'You found her, and you knew her, so you're prime suspect.'

'But I didn't …'

'You have an alibi, remember? You were with me last night.' When they'd left the club at about eleven, Donna was boogieing with a group of women, her jewelled handbag banging against her hip.

Eden hurried over the grass to the trench, where a policeman yelled at her to keep back, there was nothing to see.

'There's everything to see!' she muttered under her breath, trudging back a few yards and craning her neck to see what was going on. It was useless: the site buzzed with police uniforms. She itched to get a glimpse of the crime scene, see the orientation of the body, but it was invisible beneath the lip of the trench.

Frustrated, she walked back to her car. 'Tell me what happened,' she said to Aidan.

His face was grey and stunned. She recalled her own first experience of violent death – the shock, the guilty relief it wasn't her lying there, the fear she'd never scrub away the smell. Softly, she touched his arm. 'You OK?'

He nodded. 'Just a bit ... I never imagined there'd be a ... she was just lying there.'

'I know. How did you find her?'

'I got here first thing, and saw her lying on her front in the bottom of the trench. I thought she was hurt, so I jumped down and turned her over. That's when I realised she was dead, and that I recognised her.'

'Then what?'

'I called the police, and then I called you.'

'I wish I could have seen her before the police got here.' Eden chewed the skin around her thumb nail. 'The crime scene can tell you a lot that the police won't.'

Aidan slid his hand into his pocket. 'I thought you'd say that, so I took some photos while I waited for the police to arrive.' He handed over his mobile phone. 'They won't be great – my hands were shaking, but it's the best I could do.'

Eden gazed up at him. 'You knew I'd want to see the crime scene?'

'It's by way of an apology,' Aidan shrugged. 'I'm really sorry about dumping that stuff about Lisa on you this morning.'

'You know flowers and chocolates are more traditional peace offerings?' She opened up the folder and scanned the photographs.

Aidan turned his head away. 'I can't look at them,' he said. 'It was bad enough finding her.'

She squeezed his hand. 'You did really well, Aidan.' She skipped to the next photo. 'Any marks on the body?'

'A purple mark around her neck.' Aidan put his fingers to his throat.

'This is how you found her?' She showed him a photo of Donna face down in the mud. He shuddered.

'Pretty much. I turned her over, realised she was dead, dropped her, and she just sort of flopped back on to the soil.' He sucked in a breath. 'God, her eyes, open like that, frightened the life out of me.'

Eden nodded. 'It's all right.' She skimmed through the photos again. Aidan had zoomed in on Donna's body from various angles. 'Her skirt was ruckled up like this?'

'Yes.'

'Not shoved right up? Exposing her bottom?'

'No, just a bit … disarranged?'

She showed him one of the pictures. 'Her shoes were like this? One off, one on?'

'Yes. I didn't touch anything apart from her shoulders.'

'Did the police ask if you knew her?'

'They asked me if I recognised her. I told them I'd met her at a singles bar.'

'Did you give them her name?' Eden asked.

'I told them her name was Donna.'

'You didn't give them her surname?'

'I don't know her surname. She just told me her name was Donna.'

'Good.' Eden let out the breath she was holding. 'Say that to the police.'

'Why?'

'She was murdered, strangled from what you said about the mark on her throat, and she knew my client who also died in suspicious circumstances,' Eden said. 'At the moment the police have nothing to identify her. As soon as they know who she is, they'll be all over her home and I won't be able to get in. I want to have a look round first.'

Donna knew more about Paul Nelson than she'd let on. They'd had a relationship and it'd ended acrimoniously. Maybe there were clues to Paul's death in Donna's house.

Eden sped through the photos again. 'Spot what's missing?' she asked.

Aidan shook his head.

'Last night, Donna had an expensive jewelled evening bag. It's not on her body and it's not in the trench or nearby, so where is it?'

A quick search of the online phone directory supplied Donna Small's address. Eden rang the coroner using the hands-free set in her car while she drove there.

'Eden Grey, Cheltenham General,' she said, in the brisk tones of the harassed hospital doctor. 'A patient of mine had a post-mortem yesterday, what was the result? Paul Nelson. Yes, I'll hold.'

She listened to some manufactured music that bore a passing resemblance to Vivaldi's *Four Seasons* – surprisingly upbeat for a coroner's office – then a man's voice came on the line. Eden could hear rustling paper as he spoke to her.

'Dr … er …?'

'Grey.'

'Dr Grey, that's it, you're asking about Paul Nelson?'

'Yes. Presented with severe abdominal pain, diarrhoea and vomiting,' she said. 'Later convulsions, disorientation and coma.'

'We PM'd him and ran a full tox screen. Funny one, this. Cause of death was poisoning.'

A momentary lacuna when her thoughts stilled to silence. 'Poisoning? With what?'

Abrus precatorius.

'Say again?'

A chuckle on the end of the line. 'That was my reaction. *Abrus precatorius.* Also known as the lucky bean or the love bean. Not so lucky for this chap. That do?'

'Yes, thanks, that's helpful. Hang on a minute, when did he ingest it?'

'Difficult to say. I had to look this one up. Reaction times vary from several hours to three days.'

'Thanks.'

She repeated the name of the poison over and over to make sure she didn't forget it. Some sort of bean. Could Paul have taken it by accident? Twelve hours ago she would have accepted that explanation, just, but now that Donna was also dead – strangled – she distrusted the coincidence.

This. Deliberate. Tried to kill me.

Gut instinct told her that whoever killed Paul also killed Donna, and somehow, she'd find out who, and why.

CHAPTER
ELEVEN

Cheltenham, August 1795

Daphne remained silent about what happened that evening at Greville House, the evening when she was removed from the debauchery and taken through the tunnels. Despite persistent questioning from Rachel, she refused to reveal anything further about the tunnels, where they were, or what happened in them. Each time Rachel pressed her, she turned her face away and her mouth trembled.

'What's she got to be so secret about?' Rachel complained to Emma, as she brushed out her hair and plaited it one night. 'It's not like we haven't seen and done a hundred things together before.'

'You'd never seen that living table before,' Emma commented, reminding her of Daphne's pale body layered with jellies, oysters and fruit to be nibbled at by the gentlemen. Emma nudged her. 'Might be you next.'

'I wouldn't be able to stop giggling,' Rachel said. 'I bet it tickles.'

'Who were the men at that party, d'you suppose?'

'Rich, anyway,' Rachel said. 'But not the quality.' She snorted. 'What passes for quality in Cheltenham, anyway.'

'Might be your ticket out of here.'

'With one of them?' Rachel knotted a scrap of ribbon round the tail of her plait, calculating for a moment. 'Maybe. But not an old one. Or anyone ugly.'

'That's most of the men counted out,' Emma said, hitching up her nightgown to clamber into the high old bed. Her legs flashed palely in the candle light. 'Did you see them taking the waters the other day? So many wrinkles it reminded me of an elephant.'

Rachel sighed. She used to love visiting the Tower to marvel at the elephants and lions. The most exciting thing she'd seen in Cheltenham was a flock of pigeons jabbing at the slurry in the gutter.

Rachel caught Emma looking at her out of the corner of her eye. She knew that look.

'What?' she asked.

'Seen how much money Daphne's got all of a sudden?'

'No. How much?'

Emma whispered, 'Twenty guineas.'

'Twenty guineas!' Rachel was indignant. 'Where did that flat-faced whore get that sort of money?'

'Shh! Mrs Bedwin will hear. It's supposed to be a secret, but Daphne keeps on counting it out.'

'When did she get it?' Rachel asked, but she knew. The other night, at Greville House. She, Emma and Roseanne had only been palmed two guineas for the whole evening. Daphne, the stinky puss, got twenty guineas a trick, did she? She had to know why.

She attached herself to Daphne and wheedled herself into the girl's affections.

'You know what would look lovely on you?' Rachel said, under pretence of delousing and ragging Daphne's hair one evening. 'An emerald green shawl. It would set your hair off beautifully.'

'I don't have a green shawl,' Daphne said.

'Really?' Having raked through Daphne's box, Rachel was only too aware of the fact. She cracked a flea with her thumbnail. 'Then you must get one. They can be got quite cheap, and it would look so pretty.'

'But where?'

'There's a shop in Cheltenham. I saw it the other day when I was out walking.' Rachel gripped Daphne's shoulders and spun her round to face her. 'We could go together, and look at the fabrics and try on bonnets! Would you like that?'

'Ye-es.' Daphne didn't seem to realise the great honour that Rachel was bestowing on her, condescending to traipse about dreary Cheltenham shops and counterfeiting an interest in Daphne's scrawny appearance.

Undeterred, Rachel pasted on her brightest face. 'Then we'll go tomorrow,' she announced.

The next day, they tramped into a mercer's shop on the High Street, where Rachel set about bossing the assistant to fetch shawls and bolts of fabric and lengths of ribbon and lace. She held up each item to the light for scrutiny before assessing it against Daphne's muddy skin.

'Too bright. Too tawdry. Too cheap. Now *this* one is right for you. Very subtle.' It was a bolt of sprigged muslin. She heard the shopkeeper mutter the price and pulled a face. 'Oh, but it's very dear,' she said disingenuously, and made to return it to the counter.

'No matter,' Daphne said, foraging in her reticule. 'I can afford it. If you truly think it suits me, Rachel?'

Rachel's eyes clamped on to Daphne's purse, as she scrabbled in it and drew out a bank note. Rachel watched the note's journey across the counter to the shopkeeper's twitching fingers, and saw a sudden spark of interest flare in the man's eyes.

'You're flush,' she said, lightly.

Daphne blushed.

'Got a sweetheart, have you?' She elbowed Daphne in the ribs.

'No.' The blush deepened to an ugly rash over Daphne's neck and bosom.

'Go on! Look at you; you've got a special gentleman, spoiling you. Eh?'

Daphne fastened her eyes on the fabric as it was measured and cut. Rachel knew when her quarry had bolted into a hole, and feigned fascination in a box of buttons on the counter. While she turned them over in her hands, the shop bell rang and a couple of ladies entered. Rachel cast them a glance, dismissing them for their dowdy dress and red cheeks hatched with broken veins.

But something one of them said to the other caught her attention, and though she continued to riffle through the buttons, her whole attention was fixed on what the women were saying.

'A disgrace, that's what it is. We shan't be going.'

'No, nor us. Mr Proudfoot was most insistent that we should not go.' A wistful tone crept into the woman's voice. 'Though I should love to see the wallpaper. I heard it was specially printed.'

The other woman snorted. 'Greville House wallpaper! You'd sell your soul for a glimpse of Chinese print!'

'Well, no, but I hear the gardens are a sight.'

The other woman puffed up her chest. 'To think that such people should do such things in Cheltenham.'

'Quite.' A pause. 'What things? Exactly?'

'You must have heard the rumours. Though I never attend to gossip myself.'

'No, of course not, one would never think of doing such a thing. Mr Proudfoot spoke in such chilling terms about Greville House, but he didn't *specify*.'

Heaving-bosom leaned closer to her friend. 'You have heard of the Hellfire Club?'

Mrs Proudfoot's hand crept to her mouth. 'No!'

A sage nod. 'Women brought in from London. We can imagine why.'

'Can we?'

'Gambling. Drinking. The worst excesses. Human sacrifice and cannibalism!'

Daphne's head snapped round at this. So you've been eavesdropping, too, Rachel thought, and softened a little towards Daphne.

'Men with money and influence, the highest in the land, and they behave like animals!' Heaving-bosom declared. 'A disgrace. We certainly shall not be going.'

'No, certainly,' Mrs Proudfoot echoed, and she stroked a bolt of printed cotton and sighed with something that sounded suspiciously like regret.

Rachel could barely wait until they were out of the shop before she rounded on Daphne. 'Men with money and influence, the highest in the land – who were they the other night?' Rachel demanded.

Daphne sighed. 'Sons of dukes and earls, a foreign count, the sons of politicians, and men of fortune.'

Rachel made a swift calculation. 'But there were only four of them there. You're talking as though there were dozens and dozens.'

'There was,' Daphne said. 'Later. In the tunnels.'

But more than that, she wouldn't say.

Rachel sprawled on one of the sofas in the seraglio and calculated how she would spend twenty guineas. The stagecoach back to London for a start, then some swish new gowns and a room somewhere while she let it be known she was seeking a new keeper. She was out of the game, stuck here in fusty old Cheltenham surrounded by sick people guzzling water. A girl like her should be at the heart of the action.

Her designs were interrupted by squealing and shouts from the room above. Roseanne and Daphne were dealing with a group of schoolboys, by the look of them, who'd bundled in and announced it was some fellow's birthday and it was time he became a man. They wouldn't take long.

Mrs Bedwin poked her head round the door and tutted. She'd taken the boys' money before they even clapped eyes on the girls. And charged them double for wine and cakes, addressing them as 'gentlemen' the whole time. They were so busy giggling and shoving each other in the ribs that they never noticed the gleam in her eye. When she'd allowed them into the boudoir, they'd chosen Daphne for her youth and Roseanne for the novelty. From the expression on Roseanne's face when one addressed her as 'the blackamoor', Rachel suspected that Mistress Pain would take control upstairs. Serve the upstarts right.

A sedan chair had called for Emma that morning, and jolted her away to a ladies' bathing party. Goodness knew what that meant, Rachel shuddered. But Emma seemed to enjoy them. She'd been fetched before, and always came back looking like the cat that got the cream. And so Rachel was alone with her thoughts.

The mythical twenty guineas was almost spent in Rachel's mind when a clatter on the stairs announced a new customer. Rachel draped herself artfully over the sofa as a man of about twenty-five shuffled into the room.

'Good afternoon,' he said, with a little bow. 'I wonder, are you free?'

Rachel sat up. 'Not free, but very reasonable, sir,' she purred.

'What? Oh yes, very good. Hem.'

'Do you wish to choose me, sir?'

'You're very pretty.'

'Then come sit by me a moment.' She patted the sofa. 'Would you care for wine and cakes?'

Mrs Bedwin slid into the room and put down a tray of small cakes and a bottle of wine. She extracted money from the man and said, 'Use the pink boudoir.'

Rachel took his hand. He was trembling. 'There's no need to worry, sir. Rachel will look after you.'

She poured his wine and he gulped it down. She refilled his glass and sipped delicately at her own.

'What's your name, sir?'

'Rodney Paige.'

'Mr Paige. That's nice. Are you here for the waters?'

'Oh no, nothing wrong with me. Fine and hearty.' A bit of wine went down the wrong way and he choked. She thumped him on the back until he caught his breath. 'I'm here to make my fortune. I hope.'

'Really?' Rachel eyed him over. Fair curly hair, worn long and giving him the appearance of a small boy. Big brown eyes, gentle and soft. They gazed at her now as if she were a water sprite who'd vanish if he startled her.

She led him upstairs to the pink boudoir. Through the wall came muffled giggling and shouts of 'Go on, Horace!' as the bed springs creaked.

Rodney glanced uneasily at the wall. 'Making rather a din, aren't they?'

Rachel smiled as if it were no matter. She'd heard worse. They'd be done soon, anyway. What she had here now was a young man of pleasing countenance and pretty manners, all set to make his fortune. She glided up to him and eased him out of his coat.

'Let's make you more comfortable, sir,' she said.

'Please call me Rodney. Sir sounds so impersonal, considering what we're about to …er … become to one another.'

'As you wish, *Rodney*.' Her breath fanned against his cheek as she said his name.

'That's much better.' His fingers fumbled with his shirt, and she stepped up to help him ease it off over his head.

'Skin a rabbit,' she murmured.

'My nurse used to say that.' He blushed. Rachel hid a smirk: what would nurse say if she could see him now, in a Cheltenham cat house. No wonder the poor boy was trembling.

She helped him to undress. Naked, he was pale and vulnerable, as though only half formed, like a newborn mouse. His legs bowed and he was pigeon chested with just a tuft of sandy fluff on his breast and another at his groin.

Rachel draped herself over the bed and urged him to join her. As they lay together, the boys in the next room started to roar and thump on the wall. Roseanne's voice bellowed out, admonishing them, and there was more sniggering. Rachel glanced at Rodney. His face was sheened with sweat and his eyes darted about the room.

'Not used to us bad girls, sir? Rodney, I mean?'

'No. That is, you're not bad. I'm not used to girls at all. One of seven boys.' He glugged his wine. 'I just want to make sure that everything is … pleasurable … for you. Hem. Not just me.'

'Don't you worry about that, Rodney. My pleasure is your pleasure.' She reached over and took the wine glass from his hands. 'Now, follow me.'

'You will tell me if I do anything wrong, won't you? Or if you don't like it?'

She looked at him properly for the first time. His eyes pleaded with her. He was so anxious to please, her heart melted a little. How many men had paid for their transaction and done the business, never casting a thought to her? Yet here was Rodney Paige, begging her to tell him how to please her.

She nuzzled his neck, her teeth nipping lightly at his skin. 'Tell me, Rodney,' she murmured, 'how you propose to make your fortune here in Cheltenham?'

CHAPTER
TWELVE

Thursday, 26 February 2015

08:17 hours

Eden drummed her fingers on the steering wheel as she drew up in a long line of cars at a red light. At this rate the police would have identified Donna and searched her house before she even got there. The clock was ticking. The pathologist would already have alerted the police to Paul's suspicious death; it wouldn't be long before they made the connection between Paul and Donna, and then she'd be muscled out of the investigation altogether.

The lights changed and she accelerated, turning towards the imposing circular building that housed GCHQ, the spy base. It was known locally as the doughnut because it was built in a ring, the middle part of grass and shrubs visible from the air. Myths abounded about the place: it was haunted by spies who'd committed suicide, that there was an underground train connecting it to Downing Street, that Cheltenham was riddled with spy escape tunnels.

She'd been inside once, years ago, when she was Jackie, and had quickly become muddled by the building's layout, glad she was escorted everywhere otherwise she was convinced that she would have spent the rest of her natural life wandering in circles, trying to find her way out.

Rather than standing in isolation, new housing estates had sprung up alongside GCHQ. Strange thing to wake up to a view of the tinted curved windows and razor wire, Eden thought. This, though, was where Donna chose to live. Eden skirted a line of cars queuing to get into the GCHQ car park, and turned right into Donna's street, crawling along, hunting for the right number. She spotted it, and parked further up the street and walked back.

Donna's house was tall and narrow with a Scandinavian twang to it, overlooking a tiny front garden and a collection of wheelie bins. The grass verge outside was piled with cardboard boxes of recycling. One had tipped over, spewing plastic cartons across the tarmac.

Eden looked up at the house and its neighbours, walked to the end of the street, and slowly made her way back, her phone clamped to the side of her face as if she was making a call. No one worried about a dawdler on the phone.

When she reached Donna's house, she ducked down a side passage and tried the back gate. Unlocked. Careless, but lucky for her: she disliked scrambling over fences. She slipped inside and closed the gate firmly. The tiny garden consisted of a square of turf and a few patio slabs. Evidently Donna didn't have green fingers.

She glanced up at the windows – blank patio doors facing the garden; upstairs the curtains were still closed. No movement inside the house, no sound of a toilet flushing, a washing machine running, or a shower. No radio or TV. It seemed the house was empty.

Drawing a set of pick locks from her bag, Eden set about opening the back door. She felt a pang of nostalgia for the old days when she could open a locked door in seconds using a credit card. These days it took patience and specialist tools, or an enforcer wielded by a beefy plod, but eventually she got the door open.

She wasn't the first one to get there. The place had been turned over. Not police: even they wouldn't make this mess. Eden stepped into the kitchen over shards of glass and china. Broken plates and mugs, cupboard doors hanging askew, packets of flour and sugar burst open on the tiles. Pots of herbs had been flung to the floor and trampled, releasing a scent of basil and mint over the chaos.

Feeling in her backpack, Eden drew out a pair of latex gloves and slipped them on as she moved into the living room. Here, the sofa was tipped upside down, the webbing underneath ripped open. Drawers hung drunkenly, their contents spilling on to the floor. A handful of romcoms had been swept from the shelves and lay with their pages crumpled on the carpet.

A sideboard held a number of toppled photo frames. She righted one, seeing a photo of Donna with a teenaged boy. Other photos of the two of them, and lots of just the boy, growing steadily older and moodier in successive snaps. Where was he? A nasty feeling crawled in her stomach. Donna dead, her son missing, their house turned over: she didn't like it at all.

An expanding file lay open, the compartments plundered, the contents slewing across the carpet. Gathering up a handful of papers, Eden flicked through them. Bank statements. Donna's salary going in every month, plus a monthly deposit of a couple of hundred pounds from a B. Small. Her ex-husband, presumably. Gas bills, water bills, credit card statements. Donna spent up to her credit limit on every card, and paid all of them off in full each month. Eden looked down the list of purchases: beauty parlours, hair salons, manicures, clothes, shoes, skin preparations, botox injections.

Lawyers' letters and a decree nisi dissolving the marriage between Donna and Barry Small. Birth certificates for Donna and Wayne Small – presumably the arsey-looking teenager in the photos – indicating he was now fifteen. Wayne's school reports from the Cheltenham Park School, where he was a day pupil. Eden skim read them. Wayne Small was not a model pupil: problems with his attitude, poor attendance, a few detentions for answering back to staff and fighting with other boys. His grades were low and he was expected to get three Cs for his GCSEs and fail the rest. The starchy headmistress wouldn't like that: she seemed the sort to expect all her pupils to achieve A grades in about two hundred subjects.

A photo album had been tossed across the room. There were a few photos of a younger Donna with a man, the toddler Wayne cuddled between them, all of them gurning into the camera. The family in happier times. The man disappeared from the photos and there were several of Donna with female friends on what was evidently a singles holiday, lounging by a pool swigging drinks laden with fruit.

Eden turned the page. Donna, topless on a sun lounger, holding a cocktail. There was a man next to her, tanned and grinning. There were more photos of them together somewhere tropical, judging by the white sand and achingly blue sky. Eden blinked. She knew the man in the pictures: he was Donna's boss in the planning department, Greg Barker.

Eden whistled and dropped the photo album back on the floor, and carried on her search upstairs. A messy bathroom with a cabinet crammed with toiletries. A narrow bedroom reeking with the musty cheese odour of teenage boy. It was furnished with a single bed with a Spiderman duvet cover that he'd surely grown out of by now, a desk, laptop computer, and walls covered with photos of glamour models cut out of lads' mags. Under the bed was a stash of pornography, well thumbed. Eden blessed her rubber gloves as she shoved the hoard back under the bed.

Donna's room was decorated in pink and smelled strongly of heavy scent. The whole of one wall was given over to built-in wardrobes. Eden cracked open the doors and clothes bloomed out. Stacked at the bottom of the wardrobes were at least fifty transparent plastic boxes containing shoes. Her bed had a red satin cover and all the pillows heaped up on one side of the bed, a frilly heart-shaped cushion perched on the top. The bed looked as though it hadn't been slept in.

Eden slid open the drawer in the bedside cabinet. Headache pills, antidepressants, tissues, a small appointments diary. Eden fanned the pages and a photo tumbled out. She tucked the diary into her pocket while she retrieved it and smoothed it out on her knee – Donna and Paul Nelson, heads together, beaming into the camera.

But what was most interesting was the fracture lines across their faces. At some point, the photo had been ripped into little pieces, and then sellotaped back together again. Pieced back together with some care, Eden noted, the edges carefully aligned and the picture taped on the back to save the image. She'd love to know when it was ripped up and then so tenderly repaired.

As she was squinting at the picture, trying to make out where it was taken, the front door banged. There was no time to hide; footsteps already thumped up the stairs. Better brazen it out.

She stepped out of Donna's bedroom just as a boy rounded the top of the stairs. He jumped and let out a cry.

'Who are you?'

'I'm Eden Grey, I'm a detective. Are you Wayne?'

'What's happened? That mess downstairs …' He had black hair about four days overdue for a wash that hung past his collar. His clothes were rumpled, his trousers drooping low off his backside, and the high rank stink of alcohol came off him in waves. 'Are you from the school?'

'Where have you been, Wayne?' Eden asked, stepping towards him.

The boy looked round wildly. 'What's going on? Where's Mum?'

'I'm trying to find out what happened,' Eden began. 'Here.' She fished a business card out of her backpack and handed it to Wayne.

'A detective?' Fear chased across his face. Suddenly he turned and bolted past her, down the stairs to the front door.

Eden hurtled after him, calling, 'Wayne! Wait! What is it?'

Wayne didn't answer. He had the front door open and was sprinting up the street before she reached the bottom step.

'Wait!' she called after his receding heels. He didn't stop.

Eden was back at her flat before she remembered she'd slipped Donna's diary into her pocket. Damn! She couldn't get it back to Donna's house now: the police would be there any minute and she'd have to fess up to breaking in. That would inevitably lead to awkward questions about how she knew who the victim was, and that would get Aidan into trouble, too.

She squared it with her conscience by deciding she'd see what was in the diary, and if there was anything that could help the police, she'd get it to them somehow, even if it backfired on her.

The hair was in place across her door as she ferreted her key out of her backpack. Inside, the flat was undisturbed, but a light blinked on the answering machine. Eden pressed the play button and wandered into the kitchen, hunting for paracetamol. The morning's stress had brought on a thumping headache. As she riffled through the cupboard, the answering machine beeped and a disembodied voice echoed across the room.

'Hello there. Long time no see. Still, what with me being stuck here inside, and you being on the outside, that's no surprise.'

Eden froze, her hand in mid-air. She knew that voice, knew it all too well. Even now, the sound of it sent a sickening fear rippling through her.

Hammond. His voice in her flat, her home.

'Anyway,' he continued, in that sing-song tone that was more menacing than any overt threat, 'I just wanted to catch up with you. See how you're doing.'

She swallowed. Her throat was dry and her tongue stuck to the roof of her mouth.

'And I will catch up with you, Jackie, or whatever you're calling yourself now. I will catch up with you.' A noise in the background, a scrote swearing at the screws, something about his fucking human rights. Hammond paused. Maybe he was eyeballing the shit who'd interrupted his phone call. His voice was breathy when he spoke again, as if his mouth was very close to the receiver. 'I will catch up with you, and when I do, then we'll see how you're doing. Bye bye.'

A clunk as he hung up. Hammond ringing her here. His voice poisoning her home. How the hell had he found her? She gripped the sink and ran cold water, splashing it on to her face and into her mouth. It tasted metallic. She rinsed her mouth and spat into the sink. Just hearing Hammond's voice again had sent her pulse into overdrive.

Breathing fast, she went to the answering machine and replayed the message another three times, straining to pick up any clue from his voice or the noises in the background. He was definitely calling from inside prison; the sound quality suggested he was using the public phone. Yet surely Hammond would have got a mobile smuggled in somehow? The thought he was saving a mobile for something special didn't comfort her. Neither did the thought that he felt so untouchable he was confident to make a threatening phone call with a prison officer in earshot.

Her hand hovered over the phone. She should call Miranda, then the police. Hammond had found her somehow, like he'd found Little Jimmy. Bragging, that's what Miranda had said. Hammond was in prison yet he'd got someone to kill Little Jimmy for him. He was snubbing his nose at them. Probably pissing himself laughing.

She didn't call Miranda and she didn't call the police. It was pointless. She was on her own. No one stood in Hammond's way.

Her flat was polluted by his call. His voice lurked in the corners and made her jumpy. She had to get out. She checked the windows and fixed the hair in place across the front door as she left, taking her notebook and Donna's diary with her. The hallway was empty as she checked and double-checked the door. No one in the stairwell. No one watching her as she got into her car and drove away.

No one that she could see, anyway.

As far as she could tell, no one followed her to her office. She parked up and walked to the sandwich shop, craving normal human company and a large mocha. Tony was in there, slicing tomatoes, his hands wrinkly in protective food-handling gloves. He grinned when she came in.

'You're early,' he said. 'Hungry?'

The initial rush of adrenaline had subsided leaving her suddenly starving. 'A bacon bap, please. Lots of sauce.'

'Red or brown?'

'Surprise me.'

She leaned against the counter as Tony fried two rashers of bacon and sliced a bun.

'You hear about that woman?' Tony said.

'Woman?'

'Found dead in Cheltenham this morning. It was on the news.'

The press were on to it quickly. 'They say who she was?'

'No, don't think so. Bet you wish you'd found her, eh?'

'Oh yeah, I love starting off the day stumbling over a corpse or two,' she said, drily. 'It beats chasing round after cheating husbands.'

Tony selected a bottle and squirted sauce on to the bap. 'I think you're in a brown sauce mood.'

Eden smiled and handed over a five-pound note. 'Thanks, Tony.'

'Laters.'

Still no one lurking in the car park. She allowed herself to feel safe for a moment before reminding herself that Hammond wasn't subtle. If he wanted her dead he wouldn't waste time conducting a pattern of life analysis, he'd just pay two thugs to snatch her off the street and drive her somewhere no one would ever find her. Not until it was way too late, anyway.

She fumbled getting her office door open. She kicked it hard, imagining Hammond's face, and the door bounced back against her toe. The red graffiti, BITCH, confronted her, suddenly sinister. She'd assumed it was glued-up kids, but was it Hammond, letting her know he'd found her?

Once inside, she slammed the door shut and locked it, and flopped down in her chair. A waft of bacon fumes made her stomach rumble and she bit into the bap, licking brown sauce where it squidged on to her hand. While she chewed, she cracked open Donna's diary at that day's date.

Donna had an appointment at the school scheduled for later that day. Was that why Wayne was jumpy, because his mum had been hauled in to discuss his appalling school reports? Then again, how did Donna afford the fees at a place like the Park School? Eden had seen her salary going in every month on the bank statements, and almost all of it going straight out on the mortgage, food and bills. All Donna's luxuries were on plastic. Goodness knew how she paid the credit cards, either.

Eden did a quick internet search for the Park School's number and rang the admissions team.

'Good morning, I'm enquiring about your fees.'

'Day pupil or boarding?'

'Day pupil.'

The woman in admissions quoted a price that made Eden rock back in astonishment. For a moment, she couldn't speak; there was no way Donna could afford that. The fees were more than her annual salary.

The woman evidently guessed her dilemma, because she added, 'We do offer a number of scholarship places.'

'How many a year?'

'Two or three. There's stiff competition for them.'

I bet there is, she thought, thanking the woman and hanging up. Wayne didn't appear to be overly blessed with brains, so how *did* he get a place at the Park School?

Eden flicked back through the diary and froze when she saw the entry on Monday evening: 'P.N. 9pm'. Did that stand for Paul Nelson? Did Paul and Donna arrange to see each other after the planning meeting? And did Donna kill him?

The coroner's office had told her that the poison that killed Paul could take between a few hours and three days to take effect. That meant he took it any time between Saturday and early on Tuesday. Donna certainly fitted the time frame. But then who killed her, and why?

Eden chewed the side of her thumb. From what the barman said at the singles club the night before, Donna hated Paul and had made her feelings clear. So why would Paul agree to meet her? He didn't seem the sort of man to enjoy raking over old grievances.

Eden unlocked her drawer and took out Paul's diary, turning the pages and cross referencing it with Donna's. On New Year's Day, Paul had written 'Donna' in his diary; Donna had written 'Paul'. She flicked through the pages, noting where they corresponded. For a few weeks, they met twice a week, then the entries stopped.

Donna wasn't Paul's type. Paul, with his interest in art and preserving heritage buildings, wouldn't find much to hold him to Donna, who came across as shallow and vain with her warpaint and tight skirts and botox injections. But to Donna, Paul was a wallet, a refined gentleman who'd treat her right and with plenty of cash to spoil her. No wonder she was pissed when they split up.

Eden stood and stretched her back, the vertebrae clicking. She needed a run to get her blood pumping again and work her muscles; let the rhythm of running smooth her mind and create a capsule of peace. Maybe after work tonight.

Her mobile rang.

'Eden, bad news.' Miranda's voice came through as soon as she answered. 'Switch on the TV news.'

'How did you get this number?'

A throaty laugh. 'Friends in low places.'

'I got a call ... from him,' Eden said.

There was silence on the line and she thought Miranda had hung up. 'Watch your back,' was all she said, then static filled the line.

Eden put down her mobile. Switch on the TV news, Miranda had said. She left her office, locking the door carefully behind her, and trotted along the walkway to the TV repair shop that occupied the unit next to Tony's sandwich shop. A bell rang as she entered.

'Hi, Denny, can I borrow a telly, please?'

Denny looked up from behind the counter and pointed a remote control towards a TV fastened to a bracket on the wall.

'Which channel?'

'News, please.' She looked up at the screen as he changed the channel and yanked up the volume.

A familiar figure appeared outside the Court of Appeal. A beefy man with a bald head. A spider's web tattoo crawled up his neck, incongruous with his suit and crisp shirt. His lawyer spoke for him as a rash of microphones and recorders jostled for position and cameras rattled off photo after photo.

'This has taken two years to achieve, but at last today we have seen justice,' the lawyer said. 'The conviction against my client was always a travesty, and today has been deemed unsafe and overturned. This is a triumph for the British justice system.'

Dave the Nutter scowled at the camera, his face contorted; a pit bull with PMT. He raised his fist high in victory and screamed into the nearest microphone, 'Justice!'

Eden stared in horror as he waded into the crowd, triumphant and free. Released on a technicality, the voiceover informed her, as the camera panned over the Court of Appeal.

Dave the Nutter, out there, somewhere. He'd always hated her, and now he'd had time to nurse a grudge up to boiling point. Hammond's threat, *I'll find you*. He knew where she lived. Now his henchman was out there, free.

The net was closing around her.

'You all right, Eden? You look like you've seen a ghost.'

Dazed, Eden turned away from the TV screen.

'Earth to Eden,' Denny said.

She dragged her mind back. 'Sorry, Denny, miles away.' The news changed to a report on the woeful state of the economy. *Plus ça change.* 'Thanks for the loan of the TV.'

'My pleasure. That'll be ten quid.' She started and he cackled. 'Got you there, didn't I? The look on your face.'

She forced a smile. As she reached for the door handle, Denny said, 'You get that bloke who done your door?'

She swivelled on her heel. 'What bloke?'

Denny put down the soldering iron. 'The one with the tin of red paint and the grudge. I was working late, about midnight on Tuesday, and saw him. I ran out and shouted, but he legged it.' He caught her look and added, 'I've been round a couple of times to tell you, but you're never in.'

'You saw him? Did you tell the police?'

Denny laughed hollowly. 'Couldn't organise a fart in a curry-eating contest that lot. When my shop was done over, all I got was a crime number for the insurance. Never caught the bastards. Don't think they even tried.'

'Would you recognise him if you saw him again?' Eden asked.

'Probably. He wasn't your usual piss-artist, drunk teenager with a can of spray paint. He was middle-aged. Should've known better.' Denny shook his head. 'And he was wearing the stupidest bobble hat I've ever seen. Looked a right plonker.'

CHAPTER
THIRTEEN

Thursday, 26 February 2015

13:56 hours

Rosalind Mortimer was not pleased to see her. The fussy bow on her blouse quivered with indignation as Eden came in and took a seat in front of the headmistress's desk.

'We met before,' Rosalind said, with a quirk of her lips to indicate the memory wasn't a pleasant one.

'Yes, when those skeletons were discovered in the school grounds,' Eden said, blithely. Little Jimmy had been murdered, Dave the Nutter was out of prison, and Hammond was coming to kill her, so a huffy headmistress in a pussy bow blouse wasn't going to discompose her one jot.

'And now another body has been found in the school grounds,' Eden said.

Rosalind flinched. 'How do you know about that?'

'It was on the local news.' An outside broadcast van was huddled against the school gates when she drove up. No doubt Rosalind was calculating how to minimise the adverse publicity for the school. Eden stared at her for a moment. 'Did you know the victim?'

Rosalind crossed her legs. She was wearing the naughty librarian shoes again. 'As it happens, I do know the victim. She was one of our parents.'

'You saw the body?'

Rosalind swallowed 'I went to see what was going on.' She shuddered, too theatrically to be convincing. 'Horrible. I identified her for the police.'

'It was Donna Small, wasn't it?'

'How do you know?'

Eden sighed. 'I'm a detective, Mrs Mortimer. Tell me what you know about her.'

Rosalind straightened the green tooled-leather blotter on her desk before she deigned to answer. 'Her son, Wayne, is a pupil here.'

'I've met him. He's not a typical Cheltenham Park pupil.'

'What do you mean?' Anger flashed in her eyes.

'Wayne Small is a scruffy, unprepossessing, smelly oik, and a thick one at that,' Eden said.

'I wouldn't say that …'

'And you know it,' Eden interrupted. Rosalind flushed scarlet, though whether it was at being interrupted or because the description of Wayne was apt, she wasn't sure. 'Now I know that teenage boys are typically monosyllabic thugs, but not here. He must stick out like a chocolate éclair at a weight watchers' meeting. So how did he get a place?'

'His fees are paid.'

'I'd gathered he wasn't scholarship material.'

A pulse jerked in Rosalind's throat.

'Who pays his fees?' Eden asked. 'And don't say his mother pays them, because we both know her salary as a PA for the council won't run to the fees here, not even for a non-boarder. So who? His father?'

Rosalind glanced at her and her gaze skittered away again. 'No, his father isn't able to afford our fees.' Eden raised an eyebrow and she added, haughtily, 'I understand that Wayne's fees are paid by a benefactor. Someone concerned about his future.'

'Who's the benefactor?'

Rosalind shook her head. 'I can't say.'

Eden's voice hardened. 'Can't or won't?'

'Please.' A muscle ticked under her eye. 'Don't ask any more. I can't say.'

Interesting. A secret benefactor. Wayne's biological father? Someone in high places whose reputation would suffer if it came out that he had a bastard child?

Eden shifted in her chair and tried a different line of attack. 'Donna had an appointment booked here today. What was that about?'

Rosalind relaxed visibly. 'To discuss Wayne's progress. He wasn't the shiniest apple in the fruit bowl when he came to the school, but in the past few months his behaviour has deteriorated. He truants more than he attends, these days.'

'Why's that, do you think?'

'He's a fifteen-year-old boy out of his depth.' Rosalind turned candid eyes on her. 'As you said yourself, he doesn't really belong here.'

Rosalind stood and paced to the window, tapped on the pane to admonish a group of pupils lurking about, and turned back to Eden. When she spoke, her voice had regained its hauteur. 'Are we finished? I'm very busy, as you can see.'

Eden could see nothing of the sort. The desk was uncluttered, the phone hadn't buzzed once, and no one had tried to interrupt them. Rosalind seemed remarkably unbusy for the headmistress of a top public school where three bodies had turned up in as many days.

'There is something else,' Eden said, not making any effort to move. 'Another parent at the school, Paul Nelson, also died this week. Also in suspicious circumstances.'

Rosalind paled. 'Paul Nelson? Yes, of course, the girls' mother rang me.' Her head snapped up. 'She didn't say his death was suspicious. He was in hospital for a gastric complaint, she said. I assumed ...'

'You assumed wrong. So why is it, Mrs Mortimer, that two parents from this school have died violently this week?'

Rosalind didn't answer. Her hands shook as she rearranged the pencil tray on the desk, sorting the pens into ascending order of size.

Eden tried a different line of enquiry. 'You had a burglary here about eighteen months ago?'

Rosalind glanced up at her, surprised by the change of tack. 'A valuable painting was taken. A Constable.'

'Have you got a picture of it?'

'Somewhere, just a minute.' She picked up the phone and asked her secretary to bring in a folder. 'I don't see what this has got to do with Paul Nelson and Donna Small. Or the skeletons, for that matter.'

Neither do I, thought Eden, but said nothing.

When the file was delivered, Rosalind flicked through it and extracted a photograph. She pressed it down on the desk in front of Eden. It was of a rural idyll, a thatched cottage beside a mill pond the colour of tea, the light golden and slanting on the scene.

'We took this for insurance purposes,' she said, 'after the painting was revalued.'

'When would that be?'

Rosalind rolled her eyes, thinking. 'The painting came to the school over forty years ago. It was valued at the time, and then revalued about ten years ago, when we took out separate insurance on it.'

'And this photo was taken then?'

'Yes. A valuer came from Sotherby's and checked the provenance, and took detailed photographs.'

Eden reached in her bag and extracted a notebook. Tucked between the pages was the photo she'd borrowed from Paul's office, of his daughter standing in front of the painting. That photo was taken a couple of years ago, only a few months before the painting was stolen. She laid the pictures side by side and squinted at them, going over them inch by inch and comparing them with each other.

They weren't the same.

Eden's mobile rang as she drove away from the school. The ring-tone was still on the factory setting, though occasionally she toyed with the idea of changing it to the *Mission Impossible* theme tune.

She pulled into the side, anxious not to be driving if the phone call was Miranda, or worse, Hammond. She didn't rec-ognise the number, but it had a Cheltenham code that sent a gust of relief through her. Not Hammond, not Miranda.

'Hello, Eden Grey,' she said.

A breathy, distressed voice, the words clacking against each other. 'It's my daughter. She's gone missing and they won't take me seriously. Oh, it's Mrs Portman, Susan Portman, and my daughter's called Chelsea. She's not come home and they won't listen, say she's old enough, but I'm worried sick …'

'All right, Mrs Portman,' Eden said, sliding her notebook and pen out of her bag. 'Can you start at the beginning for me?'

Gulping, Mrs Portman told her that her eighteen-year-old daughter, Chelsea, hadn't returned home the night before. She'd waited until nine that morning and then called the police.

'They say they have to leave it twenty-four hours, that she'll just turn up, but it's not like her.' The voice cracked. 'They keep saying she's eighteen and she can do what she wants.'

'How can I help?'

'You're a private detective. Please find my daughter.'

Susan Portman lived in a neat bay-fronted bungalow in a tree-lined road. A gravel drive led to a narrow garage with shabby wooden doors in need of repainting, and a soggy circle of grass dotted with snowdrops made up the front garden.

The front door opened before Eden had a chance to ring the bell. Mrs Portman was in her late forties, and leaned heavily on a walking frame to support herself. She was dressed in jeans and a saggy brown sweater, and her hair was combed back from her face and tucked behind her ears.

'Eden Grey? Come in. Tea, coffee?'

'That'd be lovely. Let me give you a hand.'

The kitchen was neat pale oak with red canisters labelled 'tea', 'sugar', 'cake', in case you forgot the contents. Susan busied around finding cups and teabags, her hands shaking, her walking frame clunking on the tiled floor. She talked constantly, disjointed sentences interrupted by little flurries of crying.

'She went out last night with her friends. She was supposed to be back by eleven, especially on a school night, but she didn't come back.' Susan said. 'I sat up waiting for her, all night. I couldn't go to bed: I couldn't lock and bolt the door, knowing she was still out. And I couldn't leave it, could I?'

She turned desperate eyes to Eden, who asked, 'And was there any phone call? Text message at all?'

Susan shook her head. 'Nothing. It's not like her. She'd tell me if she was going to be late.'

'What about her friends?'

Susan pulled a scratty tissue from her sleeve and blew her nose. 'They said she wasn't out with them at all. Apparently they don't hang around together any more,' she said. 'I don't know who she saw last night. I've been ringing and ringing her mobile, but it's switched off. I've left I don't know how many messages.'

Susan leaned against the sink, filling the kettle until it overflowed, staring at it as though she'd never seen it before in her life. Eden gently prised it from her hands and took over.

'Why don't you sit down, Mrs Portman?' she said. She helped Susan reverse into a kitchen chair, and held her arm while she lowered herself into the seat. 'Can I ask you why you need the walking frame?'

'Arthritis,' Susan said. 'You always think old people get it, don't you, but I was diagnosed in my twenties.'

Eden's gaze dropped to Susan's ankles where they jutted beneath her trousers. Knobbly and deformed, they looked like melted blobs of toffee, and her feet twisted sideways.

'When did you last eat, Mrs Portman?'

'I'm not hungry.' Eden continued to hold her gaze until she confessed, 'Dinner last night. I just can't manage anything.'

It was after three in the afternoon. No wonder she was shaky. The house was cold, too.

'You're no good to Chelsea like this,' Eden said. 'Mind if I look in your fridge?'

The fridge confirmed what she suspected: that Susan was the sort of mother who cared what her daughter ate, the sort who never let her go out without a solid meal inside her, who cried at the thought of kids going to school without breakfast. The fridge contained salmon steaks, salad, low fat yoghurt, ham, a bag of salad leaves, and an expensive bar of high-cocoa chocolate that was evidently being savoured chunk by chunk. Eden admired her restraint: she'd have gobbled the lot in one go. She knocked together a sandwich and persuaded Susan to talk generally about Chelsea while she ate.

It was a pretty average tale: Chelsea was still at school, due to sit her A levels in June. She wasn't an outstanding student but she tried hard and was hoping to go to university to do marketing studies in September. Her older brother was away at college, and the two siblings got on well.

'Has he heard from her?'

'He said just wait, she'll come home,' Susan said, 'but it's not like her.'

Thing is, girls of eighteen can be angels one minute and devils the next, Eden thought. Staying out all night and not coming home could be completely in character for the new Chelsea. Legally she didn't have to come home at all. Eden could well imagine how claustrophobic this household could be, with a worrying, disabled mother and a brother who'd flown the nest. In the same situation, she knew she'd stay out all night occasionally, too, if she could.

'What about boyfriends?' she asked.

'She split up from her boyfriend a few months ago,' Susan said. 'He's in her class. Nice lad. I liked him. I don't know if she's got a new boyfriend, she won't tell me.'

'Any other friends?'

'Lots on Facebook. Hundreds. I don't know who they are.'

'Can I see her room?' Eden asked.

Chelsea's room was a messy nest. Clothes were draped on top of each other over the open wardrobe doors, and shoes lay scattered about the floor. Cosmetics covered the dressing table, oozing gloop on to the polished wooden top. A pinboard above her desk was covered with photos – old ones, by the look of the curling edges, the girls in them aged about fourteen, not eighteen.

'Does she have a camera phone?'

Susan pulled a face. 'Always filming on it. Every time you turn she's holding it up, posting stuff online.'

'A diary?'

Susan hesitated. 'She hides it. I found it when I was tidying her room once, and just put it back.' The answer was too quick: she'd sat down and had a good read through. It suggested she didn't know her daughter as well as she thought; felt there was something being held back or she wouldn't have snooped.

Eden outlined her daily fees and the deposit she required.

'The police are right: most people who go missing turn up again within a day. If you want to wait, that's fine. If you want me to try and find Chelsea now, and she rocks up tomorrow morning, I'll keep the deposit and charge you for the hours I've already worked on the case. It's up to you.'

Susan bit back a sob. 'I don't care about the money. I just want her back. I know what everyone's said, but I'm worried about her. Call it mother's instinct if you like, but I can't get rid of this awful feeling that something terrible's happened to her.'

'I'll need some details, a recent photo, and her laptop,' Eden said. 'Where's Chelsea's father?'

'At work.'

Her expression must have changed because Susan rushed to add, 'He's as worried as I am, but he had to go into work. His job always comes first.'

'What does he do?'

A pause. 'He's in the civil service.'

In Cheltenham-speak that meant GCHQ. 'I understand,' Eden said. 'Tell me if there's any reason why his job might be connected with Chelsea's disappearance. I'm happy to sign the Official Secrets Act.'

She'd signed it before. The memory of that time squeezed the breath out of her, a band tightening round her chest.

Susan nodded. 'You don't think ... someone took her to get to him?'

Eden squeezed her arm and said, 'It's more likely she got drunk with her mates and was too embarrassed to come home, or afraid she'd be in trouble. But I'll get cracking straight away. Call me if you hear from her.'

She tucked Chelsea's laptop into her backpack, and slotted two photos of Chelsea into her notebook. The first photo Susan offered was of Chelsea in school uniform: prim, young and dull. Eden asked for one of her dressed as she would at weekends, out with her mates. In the second photo, Chelsea had aged five years. Amazing what a bit of lacquer and slap will do to teenage bone structure.

'What do I do now?' Susan asked, hugging her big sweater close about her.

Eden took in her grey face and lank hair, and a surge of pity rippled through her. 'Have a shower, wash your hair, put a cold flannel on your face and lie down for half an hour,' she said, softly. 'You'll feel better, I promise.'

She decided to go legit on the computer, taking Chelsea's laptop to a computer repair shop rather than palming a twenty to some scrote outside the Magistrate's Court. The shop offered unlocking and resetting of computers to those who'd password protected theirs and then promptly forgotten the password. She'd used them before to virus check disks and USBs clients handed to her, and knew they were just the right side of dodgy.

'Long time, Eden,' Nat greeted her. She'd got a new tattoo on her neck – a mermaid by the look of it, sinuous scales curving into her startling red hair. 'What can I do you for?'

'Can you get into this laptop for me?'

'Easy. You want it all downloading and resetting?'

'Just open it up for me, please.'

'Might be safer if I take a copy, too, just in case.' Nat already had the laptop open and powering up. 'Jesus, this is slow. Probably got all sorts of crap on it. Want me to clean it up, make it a bit quicker for you?'

'It's not mine, it belongs to a client,' Eden said. 'Her daughter's gone AWOL. I'm trying to find her.'

Nat whistled. 'Won't take too long, Eden. Have a seat.'

The seat was a stool with a ripped vinyl top and bulging yellow foam. Eden hoiked her bum on to it and watched

Nat while she worked, trying to memorise the sequence in case it came in useful one day. Professional development, she thought, wryly.

Nat connected up an external drive to the laptop and transferred the contents of the laptop's hard drive to the external drive, then reset the laptop to factory settings.

'I'll copy this lot off here for you,' Nat said, plugging the external drive into a PC and clicking a few keys.

'Can you show me the last things she did on the computer?'

'Sure. Take a little while. How far do you want me to go back?'

'A week.'

'A week! These girls spend all day online, a print out of that is going to fill a library.'

'Two days?'

Nat harrumped and set to work. She reloaded the laptop with the data she'd downloaded and passed it to Eden. 'There's no password on it now, so you can browse through if you like. And here are her passwords.' She handed over a scrap of paper where she'd scrawled passwords for email, Facebook and Twitter accounts.

'How did you get those?'

'She kept a file on her desktop marked "passwords". It's not rocket science.' Nat grinned at her and went back to work.

Eden surfed through the laptop. Lots of activity on Facebook, including photos taken the night before at a club: Chelsea with her friends, all of them in skimpy tops and false eyelashes, clutching blue drinks, and grinning into the camera, looking closer to twenty-five than eighteen. Three girls on a night out. One now missing.

The Facebook timeline indicted the photos had been uploaded at nine thirty, presumably only seconds after they'd been taken, and the tag facility identified the subjects as Chelsea Portman, Bryony Young and Olivia Gordon. A stalker's dream.

As she was browsing, a message popped up on Chelsea's page from Bryony, 'Hey gorgeous, so you're back in the land of the living LOL. Where'd you get to last night? XXX.'

A moment, and then the other friend, Olivia, added, 'She was tooooo busy with the looovelyyyyy Zamir!'

Eden went to the settings on Chelsea's Facebook page and opened up the security feature. The phone numbers of all her friends were there, captured every time they used a smartphone to update Facebook. She scrolled down until she found Bryony and Olivia, then called.

'Hello, I'm Eden Grey, I'm a private investigator,' she said when Bryony answered. 'Chelsea didn't come home last night and her mum has hired me to find her.'

'Oh my God,' Bryony said. 'Chelsea? She was with us last night. I thought she'd ... She's not come home?'

'No, and I'd like to talk to her friends to see if they've got any idea where she might be. Will you help?'

'I don't want to get her into trouble.' Bryony played the dutiful loyalty card.

Eden sighed. 'Believe me, she won't be in trouble if she gets home safely.' She allowed a small emphasis on 'if'. 'But she might be in danger, and that's why I need to find her.'

They arranged to meet in a coffeeshop in town. Eden rang Olivia as soon as she hung up on Bryony, suspecting that Bryony's first action would be to call her, and anxious to get in first.

She paid Nat for the work on the laptop and took away a sheaf of printouts. Arriving early at the coffeeshop, she analysed Chelsea's keystrokes over the past two days. There was a lot of Facebook messaging, all of it a bit shouty; a couple of flirty emails to someone called 'PacManDude'; and a bit of homework on the Tudors, neither accurate nor well-written.

In the pictures folder of the laptop were hundreds of photos of Chelsea: at parties, with her friends, and with a couple of men in their twenties. The dates on those photos went back three months. Was one of the men 'PacManDude'?

Bryony and Olivia arrived together, their arms linked, and Eden bought them both iced coffees with swirls of squirty cream on top. The girls stared at her, wide-eyed, when she showed them her ID. Eden weighed straight in, keen to capitalise on the glamour she'd acquired through being a private investigator. In her experience, it quickly wore off.

'You were all out together last night?' Eden asked. 'Where did you go?'

'Vodka bar in Gloucester,' Bryony said. Quickly she added, 'We're all over eighteen.'

Eden smiled. 'I'm not trying to trip you up and I'm not going to go telling tales to your parents, I only want to find Chelsea and make sure she's safe.'

Olivia dandled her straw on her bottom lip. 'We left about eleven. School night.' She pulled a face to indicate the injustice of this. 'Chelsea left before us, about quarter to. She and Zamir had a row and she ran off. He went after her.'

'Zamir?'

'Chelsea's boyfriend.'

'What were they rowing about?'

'She thought he was looking at other girls,' Bryony chipped in.

'He'd never do that!' Olivia cried. 'He really likes her.'

Bryony twisted her lip, not convinced. 'He was, though. And he's tried it on with me before now.'

'No way!'

'Yes way. The other week, when we were shopping and he was buying her that top and told me to try one on, too. I came out of the changing rooms and he made all these comments about my boobs.'

Alarm bells rang. Loudly. Eden interrupted with, 'When did Chelsea meet Zamir?'

Bryony shrugged. 'A few months ago.'

'Is he at your school?'

'No, he's really old!' Olivia laughed. 'About twenty-five. Lots older than us.'

'Older men are more mature,' Bryony primly informed her.

Sure they are, Eden thought, sighing inwardly at Aidan's mood swings and grumpy silences. Way more mature. 'How did they meet?'

'We were in McDonald's and he just came over and started chatting to us. He's really nice,' Olivia said. 'He friended her on Facebook, and emailed her that she looked nice, and was really sweet.'

'When did he become her boyfriend?'

'Not for ages. He bought her nice presents and that. Tops, and a bikini, and a handbag, and a necklace. Then they got together.'

God, it got worse and worse. 'Did she meet his friends?'

'He has one he hangs round with a lot. They both take us all out and buy us pizza and we have bottles of wine,' Olivia said. 'It's really grown up.'

'What are their names?'

'Zamir is Zamir Sussman,' Bryony said. 'His friend is Vinnie Malik.'

'They took you clothes shopping?' Eden said. 'Anything else?'

'We all had makeovers one Saturday,' Bryony stabbed her straw into the ice at the bottom of her glass. 'Chelsea's dad wasn't happy about it. Said she looked cheap. And she was drunk when she got home.'

'Zamir said she looked beautiful,' Olivia said, wistfully.

'Is this Zamir here?' Eden asked, showing them the pictures on Chelsea's laptop.

'Yes, that's him. And that's Vinnie.' Bryony pointed to a man just behind Zamir.

Time for the questions she couldn't ask Chelsea's mother. 'Has Chelsea had many other boyfriends?'

'A couple, at school.'

'Did she have sex with them?'

Bryony and Olivia exchanged glances.

'I'm not going to tell,' Eden said gently.

'No, she didn't have sex,' Bryony said, 'but she wasn't a prude either. She did some stuff with boys, but not all the way. She was romantic about it, said she was saving herself for the right boy.'

Olivia slid her straw in and out of her mouth, catching Bryony's eye. Both girls blushed scarlet and giggled behind their hands.

So Chelsea was just dirty enough. Eden felt a stone in her stomach. Instinct and experience screamed that Chelsea had been singled out and groomed, reeled in over a period of weeks. And now she'd disappeared. Suddenly this stop-out teenager looked horribly like human traffic.

CHAPTER
FOURTEEN

Cheltenham, September 1795

The costume was prickly. Rachel yearned to wriggle about and scratch a spot between her shoulder blades where the fabric was rubbing her skin raw. And now her nose was itching. She'd tried twitching it, but that didn't work. If only she could move, instead of being stuck in this awkward pose. She hadn't moved a muscle for hours. It felt like hours, anyway. She sighed deeply, a gentle whinny of despair.

She was back in Greville House with the other girls. No human table this time, though, but a series of tableaux: Samson and Delilah, David and Bathsheba, Cleopatra and Mark Antony. They were all in costume: the gentlemen guests at Greville House playing the male characters, and Mrs Bedwin's girls filling the female roles. They had to maintain the poses, while the others in the room guessed what they were depicting. Rachel was Delilah, brandishing a pair of shears. Any more of this and her arm would drop off and she'd cut the gentleman's head off.

'Samson and Delilah!' someone cried, and shuddering with relief, she relaxed the pose.

No sooner had she put down the shears than 'Samson' was upon her, tearing at her costume.

'Good job you didn't cut my hair,' he said. 'I would lose my strength and not be able to love you.'

So this was love. A nameless stranger in a silly costume, rutting in the middle of a room, egged on by his friends, who piled in on the fun.

Not like Rodney. Dear, sweet, shy Rodney. He'd brought her flowers that morning. A little posy clutched in his paw and two bright red spots on his cheeks as he presented the flowers to her. He didn't stop to enjoy her favours. A business meeting, he explained, looking excited, but he wanted her to know his esteem and regard. And with his funny little bow, off he'd gone.

Samson groaned and juddered, and collapsed on her chest with a woof. Rodney never did that. He took his time – Mrs Bedwin wasn't pleased – and talked to her, and stroked and comforted her.

'When I make my fortune, Rachel, I shall take you away from all of this. Would you like that?'

Would she like that? She'd nodded at him, a fluttery feeling in her chest, and when he'd gone, she missed him immediately and started counting down the days until she could expect him again.

'Don't forget about that thief-taker and the matter of the gloves what you stole,' Mrs Bedwin reminded her, as she mooned about downstairs feeling dreamy. 'So don't get no plans about leaving, will you? You're not going nowhere.'

Rodney would rescue her. He'd pay off Mrs Bedwin and take her away and set her up in a nice little house with china tea bowls and a looking glass, and a maid to cook and clean for her. And dear Rodney would visit with his pockets full of trinkets, and he'd sit her on his lap and she'd comb her fingers through his hair and he'd tell her she was the sweetest dumpling in the world and she'd say …

She became aware that she was being pointed at.

'You and you,' someone ordered. 'Stop daydreaming.'

Ye gods, was it not enough that she was poked and prodded before all and sundry but that now she had to pay attention during it, too?

'Come on,' Emma whispered, tugging on her arm. 'They want us.'

The two girls were led out of the room and through a series of chambers. Rachel caught glimpses of gilt chairs and a huge polished dining table, sofas and draperies and walls hung with portraits, then they were pushed into a room that led off the main hall. At the far end of the room, a door stood open.

As Rachel passed through the door, a servant thrust a lit candle into her hand, and she found herself in a narrow passageway. She jumped as the door slammed shut behind her. It was cold in the passage, very dark, and smelled stale as a crypt. Groping for Emma's hand, she stumbled along the passageway and down a flight of stone steps to a tunnel lit intermittently by candles set into niches in the wall. Rachel pressed her fingertips to the side: they came away slimy with damp.

After what seemed like a long time, steps led up again, and they emerged into a small, circular room. Two mean candles burned in the centre and gave out a stink of tallow, their light puddling on contorted shapes painted on the walls. Rachel held her candle high to see. Depictions of all varieties of sexual act were painted over the walls. Every fancy, every contortion, every abhorrence.

On the far side of the room, clinging to the shadows, were four skinny girls, shackled together. Their faces were pale with black hollows carved deep beneath their eyes. One had a bruise swelling her cheekbone; another had scratches all over her arms and her head was shorn. Chains clanked against the stone floor every time one of them moved.

'Where is this?' Rachel asked in a low voice, afraid to the depths of her soul.

'The Paternoster Club,' one of the girls spat. She looked about thirteen. Tear tracks ran through the grime on her face.

'What's that?'

'You've heard of the Hellfire Club?' said the girl with the shaven head. The razor had nicked her scalp and there was a crust of blood above her ear. She scratched at a sore on her bare leg. 'Imagine all the rumours were true.'

Her tone sent an icy shiver down Rachel's spine. She'd heard the stories about the Hellfire Club. Summoning the devil, evil rites, everyone sworn to secrecy. Rachel and Emma exchanged a look. Emma's eyes were huge and frightened, and her breath came swift and shallow. Any moment she'd faint from fear.

Rachel raised her candle. 'Where are you from? You're not Mrs Bedwin's girls.'

'I was on an errand for my mistress in Bath,' the girl with the shaved head said. 'There was a bag over my head and I was in a coach before I knew it.'

'You were all snatched?' Emma echoed. The girls nodded.

'What are we here for?' Rachel said, panic building.

'The gents that want to join the club. They have a test, like a trial by ordeal,' the girl said. Her mouth worked silently for a moment before she was able to utter her next words. 'Us too.'

Dread crawled over Rachel's scalp. Desperately she calculated her chances of escape if she sped down the tunnel, out of Greville House and away. Mrs Bedwin would set the thief-taker after her for her gowns, but surely that was better than staying here. She gripped Emma's hand. 'We should run away while we can. Before someone comes for us.'

'We can't leave them here.' Emma crouched in front of the girls, studying their faces. 'How long have you been here?'

Before they could answer, a door opened behind them and they all flinched. Rachel pulled Emma to her feet and cowered back against the wall.

A squat man with grey stubble peppering his head came into the room and grabbed one of the girls by the elbow. 'Come on,' he said. 'They're ready for you.'

He dragged her through the door, forcing the others to shuffle and hop along in her wake. Rachel cast Emma an anguished glance, and they too trailed behind them, into a temple punctuated with stone columns and draped with crimson velvet. It was lit with hundreds of candles and incense burned in the corners, filling the air with perfumed fug. A table covered with black velvet stood in the centre of the room like a satanic altar. Rachel shivered. There must be some way to escape. Perhaps she could fight her way out. But no, there were six masked men already there; too many to take on. She'd have to bide her time and pray a better opportunity came along.

A man wearing a ram's head stepped forwards and held his arms high and wide.

'My children. We are gathered here together so our dear brother may be tested and show he is ready to be one of us. Brother, come forwards.'

A man wearing a wolf's mask moved into the centre of the circle.

'Are you ready to be tested?'

'I am.'

'You know that if you pass the test you will hold the power of life and death?'

'I do.'

'Are you ready for this honour?'

'I am.'

'Do you swear to keep all you see, hear and feel here tonight secret until your dying day, and to take the secrets of the Paternoster Club with you to the grave?'

'I do.'

Ram's head clapped his hands. Another man brought forth a glass of wine and a small inlaid box. He opened the box and thrust it at the initiate.

'Choose.'

Wolf man scrabbled in the box and brought out a bean. At a signal from ram's head, he plopped it into the wine, held the wine glass up high, and downed the contents in one long swallow. Everyone gasped.

'And now we will see whether you have passed the test, and whether you are worthy to join us.' Ram's head snapped his fingers. 'Choose a damsel to accompany you to heaven or hell.'

The wolf strutted up and down the line of girls, scrutinising each one in turn. Eventually he chose one of the scrawny captives, hoisting her arm high in the air as though she'd just won a prize fight. A long, low moan escaped the girl's lips. Rachel's insides turned to water. She'd heard that moan before from the captives tied in the back of the cart on their way to the gallows. It was a moan that betrayed there was no hope. She shrank back as wolf man hauled the girl away, shutting her ears to the girl's pitiful screams.

'Take your partners,' ram's head announced. 'Ladies' choice, I think.'

The men did not remove their masks as one by one the girls picked their partners with blindness born of shock. Rachel was barely aware of what was happening; her mind echoed with everything she'd witnessed. This was all play-acting, surely? It wasn't real, it couldn't be. It was just a bit of silly dramatics to amuse these silly men who had too much money and liked to feel important.

The girl wasn't really going to die, was she?

In a daze of fear, Rachel chose one of the men. They were all the same; it made no difference to her. Throughout what followed, her eyes never strayed from the doorway where the girl had disappeared. She'd punch this fellow in the guts and run to help the girl. Then they'd escape into the night and …

She wouldn't. She had no money, nowhere to go, no one to help her, and Mrs Bedwin could tell the thief-taker something that would snap Rachel's neck. They'd both be dead: her and the girl, the poor snatched girl. A tear glided over Rachel's cheek as she leaned against one of the stone columns, bracing herself on her palms while her gentleman battered into her. All the girls were silent. The only sounds came from the five men. When they were done, they slunk away, never speaking a word.

When the men were gone, the girls huddled together in the temple. Emma and Rachel sobbed, their arms tight about each other's waists. The chained girls did not cry, just stared with hollow blankness into space.

'This trial by ordeal?' Rachel asked. 'What is it?'

The girls shrugged.

'And your friend, the other girl, she'll be back tomorrow?'

'No.' One girl raised her head. 'We never see the girls again.'

CHAPTER
FIFTEEN

Thursday, 26 February 2015

17:27 hours

Eden ran a computer search on Zamir Sussman and found an address in Gloucester and a business registered to him: a takeaway food shop near the bus station. Perfect location to prey on teenagers too pissed to realise what was happening to them.

She looked again at the photos of Chelsea out shopping with her friends: overly made up, trying too hard, vulnerable, sassy, desperate to prove they were grown up. Easy prey. Zamir must have picked them out straight away: three girls on the lookout for excitement, for attention, for flattery, and he knew just how to satisfy them.

She made copies of the photos of Chelsea and drove the short distance to Gloucester, first stop Zamir's address. No one answered the bell, nor when she knocked on the door. Peering through the windows she could make out no trace of Chelsea: no coat hanging up, no shoes lying on the carpet, no handbag. A scout round the back of the property also yielded nothing. Dishes lay drying in the kitchen rack: one mug, one bowl, one spoon. She liked this less and less.

A tiff, making up, Chelsea stays the night, too loved up or embarrassed to call her mum; all of that was possible. But the way Zamir had homed in on the girls, buying them clothes and makeovers, reeling them in; that disturbed her. And if Chelsea had stayed the night, where was her mug, remains of her breakfast and lunch? If she wasn't here, where was she?

Eden climbed back into her car and headed for Zamir's shop. The takeaway had yellow lettering covering much of the front window, and a formica counter where four youths were loitering and eating their takeaways.

She pushed open the door and the smell of hot oil, garlic and chips assaulted her.

'Is Zamir in?' she asked the serving girl.

'Zamir? No, he's out at the moment.'

'When's he going to be back?'

The girl shrugged. 'He doesn't come here much. Do you want to speak to the manager? He'll be back in about an hour. He's at the cash and carry.'

Eden dug out a photo of Chelsea. 'You ever seen her?'

'No.'

'Try looking.'

A sigh, but she looked properly this time. 'No. I don't know her.'

'OK. Thanks.'

Eden tried the youths on the off-chance they'd seen Chelsea, but they all shook their heads. 'Wouldn't mind, though,' one contributed. 'She's well fit.'

She left the shop and scouted round the area. Above the takeaway was a flat: grimy windows and a square of cardboard taped over a fractured pane. The door to the flat was round the side of the building, no name underneath the bell. She pressed the buzzer.

''Lo?'

'Hi, is Zamir there?' She made her voice light and frothy, copying Olivia and Bryony's breathless manner.

'Zamir?'

'Yeah.'

A snuffle. 'No.'

'I thought this was his flat.'

'No, love. Just me here. I rent it from the council.'

'Sorry.'

Damn! Still, worth a try. What she needed now was street intelligence. A thin rain was falling as she left her car in a central car park where she knew it would be safe, and walked to an area of Gloucester where tall Victorian houses jostled next to each other. Once prosperous, the area had slid steadily downhill. Now the haughty Victorian facades were grubby and the stone steps were broken. The buildings were chopped into the sort of flats and bedsits where blankets served as curtains. Student digs, landlords who demanded key money, shabby B&Bs with brown nylon carpet tiles where a toaster and a pile of white bread constituted breakfast.

The area was well furnished with hookers, too, as shabby and broken-down as the Victorian villas. Eden knew some of the girls; knew which ones would lie and take her money, and which ones would tell the truth and take her money. Kaz fell into the latter category. She was shivering on the pavement in shorts and halter top, shoulders hunched against the rain, sucking on a fag as though it were her last breath.

'Hello, Kaz,' Eden said. 'Fancy a cup of coffee?'

'Might miss a punter.'

Eden looked up and down the empty street. 'Yeah, I can see them queuing. Come on, it'll be warm in the caff.'

Kaz sniffed.

'I'll buy you a doughnut.'

'Make it a few rounds of toast and jam and you're on.'

The caff was as dispiriting as the rest of the neighbourhood. Plastic-covered chairs bolted to the floor, chipped formica tables and a blob of tomato ketchup in the sugar bowl. It stank of bad breath and vinegar.

'So what's up?' Kaz said, when the toast and jam arrived. Her accent was pure Bristol; vowels so thick you could stand a spoon in them. She bent her face close to the plate to eat, revealing grey roots to her ebony hair.

'I'm looking for a girl.' Eden slid the photograph across.

'She don't look like a tom.'

'She isn't. Yet.' Eden sipped her coffee: it had come out of a machine not a jar and was surprisingly palatable. 'You heard of a bloke called Zamir?'

'Pimp?'

Eden shrugged. 'Could be. Could just be a supplier.'

Kaz fixed her with a look. 'Fresh meat?'

'Uh-huh.'

'Bastard.'

She showed Kaz the photo of Zamir. 'Know him?'

'Nah. Not seen him before. Could be he doesn't use cats.' Kaz poked a triangle of crust into her mouth 'Not old cats, anyway.'

'Could you do a bit of asking around for me? Just quietly?'

Kaz glanced up at 'quietly'. 'Vicious bastard, is he?'

Eden shrugged. 'I don't know yet. It could just be the old story, runaway teenager, comes home after a few days. But there's something I don't like. A feeling in my guts. And it's got …' She searched for the right word.

'Hallmarks?' Kaz supplied.

'Yes, hallmarks.' The word made her shudder.

'You all right? You look like someone just walked over your grave.'

'Perhaps they just did, Kaz. Perhaps they did.'

A return to the takeaway didn't bring her any closer to Zamir. The manager said he hadn't seen him for a couple of weeks, but did pass on a mobile number. Eden rang it and was informed that the number no longer existed. With Kaz gathering intelligence amongst her punters and colleagues, there was little more she could do, so Eden headed back to Cheltenham.

It was after seven by the time she arrived back, and on impulse decided to visit Paul Nelson's ex-wife, Zoe. Zoe had admitted seeing Paul on Monday. According to the coroner, Paul was poisoned sometime between Saturday and early Tuesday morning. That put Zoe squarely in the time frame. Time for a surprise visit.

Zoe evidently hadn't had time to change after work when Eden called round. She was still in a smart business suit and ivory silk blouse, and she padded around in stockinged feet as if she'd only just kicked off her heels. The death of her ex-husband, the father of her children, evidently hadn't kept her from work.

'Mrs Nelson? I'm Eden Grey, we spoke on the phone yesterday. I rang to tell you about Paul.'

'Yes, yes. What do you want?'

'I wanted to check you're all right. How are the girls?' Eden said.

'They're upset.'

'Of course. A terrible shock for all of you.' Eden glanced up at the rain. 'Can I come in for a minute, please? I wondered if I could have a word.'

Zoe seemed distracted but opened the door wide to let her in. It was a beautiful house: a Regency terrace with two clipped shrubs standing sentinel either side of a generous front door. The hallway was light and airy, the floorboards had been sanded and varnished to a deep patina, and the walls were palest cream. She could imagine Paul being happy here, with these classic lines and the feeling of space.

Eden's nose twitched as she entered the hall and Zoe swung the door shut. A scent, familiar and yet elusive. What was it? The same perfume her primary teacher wore? The scent that spoke to her of stories about owls and illustrations in primary colours. Learning to read.

The sitting room, which Zoe referred to as the 'drawing room' was large and square, with a pale blue rug in the centre. The furniture was a discreet wheat colour, and obviously expensive. No Ikea tables or sofas here. Eden was directed to a deep corded armchair.

'What do you want?' Zoe asked, sitting opposite her with her legs demurely bent to one side.

'I'm investigating Paul's death,' Eden said. 'The coroner believes it's suspicious.'

Zoe's hand crept to her throat. Her fingernails were freshly manicured in palest pink, the half-moons picked out in white. 'Suspicious? I thought he ...'

'Thought he what?'

Zoe swallowed. 'He said he couldn't afford to pay more maintenance for me or the girls. I assumed his business was in trouble. You know how men can react.'

Eden didn't reply, intrigued by the sudden appeal to complicity.

'I assumed he'd done something silly. Taken his own life.'

'When did you last see him?'

'Monday evening, just after six. We'd arranged for him to come over and see the girls, but also he wanted to talk about the maintenance. I was asking him for more. He refused, said he couldn't afford it.'

'How did he seem?'

Zoe spread her hands wide. 'Wary. He seemed to think I had a live-in lover who ought to contribute to my upkeep.'

'Do you?'

Zoe stared at her. 'That's not the point. He's the girls' father. He ought to pay for their upkeep.'

She stood and paced to the mantelpiece, adjusting a photo in a silver frame: her and two girls; matching hair and eyes, a smile printed from the same block. There were no photos of Paul on the mantelpiece; maybe his daughters kept pictures of him in their rooms. Zoe returned to her chair. That scent again, but now Eden knew why it was familiar.

'Do you have a key to Paul's apartment?' she asked.

'Yes, as it happens.'

'When were you last there?'

Zoe looked up at the ceiling, thinking back. 'A while ago. Christmas, perhaps. I don't go there as a rule. Paul comes here to collect the girls.'

'You went to his apartment yesterday morning, early. You let yourself in with a key. Why?'

'What? I wasn't … how do you know?'

'Someone saw you.' Not strictly true, but easier than explaining that Eden herself was in Paul's flat when Zoe called. Eden's voice hardened. 'So I'll ask you again, why were you in Paul's flat the morning he died?'

Zoe sighed and crumpled against the cushions. 'He always goes running early in the mornings. I knew he'd be out. I wanted to look at his bank statements. We shouted at each other when I saw him on Monday. He refused to pay any more for the girls, accused me of spending the money on myself. I called him terrible things. I wish I hadn't. He is their father, after all. Anyway, I know his routine, so I thought I'd go and find the evidence I needed to get the maintenance increased.'

'And did you?'

'Yes, I took some of his statements away with me. I returned them after you'd called and said he was dead. No point anyway, the statements showed he was broke.' Her voice cracked. She pressed her hand to her eyes and visibly composed herself. 'And now he's dead. I wish we hadn't parted like that.'

'Did Paul leave a will?'

'He remade it after we divorced. He's left money in trust for the girls.'

'Are you a trustee?'

'Yes, I am. I'm their mother ...'

'How much is the trust worth?'

Zoe licked her lips. 'Three and a half million pounds.'

19:38 hours

Unfinished business beckoned, and this time it was going to be sweet. She pulled up at the end of the street and made her way on foot to the house. A ring on the bell brought a skinny woman with a fake tan. Eden flashed her ID and put on her most menacing 'don't mess with me' face.

'I want to speak to Chris Wilde.'

'He's eating his tea.'

'No, he isn't. You eat early, about six-ish.'

'How the hell do you know ...?'

Eden sighed theatrically. 'I'm a detective. Where is he?' She jammed her foot in the door. 'Get him here now.'

Chris Wilde's missus shot her a venomous look but scuttled off to fetch him. There was a babble of voices; recriminations by the tone of it; then Chris Wilde's bulk filled the hallway.

'Mr Wilde, I'm Eden Grey, we've met before. I'm here to ask you to do some work for me.'

Chris's gaze shuttled between her and his wife, wrong-footed. 'Some work? I thought ...'

'I want you to sand down, clean and repaint my office door, and then I'd like a pot of bright spring flowers, preferably a mixture of narcissi and hyacinths, to place outside it. The pot should be frost-resistant, heavy, so it's less easy to pinch, and at least twenty inches wide. And I want it crammed with scented flowers.'

Chris scratched his ear. 'Sure, no problem. That'll be ... let me see.'

Eden stepped so close to him their noses almost touched. In a low, deadly tone, she said, 'It will be free, and you will do this by Monday morning, latest, or I take the CCTV footage to the police.'

'CCTV?' Chris stuttered.

'Of you scrawling an offensive slogan on my office door. That's criminal damage. You will receive a fine and be ordered to pay compensation. You will have a criminal record. Not helpful when you've recently been made unemployed.' She paused. 'Or you could put it right and I won't bring the force of the law crashing down on your pathetic head.'

Chris's mouth worked and gibberish came out.

Eden turned on her heel. 'By Monday 9am, latest. I think you'll find it's a better solution than going to court.'

She allowed herself a snicker as she drove away. The old CCTV wedge of persuasion. Worked every time.

Aidan was waiting outside in his car when she returned home. He sprang out and rushed over to kiss her cheek the moment she unclipped her seat belt.

'What are you doing here?' It came out more churlish than she expected; she'd evidently picked up some young person's attitude talking to Bryony and Olivia.

Aidan didn't flinch. 'I'm offering to make you dinner.'

'Dinner? You're going to cook?'

'Yes.'

How wonderful that sounded: someone cooking her dinner. Just what she needed after the day she'd had. Hammond's voice had echoed in her mind, haunting her every move. Every time she closed her eyes she saw Dave the Nutter with his fist high in salute outside the Court of Appeal. Free.

'OK, I'll be round in about an hour. I'm all grungy and stinky,' she said. 'Been to Gloucester today.'

'I'm going to cook for you.' Aidan held up a supermarket carrier bag. 'In your place.'

'Oh.' What if there was another message on the answering machine? Another threat from Hammond? Impossible to laugh it off to Aidan, and explaining would mean revealing too much about herself. She was aware she sounded ungrateful; he was offering to cook her dinner, after all. Trying hard to smile naturally, she said, 'That sounds nice. Come on up.'

She pretended the door was stiff; turning her back on him so she could check the hair was still in place. It was. She heaved open the door with an over-bright cry of, 'Here we are!' and stepped inside with trepidation fizzing in her veins.

Nothing had been moved; the flat was silent and still. She breathed out a long, deep breath she hadn't even realised she'd been holding.

Aidan bustled into the kitchen with carrier bags of ingredients, and set about hauling out frying pans and saucepans. Typical man, can only cook something if he uses every pan, plate and utensil in the place, she thought. At least his pernickety nature meant he cleaned up after himself and she wouldn't be faced with a leaning tower of washing up at the end of the meal.

'I'm just going to have a shower and get changed,' Eden called. He nodded back, putting on a CD of Beethoven and singing along while he chopped onions. He'd brought the CD with him, too.

Eden went into the bedroom, stripped, and tossed her mucky clothes into the washing basket. She stood for a long time under the shower, scrubbing away the stress and misery of the day until the water began to run cold.

With a fresh towel wrapped around her, she returned to the bedroom. She cracked open the door: Aidan was still singing, and she could hear pans sizzling in the kitchen. The occasional burst of staccato swearing indicated he was happily employed. She was safe to make a phone call.

Underneath a layer of t-shirts in the bottom drawer of her wardrobe was a box. She lifted it out on to the bed and raised the lid. Eight mobile phone handsets, fifteen used SIM cards, and twenty SIM cards still in their packets. Underneath it all was a plain exercise book with a blue cover. She flipped the pages until she found the number she wanted, the name 'Roger the Dodger' and his phone number written in her own slanting script.

She selected a handset, inserted a new SIM card, and dialled a number she hadn't used for years.

'Roger, it's Isabel.'

'Isabel?'

'We met a few years ago. About a Monet.'

'Isabel! How you doing, girl?'

'I'm good, thanks, how are you?'

'Bold and breezy, just the same. What can I do you for, girl?'

She doodled a cat on the cover of the exercise book. 'I need some info on a bent Constable.'

'Plenty of them about, girl. You tried Scotland Yard?' Roger chuckled.

'Not a bent copper, Roger, a bent Constable of *Hay Wain* repute.'

'Oh him. What you got?'

She pulled her notes on the Paul Nelson case towards her. 'I want to know if a Constable entered the black market, some-time between ten years ago and eighteen months ago. Also, was someone asked to do a copy around the same time it went to market?'

Roger breathed heavily down the phone. 'Any bent Constable, or have you got more details?'

'I can send you a picture of the original, and of the copy,' Eden said.

'How you thinking of getting it to me?' Roger's voice was dark.

'I'll put the images password protected on the Cloud, and text you the password. All right?'

'Should be safe enough,' Roger grumbled. 'I'll ask around. Call you back on this number?'

'Sure.' She paused, then added, 'Roger? Be careful, the last person who spotted that this picture was bent is dead.'

'Got you. Bye, Isabel.'

She hung up. As she was about to stow the phone, a noise behind made her jump. Whipping round so fast her neck twanged, she saw Aidan lurking in the doorway.

'Just who the fuck is Isabel?' he asked.

'Aidan, I didn't see you there!' Eden said. 'Is dinner ready? Smells wonderful.'

'Who is Isabel?'

'What?'

'I heard you talking, Eden. You introduced yourself as Isabel. Now are you going to tell me why, or are you going to leave me to make up my own ideas? Because believe me, I already have some, and they're not flattering.'

His face was pinched and white with anger and hurt.

'Whatever it is you think you know, that's not it,' she said, at last.

'You tell me now what's going on, or I'm leaving.'

He meant it. She rose from the bed and went over to him, and held his arms, looking up at him. He didn't respond. His face was choked with emotion.

'I mean it, Eden.'

She had lost Molly, her old life, her friends, her family; lost everything for her job. It wasn't a conscious sacrifice. It wasn't willingly made. She was damned if that old life would force her to relinquish Aidan, too.

'Sit down. No, come on, sit down.' He perched on the end of the bed, stiff and reluctant. She slid the box over to him.

'Take a look inside.'

He frowned at her then opened the lid and lifted out the mobile phones, the SIM cards, the virgin SIM cards and lined them up on the bed. 'What's this?'

'I have a different identity for each phone. I swap the SIM cards around, use some of them only once, so I can't be traced. I sometimes use a phone once and then dump it so I can't be tracked.'

He glanced up at her, his eyes dark and afraid. 'Are you in trouble?'

She gave a short humourless laugh. 'I'm in deep trouble. Aidan, if I tell you why, I'll be putting myself at risk, and I might be risking you, too. So walk away now, before it's too late.'

He got up and left the room. She packed the phone and SIM cards back into the box, her hands trembling. That was that, then. She heard Aidan clattering about in the kitchen for a few moments, then he reappeared holding two glasses of wine.

'I've turned down the oven,' he said, handing her a glass of wine. He sat down and swung his legs up on to the bed.

'Are you sure?' she asked.

He tucked a strand of hair behind her ear, a gesture so tender it almost made her sob. 'I'm sure.'

'I meant it about the danger.'

'Tell me.'

Eden took a deep glug of the wine, then stretched her legs out beside him. Side by side, she told him the story.

'Years ago I worked in Customs and Excise, not doing VAT or checking for dodgy fags, but working undercover. I infiltrated a gang that was bringing in arms to the UK. They didn't just do arms, obviously, like most of those gangs they also handled drugs, and human traffic. I worked undercover with them for two years.

A big arms consignment was due to come in and I'd tipped off the authorities, but somehow the gang leader found out.' She tried to take a drink of wine, but it caught the back of her throat and she choked. 'He knew it was me, God knows how, and he tried to kill me.'

A slash across each arm, a cut across each thigh, a stab in the stomach.

'Those scars I've got,' she started.

'You told me that you fell through a window.'

She shook her head. 'I didn't. He … cut me.'

'My God, Eden!' Aidan's face twisted with shock.

'I was rescued just in time.' *Little Jimmy saved your life.* 'I testified against the gang. They heard in court who I worked for, that I was undercover, and that I'd duped them and got them all arrested. They got huge prison sentences.'

'Good.'

She sipped her wine, her hands juddering so much she missed her lips and wine trickled down her chin. She wiped it away with her palm. 'I couldn't carry on working undercover: I'd been busted, and to be honest I wasn't in great physical or mental shape after what happened.' Aidan squeezed her hand. 'I didn't want to stay in the office checking VAT returns, so I left the service. I was put under the witness protection programme: I got a new start, but I had to leave my old life behind. All of it.'

She paused. *How are Mum and Dad?* She'd asked Miranda. Been told, *I don't know and I can't find out. You know the rules.* Her parents. They'd been told she was dead, died as part of a security operation. Heroic, brave, given this shred to comfort them in their grief. She wondered who they'd buried in her place – someone without a name, unmourned – or if they'd clustered at a yawning grave and sobbed while a box of stones was lowered into the earth.

She continued, 'I came to Cheltenham and set up as a professional investigator. It's what I've been trained to do.'

'So that time when I locked myself out of my flat,' Aidan said, recalling an incident early on in their relationship, 'and you managed to get the door open in seconds, that was your training?'

'You need better locks on your door,' Eden said, trying to lighten things. She wanted to weep, reliving it all again now.

Aidan turned to face her. 'So what's the trouble that you're in?'

She sucked in a deep breath, feeling broken and afraid. 'One of the gang members has been released: an unsafe conviction, apparently. And the gang's boss has connections on the outside. He had someone killed.'

Aidan gaped at her in horror. 'Are you in danger?'

I'll catch up with you. No point frightening him. There was nothing Aidan could do if Hammond was determined to get her. 'I have to be careful,' she said. 'And so do you. You can't tell anyone what I've just told you.'

He was staring at her, his eyes searching her face as if he'd never seen her before. Eventually he spoke. 'Is Eden Grey your real name?'

'It is now.'

It is now. How could she be so calm? Just blithely tell him that she used to work undercover and someone tried to kill her. That she isn't who he thought she was, that the past few months together had been a lie. He didn't know who or what she was any more. Everything he thought he knew about her tilted.

He swung his legs off the bed. 'I'd better check on dinner,' he said, with false brightness. He had to get out of there; his head was spinning. The world had shifted and he didn't know anything anymore. 'Don't want burnt offerings.'

How well do you know her? Lisa's mocking tone, asking him whether Eden had brothers and sisters, where she went to university. Was anything Eden had told him true?

He lifted the pot out of the oven, gave it a stir, licked the spoon and added a squidge of juice from a jar of red jalapeno peppers. Tasted again. The sauce was too spicy now. Bugger it, it'd have to do.

Does she carry a gun? Blasted Lisa. Asking all the right questions. Was there a gun in Eden's flat? Eden, or whatever her name was. All those times he'd spoken her name, liking the feel of it on his tongue. Aidan and Eden, the rhythm of their names, corresponding. All of it lies. She wasn't Eden, she was … who? He didn't know her at all.

He tipped rice into a sieve and rinsed it under the tap, his mind whirling. From the bedroom came the buzz of the hairdryer. Eden carrying on as if nothing had happened, as if she hadn't pulled the pin from a hand grenade and tossed it into his life.

He thunked the rice into another pan and topped it up with water. Foraging in the drawer for a fresh wooden spoon, his hands met cold metal. Hidden at the back of the drawer, behind the nutmeg grater and the salad servers that were so clunky they were inoperable, was a set of keys. He drew them out, casting a glance behind him. The hairdryer droned on.

The keys squatted in the palm of his hand. One key to open the main door, one for the door in the sitting room that opened on to a small balcony, one for the front door to Eden's flat. A blue plastic tag bent on the ring. He stared at the keys for a long moment, then closed his fist over them and slid them into his pocket.

CHAPTER
SIXTEEN

Cheltenham, October 1795

Rachel came out of the spa feeling queasy. The waters tasted revolting, like the smell of rotten eggs and ordure, and she couldn't wait to get back to Mrs Bedwin's and guzzle down a pint of porter to take the taste away. Not that the waters were doing her any good. The sore that had started as a small spot on her neck was growing, and more sores had appeared on her scalp. Fortunately she could hide them with her hair for now, but she dreaded waking each morning and discovering a new one had erupted overnight.

So, each day she traipsed to the spa, paid her penny, and drank a pint of the disgusting water amongst the gout-ridden, the coughers of blood, the faint and weary, and the frankly mad.

As she hurried away from the porticoes of the spa, she caught a glimpse of a familiar figure ahead of her. Her heart leapt. Darby Roach! For a moment she considered rushing after him, calling his name, then hesitated. Their last meeting still rankled. How he'd tossed her out on to the street, how she'd lost her home, her gowns, her possessions and her little maid, Kitty.

Darby Roach in Cheltenham. His health ruined after losing his father's money? Or had that life of dissipation finally caught up with him? She knew Darby, and knew that whatever his disease, he'd seek out the local cat house. They'd be face to face eventually and she braced herself for their first interview.

She didn't have long to wait. Darby Roach and a couple of cronies swaggered into the seraglio the next day. Rachel cringed at the surprise on Darby's face when he recognised her.

'Rachel!' he cried. 'You're here in Cheltenham! I knew you'd fall on your feet.'

'Darby,' she said, coolly, pouring him a glass of wine.

'I'll choose you,' he announced, gallantly, 'for old times' sake.' He turned to his chums. 'But you should take a turn, too. I've had her myself, I know she'll see you have a good time. In fact, Rachel was my own special darling for a while. That's how accomplished she is.'

He chortled and dug the friends in the ribs. The other whores looked at Rachel with interest. Now they knew she'd been thrown over by this prancing booby. Humiliation scorched her.

'This way, sir,' she said, scraping together every shred of dignity she could muster.

Mrs Bedwin, sucking her gums with avarice, pounced as they left the room. 'That'll be two guineas, sir,' she said, her hand cupped. He opened his pocket book and withdrew a five-pound note.

Rachel cringed as he said, mockingly, 'Two whole guineas, eh?' and knew he was scorning how far her price had dropped. Mrs Dukes had never sold her for less than five.

As her foot touched the first stair, Mrs Bedwin said loudly, 'And it's two guineas for the wine.'

Her mortification was complete. Silently she led Darby to the boudoir and yanked his coat from his shoulders.

'This cost a pretty penny,' she remarked, noting the scarlet silk lining and the braided buttonholes on his coat.

'Yes, I had a stroke of luck,' Darby said, sitting to pull off his boots. His feet stank and his stockings were wet with sweat. She wrinkled her nose as she tugged them off his feet.

Darby continued, 'Quite a stroke of luck: my father died.'

She glanced up at him, unsure how to respond.

'He'd paid off all my debts and was keeping me on a tight leash. Couldn't even have my horse. The old man was incandescent with fury over that spot of trouble I had. You remember?'

She remembered. A moment's notice to leave her home, leave all her jewels, her gowns, her beautiful furniture. Leave Darby forever, because he'd lost a fortune at a card game.

'My debts were all paid off, then he died and I inherited the title and the estate. I mortgaged the estate and I was back in business.' He grinned at her. 'Change of luck just like that.' He snapped his fingers.

A change of luck. Wasn't it just.

'How did your father die?' she asked.

'Broken heart. Not me, well, not all me. My sisters died of the smallpox, one after another. All gone within a month. It killed my father, especially when Lizzy died. He adored Lizzy.' Darby puffed out his cheeks. 'But it meant the money that had been set aside for their dowries was back in the family coffers. I've only got mother left to support now. She's moved into the Dower House, and to be honest, she's so upset about father's death and the girls, that I wouldn't be surprised if she goes to meet them soon.'

Rachel could think of nothing to say. She thought of her own mother, dead ten years ago now. If her mother had lived, she wouldn't be here, at Mrs Bedwin's, haunted by the shadow of the thief-taker.

'Still, it's an ill wind, as they say,' Darby added, breezily. 'So I'm here on a spot of business. Made some money at cards. I used to do card tricks at school. Kept the boys off me and I made a few shillings. Turned those skills to good use.'

'Cheating?' Rachel said.

Darby grinned. 'Sleight of hand.'

He pulled his shirt over his head. 'There's a fellow here, Ellison, into property. That's where the money is, you know, building the new town. He's got it all sewn up. If you're not part of his circle, you get nowhere.'

Darby flopped on to the bed. 'Come to me, sweet Rachel. How I've missed you.'

She joined him. 'Do you, Darby? Do you miss our old home together?'

'Oh, I do, my angel,' he said, nuzzling her neck.

'We could make a new one, just like the old one. You could visit and we'd be together again, with our funny little maid Kitty to look after us.'

Darby barked with laughter. 'Kitty? That wretch? She's long gone.'

Rachel stilled. 'What do you mean?'

'She stole from me, when she left the house. Took some silver and some of the jewellery I'd bought you. Bangles and rings and such like. Quite a haul.'

Rachel bit the inside of her cheek. The girl had learned some tricks from her, it seemed. But not all of the missing jewellery was pinched by Kitty; she'd made off with some of it herself. Good job, too, or she'd have been in the gutter and probably dead by now.

'I soon found out what was missing and sent the thief-taker after her,' Darby continued. 'She wasn't hard to find. Stupid girl still had a silver carving set and some rings on her when he caught her.'

Rachel's throat was dry. 'What happened to her?'

'She was lucky. Seven years.'

'Prison for seven years?' That was lucky: Kitty could have been hanged.

Darby gave a short laugh. 'No, transported for seven years.'

A stone fell in Rachel's heart. Kitty would never come home.

She'd never raise the money for the ship back to England. The shadow of the thief-taker taunted her again. It could be her.

Darby's face hardened. 'She deserved it. She should've hanged.'

She used to adore this face. Used to wait to hear his step on the stairs. Now she looked at the weak chin and hard eyes and wondered what she'd ever found to love. His money, she supposed. But now he'd told her what he'd done to Kitty, even his money wasn't enough to make her love him. He'd thrown her out on the street once, he could throw her over, or worse, again. She saw, at last, the man he was.

Still, he had his uses.

'Mr Ellison is the man to know, you say?' she murmured in his ear, her breath fluffing his hair in the way he couldn't resist. 'What makes him the big man, eh?'

And Darby talked. When he left, he said suddenly, 'You know, Rachel, what I've said, it's supposed to be a secret. Ellison would be furious if he knew what I'd told you.'

'Oh, Darby, don't be silly,' she said, planting a kiss on his cheek and ushering him out of the room.

'I'll send up my friend,' he said at the door. 'Be ready for him, won't you, he's a good fellow and likes a bit of rough.'

And with those words, any last vestige of fond memory was gone.

'Does he?' Rachel thought to herself. 'We'll see about that.'

Darby's friends did like it rough, and she gave it to them, beating out of them more details about Mr Ellison and his select group who stood to make a mint out of building the new town of Cheltenham. And with that information, Rachel intended to secure her future.

'The person to get to know is Mr Ellison,' she told Rodney, when he called to see her the following day.

'Mr Ellison? The man who owns Greville House?'

'Yes.'

'I've heard some odd things happen there,' Rodney said.

Rachel's mind slid back to the Paternoster Club, to the chained-up girls, and something stalked over her grave. At the end of the night she'd been handed twenty guineas and told to keep quiet. Not talking about it was easy, not remembering was quite another.

'You don't have to be involved in that,' she said to Rodney. 'You've got the money to buy land, haven't you?'

'I've seen just the parcel of land that I want.'

'I've heard that Mr Ellison is the man who controls who can buy land and develop round here. If you're not one of his friends then the land goes for inflated prices so whoever buys it can't make a profit. If you get to know Mr Ellison, as a businessman, then he could see you get the land for a fair price.'

Rodney tugged his upper lip. 'You're very good at this. You've got a good business head, sweet Rachel.'

I'm a whore, Rachel thought, it's all about business. But that wasn't strictly true. She was growing fond of Rodney, with his gentle manners and soft words. His concern for her pleasure was touching, too, in a life where most clients thought only of their own. She wanted him to get on in life, to do well for himself. Besides, he'd promised to take her away from all this once he made his fortune.

'And when you make your fortune and build the nicest houses in Cheltenham, perhaps we could live together in one of them,' she murmured in his ear. 'You could be my own special Rodney, and I would be your own dear Rachel.'

'I would like that, Rachel. I want you to have everything,' he said. 'A carriage and a maid to look after you, and I don't want you to worry about a thing.' He set his mouth. 'I shall find out Mr Ellison, and see what the deal is with this land.'

'That's my Rodney,' she said, and lay down quietly beside him.

CHAPTER
SEVENTEEN

Friday, 27 February 2015

07:56 hours

The phone ringing awoke her. Eden lifted her head from the pillow, groggy and disorientated. For a heightened moment she couldn't work out who or where she was. Memory crashed back in place.

Close by her ear, the phone rang on. She hesitated before she answered, checking the caller ID. Not a number she recognised. She pressed connect, praying it was neither Hammond nor Miranda.

'Hello?' She struggled to sit up in bed, squinting at the clock. She couldn't remember the last time she'd slept so long.

'Is that Eden Grey, the detective?' A male voice, young, rough.

'Who's asking?' Not the best way to start a conversation with what might be a potential client, but after the past few days she was cautious. It could be another of Hammond's lackeys, trying to frighten her. If so, it was working.

'You were at my house yesterday. My mum …' The voice broke. 'They told me she … someone's killed her. You said you'd help.'

She chased the connection round her mind for a second before realising who the caller was. 'Is that Wayne?'

A gulp the other end. 'Yeah.'

'What's happened?'

'I can't tell you on the phone.'

'Are you at home?'

'Nah, I daren't go there. The police …' His voice trailed away.

'What about the police?' Eden asked.

'They'll think I did it. You said you could help.'

'Where can I meet you?'

'Not here,' he said, quickly. 'I'll come to you.'

Eden scooped back her hair with her hand and scratched her scalp. 'I've got an office off the High Street. Want to come there in about an hour?' She gave him directions and Wayne hung up.

Wayne Small was the sort of boy whose mouth hung open loosely when he wasn't using it, adding to the overall impression of gormlessness. He sloped into her office, banging the door shut behind him. Despite the nip in the air, Eden wished they could keep the door open: Wayne was rank.

He slumped into the clients' chair opposite her desk. His hair hung in lank ropes about his face, and his eyes, sunk into grey pouches, were like poached eggs in a pan of salted water.

'You were in my house yesterday,' he started.

'I wanted to find out what happened there,' she said. 'Where've you been?'

Wayne shrugged. 'About.'

'Why did you call me?'

'The house … it's a right mess … and what happened to Mum …' Wayne sniffed. 'I'm frightened. I don't know what to do.'

Eden rose from behind the desk. Wayne flinched. She softened her voice. 'Would you like a coffee?'

'Yeah. Thanks,' he added, as an afterthought.

'When did you last eat?'

Wayne pulled a face.

'Hungry?'

He nodded.

'Come on, I'll get you a sandwich. There's a place just along here.'

She left the kettle to boil and took Wayne to Tony's sandwich bar. Tony raised his eyebrows at Wayne but said nothing when Eden ordered him a breakfast bap and a carton of orange juice.

Back in her office, Wayne set about the breakfast bap in a way that would impress a starving tyrannosaurus. Maybe he hadn't eaten for days, Eden wondered. He even guzzled the orange juice, tipping it down his throat as though parched, and finishing it off with an orotund belch.

'Pardon,' Wayne said, wiping his mouth with his fingers. 'That was great. Thanks.'

He looked better. Looked as though he could take a bit of questioning now, anyway.

'What is it you want me to do, Wayne?'

'They told me Mum died.' He choked on the word. 'Someone killed her.'

'Who's they?'

'The police. They called my mobile. I don't know how they knew the number.'

Eden hid a smile. 'They can find out stuff like that really easily, Wayne. What else did the police say?'

'They said they needed to talk to me. I can't do that. They think I killed Mum.'

Eden sipped her coffee. 'Why should they think that?'

Wayne's gaze skittered away, his hand creeping up to his cheek. 'We had a fight,' he mumbled.

'A fight? An argument?'

'Yeah, and a … fight. She got a bruise and the police will think I killed her.'

'You hit her?' She fought to keep the distaste out of her voice. 'You hit your mother?'

Wayne nodded, unable to meet her eye.

'Did you kill her?'

Wayne shot to his feet, shouting, 'You're as bad as everyone else! I thought you'd help me, but you think I killed her!'

'Sit down, Wayne,' Eden said, quietly. He slumped back in the chair, rubbing away tears with a grubby paw. 'I had to ask. Tell me what you were fighting about.'

'She said I wasn't working hard enough at school. Just kept nagging me and nagging me. Saying it was the best opportunity I'd ever get in my life and I shouldn't throw it away.'

'Sounds like most mums,' Eden said, a memory of her own mother doing the same bringing a wave of homesickness.

'It was every day, on and on and on. It was always "Do your homework, you're not going out until you show me your homework". She drove me mad. She wouldn't even let me go out at weekends. It was all just school, all the time.

'I wanted to go and see my mates. My *real* mates, not people from that school, and she tried to stop me. The school had rung her and said I'd been playing truant. She was really mad. She stood in front of me, with her hands on her hips, trying to stop me leaving, and I pushed past her. She grabbed hold of me, and I was trying to get away, I just wanted to see my mates, and we're there struggling by the door, and … I hit her.'

'When was this?'

'Wednesday evening. *She* was ready to go out, all dressed up, and she was saying *I* couldn't. It's not fair.'

'Did she go out much?'

'All the time. Some bloke or another.'

'How was she when she was at home? Anything worrying her?'

'She wouldn't listen. I tried to tell her about that school and she wouldn't listen! She was always out, or at home drinking, or crying. She wouldn't listen to me.'

Eden topped up his coffee cup. 'All right, Wayne. So your mum was stressed and drinking and crying a lot. When did that start?'

He shrugged. 'A few months ago, maybe? I don't know.'

'After you hit her on Wednesday, what happened then?'

Wayne rubbed his hands together between his knees, avoiding her eye. 'Everything just sort of went into slow motion, you know? I think my heart stopped. I've never hit her before. It was horrible. She was all soft, like a girl is, you know, so soft, and I'd hit her. My mum. And she gave me this look. I'll never forget it. She didn't say anything, just looked at me. I couldn't stand her looking at me like that, not saying anything, so I ran out the house and away.'

'Where did you go?'

'I got the bus to Gloucester and met up with some mates and got drunk, slept on someone's floor.'

'What were you doing back home on Thursday morning?'

'I'd come for my stuff.' Wayne sniffed. 'I knew she'd be at work, and I was just going to leave her a note, say sorry, and get out of there.'

She watched him crying and silently handed him a tissue. He took it without a word and scrubbed his face.

'Wayne, when did you start at the Park School?'

'After primary school. I thought I was going to Bournside with my friends, but then one day Mum announces I've got a place at the Park School.'

'Who pays your fees? Is it your dad?'

'Dad?' Wayne spluttered. 'Hardly. He pays child support to Mum for me, but he can't afford what they charge there.'

'What does your dad do?'

'He's a plumber. He's remarried now. Got a kid.' Wayne glanced up, his face pinched with fear. 'He didn't kill Mum, did he?'

Eden shook her head. 'I don't know, Wayne. Why should he? Did they argue?'

'Didn't have anything to do with each other. I used to go and stay with him, but she never saw Dad.'

'So if it's not your dad, who pays your school fees?'

Wayne shrugged. 'Dunno. I wish they wouldn't. I hate that place.'

Eden drummed on the desk with the end of her pen. 'You said your mum was drinking and crying a lot. What was that about?'

'She wouldn't say. She was jumpy, too. Jumped out of her skin if the phone rang, wouldn't answer it half the time, just let it ring. One time she ignored it like that and her boss came round, all mad, and gave her a load of work to do. Shouting that he'd been ringing her for ages and why didn't she answer.'

'Her boss?'

'Greg. Right ponce.'

'How often did he come to the house?'

'A couple of times that I saw. He'd give Mum work to do at home.'

Eden recalled the photos of Donna and Greg together on holiday. 'Did she and Greg have a relationship?'

Wayne flushed scarlet. 'Yeah,' he said. 'Stupid. He's married. I think his wife found out and he ended it with Mum.'

'When was that?'

'Last summer.'

Before she started seeing Paul. A relationship with her boss, who then thought he could call round at her house and deliver work. Work? She was a secretary, what did she need to do at home that couldn't be done in the office?

'There was something else,' Wayne said. 'Mum kept on telling me about insurance. If she'd been drinking, she'd get all scared and crying and start telling me she had insurance.'

'Life insurance?'

Wayne shook his head. 'She said once, "They can't touch me. I've got insurance. I know too much and I've written it all down. And they know it. Anything happens to me, it's all there. That's why I'm safe."'

She wasn't safe, though, was she? Someone killed her, and someone turned her house over. Looking for the 'insurance'?

Eden stood and grabbed her coat. 'Come on, Wayne. We've got work to do.'

'Where are we going?'

'We're going to find out what your mum knew that got her killed.'

Wayne let them in through the back door. The house was in the same mess as before: drawers emptied on to the floor, cupboards swinging open, the sofa tipped upside down. Wayne gave a low moan when confronted by the state of the house. He crouched down in the middle of the floor and picked up shards of china and glass. He was still for a long time. Eventually Eden touched his shoulder, and said, kindly, 'Come on, Wayne, help me find out who did this, huh?'

He swiped his sleeve across his eyes and watched her wriggle her fingers into latex gloves.

'Why do you need those?'

'Just in case we find something with someone else's prints on it.'

'The person who killed Mum?'

Eden didn't answer. Wayne picked up a bowl from the floor and placed it on the shelf, a futile, tender gesture that flooded her heart with sympathy. He was only fifteen, his mother had been killed; he was facing this alone.

'Your mum said she had insurance,' Eden said. 'She must have hidden it somewhere: I think that's what whoever turned over the house was looking for.'

'Do you think they found it?'

Eden looked at the mess. 'No, because if they had, I think they just would have scarpered with it. Someone searched every room, so unless they only found it in the last place left to look, I think they left empty handed.'

She started in the sitting room, feeling behind and underneath cupboards and shelves, pulling drawers right out and checking whether anything was taped to the underside. She removed cushion covers and squeezed the cushions, listening for a tell-tale rustle. She lifted the rugs, flipped them over, and checked the flooring underneath. Nothing.

She worked from room to room, Wayne watching her from the doorway.

'What do you want me to do?'

'Watch me, and tell me if I miss anything.' She turned to him with a gentle smile. 'Tell me about your mum.'

'Like what?'

'What was she like?'

Hesitating at first, Wayne started to speak. 'She was just an ordinary mum, really. Shouted at me, made me pick up my clothes off the floor. When she and Dad were together, we used to go to the seaside on holidays. Nowhere flash, just Cornwall and places like that. She used to collect all sorts of crap. Leaves and shells and postcards, photos of all of us together, tickets for the steam train and stuff like that, and when we got home, she'd make a collage out of it. Like a little kid, with glue and a piece of card, and she'd call it the holiday collage, and put it up where we'd all see it to remind us of our holiday.' Wayne stopped. When he continued, his voice was gravelly, 'She didn't do that any more after Dad left.'

'Why did your dad leave?'

'She kicked him out. Found out he'd had an affair. She couldn't stand being near him after that. Dad married the other woman, Cora, after the divorce. I think that's why Mum never went to their place: she didn't want to see Cora.'

The woman who'd broken up their marriage. It made sense. Also explained why she might have an affair with a married man herself: it had been done to her, why not suit herself from now on.

Eden moved into the kitchen and searched the cupboards, one by one. There was a little utility room off the kitchen, with a washing machine and small sink. Hanging above the sink was a collage: a mess of ticket stubs, bits of shell, photos of Wayne when he was small, framed in a light wood.

'Did your mum make this?'

'Yeah. Horrible, isn't it?'

She was surprised that Donna kept it on display. It must be hurtful, looking at these memories of a happier time day after day, a daily reminder of everything she'd lost.

She opened the cupboard and began to take out the box of washing powder and bottles of stain remover, then glanced again at the collage. She reached up and lifted it down. Turning it over, she saw it was backed with a piece of stiff hardboard held firm with four metal clips. She eased them off one by one and prised off the backing.

'Bingo,' she breathed, as she picked up an envelope concealed behind the backing. 'The best place to hide anything is in plain view.'

She replaced the backing and rehung the collage then opened the envelope. It wasn't sealed. Inside was a sheet of paper with entries written in different pens as though it had been compiled over a period of time. Eden turned the paper over. Writing covered both sides. It was in the form of a rough table. Date, then a name, then an amount, then a Y or N, which she presumed stood for yes or no. But yes or no to which question?

She handed the sheet over to Wayne. 'This make any sense to you?'

Wayne studied it. 'No. Whose names are they?'

'I was going to ask you that. Butler, Carsons, Keble?' She looked at Wayne and asked gently, 'Your mum's boyfriends? Men she dated once or twice even?'

Wayne shook his head. 'No. She went out with someone called Paul not long ago. He was all right. He took me to the football.' He flicked down the list. 'His name's here. Look, at the bottom.'

Not quite the bottom. Underneath was a date two weeks away, the name Shearer, and an amount. Over a million pounds. Next to it was an N.

'What are you going to do?' Wayne asked.

'I'll take it with me, if that's all right with you,' Eden said. 'It doesn't make sense to me yet, but I'll see what I can work out.'

'What about me?'

'I think you should go to stay with your dad. The people who searched the house might come back. Anyway, you can't stay here on your own.'

'Dad'll call the police if I turn up.'

'You'll have to speak to them eventually.' She squeezed his arm. 'Tell the truth and you'll be fine.'

They left the house, locked up, and Eden drove him to the station where she bought him a ticket. 'Ring your dad and ask him to pick you up. And let me know how you get on.'

She put him on to the train, fearing he'd skip and cash in the ticket, thinking he could run forever. As the doors closed, he poked his head out and asked, 'What if they come after you?'

'Don't worry about me, Wayne,' she said, 'I can take care of myself.'

The receptionist at the planning office told her Greg Barker was out. 'Working from home today,' was her specific allegation. If that was meant to put her off, it didn't work. She simply looked up Greg's home address and tootled round there.

The woman who answered the door wasn't what she was expecting. Having met Greg: macho, brash and overbearing, she'd expected a woman clad in leather trousers and a zebra-print top, not the gentle-faced woman in a pink wrap-around sweater who greeted her.

'Hello?'

'Mrs Barker?'

'Yes.'

'Is Greg in?'

'No, he's at work.' The woman frowned at such an elementary mistake.

'Then can I talk to you?' Eden fished out her ID and flashed it like they do in movies. The woman took the ID from her hand and studied it before stepping aside and inviting her in.

Sally Barker had mousy brown hair hanging straight to her shoulders. She tucked it behind her ears as they sat down in her sitting room. A toybox spilled dolls and dolls' clothes over the carpet; Eden trod one underfoot accidentally as she made her way to the seat Sally indicated. She bent and picked up a small plastic doll with long blond hair.

'Sorry,' Sally said. 'Excuse the mess. Children, you know.'

Eden balanced the doll on the arm of the chair. 'How old are they?'

'Eight. Twin girls, Abigail and Amy.' Her gaze strayed to a photograph above the fireplace: a studio portrait of Sally and Greg with two girls, dressed identically.

The house was modest: a simple three-bed semi on a modern estate. She'd imagined Greg to have a large detached house in a gated community. The sitting and dining room were open plan, with doors at the back of the house leading out on to a compact garden. A plastic slide dominated the square of lawn, but someone had created imaginative flowerbeds that made the most of the small space.

'Are you the gardener?' Eden asked.

'What? Oh yes, I love gardening. I love being out there.' She turned back to Eden. 'You didn't come here to talk about gardening.'

'I'm investigating the death of Paul Nelson. Did you know him?'

'Paul Nelson? No, I don't recognise the name. How did he die?'

'He was poisoned.'

Wide blue eyes fixed on her. 'You mean food poisoning?'

Eden ignored her question. 'Are you sure you don't know him? Your husband might have mentioned him. Paul was a property developer.'

'I don't have anything to do with all of that.'

'All of what?'

'Business. Greg's work.' Sally gave a small laugh. 'I just look after the house and the girls.'

'So he never brought Paul here, for a party or drinks? He never mentioned him?'

Sally shrugged. 'No, sorry.'

'Does Greg ever talk about work?'

'A bit. You know, complaining about stress, talking about people I don't know. I just nod and sympathise.' She fingered the beads on her red and black bracelet abstractly.

She wasn't getting anywhere; time to try an appeal to chumminess. Nodding at Sally's bracelet, Eden said, 'Snap.' She jutted out her wrist to show her. 'Got mine from a music festival.'

It took Sally a moment to catch up. 'Oh yes,' she breathed, 'Greg bought this for me. We got it from the Eden project years ago.'

'Nice.'

'I had a necklace that matched, but the string broke. Greg was going to fix it but …' Sally dribbled to a halt. 'Anyway, sorry I can't help you.'

'Where was Greg on Monday night?'

'Monday?' Sally screwed up her face. 'Monday's always the planning meeting.'

'What time did he get home?'

Sally smoothed her skirt over her knees. 'The usual time, about half past nine. Look, what's this about?'

Eden persisted. 'And Wednesday night? Where was he then?'

Sally's face closed. 'He was here, with me. Where else would he be?' She crossed her arms over her chest.

Liar, Eden thought. Time to play dirty. 'What about Donna Small?'

Sally stiffened slightly, and brushed an invisible piece of lint from her sweater. 'She's Greg's PA,' she said.

'How long has she worked for him?'

'Why don't you ask her?'

'I would, Sally, but Donna was killed a couple of days ago.'

Sally slumped back in her chair. 'Killed? How?'

She wasn't going to answer that question. Surely Greg would have told his wife his PA had been killed? 'How well did you know her?'

Sally was staring into space, her fingers working at her bracelet, and Eden had to repeat the question.

'Not very well,' Sally said, her words hollow. 'I saw her occasionally at the work do at Christmas.'

'When did you last see her?'

'The Christmas party, probably.'

'How well did Greg know her?'

Sally bit her bottom lip. 'She was his PA.' Her voice hardened. 'She was his colleague, that's all.'

'You didn't socialise with her?'

Sally shook her head. 'Why should we?'

'I got the feeling you all went on holiday together.'

A pause. When Sally spoke, her voice was hoarse. 'What makes you think that?'

'Donna Small had a photo of her and Greg together, somewhere tropical, hotel pool, cocktails with fruit in. I assumed that your family and hers went as a group.'

Sally jumped up. 'Get out,' she said in a low voice. 'Get out!'

Eden stood. 'Where were you on Wednesday night, Sally?'

'Here. I was here with the children. I don't know anything.'

She grabbed Eden's elbow and hustled her to the door. 'Now go!' she cried, opening the door and shoving Eden out.

As Eden walked back to her car, she turned and saw Sally framed in the window, watching her go, tears pouring down her face. For a second, Eden toyed with going back, apologising, comforting her; then she dismissed the idea. She had work to do.

She drove back home and parked in her allotted space outside the block of flats. Hoisting her bag on to her shoulder, she opened the front door and cantered up the stairs to her floor. No one about. She dug out her front door keys and froze.

The hair she placed carefully every time she left the flat was missing. Someone had got in.

She opened the door cautiously and slunk inside, her senses taut. The air in the flat was different; it had shifted since she'd last been here; accommodated the space of another human being.

Standing frozen, she strained her ears for any sound, any breath that would tell her the intruder was still there. Nothing. The sitting room was empty, as was the kitchen leading off it. She edged from room to room, scouting out signs of an intruder. Her nerves were at full alert, tensed to any shiver in the air that betrayed she wasn't alone.

The dust she left on purpose on the bookshelf was disturbed: the books had been pulled out and replaced. No one in the bathroom, but the mirrored door on the medicine cabinet was closed tight shut: she always left it slightly ajar. She opened it: the medicines had been stirred around. Someone had searched her flat.

She screwed up her courage to open the wardrobe door in her bedroom, taunted by images of someone jumping out at her. It was Hammond's style to lurk in her bedroom and frighten her, get the upper hand and shred her nerves before he even started.

She swallowed. She couldn't think about what he'd start if he ever caught up with her.

No one in the wardrobe, but her clothes had shuffled along the rail. The hair across the top drawer of the chest of drawers was missing. The rooms were empty, that only left the balcony. She peered out on to it, craning her neck as far as she could. There was a blind spot where the balcony curved away round the side of building. He could be skulking there. The hair across the door had gone: whoever had searched the place had done a thorough job if he'd frisked the daffodils in their pot, too.

Yanking open the door, she leapt out on to the balcony and sprinted to the corner. Nothing. Her heart banging against her chest, she leaned on the balcony rail and looked out over the velvety grass and cedars that surrounded the block of flats to the shops, and beyond them, to the hills.

Her hand shook so hard she could only cling to the rail while she fought to calm her breathing. Someone in her flat. No sign of a forced entry, so it was someone who knew how to pick a lock. Someone with skills. Someone who knew what he was doing. She let go of the rail and ran back inside, slamming the door and locking it.

It was only then she realised that whoever had searched her flat had made a mistake: he'd left the balcony door unlocked. Was it a mistake, or a threat? Done deliberately to let her know someone had breached her sanctuary? Someone letting her know he'd found her and he'd come back for her one day?

A shudder rattled through her body. Hammond.

CHAPTER
EIGHTEEN

Friday, 27 February 2015

13:09 hours

She made herself a cup of tea, and left it untasted on the table while she sat, arms hugging her knees, frozen with fear. Her nerves were at snapping point, and she screamed when an alarm sounded in her flat. After a second or two, she realised it was only a phone ringing; not her usual phone, but one of the undercover handsets she stashed in the bottom of her wardrobe. Leaden legs carried her into the bedroom. As she pressed connect, she realised she couldn't remember which persona she was meant to be on this number.

'Hello?' she said.

'Isabel, it's Roger. How you doing, girl?'

She let go of her breath. 'I'm well, thanks, Roger. How are you?'

'Mustn't grumble. No one takes any notice anyway.'

She forced a laugh. 'You got some information for me?'

'Yeah, and it's good. You ready?'

She tucked the phone under her chin and reached for a pen. Roger's voice dipped as he passed on the information, as if that would fox any attempt at interception. 'There was a Constable up for sale on the quiet eight years ago,' he said. 'The same one in that photo you sent me.'

'Who sold it?'

'Well, it wasn't Christie's, I can tell you.' He broke off to cough. 'Went underground and ended up with one of them Russian billionaires what can't find enough to spend their cash on.'

'Where is it?'

'Some palace in Russia.' Roger tutted. 'They have that revolution to overthrow the big I ams, and what do they do, but go and make a mint and live in the palaces themselves. I ask you.'

'Who facilitated the sale?' Roger knew too much about Russian history and could drone on with his interpretation of the wrongs of Bolshevism for hours if unchecked.

'Inside job. Knew who to go to to get it shifted, though.' Roger coughed again. ''Scuse me. Been hacking like an asbestos miner since I gave up the fags. Interesting thing is, the owners got someone to do a copy of the painting before they sold it.'

'I'm not surprised.'

'This bit is. That painting, copy or forgery whatever you want to call it, was nicked about a year and a half ago.'

She tapped her pen on the notebook. 'Who bought it?'

'Collector who knew it was a fake. Didn't pay top dosh for it, knew it was bent as a marmite sandwich.'

That surprised her. 'They knew it was a fake? Surely whoever stole it would've made more passing it off as real?'

'That's the thing, Isabel. It was stolen to order. Insurance job, no questions, collector keeping shtum.'

'Stolen to order?' she echoed.

'Very helpful they were, too. A bit careless where they left the security codes, that sort of thing. That's the rumour on the streets, anyway. Might not be true, but the story doing the rounds is it was the easiest heist in Christendom.'

'Thanks, Roger, that's really helpful.'

'So when am I going to see you, girl? It's been ages. You used to take me some nice restaurants in Soho, as I recall.'

'Next time I'm in London, I promise,' she laughed. Thanking him again, she hung up, removed the SIM card from the phone and snapped it in two.

An insurance job. If the painting was a copy, the school must've been in on the sale and the insurance scam. It seemed they'd been paid twice: once when the painting was sold to the Russian collector eight years before, and again eighteen months ago when the insurance paid the full amount of the painting's value. It was an audacious plan.

Armed with this new information, she set off to the Cheltenham Park School to confront Rosalind Mortimer. Her secretary tried to bar the way, but Rosalind herself came out of her office and allowed Eden inside.

'I want to talk to you about the painting,' Eden began. 'The stolen Constable.'

'I thought you might, when you asked about it and took that photograph away with you.' The skin around Rosalind's jaw was pouchy, and lack of sleep carved dark hollows around her eyes. 'What do you want?'

This wasn't the feisty madam Eden had become accustomed to; this was a pallid mannequin with its strings cut.

'The painting that was stolen eighteen months ago was a fake, and that fake was painted to replace the original about eight years ago.'

Rosalind glanced up sharply. 'How do you know all this?'

'I have friends on the wrong side of the law,' Eden said, simply.

Rosalind pressed her fingertips into her eyes. Muffled, she said, 'I wasn't here when the original was sold and the replacement painted. That was my predecessor's idea. I had no idea for quite some time, actually, and it was only a few years ago that she told me what she'd done. She was dying of cancer and felt the urge to confess.' A humourless smile. 'She said that they'd sold the painting for good reasons. The school needed new buildings, it didn't have the money, parents were expecting more from the school but weren't prepared to pay higher fees for improved facilities. So, they sold the painting and had a copy made.'

'Why sell it on the black market? Why not take it to Sotheby's or Christies?'

Rosalind's mouth twisted. 'The painting wasn't the school's to sell. It was gifted to us by a benefactor to hang in the school, but wasn't ours to do with as we liked. That's why there was a copy made, and the original was sold quietly.' She barked a short laugh. 'All we got from that painting was massive insurance bills and the need for state-of-the-art security. The privilege of hanging it on our walls cost us a fortune. Some benefactor. But the parents liked the kudos the painting lent the school, and by extension, them.'

She sucked in a deep breath and lolled her head back on her leather seat, as though weary of the whole thing. In a tired voice she continued, 'The school did all right for a few years, then the same issues cropped up. New accommodation, parents demanding new classes, new labs, new sports facilities. You can't just educate a child these days, stuff their brains with Latin conjugations and dates of battles, teach them how to do long division. They have to be fit and creative, have to do fencing and gymnastics and rowing and drama. We have to have facilities to do all of that on site: no sharing a stage with the local comprehensive. It all has to be here.' She stared glumly out of the window where the diggers stood idle like frozen dinosaurs.

'If these facilities ever get built, if people could stop digging up corpses every time they turn a sod, we might just have some new science labs by the next academic year.'

'Paid for with the insurance on the stolen painting?'

'By a squeak. We couldn't increase the insurance on the painting because that would have meant having it valued, and any art expert trotting out here and taking one look at that painting would have known it was a copy. We got what it was valued at ten years ago: a fraction of what it was worth. It was just enough for the new building work.'

'How much?'

'Two million.'

Eden's mind reeled. 'Two million? That's all?'

Rosalind shrugged. 'It was a very competitive quote.' She held Eden's eye. 'What are you going to do now?'

'I'm still making enquiries, but I'll have to pass my findings on to the police.'

'About the painting?'

'What else?'

Rosalind swivelled her attention back to the window, to the churned up soil and incipient foundations of the new buildings and didn't speak again. Eden saw herself out.

Back at her car, she called Janice, Paul Nelson's PA. She'd worked for him for years, presumably she knew a thing or two about large building contract jobs. After a few preliminaries, she asked outright, 'Ball park figure to build from scratch a science block and gymnasium.'

Janice sucked in a breath. 'You'd need a specialist firm. You wouldn't get Joe Blogs who does your conservatory for that.'

'Can you give me a rough idea what Paul's company would price it at?'

Janice harrumphed a couple of times while she thought. 'Depends on how big and how quickly, but you wouldn't get much change from five million pounds.'

Eden only stayed long enough in her flat to shower and change her clothes. Assassins lurked in every corner; when a floorboard creaked she jumped out of her skin. Even stepping out of the shower took courage; she was convinced that a hand was about to spring out and grab her by the throat. Fear coopered her chest; every breath was tight.

She needed warmth and companionship, and the kind of reassurance that could only be found in six feet of archaeologist. Aidan found her sitting on the doorstep to his flat when he came home from work.

'What're you doing here?' he said. 'Pretending to be an orphan?'

'Please can I come in, Aidan? I'm frightened.'

His face changed immediately, softening into concern. 'Come on, you,' he said, ushering her inside and up the winding stone staircase to his flat. She flung herself down on his settee. 'What's happened? God, Eden, you're shaking!'

'That phone message you heard the other day.' The message from Miranda, telling her Little Jimmy was dead.

'The spooky one?' His hand was warm, holding hers as they sat side by side on the settee.

She nodded. 'I got another one, threatening me. They mean it, and they can get to me, too. Especially now one of the gang's been released.'

'Shit.'

'They're trying to scare me, and it's working.'

'Oh, Eden.' He wrapped his arms round her, pressing her face against his shoulder. He smelled of sandalwood and earth; his shirt was soft against her skin. 'What are you going to do?'

'I can move, change identity again, and pray they don't catch up with me,' she said. 'Or I can stick it out. They're the sort that will be inside again before long. Hopefully they'll manage to keep hold of them this time.' She puffed out her cheeks, fighting exhausted tears. 'They killed the man who saved my life.'

'Saved your life? How?'

Disentangling herself, she unbuttoned her blouse and slipped it off her shoulders. 'This scar here: where my spleen was removed. He stabbed me in the stomach and nicked it. Internal bleeding.' She pointed to two faint lines across her arms. 'Here is where he sliced across my arms before he stabbed me.' She unzipped her jeans and stepped out of them to show the two scars across her thighs. 'And he cut me here. Then they tied me up and threw me in the back of a lorry. The driver was ordered to dump me in the Thames.'

'Bloody hell, Eden.' His fingertips traced the scars and her skin prickled. 'And I believed for so long that you fell through a window as a child.'

'I could hardly tell you the truth, could I?' she said. 'One of the gang got away and raised the alarm. Had even memorised the registration number of the lorry, that's how they got to me in time.' Her voice cracked. 'He was a thick little shit, but he did that for me. He took the whole gang down, and they killed him.'

'And now they're after you?'

Eden nodded. She reached for her jeans and started to pull them back on. Aidan reached across and held her wrist. 'Not so fast,' he said, gently.

He stood and wrapped her in his arms, his breath feathering her hair. 'You're not in this alone,' he whispered. 'If you want us to run away, we'll run away.'

'Us?'

'Yes, us.'

Her heart contracted. It had been so long since anyone had cared for her like this. A long time since she'd felt this safe.

Aidan continued. 'It's the weekend, so I'm going to run you a bath, and even put in some of my favourite bath oil, and I'm going to bring you a glass of wine and hand feed you peanut M&M's while you have a soak. OK?'

'Sounds good.' As he went towards the bathroom, she called after him, 'Can I play with your rubber ducks?'

He laughed. 'No. The ducks are off limits. You always put them back in the wrong order.'

The bath water came up to her chin: deliciously scented and just the right side of hot. Eden knocked the plastic ducks with her toe and poked them about on the waves. Aidan frowned and popped another chocolate in her mouth, then two in his own.

'I like the fact you're a chocoholic,' Eden said. 'Some men don't see the point of chocolate.'

'I'm not some men,' he said. Tracing the line of the scar on her arm, he said, sombrely, 'You must've been so scared.'

'I thought my time was up,' she said. 'I died in the operating theatre – twice – apparently. They wouldn't let me go.'

Her gaze met his. His eyes were dark and serious. 'I'm glad they didn't,' he said. 'Wash your hair?'

She dunked her head under the water and he poured shampoo into his palm and massaged it over her scalp, working it in behind her ears and soaping the length of her hair.

She studied his face as he washed and rinsed her hair: that tender dimple in his cheek when he smiled, the thick dark hair that he wore just slightly too short; and a surge of affection caught her unawares.

'Are you going to have a baby with your ex?' she asked.

He put down the cup he was using to rinse her hair and knelt beside the bath, his face close to hers. 'No.'

'You said you'd think about it.'

'I'm an idiot. I didn't know what to say. She caught me completely by surprise. What should I have said?'

Eden shrugged. 'Depends on whether you want to be a father or not.'

'Do you? Want kids?'

Her heart thumped, she saw her skin jerking beneath the water. 'I had one, once.'

The blood drained out of his face. 'What? You have a child? Eden, how come …'

She cut him off. 'I lost her.'

He slumped against the bath, his shirt spotting dark blue with water.

'I was pregnant, had the scan, knew I was expecting a girl. We called her Molly. She died when I was six months gone. The hospital induced me, and we held her for hours. She was tiny and beautiful, and like a wax flower.'

'We?'

'I was married. Nick. Nice man.'

'What happened?'

'He hated my work, said he worried about me, that it was dangerous. It wasn't: I met scumbags but I wasn't doing the really hardcore undercover work then. He blamed me for Molly's death, found someone else, and we got divorced.'

'When was this?'

'Molly died six years ago.' She brushed away a tear. After she'd gone and Nick had gone, I went into undercover work, living full time with the gang.' She glanced up at Aidan and saw his face was seared with pain. 'I dream about Molly.'

'Are you still in touch with Nick?'

'No. I don't exist anymore, remember? He was told the same thing as my parents: that I died. I am dead.'

Aidan rubbed away her tears with his thumbs. 'I don't know anything about you,' he said, despair crackling in his voice. 'All this time, I didn't know a thing.'

'It had to be like that, for my safety.' The water sloshed on to the floor as she sat up and reached for the soap. 'What do you want to know?'

'Where you were born, where you grew up, went to school. Everything. You said you went to university in London, was that true?'

'Yes, I did go there. But I went to Oxford first, then Edinburgh for my MA, and did my PhD in London.'

Aidan's mouth hung open. 'You've got a PhD?'

She flicked water at him. 'You're not the only one, you know.'

'What in?'

'First degree in Psychology, MA in Forensic Psychology, then a PhD in Criminology. It tied in with work.'

'You worked and did a PhD?' Admiration shone in his voice. 'I studied full time for mine and whinged about how hard it was.'

'I enjoyed it.' She shrugged and began to soap her arms. The hot water transformed her scars into bright red welts.

Aidan posted more chocolate into her mouth. 'So you're Dr Grey?'

'No, Eden Grey doesn't have a PhD. The woman who did all of those things is dead now, remember?'

He rang for takeaway while she dried herself and dressed.

'Thai meal for two on its way. Will be about forty minutes.'

'Lovely, I'm starving.'

He took the towel from her hands and sat behind her and rubbed her hair dry. As she knelt there, between his feet, she looked round the room, at his books in colour order, at the precise distances between the candlesticks on the mantelpiece, the perfectly straight pictures on the walls, the symmetry to everything in the room.

'You're good at puzzles, aren't you?' she said. Dragging her bag over to her, she dug out the paper she'd uncovered in Donna Small's house: her 'insurance', the list of dates and names and yes/no. 'What do you make of this?'

He scanned the piece of paper, flipped it over and read the other side. 'What is it?'

'Don't know, except it's valuable to someone. Anything jump out at you?'

'All the dates listed are a Monday,' he said.

She snatched the paper from him. 'How do you know that?'

He shrugged. 'Don't know. Check if you like.'

She foraged her diary out of her bag and started to check the dates. He was right: they were all Mondays.

'Anything else?'

'I recognise some of these names. Keble's a developer. So's Osbourne. Might be a coincidence. Not sure about the others. Have you run them through a search engine?'

'Er, no.'

He grinned at her. 'And you with a PhD. Elementary, my dear Doctor.'

She thumped his arm playfully. 'Can I use your computer, please?'

He powered up his laptop and balanced it on his knee. 'Read out the names.'

Cross-legged beside him on the settee, she read out the names from the paper and he ran a search on each one in turn.

'Property developers.'

Eden scrubbed at her face with the palms of her hands. 'What's all of this about, Aidan? My client, Paul, who was a property developer, was poisoned some time between Saturday evening and Tuesday morning.'

'Poisoned?'

'Yes, some sort of bean.' She scrabbled through pages of notes to find the name. 'According to the coroner's office it was lucky bean or love bean.'

'Not that lucky.'

'Or loving. He'd been dating Donna Small until a few weeks ago, and she turned up dead on Thursday morning. They were both members of the same singles club. Donna was PA to the planning committee at the council.' She stopped. 'Hang on, the planning meeting is always on a Monday. Coincidence?'

'How did you get this paper?'

'Donna hid it and told her son she had "insurance" in case anything happened to her.'

'Which it did.'

Eden nibbled a bit of dead skin round her thumbnail. 'Maybe the two deaths aren't related. Maybe Paul was poisoned by his ex-wife, or by Donna. We know she hated him.'

'So who killed Donna?'

Eden shrugged. 'Her son, Wayne, had a fight with her and then ran away. And she had an affair with her boss: maybe his wife did her in.'

Aidan traced his finger along her jawline. 'What a job you do. Poisonings and jealous spouses and people being done in.'

'Normally it's divorce work and proving adultery, or people fiddling insurance claims,' Eden said, stroking his face in return, tracing the outline of his lips. 'Which reminds me. The Cheltenham Park School is into something dodgy, too.'

She told him about the sale of the real Constable and the theft of the fake. 'It was to pay for the new buildings they're doing there, where you dug up your skeletons,' she said. 'But the whole project is only costing them two million quid. I asked someone in the business how much a project like that would normally cost and they said about five million. So how is the school able to get that sort of building done at such a discount?'

'A parent in the building trade, willing to tender at a low price?'

'Could be. Paul tipped me off about the painting. He'd spotted there was something wrong with it because he'd seen the original. Maybe he confronted Rosalind Mortimer and she fed him a love bean.'

The doorbell buzzed and she froze.

'That'll be the takeaway,' Aidan said. 'I'll buzz them up.'

'No, go down and open the street door,' she said. 'I'll watch from the landing.'

He frowned at her. 'It's only a Thai meal for two.'

'You don't know that, Aidan. Go on, I'll stay out of sight, but I'll be able to suss them out.'

'You don't really think that they know about us, that they know where I live and have turned up with a shotgun in a takeaway bag?'

She fixed him with a look. 'Don't underestimate Hammond,' she said, quietly. He hesitated, and the doorbell rang again. 'Go on.'

Aidan trudged downstairs. As he reached the bottom, he glanced up at the stone staircase, his eyes searching for her. Eden waved him on, then slid behind the curve of the wall and watched as he opened the door, got out his wallet, and handed over cash.

'Thanks,' he called, too loudly, as the delivery man went back to his car. He carried the plastic bag back upstairs and brandished it aloft. 'Hungry?'

'Always.' She took the bag from him and started sorting out plates and spoons in the tiny kitchen. 'Aidan?'

'Hm?'

'Thanks.'

'It's only a takeaway.'

'Not just this. For everything.'

Saturday, 28 February 2015

08:01 hours

Pale light filtered through the curtains and played across her face. She flopped on to her side and bumped up against Aidan's back. Curving her arm round his waist, she kissed the tender spot between his shoulder blades, peppering tiny kisses up his spine to the nape of his neck and back down again. His fingers entwined with hers.

'Sleep OK?' he mumbled.

'Like a log. You?'

Yawning, he shuffled round to face her. 'All right. A few odd dreams, I think it was the curry.'

'Tea?'

'Yes, please.'

She kissed him and slid out of bed, padding to the kitchen and filling and setting the kettle to boil. Aidan liked toast for breakfast: made under the grill not in a toaster. He was emphatic about that, insisting the grill was properly warmed up before the bread went under, and demanding that his toast was slathered in butter. She switched on the grill to heat up and fossicked in the fridge for butter, marmalade and marmite.

She'd left her bag tossed on to the end of the settee. She dug out her phone and switched it on. Immediately it beeped with a voicemail message. She stood at the tall windows, gazing out at the sweep of tawny buildings opposite and the imposing square tower of Christ Church, her phone pressed to her ear.

A message from Kaz, the hooker in Gloucester. She thought she'd seen the missing schoolgirl, Chelsea, outside a club the night before. The girl'd been with a couple of men, older than her, and she'd been crying.

No point ringing Kaz back just yet, she'd still be sleeping off her Friday night, but Eden needed to find out what Kaz saw before she started on today's bender and forgot all about it. She reckoned she had a window of about two hours before the first vodka of the day sluiced down Kaz's throat.

She made breakfast and carried it into the bedroom. Aidan propped himself up against the pillows and helped himself to toast as she slipped back into bed beside him.

'I've got to go,' she said, pulling down the corners of her mouth.

'Someone else been murdered?'

'Missing schoolgirl been seen in Gloucester. It smacks of a grooming case and I think she's in real danger.' She pulled a face. 'I'm sorry, I'd hoped we could spend the day together. I won't be too long, though.'

'That's all right. See you when you get back. I'm just going to have a quiet morning, I think.'

'Tired?'

'Bit of a headache, that's all.'

She showered and dressed, and kissed him deeply before she left. 'You feel a bit hot, Aidan,' she said, smoothing his hair back.

'Just a headache,' he said.

She left him flipping the pillows over in search of a cool spot, and went to hunt down a missing schoolgirl.

CHAPTER
NINETEEN

Saturday, 28 February 2015

09:15 hours

The other side of the pillow was cool against his cheek and he sank his head into it. The headache pulsed behind his eyes and throbbed down the side of his face. He took another pillow and pressed it on top of his head, smelling Eden's coconut shampoo on the cotton.

He slept, waking an hour later. The headache had receded and his mind was whirring with ideas. Aidan threw back the covers and wandered into the kitchen, hopping from foot to foot on the chilly tiles while he made coffee. Eden's piece of paper with the names of the property developers was lying on the table. He carried it to the window and studied it. There was a pattern here, he knew it, he just couldn't quite see it.

Patterns had always mocked, intrigued and irritated him in equal measure. As a child, he'd rearranged the decorations on the Christmas tree to make them symmetrical: the weighting of blue baubles to the left of the tree had been intolerable. His grandmother's fireplace induced unbearable scratchiness in him: unable to shuffle the thirteen tiles across the top into any pattern. Four threes and then a left over one. Impossible. He started to sit where he couldn't see the tiles, knowing that he'd be compelled to count them over and over, the frustration rising in him as they refused to be put into order. Even when he sat at the other side of the room, knowing that the tiles were there in all their thirteenly inadequacy nagged away at him.

His flat in a Regency building was perfect for him: tall windows (two sets of eight, a divine sixteen), the elegant proportions, the black and white tiling that could be mentally grouped into small squares and larger squares. And though he saw the same objects day after day, still he counted. Eleven mugs on the tray at work distressed him until a new person joined and suddenly there were twelve, and it was as though his brain smoothed out, fell into a shallow wave of comfort.

Now here, a list of property developers, a list of amounts, yes and no, and a set of Mondays. No discernible pattern. He slugged a couple of paracetamol with his coffee; the headache was lurking at the back of his mind like a ghost, a shadow on his brain, but he must find the pattern, had to find the organising principle behind the list.

Logging on to his laptop, he drew a pad of paper and a fountain pen towards him and started to search. The names were all property developers, and Eden said the planning meetings were on Mondays, so he started with the planning reports, writing down every application that related to the companies listed on the paper, the amount involved, and whether or not it was successful. Working back over two years, painstakingly tabling every one, a pattern emerged.

Aidan sat back in his chair, his neck stiff from hunching over the laptop for so long. His headache was worse now. When he stood, his spine creaked. Time for a shower, another coffee, then look at the results again.

The pattern was there. He transcribed it into a spreadsheet so he could manipulate the data and show Eden, and so he could double-check what was already evident to him. He could see precisely what this list meant, and exactly why someone would kill to get it.

He rubbed his hands over his face and yellow flashes sparked before his eyes. His headache flared and he watched his thoughts swirling. A migraine on its way. It always started like this, when he could see his thoughts, could see his mind making connections, dragging up esoteric facts he didn't know he knew. When he went back to the spreadsheet, he was automatically finding the middle letter of every word, dividing each word up into equal pockets of letters. Counting.

He knew he didn't have long before the migraine exploded. His hands trembling, Aidan went back to the search engine, looking for patterns, searching for connections between the building firms on the list. Some were based in Cheltenham, some Bristol, others from London.

He tried another line of attack and this time hit pay dirt. An hour later he had a diagram that proved the pattern. He'd cracked it.

The migraine knifed the side of Aidan's face. He flinched at the light and tugged the curtains closed, then crawled back into bed. Just before the agony struck, he sent a one-word text to Eden: migraine.

Eden. What was it she'd said about Paul Nelson and how he died? Lucky bean. Love bean. He watched his thoughts churning and making connections as though he was viewing the operation of a massive computer.

Just before he died, he said 'Paternoster'.

It means 'Our Father'. The Lord's Prayer.

I didn't know you were a Catholic.

I'm very, very lapsed.

Paternoster. He'd heard that before. Where?

The words swirled and connected and the pattern resolved before his eyes. Foraging a pen out of his bedside cabinet, he scrawled a note on a sheet of paper, then collapsed. Words were gone, only pain remained. Agony behind his eyes and crushing his skull. Even to rest on the pillow was torture.

He closed his eyes and resigned himself to the migraine's power.

09:34 hours

Kaz was in her usual haunt, her bony shoulders hunched into a ratty fur coat of such a dubious orange hue it must've originally been a large ginger cat. As Eden pulled up, Kaz was bending to speak to a punter in a battered yellow Vauxhall. He scarpered the moment Eden got out of her car, his tyres squealing as he turned the corner.

'What d'you do that for?' Kaz spat, her hands on her hips. 'Lost me good money!'

Eden ignored this. 'You rang and said you'd seen the missing girl.'

'Yeah, well, I don't know whether I did now.' Kaz sniffed and ground her fist against her nose. 'I might have been mistaken.'

Eden bit back her irritation. Saturday mornings were for lazing in bed, browsing second-hand bookshops and reading the newspapers in coffeeshops. Not dodging vomit pancakes in the Gloucester red-light district and being smart-mouthed by a raddled tart.

'Course, I might remember, if I had some incentive,' Kaz said, a sly look shivering her face.

Eden walked back to her car and unlocked the door. 'See you, Kaz!'

She climbed in and started the engine, tugging the seat belt around her. Kaz scuttled round to the driver's door, rapping on the window. Eden didn't lower the window, just let Kaz shout through it.

'I did see her! I remember now. It's just with being a bit peckish and everything I'd forgotten.'

'Peckish?'

'No milk for me tea this morning.' Kaz's Bristol accent thickened. 'Or me cornflakes.'

'You should've had toast.'

Kaz scowled. 'Funny. Maybe I didn't see that girl after all.'

'That's what I thought.' Eden let out the clutch and the car jerked forwards. Kaz banged on the roof.

'Stop! I saw a girl who looked just like that missing girl last night. Very pretty she is.'

Eden leaned over and swung open the passenger door. 'Get in.'

'I'm not going anywhere with you. You could be anyone.'

At that, Eden lost her temper. 'You get in and out of strangers' cars all day long, Kaz. The risks are part of your job description. I'm not going to rape you, beat you or kill you. I'm not going to give you any money, either, but if you want some breakfast then get in the fucking car because I'm not leaving it here while we find somewhere to eat. OK?'

Kaz got in and silently fastened the seat belt.

A greasy breakfast and a gallon of sugary tea later and Eden was little the wiser. She'd learned that Kaz fancied a bacon sandwich, that she wanted one with so much red sauce it dripped down her top, and that she had a punter coming later who always treated her right. As to Chelsea, the missing school-girl, she was less forthcoming. She'd seen a girl about the right age and with the same hair in a club the night before.

Big deal. It could have been Chelsea or any one of her friends and schoolmates: for all their asserted individuality they all had the same hair and wore the same clothes. For a brief moment, Eden wished that Chelsea was a Goth or into vintage clothes, or always wore lace gloves. Anything to mark her out as different from all the other teenage girls.

'So, I saw her in Rodrigo's last night,' Kaz said, licking ketchup from her fingers. 'That must be worth something, eh?'

'Who was she with?'

'A group of girls about the same age?' Kaz's inflection betrayed what Eden already suspected: she hadn't seen her and was making up what she thought Eden would buy. Time for a bit of fun.

'That's great, Kaz. About four of them were there?'

Kaz nodded enthusiastically. 'Yep, four, that was it. I definitely saw four.'

'Did one of the girls have ginger hair? Lots of ginger hair?'

'Right down her back it was.'

'And one with a big nose, and one with sticky out ears?'

Kaz stared into space as if she was shuffling the girls round in her memory. 'Now you mention it, they weren't oil paintings, no. Your girl, she was the best looking by a long way.'

'Did one of the girls have scales all over her face and three eyes and boobs down to her knees?' Eden asked, leaning forwards. 'And Chelsea, was she wearing a Guantanamo Bay jumpsuit and a spaceman's helmet?'

Kaz glared at her. 'I was trying to be helpful.'

'You were trying to help yourself, Kaz.' Eden scraped her chair back. 'Goodbye.'

She left Kaz to finish the mound of toast and went back to her car. She'd try Rodrigo's anyway, just in case Kaz had by accident seen the girl. No joy: the club had been closed for a private function the night before: someone's fiftieth birthday party. Unlikely that Chelsea would have been there, but she left a photo and her contact number just in case.

Driving back to Cheltenham, she had the distinct impression that she was being followed. A red Skoda Octavia drew up behind her as she left Gloucester, and clung tight to her bumper down the Golden Valley bypass. It indicated at the turn off for

Tewkesbury, then at the last minute swerved back into the lane again. Time to see whether this joker was really following her.

Moving into the outside lane, she cut round the roundabout as if she was heading for the supermarket referred to locally as the 'new' Asda. The red car followed. She went into the supermarket's car park, drove round, parked, waited, and then drove off again. Thinking she'd lost him, she cut around the back of Benhall and headed towards Aidan's flat in Lansdown. When she stopped at traffic lights and looked in her rear view mirror, the red Skoda was three cars behind her. She was being tailed.

Dodging across the traffic just as the lights changed, she cut away towards the university. Hurtling through the maze of streets around Tivoli, she managed to shake off the red Skoda by dashing down a rutted lane behind a terrace of houses, but it was a close call.

She'd got a partial view of the driver: square head, possibly late thirties, hair clipped very short. He knew how to handle a car, that was for sure.

She reversed back up the lane and out on to the street. No sign of the red Skoda. She was pretty sure there wasn't a second car: it would have tailed her from when she went into the supermarket car park if so, but she still needed to be careful. Checking the road was clear, she drove away, parking her car several streets away from her flat and walking the rest of the way. There was nothing like a vehicle parked outside a block of flats to announce that's where the owner lived.

The hair was in place across her door and there was no sign that anyone had been in the flat. She let out a long, pent-up breath and her muscles sagged. The message light was blinking on her answering machine. Hitting the play button, it was a while before she could identify the voice, and had only just worked it out when the message ended with, 'Oh, it's Sally Barker, by the way.'

Eden called her back. A puffy-sounding Sally answered after two rings, as if she'd galloped to pick up the phone.

'Hello, thanks for calling me back.' Her voice was low, as if she didn't want to be overheard. It was soon apparent why. 'Listen, I've been thinking about what you said, about Greg and Donna. I've had enough. I want to tell you everything.'

'Is he there?' Eden asked.

'Yes.'

'Does he know you're on the phone?'

'Yes, but he doesn't know I'm talking to you.'

'Speak normally, and pretend I'm a friend who's having some sort of relationship breakdown. Say I'm in a state and you're popping out to see me.'

'Where should I meet you?'

Eden named a coffeeshop in the town centre and arranged to meet Sally there in twenty minutes' time. She prayed that Sally would be able to keep a straight face in front of her husband.

She found a corner table and waited for Sally to arrive. By the time she bustled in, she was red-faced and flustered, harassed because she'd had trouble finding a parking space, and then didn't have change for the ticket machine.

'It's all right,' Eden said. 'Stay here and I'll buy you a drink. Coffee?'

'Tea, please.' Sally unwound a long scarf from around her neck. She slipped her arms out of her coat and adjusted the sleeves of her sweater so her black and red bead bracelet hung free.

'What is it you want to tell me?' Eden asked, when she returned with the tea.

'You said you'd seen a photo of Greg and that Donna Small together on holiday?' Sally started. Eden winced. She shouldn't have been so brutal. Before she could explain, Sally ran on, 'I confronted him about it. He's had affairs the whole time we've been married, and I've had enough. I *knew* there was something between him and Donna. I challenged him about it hundreds of times and he denied it. I started to think I was paranoid, seeing things that weren't there. Only I wasn't, was I? He was a lying, cheating scumbag, and he's been found out.'

Sally sipped her tea and took another breath. Years of pent-up anger, frustration and jealousy poured out of her.

'You asked where Greg was on Monday and Wednesday nights. I lied.' Sally tucked her mousy hair back behind her ears and looked Eden straight in the eye. 'He was home at the usual time on Monday night, but it's not nine thirty, closer to one in the morning. And on Wednesday he wasn't home with me. I don't know what time he came in.'

'What time did you go to bed?'

'About ten, then I read for about an hour and he still hadn't come in. In the morning he was asleep in the spare room.'

'Did you ask him where he was?'

'No.' Sally's eyes dropped, and she twisted her wedding ring round her finger. 'When he's late like that, without telling me, it's because he's off with some other woman. It's better not to ask, he only lies to me.' Sally reached into a large bag on the chair next to her. 'On Thursday morning, he gave me this. A present – no reason, he said, just thought I'd like it. Guilt, I think.'

She lifted out a jewelled evening bag. Eden gawked at it. The last time she'd seen it, it was hanging off Donna Small's shoulder at the singles club. She took the bag from Sally's hands and examined it. The bag looked new: there were no makeup stains or rips in the lining to suggest it was second-hand, and there was nothing to show it was Donna's bag. Maybe it was a purely tasteless present: giving his wife a bag identical to the one his mistress had.

Her mind whirling, Eden asked, 'Where was Greg on Monday night?'

'He always goes to some sort of club on Mondays. After the planning meeting.'

'Which club?'

Sally smothered a sob. 'He won't tell me. He says it's private. I think it's the sort of club where women are the entertainment, the way he smells, his clothes smell, when he gets in.'

It could all be a bluff. The bag, Greg not coming home on Wednesday night. It left Sally without an alibi that evening, unless her eight-year-old twins could vouch for her. Maybe Sally killed Donna out of pure jealousy and was trying to cover her tracks and implicate Greg into the bargain. But watching Sally weeping, fragile and broken as a bird, with her mousy hair and cheap bracelet, Eden didn't think so. She was a wronged wife, as devastating and quotidian as that.

'You know that what you've said could get Greg into trouble?' she asked Sally. 'He doesn't have an alibi now for Wednesday night.'

'I know.' Sally's lip wobbled.

'So why …?'

'Revenge,' Sally said, simply.

11:48 hours

'I'm sorry to just turn up like this,' Eden said, 'but I thought I'd update you.'

Susan Portman inched away from the front door, moving her walking frame aside so Eden could come in. Her skirt hung lower at the front than at the back, and her petticoat flashed when she turned. Eden followed her into the sitting room.

A bearded man sat in an armchair, the TV remote propped on the arm. His head swivelled to Eden when she came in.

'My husband, Ian,' Susan said. 'Ian, this is the detective I asked to find Chelsea.'

'How are you coping?' Eden asked, taking a seat on the end of the settee. Neither of them answered, just met Eden with blank stares.

'Have the police contacted you?'

'Police?' Ian huffed. 'Fat lot of use they've been.'

'Chelsea has been missing for over twenty-four hours now,' Eden said. There was something wrong here. She intercepted a look that shivered between Ian and Susan. Ian pressed the mute button on the TV remote, but his gaze never wavered from the screen. 'Mrs Portman?'

Susan arranged her skirt over her knees, stalling for time. When she spoke, her voice squeaked with emotion. 'They're not interested. Because she's eighteen, and because ...' She choked and halted.

'What haven't you told me?' Eden said, quietly. 'Why aren't the police treating this as a missing person's case?'

'They say she's run away before and she'll be back soon,' Susan said, her words tumbling out in a rush. 'But it was all years ago, she's been a different girl since then.'

Eden slumped back against the cushions. 'Why didn't you tell me before?'

'Because I know something's wrong!' Susan cried. She wriggled a tissue out of her sleeve and patted at her eyes. 'I just know it.'

'All right,' Eden said, her mind whirring. 'Chelsea's run away from home before? When was this?'

'About a year ago. She didn't come home after school. We found out she'd never gone to school, but had taken a bus to Bristol. She came back after a few days.'

'Where did she stay in Bristol?'

'A bus shelter. I think it frightened her and she came home.'

'Was that the first time she'd run away?'

Susan twisted the tissue round her finger. Her hands were swollen, the skin shiny over the knuckles, her finger joints lumpy marbles. 'No, she ran away when she was fifteen, up to Scotland to stay with her cousin.'

'And when she was ten,' Ian interrupted. 'Gone for twelve hours, just walking around, sitting on the swings.'

Eden glanced from Susan to Ian and chose her words carefully. 'Why did she run away?'

Ian shrugged. 'Because she's an ungrateful little madam,' he volunteered. Susan winced.

'We've done everything for her. I don't know why she would run away. She seemed happy. She's been really happy the last few months.'

Since Chelsea met Zamir. He made her feel special, she saw a way to escape this smothering house, and then one day, she simply disappeared. True love story? Or cynical grooming? The line between them blurred as Eden's eyes travelled round the room, taking in Ian and the mute TV, Susan and her worried eyes, the stultifying atmosphere in the house, and she knew that if she'd been Chelsea, she'd run away, too.

Eden stood. 'I'm still making enquiries,' she said. 'I'm chasing up a few leads at the moment, and I'm happy to share them with the police if they become involved.' She hoiked her bag on to her shoulder. 'I just wanted to check that you were doing OK. I'll see myself out.'

On her way back home, she picked up a text message from Aidan. There was no point going back to his flat. He'd be prostrate for the rest of the day if previous migraines were any indication. The afternoon was hers, so she headed to a place where she knew that chaos reigned and she'd be able to forget her problems in an atmosphere of absolute bedlam. Judy's.

The house was a Victorian terrace a stone's throw from the town centre, a handkerchief of front garden separating the house from the pavement. It took three rings on the doorbell before Judy answered. Eden knew she was in, because she could hear shrieks from inside when she was within twenty feet of the house. At last the door swung open, and there was Judy, an Amazon framed in the doorway. She stepped forwards and enveloped Eden in a rib-crushing hug.

'Please say you've come to take me away from all this,' Judy declared.

'No, but I have brought a box of chocolates.'

'That'll do. Come in. Please excuse the mess. I'll clear it up in fifteen years when they've all gone to uni and I can have my sanity back.'

Eden stepped into the tall, narrow hall, the stairs stretching up steeply before her. From upstairs came the sound of boys squabbling. Judy rolled her eyes. 'Marcus bought them a new computer game,' she said. 'Where's lovely Aidan?'

'In bed with a migraine.'

Judy pulled a face. 'So you're slumming it with me?'

'Yep,' Eden said, laughing.

Judy ushered her into the open-plan sitting-dining room. The dining table was heaped with laundry, and an iron hissed steam on a board by a window that looked out over the long, pinched garden. She took a seat at the table as Judy picked up the iron.

'You don't mind if I carry on with this, do you?' she said. 'Only it'll have its own postcode if I don't keep on top of it.' She smiled at Eden and asked, 'So, what's new with you? Can't believe you skived Zumba. I hope you've got a good excuse and a note from Matron.'

'A pretty good excuse. I told you I was with my client when he died?' Eden said. 'Well, turns out he was poisoned, and it looks like murder. Then the day after he died, a woman he'd had a relationship with was found dead. Strangled. There are lots of connections between them, but nothing that would seem to add up to murder. And then I'm trying to trace a missing schoolgirl, and it smells to me like a grooming case, only I've got no evidence yet.' Eden paused for breath. It felt good to get it all off her chest, but when she glanced at Judy, she saw she was holding the iron aloft, staring at her while steam gushed on to the shirt she was ironing.

'Blimey,' Judy said at last. 'That's what passes for small talk these days, is it? I was hoping for "Judy, I've seen these shoes that I simply must have but they're expensive. Please persuade me I must buy them".'

Eden wrinkled her nose. 'I don't like shopping for shoes.'

Judy waved the iron about. 'Handbags? Lampshades, even, not "Judy, everyone's being murdered this week".'

She didn't know the half of it, Eden thought ruefully. Little Jimmy murdered, Hammond's hallmarks, a car that tailed her home. Goosebumps shivered over her skin.

'Sorry,' she said. 'Shall I open the chocolates?'

'Good idea.' Judy threaded a new shirt on to the ironing board. 'So, tell me about this client of yours.'

'He was a nice man,' Eden said. 'I liked him, but there are too many people who could have wanted him dead.'

'Bloody hell.' Judy's eyes bulged. 'Seriously? Like who?'

'His ex-wife, who stands to be trustee for a fund worth three and a half million pounds. His ex-lover, who was pretty pissed off when he dumped her, except she's been killed, too. Then there's an employee he had to sack for fraud. And then there's an art theft he was starting to work out, but I don't think that's what got him killed.'

'And they poisoned him?' Judy said. 'What with? Cyanide?'

Eden snaffled another chocolate from the box. 'No, it was something unusual. Even the coroner hadn't come across it before. Some sort of bean.'

'How do you get hold of it?'

She shrugged.

'What does truth according to the internet say?' Judy's eyes widened. 'You haven't looked it up yet? Wait there!' She propped the iron on its end and dashed to the door, popped her head back into the room and said, 'If anyone under five feet tall asks for something, the answer is no. Back in a mo.'

Eden picked up the iron and pressed a couple of school uniforms, listening to the bickering upstairs. After a few minutes, feet clumped back downstairs and Judy burst into the room clutching a laptop.

'Got it! Marcus is going to take them to the park.' She shoved the laundry aside and plonked the laptop on the table. Eden folded a pair of grey trousers and reached for a polo shirt.

Judy looked up from the laptop, her eyes dancing. 'Right. What was this called again?'

'What are you doing?'

'Checking what it looks like. I don't want to find it growing in my beautifully tended oasis of calm.'

They both glanced down the garden, at the jungle of plastic swings, bolting spinach and dead clematis.

Eden hid a smile. 'It's called a lucky bean or love bean. I can't remember the Latin name.'

Judy clicked a few keys and frowned at the screen. 'There's a lot of filth out there,' she said, mildly. 'Ah, here we are. Also known as Paternoster pea.'

'What?' Eden put down the iron and slid into the seat next to Judy. 'Show me.'

Judy tilted the laptop so Eden could see the screen. She scrolled down the page. 'It's quite pretty, isn't it, Eden? Eden?'

Eden couldn't speak. Her mouth was dry as she gazed at the photograph. Suddenly she knew who had killed Paul. Trouble was she didn't know why, and she couldn't prove it.

Not yet, anyway.

CHAPTER
TWENTY

Cheltenham, October 1795

'I should never have let you go,' Darby said, twirling a strand of her hair around his finger. Beads of sweat glistened on his chest.

Rachel heard her heart bump. 'You did, though.'

'I was a fool. I should have stood up to my father and refused to let you go.'

'Too late now.'

'Is it?'

She sat up, the sheet clutched to her chest, suddenly vulnerable. A customer grunted in the room next door; the wall rebounding with the crash of the bedstead. 'Isn't it?'

'I had to let you go because I lost my money and my father insisted I give up everything I loved,' Darby said, his fingertips tracing a line down her arm. 'Now I have money again, and I'm about to be a very rich man.' He nipped her shoulder with his teeth. 'It would be as if we'd never been apart.'

'What would?'

'If you were mine alone. In a house, with fine furniture and a maid, and a carriage at your beck and call.'

'A house where? In Cheltenham?' She was *not* going to stay in this backwater. The king had visited to take the waters, but that didn't make the place exciting. For a start, it was crawling with sick people, and though there were fine houses, it was a dull place, with as many churches as shops springing up every-where. And Cheltenham people would never accept a woman like her, a mistress, not like in London, where people understood what was what. Only the other day, a woman hawking a basket of bread had spat at her in the street.

'Not Cheltenham,' she said firmly.

'If you like,' Darby said, airily. 'Perhaps London?'

She rounded on him. 'London or nothing.'

Darby laughed. 'Then London it is.'

'With my furniture back, and a carriage, and a maid.' She bit her lip as she remembered Kitty. The girl wasn't much good but even so Rachel winced to think of her toiling in the Australian sun. How could Darby set the thief-taker on a scrap of girl like that?

'Not your own furniture, that's gone, my sweet, but new furniture, better furniture.'

'And a carriage.'

'Everything.' He nuzzled the hollow beneath her collarbone. 'Tell me you'll come back to me.'

She considered. 'When you've made your money,' she said. 'And don't say anything to Mrs Bedwin beforehand.' No point complicating matters.

'You're mad,' Emma said, in their room later. 'He's already thrown you over once, and now you want to give him the chance to do it again.'

She was brushing Rachel's hair and plaiting it ready for bed. The bristles scraped Rachel's scalp and she winced as it grated against the sores there.

'What's the matter?' Emma said. 'Is it a knot?'

'No, my skin's sore, that's all.'

'Here, let me see.'

Before Rachel could stop her, Emma had parted her hair and was moving her fingers through it as though searching for lice. 'What is it, a spot? Flea bite ...'

Her fingers stilled.

'Is it bad?' Rachel whispered.

Emma dropped the hank of hair. 'Yes, it's bad. Have you bathed it?'

'Of course I have. It doesn't make no difference.' Rachel snatched the hairbrush from Emma's hands and flung it against the wall. 'I've been drinking that foul water, too, trying to make it go away.'

'You need the mercury cure. You know that, don't you?'

Tears burned at the back of Rachel's throat. She refused to let them fall. 'Hardly got the money for that. Besides, who's going to do mercury here? I need to be back in London.'

'It's twenty guineas every time you do ... you know ... at Greville House,' Emma whispered. 'That would give you enough, wouldn't it?'

'If Mrs Dedwin let me do it again.' None of the girls had gone through the tunnel more than once. Once was enough, they agreed, speaking amongst themselves in frightened whispers. 'I can hardly tell her I need the money for the pox cure, can I?'

'You could have a sick relative you need medicine for. Or tell her you're going to have a baby.'

Rachel snorted. 'She'd just come at me with a knitting needle, not let me earn the money for the baby farmer.' She sighed and rubbed her face with her hands. Her eyes were sore and dry. Emma pulled her against her shoulder and stroked her back like a fractious baby.

'Maybe one of your young men, Rodney or Darby, would give you some money.'

'I can't hardly tell them, either, can I?'

Emma studied her face, her eyes dark with compassion. 'Which one are you going to choose?'

Rachel shook her head. 'I don't know. Whichever one gets rich first, I suppose.'

'Rodney's your favourite, though, isn't he?'

'He's kind and sweet, and Darby threw me out on the street before. But you know what they say. Beggars can't be choosers.'

'You're not a beggar,' Emma said, planting a kiss on her forehead.

'Will be soon, if I don't get rid of this pox.'

The way back into Greville House, it turned out, was to drip poison into Daphne's ears about cannibalism and devil worship, the blood drinking and baby sacrifice going on there, until the mere mention of Greville House was enough to send the girl into hysterics.

Mrs Bedwin slapped Daphne's face. 'Stupid girl, whose tales have you been listening to?'

'They were talking about it in the town, Mrs Bedwin. Everyone knows what horrors go on there.'

'Hm.' Mrs Bedwin's eyes snapped round the room. 'Rachel, you'll have to go. I'm sure the money will persuade you.'

'Yes, Mrs Bedwin,' she said, meekly, dropping a curtsey. 'I'll do my best.'

Mrs Bedwin wasn't taken in and clouted her for her cheek. Clutching her face, Rachel ran from the room and went to dress for the evening at Greville House.

There was no anticipation and excitement as she was led through the tunnel. Not like last time. Now she knew what was to happen, her neck shuddered with fear. This time there were five girls chained up in the chamber: three she recognised from last time, their clothes ragged and dirty. Two of them had black eyes. The newcomers' clothes were cleaner, but their legs and arms were mottled with bruises, and one girl had lost her front teeth.

'You again,' one of the girls said.

'Me again.' Rachel shivered. 'Where's the other girl, the one who was with you last time?'

'Not seen her.' The girl's voice was hoarse, as though she'd been screaming all day and all night. Perhaps she had.

'Got some new friends?' Rachel twitched her head at the new girls.

'For now,' the girl said. Her eyes were huge and dark, the pupils cavernous.

As last time, they were led into the temple, to the men with masks over their faces. Rachel recognised Mr Ellison's voice in charge of the proceedings, high priest and king, the ram's head mask terrifying in the candle flames. When the initiate stepped forwards, she recognised his walk, the shape of his shoulders, the angle he held his head.

'Darby!' she breathed. He was wearing a lion mask, but she knew him. He glanced in her direction just for a moment, before turning back to the figure in the centre of the circle.

Ellison held out a small box, and Darby selected a bean, which he dropped into a goblet of wine.

'Let's see if this one makes it,' one of the chained girls muttered.

'What do you mean?' Rachel hissed back.

'The bean's poisonous. If he survives, he's passed the test. If he dies ...' She shrugged.

Rachel watched in terror as Darby tipped the goblet to his lips and started to drink. Don't die, Darby, she thought. We've only just found each other again. You're going to make your fortune and take me away from all this. I want to be your own sweet Rachel again. Don't die, please don't die.

Darby drained the goblet and held it aloft, triumphantly.

Rachel clutched the girl's arm, petrified that at any moment, Darby would choke and fall down dead at her feet.

'Now choose your prize,' the ram's head instructed him.

Darby paced the temple, sizing up each girl in turn. He paused in front of Rachel and she tipped up her face to his. He gazed down at her, his eyes glinting. He knew her. Her lips parted to whisper his name, then he stalked past her and chose one of the chained girls and led her away.

She hardly knew what happened next. A man picked her: she neither knew nor cared who he was. Her heart seethed with anger. How dare Darby choose another girl, when he knew it was her in front of him. When he'd said he loved her and wanted to set her up in a house of her own in London. With a carriage, and a servant, and all her furniture back.

She braced herself against the chill stone wall and vowed revenge. She'd teach Darby Roach to overlook her.

'Rodney, you must speak to Mr Ellison. He's the one who controls the land around here.'

He was lying, sated, against her pillows. They didn't have long for conversation and tenderness. Soon Mrs Bedwin, aware that the bedroom percussion had stopped, would evict Rodney and set Rachel to work satisfying another hungry customer.

Rodney frowned. 'It doesn't seem right. All men are free, after all.'

Rachel dragged herself off the bed and went to the washstand to sponge herself down. Free! All very well for him to speak of freedom.

'But that's not so, Rodney, dearest,' she said, biting back her irritation. 'There are the slaves, and men who cannot leave their masters' employment.'

And whores who can't escape from Mrs Bedwin's clutches for fear they'll be hanged.

Rodney pouted at the mention of slaves. 'In America, yes. But not here in England.'

Rachel sensed they were moving away from her purpose. 'It's how it is, Rodney. I've heard about it from … people in the town.' No point reminding him that she wasn't exclusively his. Not yet, anyway. 'Mr Ellison is the one who says who can buy land, and who can build.'

'I heard he was a devil worshipper,' Rodney said, sprawling naked on the bed, his penis a soggy worm glued to his groin. 'The Hellfire Club meets at his house. Human sacrifice, that's what they're saying.'

Rachel's hand stilled. What had happened to the girl that Darby had taken away at his initiation? They had disappeared back into the tunnel, and she hadn't seen either of them again. The other girls – the stolen girls – had watched them go, a deep sigh rumbling from them all. Was it relief? Knowing that their lives were safe for now. *We never see the girls again.* That's what they'd told her, that first time. And the girl wasn't there last time she went back. Maybe they set them free, let them go home? Deep in her bones she knew this wasn't so. Maybe Darby had saved her life by not choosing her at his initiation.

'Rachel?' Rodney had risen from the bed and had his arms about her waist. 'I didn't mean to frighten you.'

She twirled in his arms and kissed him. 'You're my sweet Rodney, and I can't wait until we can be together, forever.' She gazed at him meaningfully.

'Neither can I,' Rodney said, burrowing his head in her neck. 'I want us to have our own little home.'

'Not so little,' she murmured, 'what with you being a rich man, surely.'

'It'll be as cosy as a cottage if you're there,' Rodney declared. 'Though it might have silk curtain and golden pillars and chairs that the king himself would be proud to own.'

That was more like it. Rachel smiled at him fondly and stroked his hair. 'In London, of course.'

'You want to leave here?'

Rachel lowered her eyes. 'I want to forget about all of this,' she said, sweeping her hand about the room.

Rodney followed her gaze and blushed. 'Anything for you, my sweet Rachel,' he said.

'Then you'll speak to Mr Ellison?' she asked.

'I'll call on him this afternoon.' Rodney puffed out his chest and strutted about the room collecting his clothes. Rachel clasped her hands together and gazed at him with her most adoring expression from her repertoire.

When he left her, she kissed him tenderly and whispered, 'Until we can be together forever, my darling.'

Rodney thundered downstairs, filled with new resolve. Rachel watched him go, her heart fond and her mind working.

CHAPTER
TWENTY-ONE

Sunday, 1 March 2015

10:36 hours

The first time Aidan had had a migraine, she'd teased him.

'You men!' she'd said, exasperated. 'You never have a cold, it's always flu. A headache's always a migraine, or a brain tumour.'

'It's not a tumour,' he'd mumbled, 'they checked me out for that. Did one of those scan things where you're locked in a metal tube.' He shuddered.

'When was that?'

'Years ago. They tested me because I get these headaches, and because I see patterns. You know.'

She glanced at the peculiar order and neatness in his flat on a scale way beyond tidiness. 'So it really is a migraine, then?'

He nodded and winced. 'Ow. Yes.'

'What do you need?'

'Darkness, quiet, and something cold to put on my eyes.'

She slipped from the room, found a washcloth and soaked it in cold water, folded it, and pressed it on to his forehead.

'Thanks,' he whispered. 'It's just about to hit. I might not be able to speak for a while.'

He groaned as the first wave of the migraine crashed over him, and clasped the pillow around his head. Eden stroked his back and replenished the cloth with cold water. It was the only thing that seemed to ease the pain for him. She sat beside him in the gloom, desperate to comfort him, fetching cold drinks when he croaked out a request, standing sentinel over him while he slept.

At one point he woke, asked, 'What happened to Katherine Parr's daughter by Thomas Seymour?' and fell back on the pillow.

When Aidan came round, several hours later, she fed him tomato soup and toast soldiers, regretting her scorn when he'd said his headache was a migraine. He was putty-coloured and weak, and slurred his words as if drunk.

'My mum used to make this for me after I'd been to the dentist,' he said. He leaned forwards and kissed her forehead. He smelled stale and poorly. 'Thanks for looking after me.'

'That's all right. You gave me a puzzle to sort out, anyway.'

His brow creased.

'Katherine Parr's daughter, Mary Seymour, probably died when she was a toddler.'

'Katherine Parr?' He scrubbed his palms in his eyes. 'My brain was swirling. I've been reading a biography of Henry VIII. It must've come from that.'

When he felt better, he explained to her how the migraines affected him, how his thoughts went into freefall and he could see them swirling and making connections, asking questions that would never normally occur to him.

'Even when I'm in agony my brain's trying to put everything into patterns,' he'd said, ruefully.

Now Eden rang and asked if he was back in the land of the living.

'I'm much better,' he said, sounding terrible. 'Just a bit fragile. I've worked out your list.'

'What list?'

'The list of property developers you left here. I've worked out the link. Want to come over?'

He was pale and sick, but upright, at least, and able to contemplate food again. When she held up a bag of croissants for brunch, he didn't blanch. As she unpacked butter and eggs, and set about hunting for a pan, her eye caught a notepad he'd left on the table. On it, in scrawly writing, was a single word: *Paternoster*. The sight gave her a jolt.

'Aidan, what's this?' She held it up.

He glanced at the paper. 'I knew I'd seen the word Paternoster recently. There used to be a Paternoster Club in Cheltenham. A sort of Hellfire Club. Secret meetings and orgies.'

'Where did you find that out?'

'A diary in the records office, written in 1795. I was doing some research into the Park School, trying to find out where those skeletons came from. In 1795, the Park School was Greville House, and it hosted the Paternoster Club.' He tickled the back of her neck and whispered close to her ear. 'The townspeople were scandalised. And a bit jealous, I suspect.'

Eden frowned while she thought. 'Paternoster is the last thing Paul said before he died,' she said. 'And Paternoster is the name of what killed him. The love bean or lucky bean, is also called the Paternoster pea.'

Aidan snapped his fingers. 'Trial by ordeal!'

Eden blinked at him. 'Are you still having a migraine?' she asked.

'Probably. Paternoster pea – it was made into rosaries, but in trial by ordeal, the victim swallowed one of the peas and if they lived they were innocent.'

'And if they died?'

'They were obviously guilty. Sometimes they tipped off the victim to swallow it whole. The poison's only released when it's chewed.'

'Where the hell did you learn that?' Sometimes Aidan's magpie mind blew her away and she felt dull beside him.

He shrugged. 'History classes at school. The teacher had to find some way to make it interesting. We did a lot on executions and battles.'

Eden chewed the skin at the side of her thumb. 'So why would Paul say Paternoster before he died?' she mused aloud. 'Did he recognise what killed him?'

'Or perhaps the Paternoster Club still exists.'

'An orgy club in Cheltenham?' Eden said. 'That wouldn't be Paul's scene at all. Donna Small, perhaps: the barman at the singles club said she was a bunny boiler, maybe she was a swinger, too.' She paused as a fleeting thought snagged and slipped away. Her mind chased it, sure it was something about Donna's diary, something she'd missed. The thought eluded her and she pressed her fingertips to her eyes. She turned to Aidan. 'You said you'd cracked the list?'

He powered up his laptop while she scrambled eggs, snaffling chives from the pots on his windowsill and chopping them into the creamy mix. They sat side by side, the laptop between them on the table, forking up scrambled eggs and buttery croissants, and Aidan showed her the spreadsheet he'd devised.

'Every planning application for all of these companies on the list,' he said. 'Now watch.'

He sorted the data columns by property developer. Three applications accepted, one rejected; five accepted, two rejected; seven accepted, two rejected. He re-sorted the spreadsheet to show the results for a different developer and the pattern repeated. One by one he went through the list of companies. The pattern was there for every single one.

'My God,' Eden breathed. 'This isn't a coincidence.'

'I checked what happened to other planning applications, from companies not on the list, and none of them follow that pattern. Evidently these companies know the pattern, because when they know it's time for one to be rejected, they always submit an application for a much smaller project.'

'So it looks as though the planning process is fair and impartial, but actually these companies have got it sewn up.' She ran her finger over her plate, scooping up the remains of the melted butter. 'Donna Small saw what was going on, and wrote it all down, just in case.' She sucked the butter off her finger. 'Why these companies, though?'

'I wondered that,' Aidan said, whisking the plates away and moving the laptop so she couldn't touch the keys with her buttery digits. 'All the names on that list are property development companies: not extensions and garages turned into granny flats, but major building projects. If you trace back the parent companies and directors of each company, they're all owned by one company, Peterman Developments, and it's all in the hands of three men.' He unfolded his diagram of how all the companies were linked in front of her.

She traced the lines on the diagram and read out the names of the three men. 'Greg Barker, James Wallis, Don Sussman.' She puffed out her cheeks. 'Greg Barker, head of the planning committee, raking it in while no one knows he part-owns the companies.' She shoved back her chair and stretched her arms high above her head, feeling a snap in her spine. 'Cup of tea?' she offered, already heading into the kitchen. 'My brain's starting to ache with all of this.'

'That'll be grand,' Aidan called back.

She took the canister of tea down from the shelf in the kitchen and fetched the teapot from the cupboard. The shelf held twelve identical mugs regimented in three rows of four. She smiled fondly at the twelve handles all pointing the same way. Typical Aidan, brilliant and infuriating.

The tea canister needed filling, just a few black grains in the metal seam at the bottom. Trust him not to deign to use a teabag like normal people. She collected a fresh packet of tea from the pantry, and rummaged in the kitchen drawer for scissors to cut it open. The scissors were wedged at the back behind a grater. As she groped for the scissors, her hand closed around a set of keys. She drew them out and stared.

Her keys. Her spare keys, the ones she kept in her flat. Main door, front door, door to the balcony. The blue plastic tag mangled on the ring. She'd never given Aidan keys to her place, yet here were her keys.

'Aidan.'

'Um-hum?'

'Why have you got my spare keys in your kitchen drawer?'

He stood in the doorway, flushing to the roots of his hair. 'I meant to put them back,' he said, foolishly.

'I asked why have you got my keys.' The menace in her voice was unmistakeable.

Aidan recoiled. 'I wanted to find out more about you. When you said you weren't really called Eden, I felt I didn't know you at all. Lisa had said the same thing, and it bothered me.'

'So you stole my keys? Why?'

He hesitated. 'I went to your flat and had a look round. Trying to understand you.'

The world tilted. For a moment she was so shocked she couldn't speak. 'You broke into my flat and searched it?'

The hair across the door, the drawer pushed right in instead of being left partly ajar, the dust disturbed on the shelf. The sensation that the air had shifted and settled back in a different form to how she'd left it. The terror these things had evoked.

Aidan was speaking. From his tone it was excuses, reasons, apologies. She didn't hear a word.

She'd thought it was Hammond. Him, or one of his goons, in her flat, trying to frighten her. She'd barely slept, waiting for the door to come crashing down, for the strangler to step out of the shadows. Hammond's hallmark. She'd be fish food, minced into bloody gobs, before he'd let her die.

But it wasn't Hammond. The fear, the anticipation of violence were for nothing. It was Aidan, who was still blabbing.

'Shut up!' she shouted. 'You violated my home. You made me think someone had broken in.'

'I locked up. I was careful. There's no way you knew I'd been there.'

Her tone a deadly quiet, she said, 'My life is in danger. I leave traps in my flat so I know if someone's been in there. For the past few days I thought the gang had caught up with me. How do you think that's been, Aidan? And all along it was you, with your ridiculous need to know what I was christened.'

'That's not it. I want to know *you*. Everything about you.'

She twisted and reached into the cupboard. Twelve mugs, three lines of four, their handles all pointing south-east. She grabbed one and smashed it on the floor.

'Oh dear, now you've only got eleven,' she said. Eleven would torment him. He couldn't get eleven into any sort of pattern; it would drive him mad, counting them over and over. Good, let him know a fraction of what she'd suffered in the past few days, thinking Hammond had infiltrated her home.

She snatched up her things and stormed out of his flat.

CHAPTER
TWENTY-TWO

Sunday, 1 March 2015

11:52 hours

She flew home, sobbing with anger and relief. How could he? How could he break into her flat and search her belongings, determined to know everything about her as though he had a right to it? Dismay lurked beneath her fury. She'd dared to start thinking that their relationship wasn't a short-term thing, that they might even – eventually – have a future together.

She pushed inside her flat, sniffing the air, her senses on hyper-alert. Instinct told her the air hadn't shifted to accommodate someone else and she sighed with relief. Years before, when she was training – learning how to enter premises, hide a listening device, and get out again – she'd learned the science of intuition. People can sense when someone has been in their home. Nothing needed to be touched, nothing moved, but they knew. It reminded her of a time as a postgraduate student when she was sure her landlord let himself into her house to check up on the place. She never had proof, but she'd return and find the air subtly loosened, and just know.

They'd taught her to not to wear perfume or deodorant, not to shower immediately before accessing premises as even shower gel leaves a delicate trace. Someone returning to the place hours later could still detect a ghost of it. An atavistic instinct that their sanctuary had been breached.

Hammond probably knew these things, too. Knew them well enough to manipulate them to unsettle his enemies. Go in, stir the air, leave a waft of unfamiliar washing powder and leave without touching a thing. It freaked people out. It had freaked her out, thinking Hammond's men had been in her flat. But it wasn't them, it was Aidan.

She glugged down a glass of white wine, gazing out over the rooftops to the Gothic church on the square by her flat. It had long ago been turned into a restaurant. Maybe she'd take herself there for a meal, a consolation, wrap herself round a bottle of wine. Flirt with the waiters, just to piss Aidan off, even if he wasn't there to witness it. She toyed with the idea of ringing Judy, spilling to her how hurt and angry she was. And say what? That she'd been forced to tell Aidan that she wasn't really Eden Grey, that she had a new identity to protect her from the people she helped to put in prison, that Aidan had searched her flat to find out who she really was? That she was hurt by his lack of trust in her? She groaned and wrapped her arms around her head. What a bloody mess.

The phone rang. She let the machine pick it up. Aidan's voice filled the flat.

'Eden, if you're there, please pick up. I'm so sorry. I'm an absolute shit, and I know it. But I did it because I'm falling for you. Dammit, I hate these things. I'd rather tell you this to your face. It doesn't seem right telling your answering machine that I think I've fallen in love with you. Look, I'll call later. Talk to me. Please.'

She deleted the message. Love. They'd never even played at saying the L word together; was glad it hadn't ever raised its complicated, bitter-sweet head. Love was too difficult: it made demands as much as promises.

The phone rang again. Aidan.

'Eden, me again. Still talking to your machine. I love you, OK? Please let me tell you to your face.'

I love you. The last person who'd said that to her was Nick. As he was leaving, his suitcase in his hand, he'd turned at the door, looked her full in the face, and said, 'I love you. I don't think you realise how much.'

'Then don't leave,' she'd said, her heart breaking.

'I have to. I can't deal with who you've become.'

'I'm still me.'

He shook his head. 'You're not,' he'd said, gently. 'The tragedy is you can't see it.'

She was no one now. A woman with a temporary name, a transient existence, buffeted and blown on the whims of a thug she thought she'd put away forever. She'd never feel safe again. Madness to even flirt with the idea of being with Aidan long term. Hammond's web could catch up with her eventually, and she'd be off. New place, new life, new identity. As she refilled her wine glass she realised what hurt her most was the loss of what might have been. That tantalising glimpse of normality, a regular life with a decent guy, had seduced her. She'd dared to dream, and it was all gone now.

'Mummy? Mummy, wake up.'

She was underwater. The murky Thames sucked her under, filling her mouth with foulness. She kicked and struggled, desperate for breath.

'Mummy. Mummy, help me!'

'Molly!' Her lungs screamed with pain. The water dragged her under, the weight of her clothes sending her to the bottom.

Molly's face materialised in front of her, a ghostly oval. Her mouth worked a long silent scream.

'Molly, I'm coming to get you.'

She fought the water, unable to get closer. The water drew Molly further away, always out of reach. She lunged for her, saw her hands in front of her and it was a moment before she realised what was wrong. A white fan of bones, her flesh all nibbled away. She swung them uselessly, clutching at water, feeling it slip between her fingers.

Molly shrank, her legs kicking and her hair billowing around her as the water carried her off. Her scream echoed long after she'd vanished from sight.

'Molly!'

Eden jolted awake, panting, and switched on the bedside light. Three o'clock. Flopping back on the pillows, she listened to her heart thumping. Just a dream. A horrible nightmare, that's all. Nothing to be afraid of. But she didn't switch the light off when she settled back down to sleep, and it was a long time before her eyes closed again.

When she woke, groping for her alarm clock, a thin light was creeping through the curtains. Groaning, she crawled out of bed and into the shower, and ate her breakfast standing at the window, gazing out over grey, wet rooftops and the rain-blackened skeletons of trees. She switched on her mobile phone, expecting a slew of messages from Aidan. There wasn't a single one, and she was unsure whether to be relieved or annoyed. All she felt was a terrible hollow loss.

The local television breakfast news had a short feature on missing schoolgirl Chelsea. Eden heard the news report start while she was brushing her teeth, and ran into the sitting room to catch it, toothbrush in hand, her mouth full of peppermint froth. It seemed the police were at least going through the motions of launching a missing person case, even if they believed she was just a mardy runaway. The screen flashed up Chelsea's school photo. She looked young and impressionable and very, very vulnerable. A sicko's wet dream.

'Police ask anyone who's seen Chelsea to call this number,' the news reporter stated.

'Pity they didn't show a photo of her as she was that night,' Eden said aloud. In school uniform, her hair sedately fastened with a barrette, Chelsea was completely different from the photos her friends had posted up on Facebook. No one who saw her the evening she disappeared, with false eyelashes, shocking pink top and hair backcombed into a nest would equate her with the schoolgirl in the photo.

The news item changed to a report on local hospitals, and she went to rinse her mouth. There was an unpleasant metallic taste on her tongue; the taste of fear.

Monday, 2 March 2015

09:36 hours

Her threat to Chris Wilde had paid dividends. Every trace of the graffiti was gone and her office door was now a smart shiny blue, flanked by terracotta planters filled with narcissi and hyacinths. Just as she'd ordered. The heady scent of the hyacinths wafted over her, lifting her mood. After a weekend left to its own devices, though, her office ponged of damp and she left the door ajar to air it out.

Bent over her desk, working on her accounts and trying not to despair at the dwindling amount in the bank, she didn't hear them come in. When there was a cough, she jerked so violently she jarred her elbow on the desk. Excruciating pain shot down her arm to her fingertips.

'Sorry, the door was open,' the man said. He had black hair cut short, and was wearing jeans and a khaki polo shirt under a tan leather jacket. 'I did knock, but you didn't hear.'

Eden grimaced through the pain and peered past the man to the youth lurking behind him. 'Hello again, Wayne.'

Wayne Small nodded at her. His hands were stuck in his pockets and his mouth was set in a line.

'What can I do for you?' Eden asked.

'I'm Wayne's dad,' the man said. 'Barry.' He stuck out a meaty paw to shake.

'Pleased to meet you. Have a seat.' She rose and closed the door. 'Bit more private.'

As he installed himself in her client's chair, Barry continued. 'Wayne's upset about something he saw at the school last Monday. It's taken me all weekend to get it out of him, and the only person he's prepared to talk to is you.'

Barry raised his eyebrows at Eden and spread his hands as if to say 'teenagers, eh?'

She glowered at the boy, altogether out of patience with the vagaries of men and their moods. 'What happened, Wayne?'

He dropped his chin and examined his hands, giving her a view of his greasy parting. His voice came out as a mumble and she strained to hear him. 'I was mucking around with a mate. Someone from my old school.'

'What were you doing?' She spoke sharply. The shifty way he wouldn't meet her eye told its own story.

There was a swift glance at his dad before he answered her in a reluctant drone. 'We were nicking stuff.'

'You little …' Barry started. She held up her hand to warn him to let Wayne continue. There'd be time for rows later.

'We'd grabbed a couple of mobile phones and an iPad. Those kids have so much money they don't know what to do with it! It's not like we were nicking from kids whose parents saved up for things.'

'A latter-day Robin Hood,' she remarked. 'Then what?'

'Someone came, so we hid in one of the staff rooms. There was no one in there.'

'What time was it?'

He shrugged. 'About midnight.'

'Midnight!' Barry cried. 'What did your mum think you were doing?'

'I tried to tell her what happened,' Wayne said, grinding his fist into his nose. 'She never listened.'

Barry looked ready to launch a bollocking. Eden stalled him with a stare and he huffed back in his seat.

'How did you get in, Wayne?' she asked.

'Bogs window.'

So much for Rosalind Mortimer's state-of-the-art security, Eden thought. 'What happened?'

His eyes swivelled sideways to his father for a second, then Wayne continued. 'This bloke came in, with a group of girls, five of them. They were all in school uniform, like, the school's uniform, but I didn't recognise none of them.'

'How old were they?'

'Sixteen, seventeen maybe.'

'Who was the man with them?'

'I don't know.'

'A teacher at the school?'

'Never seen him before, either. The girls, they were crying and upset. All of them. And they looked weird.'

'Weird? How?'

He shook his head. 'I can't explain. Just, they looked out of it, like sleepwalking or something, but not that.'

'Drunk? Drugged?'

Wayne's eyes were dark with misery. 'I don't know, just, they weren't happy. Definitely weren't happy.'

'What happened?' Eden asked.

'They came across the room, and we ducked down and hid. I heard them go past, and a door opened, and it went quiet, and when we came out the room was empty.'

'They went back out of the room?'

'No, they came into the room, and vanished.'

Wayne's dad rubbed his eyes and shared a glance with Eden.

'Five girls, upset, aged about sixteen,' she mused, tapping her pencil on her notebook. 'The man who was with them, can you describe him?'

Wayne shrugged again. Her temper flared. The boy was as much use as a narcoleptic guide dog.

'Very helpful,' she snapped. 'How old was he? Thirty? Forty?'

'More like twenty-five.'

'Tall? Short?' When Wayne didn't answer, she asked, 'Was he taller than the girls?'

'Not much.' Wayne scratched a scab on his knuckle for a moment, then volunteered, 'He had dark hair. And dark skin, like he was Asian or something.'

'Just a moment.' An idea suddenly came to her, the slotting together of several pieces of the puzzle. It was a long shot, and didn't make much sense, but it was worth a try. She clicked through the folders on her laptop and pulled up a photograph. Twisting the laptop round so Wayne could see, she asked, 'Is this the man?'

Wayne screwed up his face and tilted his head from one side to the other while the cogs clunked round. 'Could be,' he said, finally.

Aidan rearranged the pens on his desk into size order and counted them. Then he found the middle pen, and counted the pens each side. Put them in pairs, then threes, then bundled them all together and started over again.

'All right, Aidan?' Trev asked. A blob of tomato sauce clung to the edge of his lip and there was a smear of grease on his sleeve. The office stank of the bacon butties the team had brought in to kick the week off to a good start. Aidan had barely managed a bite of his; his stomach was sour after the emotional weekend. He bagged the remains of the butty ready for the bin; revolted when Trev snaffled it and scoffed it.

Aidan scooped the pens together in his fist. 'Just thinking about something.'

'You going to the coroner's court this morning?'

'I'd better get over there.' He gathered his papers together and bundled them into a document case.

'Will that Lisa be there?' Trev asked. 'Bit of all right, isn't she? I wouldn't mind being stuck in a trench with her.'

'She's all yours, Trev, and good luck to you,' Aidan muttered.

He stewed as he drove to Gloucester for the coroner's inquest into the skeletons they'd unearthed the week before. Of course Lisa would be there, keen for a day out of the lab and a chance to wind him up. And knowing him, he'd fall for it. Again. He was thirty-six, he should be better with women by now, understand them more, but no. He was a complete twat who didn't have a clue how their minds worked and managed to fall foul of every single trap they set him.

Eden didn't set traps, a small voice at the back of his mind told him. She never lied, she just didn't give you the whole truth in a bucket when she first met you. It was Lisa who stirred it up, and you let her.

He thumped the steering wheel. He was a total loser. Lisa had insinuated herself into his life, dropping poison just as she had years ago when they were a couple. She'd gone to work on his insecurities. How well do you know Eden? Where did she go to university? Has she got brothers and sisters? She knew just how to get to him. It was the same when they were students. Going away on a dig in Italy, her cunning remarks about how handsome and attentive the Italian men were, worming away at his jealousy until he saw rivals everywhere. Totally toxic.

Now she wanted him back. Or if not him, then his child, and she'd quickly realised that Eden stood in the way. So she chipped away at him, undermining his relationship with Eden. No doubt hoping his imagination would do the rest and before long he and Eden would be history. It had bloody well worked.

Aidan groaned, certain that if he'd told Trev what Lisa had said, he'd have laughed heartily, clapped him on the shoulder and announced, 'The cunning bitch! She's trying to split you up. Tell her to fuck off, mate. I would.'

Knowing – or not knowing – about Eden's background hadn't been an issue until Lisa waltzed in with her questions and arch disbelief. He simply enjoyed Eden's company. She didn't think he was weird, she teased him affectionately about his obsessions and seemed interested in the myriad odd facts he'd squirrelled away over the years. Eden didn't mind walking over a field with a set of dowsing rods, hunting for deserted mediaeval villages. Or rummaging through second-hand book shops searching for a particular translation of Pliny that he'd set his heart on.

And he'd lost her. She was bright and intelligent and fiercely independent. She never questioned him about his friends or where he went when he wasn't with her. She didn't cling or nag or insist their weekends were spent in shoe shops or looking at clothes. She didn't expect him to spend all his free time with her, nor did she see a daily phone call as her due. She never gazed meaningfully into jewellers' windows, as Lisa had, urging him with her eyes to propose marriage, simply, he now suspected, so she could have the triumph of refusing him. No, Eden was above all that, she led her own life, and let his dovetail with hers just sufficiently that neither was stifled. And yet it was her independence, the thing he respected the most about her, that had curdled the whole relationship.

He had to get her back. Had to prove she was special to him, that he was sorry and would never, ever, do anything so crass again. He had to earn her trust.

Lisa was waiting in the reception area at the coroner's court. He bid her a brisk good morning and strode past. She let him go, but when he bought a coffee from the vending machine, she materialised at his elbow, peppering him with questions about his weekend and what he and Eden had got up to.

'You'd think they'd do these things by video link-up,' he said, not even bothering to face her. 'Save everyone a lot of time.'

He slid the cup of grey sludge from the machine and went to talk to the site foreman. When they were called in, he gave his evidence clearly, describing how he'd received a call to give an initial assessment of the skeleton that had been found, and how another skeleton had been uncovered during its retrieval. The coroner asked a few questions, then Lisa was called.

He barely heard her evidence, though he was aware that she cast a glance in his direction and simpered every so often. He was thinking about Ezekiel Proudfoot's diary, about the research he'd done in the records office, and about the Paternoster Club. When the coroner stood and dismissed them, he sprinted from the court and drove straight to the records office. Suddenly he knew how to win Eden back.

'Can I have another look at those plans you showed me last week?' he asked the archivist. 'Plans of Greville House.'

'I remember. It was the plans for the pleasure gardens, wasn't it?'

'Yes, but also the plans for the house itself, please.'

'Take a seat, I'll have to dig them out.'

When she brought them, in a huge roll, he wished his older brother was there. Patrick was an architect, and he could read these plans effortlessly. Aidan squinted and peered at them, trying to orientate the interior plans with the exterior drafts of the pleasure gardens. He stared until he saw what he was searching for.

A quick scout round the room to check he wasn't observed. The other researchers were absorbed in their reading. He drew his phone out of his jacket pocket and quickly photographed the sets of plans. He checked the photos captured what he needed, then thanked the archivist and headed back to Cheltenham with his heart quickening.

He had something that Eden would kill for.

CHAPTER
TWENTY-THREE

Monday, 2 March 2015

23:40 hours

The streets were empty this late in the evening, not even a solitary dog walker. Eden parked her car away from the arc of the street lamps, zipped up her dark jacket, and stuffed a torch in her pocket. The pavement sparkled with frost and a halo glowed around the moon. She was glad to wriggle her fingers into thermal gloves and tug on a woollen hat.

She hunched her shoulders against the cold and hurried to the Park School. The stagnant JCBs loomed as denser patches against the black. She skirted them, sprinting up the driveway to the school. The upper windows were lit but the ground floor skulked in darkness apart from a single lamp burning by the front portico. None of the pupils lived in the main house, she'd found out, but a couple of the teachers had bedsits there. It must be them, burning the lights in the upper storey.

She made a quick tour of the outside of the building, checking in case anyone was lurking. No one was about, not even a teacher grabbing a crafty fag. The satellite buildings were in darkness, but she thought she saw a light far off in the gardens, then it was extinguished.

There was a small, frosted-glass window round the side of the main building. A sash, and someone had left it unhooked. Maybe the school now had a fake Vermeer they wanted to claim on the insurance. Too easy to slide up the window and climb inside. She dropped down on to a linoleum floor, flexing her ankles and knees to land cleanly and quietly. She strained her ears for footsteps coming towards her. Silence. She clicked on the torch. She was in a small lavatory: an old fashioned cistern with a chain, and a washbasin on a wrought-iron stand. She snapped the torch off again.

Easing the door open, she peeked out. A short corridor led to the main entrance hall, where a magnificent staircase curved up towards a domed skylight. Rosalind Mortimer's office lay through a doorway to one side of the huge stone fireplace. A door on the other side bore a brass nameplate that stated 'Reception'. The far side of the entrance hall had a door marked 'Common Room'. She went in.

The room was gloomy: the curtains had been drawn but were thin and didn't quite meet in the middle. A vague light came from outside, enough to make out a fireplace, sofas and chairs arranged in clusters, a bookcase and a stack of magazines. The room smelled of old upholstery and toast, and the ghosts of many cigarettes from long ago.

Eden padded across the room, imagining where Wayne and his light-fingered friend might have hidden. Possibly behind this large sofa. She crouched down to establish his field of vision. She could see the door from there, but nothing else unless she stood up. Wayne said that he heard the girls and the man with them pass him by, then a door opening. There must be another door. She was crawling out from behind the sofa when a hand grabbed her shoulder.

She stifled a scream. Clutching the hand on her shoulder, in one move she twisted down and away, springing to her feet with the stranger bent over, keeping the arm taut and the wrist under pressure.

'Eden, let me go, please. You're breaking my wrist.'

She was so astonished she dropped his hand. He curled away, rubbing his arm. 'That really hurt.'

'Aidan!' she hissed. 'What are you doing here?'

'Waiting for you.' She saw his teeth flash in a smile. 'Where else would you be on a Monday night but breaking into Cheltenham's most exclusive school?'

'How did you get in?'

'Front door was open. You?'

She flicked the torch briefly, and scowled at his grin. 'What are you doing here?' she whispered.

'Looking for you. I've found something I think you're going to like.'

'Sh!' She stiffened. 'A car. Quick.'

She pulled him down behind the sofa as a car's headlights swept across the windows. Voices outside; doors opening and slamming. She ducked down further as the door to the common room opened.

'Right, girls, in you go,' a male voice said.

Long, pale bare legs passed inches in front of her. Three girls in school uniform, dragging their feet, stumbling and unsteady. She held her breath as the footsteps moved down the room. A door opened and closed, and the air in the room flowed back in to fill the gap.

Slowly she raised her head. The room was empty. She turned to Aidan and pressed her fingers to her lips.

'Do you want to follow them?' Aidan mouthed.

She nodded. 'Give them a few minutes. I'm not sure what we're getting into here but I suspect it's not going to be nice.'

'Should I have brought my service revolver?' Aidan asked, 'so I can be Watson to your Holmes?'

'Do you have one?'

'No. Do you?'

'Not any more.' She sighed. 'You'd better go home, Aidan, this could get nasty.'

'You're not doing this on your own.'

'It's my job and my case. And I've had training for this sort of thing.'

'Whereas I can't even break into your flat without your knowing.' He caught her hand. 'I'm a complete shit, and I'll piss off out of your life if that's what you want, but only after we finish this. You might hate me but I'm not letting you go in there on your own.'

'Why?'

'Because I have an idea what they're up to,' he said. 'And I love you.'

She got to her feet and moved about the room, hunting for a doorway, tapping on the panelling and running her hand around the decorative mantelpiece.

'Is this what you're looking for?' Aidan said, at the far end of the room, holding a door open. It was hidden behind a bookcase, a front of leather-bound tomes that swung out into the room.

'How did you know where it was?' Eden asked.

'Looked up the architect's plans this morning. Come on.'

The door led into a dark passageway that ran a short distance along the side of the house, then dipped down a flight of stone stairs. They inched down them, deeper and deeper, until they reached a hard floor. Eden pointed her torch down and flicked it on and off, just enough to make out a narrow tunnel stretching in front of them. They stood silently in the dark for a moment, listening. No sound of the girls or the man.

'Where does this lead to?' Eden asked, her mouth close to Aidan's ear.

'To the Temple of Venus on the other side of the gardens,' he whispered back.

'The Paternoster Club,' Eden said. 'Donna wrote P.N. in her diary every Monday. I thought it stood for Paul Nelson.'

She gripped the torch firmly and set off down the tunnel, keeping one hand on the slimy stone wall to steady herself. She daren't switch on the torch. With Aidan close behind, they crept along the tunnel until they bumped into another set of stone steps, leading up. At the top of the steps was a small room lit by two candles. The meagre light revealed more than enough. Every inch of wall was painted with grotesque images.

'Regency snuff,' she breathed, her stomach churning. A year working on illegal pornography hadn't hardened her to face this. Out of the corner of her eye, she caught Aidan flinching.

On the far side of the room was a doorway. A line of light seeped underneath it. She edged towards it and bent her ear to the door. Voices and moans. Girls crying. She counted the different voices and her heart sank.

'Four men,' she told Aidan in a whisper. 'I've got to go in, those girls are in danger. Go back through the tunnel and call the police. Tell them it's a Code Tango Sierra. Got that?'

'No, we're going in together,' he said.

'Aidan, I'm serious.'

'So am I.'

One glance at his face showed her he wasn't going to budge.

'OK,' she said. 'On my signal. Ready?'

As they burst into the room, she had a split second to take in the candlesticks burning along each wall; two girls, huddled together in a corner, crying; the sadism depicted on every wall; and a long velvet chaise in the centre of the room occupied by a man in his early fifties and a girl of about fifteen. She was screaming.

Aidan lunged at the man and dragged him off the girl. Eden was aware of the two men grappling on the floor, but before she could help another man leapt at her. She swung the torch and smashed it into his temple. He staggered and came at her again. This time she cracked him hard across the face, spinning him back against the wall. He crumpled against it and lay still.

Arms clamped round her arms, dragging her backwards, lifting her off her feet. She snapped her head back and her skull connected, hard, with bony skull. Dazed, it was a moment before her vision cleared but the grip around her body had loosened. She hooked her foot behind her and twisted it around his ankle. Jabbing both elbows down with as much force as she could muster, and stabbing her heel into his instep, she managed to topple him. They both crashed to the floor. She heard the explosion of air as he landed hard on the stone floor, but his arm was still round her neck.

As the pressure on her windpipe increased, stars exploded in her eyes and the edges of her vision narrowed. Stretching behind her head, she rammed her fingers into his eye sockets. He screamed and the pressure on her neck released just enough for her to wriggle round. Sitting astride him, she swung the torch across his face, busting his nose in an arc of blood, and sending a tooth flying. His head lolled. She swung again, but the fourth man grabbed her wrist, bending it back until she released the torch. It rattled away across the floor.

He dragged her to her feet. She ducked and twisted, pain searing her shoulder socket, but it loosened his grip. She chopped the back of his neck and he let go of her. Straightening, she found herself looking at the blade of a knife.

'Game, set and match to me, I think,' Greg Barker said.

Two of the men were still unconscious on the floor. She glanced round for Aidan. He'd gone. So had the man he was fighting. Her guts twisted with fear.

Don't look at the blade. That's what she'd been taught. Look them straight in the eyes. She fixed her gaze on Greg's eyes, chilled to find nothing there. His eyes were blank and cold and devoid of emotion, like a shark.

'Why did you kill Paul?' she asked, playing for time. Please God let Aidan be calling the police right now. 'Didn't you want him to join your little club?'

'Of course we didn't want him!' Greg laughed without humour. 'Do you really think he'd fit in here?' He cast a glance at the paintings on the walls: a vision of hell.

'So why invite him to join?'

'We didn't. He found out about the Paternoster Club, found out that members enjoyed a certain level of business success. He thought it was some sort of networking group, business leaders working together for the common good and inspiring each other with entrepreneurship.' He laughed again. 'That's not what we're about. But he'd heard about the club so we went through with a certain amount of formality, for form's sake.'

'An initiation ceremony,' Eden said. 'You killed him.'

'That kind of talk's slander.' The blade swung close to her eyes. She fought the urge to step back. Play for time, keep him talking. Where the hell was Aidan? Please God, let him be safe.

'Not if you have proof,' Eden spat back at him. 'Paul was killed with a lucky bean, a Paternoster pea. It's poisonous if you chew it. You didn't tell him to swallow it whole.'

'A lucky bean? A poisonous pea?' Greg mocked. 'Where would I get such a thing? A fairy tale?'

'Your wife's necklace. Those red and black beans are Paternoster peas. The necklace broke. You didn't throw the beans away, did you?'

'You have no proof.'

'It'll be in your house, Greg. And your wife still has the matching bracelet.' Her vision swam. 'Did Donna Small tell you to kill Paul?'

'Donna! What a pain she was. No, she wanted Paul to join the club, thought it was a good business idea.'

'She knew about the planning applications, didn't she?' Eden said.

'Yeah,' Greg sniffed, 'and she made me pay. I paid for her gormless son to go to the Park School, paid her credit card bills every month and by God could that woman spend.'

'What happened?'

'She fancied herself as Paul's new wife, spending his money as well as mine. Thought if he joined the Paternoster Club, he could keep her in style. Thought telling him about it was a way to win him back.' He shook his head. 'Silly bitch.'

Eden let her gaze travel round the room. The two men were stirring, lifting their heads and rubbing blood from their eyes. She didn't have long.

'Did Donna know about the girls?' Eden asked.

'No, she challenged me about Paul, and started blabbing about seeing something suspicious at the school.'

Wayne was wrong: Donna had listened to him. If only she'd gone to the police instead of confronting Greg, she would still be alive.

'So you strangled her.'

Greg flashed his teeth. He stepped towards her, and pressed the blade against her throat. 'Donna didn't approve of our little love nest here.'

'I wonder why.' Eden fixed her eyes on his as the blade pushed cold against her skin. 'Now!'

At her word, a candlestick crashed down hard on Greg's skull. He staggered and fell, the knife clattering from his hand. Gasping and brandishing the candlestick, stood one of the girls.

'Well done, Chelsea,' Eden said. The girl collapsed in tears on the floor. Eden wrapped her arms around her and stroked her hair. 'It's fine, you're safe. You're all safe.'

Eden yanked the belts from the three men and pinioned their arms to their sides. Greg cursed as she fastened him to the chaise in the middle of the room. Chelsea helped her secure the men, tugging the belts tight, tears dropping from her eyes as she worked. Her left eye was swollen, a cut splitting her eyebrow like a burst plum. The other two girls hunkered in the corner of the room, eyes staring, too shocked to move.

'You must be daddy Sussman,' Eden said, pulling the belt so tight around him that his eyes popped. 'And you must be Zamir. Nice family business you've got here. The people trafficker and the paedophile.'

In the distance came the sound of sirens. Thank God, Aidan must've called the police. Eden straightened and spoke to the girls. 'I'm going to give you a few moments alone. You don't have long: the police will be here soon.'

She stepped out of the temple into the cold night and watched the blue lights swarm up the driveway. She didn't hear three terrified girls taking revenge on the men who'd brutalised and sold them. She didn't hear the men screaming or the girls swearing. She didn't hear a thing.

She was giving a brief summary of the evening's events to a police officer when Aidan returned, dishevelled and bleeding. His coat was torn and his lip split open. She ran into his arms, choking with relief.

'I lost him,' he said.

'James Wallis is the man you're looking for, officer,' she said. 'And you should arrest the headmistress, Rosalind Mortimer, too, for defrauding her insurance company over a faked Constable painting, and she knew about the girls being brought here.'

'How do you know?' Aidan asked, touching his tip of his tongue to his lip and wincing.

'When the skeletons were found, she assumed there'd been a murder. Her reaction was to say "the girls", not "the pupils". I think she assumed one of the trafficked girls had been killed.'

'What would have happened to the girls after tonight?' Aidan asked.

'Sold on,' Eden said, shuddering inside.

She looked across at the flashing blue lights, where Zamir, Greg and Don were being loaded, handcuffed, into a police van. The three girls, cocooned in silver blankets, were in the back of an ambulance. They had the rest of their lives to try and forget what happened that night. She understood how that felt.

'Take you home?' Aidan asked quietly.

'Yes, please,' she said, slipping her hand in his. 'Take me home.'

CHAPTER
TWENTY-FOUR

Cheltenham, November 1795

The girl at the water fountain wore a mob cap that slipped down over her eyes. She smiled constantly as she poured glasses of water and handed them to patrons, hardly seeming aware of their grimaces as they drank the foul stuff.

Rachel received her glass of water and slid her penny on to the cool marble counter. She carried the glass away from the braying crowds and sucked in a deep breath before she downed it. Over the weeks she'd been coming to the spa for the waters, she'd experimented with a variety of ways to drink the water: sipping it down drop by drop, glugging it in stages, and now, sluicing it down in one. She tipped the glass back, closed her eyes, and swallowed.

When she came up for air, her eyes were smarting and she fought the urge to shake her head like a dog that's been fed mustard. She shuddered as the water caught the back of her throat and the whole lot threatened to reappear in a rainbow on the spa's marble floor. She probably wouldn't be the first person to be sick after drinking the water. The clenching in her stomach receded and she breathed easily. Another dose done. If only it would have some effect.

She glanced around the spa, at the women wincing as they sipped the water, at the men guffawing and affecting bravery, and misery washed over her. Nineteen, pox-ridden and in need of the mercury cure; a whore held captive by Mrs Bedwin's evil tongue. She suddenly yearned for her old life: poor, simple and hard though it was. For a second, Rachel wished the water would be the end of her.

The mood passed as quickly as it had come when she saw the women eyeing her gown and reticule. Fine fabrics in the latest colours, not like these frumps. She smoothed her gown and affected not to notice their stares. As she gazed steadily in the opposite direction, her attention was caught by a familiar figure. Darby Roach. She twisted away but it was too late, he'd seen her.

'Rachel. Miss Lovett,' he said, trotting up to her side and bowing.

She bobbed a curtsey. 'Mr Roach.'

'What are you doing here?' He saw the glass in her hand and his eyes widened. 'You're not ill?'

'Oh no,' she said, smiling prettily, pushing aside thoughts of the sores blooming under her hair. 'The water is said to keep you young and beautiful.' She fluttered her eyelashes at him.

He wasn't taken in. 'I would have thought you'd know more tricks than evil tasting water for that,' he said. He gripped her arm and pulled her aside. His mouth was so close to her face, she could smell violet cashews on his breath. 'Only I've heard some people take the waters if they have the pox.'

He stared meaningfully at her. She stared back, defying him to contradict her.

'Is that why you're here, Darby?' she asked.

That wrong-footed him. 'No, no,' he said, releasing her arm. 'Meeting my banker. My building plans are going so quickly I need to withdraw more funds to pay the builders.'

'So you'll be rich soon?'

'I'm rich now,' he said.

Rich now? Then where was the house for them, with the maid and the carriage and the prettiest furniture money could buy?

He didn't notice her silence, but continued, 'There's some upstart trying to get into the game. Wants to buy some land and start building.' He laughed. 'The club will see to him.'

'Oh?'

'He can't buy unless he's in the club. The club controls who buys and sells the land.'

'Isn't that up to the person who owns the land?' she asked.

Darby snorted. 'Poor innocent Rachel! The club can be very persuasive, if you understand me.'

A look she didn't like shivered across his face, and she recalled a rumour of a local farmer who refused to sell his land being found hanged in his field. The coroner's verdict was suicide, but the land passed to his son, who immediately sold it to Mr Ellison. Rachel tugged her shawl tighter around her.

'And will you let this new man into the club?' she asked.

'No,' Darby said scornfully. 'He'll have to pass the initiation, and we'll make sure he doesn't.'

'How?'

Darby wheeled her away from the crowds. Speaking in a low voice, he said, 'You remember the part with the bean in the glass of wine?'

She nodded.

'It's poisonous,' Darby breathed.

'Poisonous? Then how did you manage to eat it and survive?'

His breath sent ice across her skin as he whispered, 'It's only poisonous if you chew it. They told me to swallow it whole. This new fellow … well, they might forget his instructions.'

It was Rodney he was talking about, she knew it. Poor Rodney. Dear, kind Rodney, who loved her and who wanted to take her away from all this. She'd sent him to Mr Ellison, led him straight into the lion's den. Poor booby probably thought it was all just a bit of high jinks, like boys at school. Little did he realise the danger he was in. She had to warn him, and soon. The next meeting was that very night.

Mrs Bedwin cast an experienced eye round the girls and selected Roseanne and Felicity to attend Greville House.

'I'll go,' Rachel said. 'I don't mind.' She had to get in there somehow, she had to warn Rodney. She couldn't bear it if anything happened to him. It wasn't just his promises to take her away, set her up in her own house, she loved him. She loved him and she'd sent him into the jaws of death. All because he wanted to be rich enough for her.

I'd have him even if he was poor, she swore to herself, as she begged Mrs Bedwin to let her attend Greville House that evening.

'You is too lascivious for words,' Mrs Bedwin declared, her brown hairpiece waggling. 'And greedy. You only went the last time because Daphne got herself in a state.'

'No, truly, Mrs Bedwin,' she said, but Mrs Bedwin wasn't having any of it.

'It's Roseanne and Felicity, and that's an end to it. You can look after the regular customers here. Make your twenty guineas that way.' And she went off cackling.

Undeterred, Rachel went to Roseanne and begged to go in her place.

Roseanne shrugged. 'They'll notice, won't they? They ask for me,' she indicated her mahogany skin, 'they're going to notice if a fair girl turns up.'

So she tried Felicity. Tried tales of murder and sacrifice, of blood drinking and summoning the devil, but Felicity wasn't swayed.

'I've heard you get twenty guineas for going there for one evening,' she said. 'I'm not losing twenty guineas for you.'

Desperately, Rachel said, 'I'll give you the twenty guineas. Please, Felicity.'

Felicity goggled at the offer. 'Mrs Bedwin's right,' she said. 'You do like it strange. What, is a bit of slapping and pinching not enough for you?'

Rachel didn't reply. She fetched the money from where she'd hidden it and handed it over. Felicity tucked the money into her bosom, where it was well concealed, and agreed to change places.

That evening, Felicity and Roseanne dressed for Greville House. As the carriage waited for them in front of the house, Rachel slipped out of the back door and scurried round to the far side of the carriage. When Felicity entered the carriage, her hood pulled over her head, she scuttled across the seats and out of the far door, and Rachel climbed up inside in her place. Emma had been primed to create a disturbance so Mrs Bedwin was distracted, and the carriage moved off without Mrs Bedwin noticing the switch.

Once in the house, Rachel searched for Rodney amongst the men at the feast. He wasn't there. He would be in the tunnel, she thought to herself, or waiting to enter the temple. Probably getting into robes and a mask right now. She'd see him soon, and could warn him. Whisper to him not to chew the bean; save his life.

Her thoughts rattled on. When Rodney passed the initiation test, they'd have to let him into the Paternoster Club, and then he could buy the land he wanted. So much for Darby and Mr Ellison thinking they controlled it all. She hid a smirk as she imagined Darby's dismay when Rodney survived his initiation.

As before, she went through the tunnel and met the bedraggled girls. One was coughing horribly, spitting bloody phlegm on to the earth floor. Her eyes were sunken and her skin was grey. The odour of the grave already hung about her like a miasma. None of the girls spoke, whipped into silent despair.

They didn't have to wait long in the cold antechamber before they were taken into the temple. Mr Ellison presided over the initiation, his ram's head mask terrifying. The candles created pools of light and dark, and the men clung to the shadows. Rachel peered into the darkness, struggling to see Rodney. The men were all masked, grotesque in the gloom, and she could barely see. Maybe Rodney wasn't here at all?

Mr Ellison intoned the words, and the initiate stepped forwards. Rachel inched closer, squinting. Surely that was Rodney's walk? It must be him under that mask. They'd given him a rabbit mask; not a fox or lion like the other initiates. Her heart twisted. Poor Rodney, he probably didn't even realise they were laughing at him, in his rabbit's mask with droopy ears.

She swished her skirts about her, trying to draw his attention. He turned briefly towards her, and she started to mouth, 'Don't chew the bean,' but he'd turned away again before she finished.

Rodney was slowly circling the temple. As he approached, she stared boldly at him, trying to catch his eye. Did he see her? She couldn't tell, not with that ridiculous rabbit mask. Desperately she mouthed, 'Don't chew the bean. Rodney, don't chew the bean.'

His steps neither slowed nor faltered. Had he seen her? Did he understand what she was trying to tell him? Her heart thudded against her ribs. What if he didn't see her, didn't understand, and chewed the bean. He'd die. Her heart wrenched at the thought. He couldn't die, not her own sweet Rodney.

Mr Ellison, his ram's head mask looming above them all, poured wine into a goblet. Instead of offering the box of beans to Rodney and dropping it into the wine, he proffered the box, and when Rodney selected one, he said, firmly, 'Chew this bean twenty times. Though it be bitter, the wine will wash the bitterness away.'

Rodney's hand hovered over the box. His fingers dipped in, and he pulled out a bean and held it aloft. Rachel stared in horror as he put it into his mouth.

She lunged forwards, shrieking, 'Don't chew it! It's poisonous! Rodney, don't eat it!'

Mr Ellison whipped round and struck her across the face. She collapsed on the stone floor, screaming, 'Don't eat it! It'll kill you!'

Ellison kicked her in the stomach. She curled into a ball, her arms around her head as he kicked again. 'Shut up, whore!'

Rodney dropped the bean and ran over to Rachel. Shoving Mr Ellison aside, he dropped to his knees beside her, throwing off the rabbit mask, and gathering her into his arms.

'Rachel.'

His face was blurred through her tears. 'You didn't eat it, did you? It's poisonous.'

Rodney shook his head. 'No. My God, Rachel.' He clamped her against his breast.

'Get them out of here,' Mr Ellison snapped.

Four masked men dragged them through the antechamber and down into the tunnel, Mr Ellison following. The men dumped them on the floor, then at a signal from Ellison, they vanished into the darkness. He towered over them, his ram's head mask an evil shadow on the wall, then raised his hands and lifted off the mask. Rachel's heart stuttered. She'd assumed the mask concealed Mr Ellison. She was wrong.

'Darby!' Rachel breathed.

'You meddling whore.'

'Don't speak to her like that,' Rodney said. 'Is it true, about the bean being poisonous?'

Darby rounded on him. 'As if we'd let an upstart like you in the Paternoster Club.'

Rodney sprang to his feet, his fists bunched in front of his face.

Darby snickered as Rodney bounced on the balls of his feet. 'You think you can fight me?'

'Come on, then.'

Darby ignored him. 'What am I going to do about you two? You know far too much.' He pressed his hands together, as if praying, and set his fingers against his lips. He looked from Rachel to Rodney with an expression that turned her insides to water.

Rodney flew to Rachel and shoved her behind him. 'Don't hurt her.'

'Do be quiet,' Darby said.

In one smooth movement he drew a knife out of his belt and stabbed Rodney in the chest. Rodney collapsed to his knees, blood bubbling from his mouth. Darby forced the knife in to the hilt and twisted it. He tugged the knife free and wiped it clean on Rodney's coat. Holding the blade up to the light, Darby spat in disgust. The tip of the knife had snapped off.

Rachel stared in horror as Rodney twitched in a pool of his own blood. Eventually he gargled, sprayed a gout of blood, and was still.

'Rodney!' she whispered, too shocked to cry.

She made to run to him, but Darby held her back.

'That's enough trouble from you,' he said.

She had no time to scream. His hands were round her neck. His rank breath on her face. She struggled and kicked as the blackness overcame her, then kicked no more.

CHAPTER
TWENTY-FIVE

Tuesday, 3 March 2015

09:26 hours

Her arms and legs ached and her body was a mass of bruises. She felt as though she was ninety years old, it hurt to move so desperately. Yet the memory of Chelsea's mother's face, when she was told the news that her daughter was safe, cheered and comforted her. Chelsea and the other girls were in hospital, being checked over and assessed, and would receive counselling to get over their trauma. The nightmares would stop. Eventually. And Chelsea was a fighter. Eden grinned at the expression on Greg's face when Chelsea decked him with the candlestick. The girl had guts.

Eden had an appointment to go into the police station to make a statement later that morning, but for now there was a pile of receipts to reconcile, and her case notes on Paul, Donna and Chelsea to write up.

First things first. Today had an air of celebration about it: a nasty swag of villains banged up. In her old job that would have meant an evening down the pub getting absolutely bladdered, and a big fry-up to compensate the next morning before they went back to business as usual.

This was no time to break with tradition. She headed out of her office and along to Tony's sandwich shop. He was standing in the doorway soaking up the early spring sunshine.

'Global warming,' he greeted her.

'Egg and bacon butty, please,' she said.

He peeled himself away from the sun and they went into the steamy sandwich shop.

'You catch many scumbags lately, Eden?' he asked, as he always did.

'One or two,' she said, with a smile. 'Loads of brown sauce on the bap, please, Tony. I've earned it.'

She watched him frying the bacon and flipping the egg, the white frilling and crisping at the edges, just how she liked it. She hummed to herself as she carried the paper package back to her office. Today was a good day and she was happy and light. The sun was shining, the hyacinths in their planter were pumping out a heady scent of spring, and there was a bacon and egg bap in her hand. Life couldn't get any better.

As she pushed open the office door, she cast an eye over the car park. Two spaces down from her car was a red Skoda Octavia. Her heart stuttered. The car that had followed her was a red Skoda Octavia. She stared at it for a moment, then chided herself it was only a car, one of hundreds like it. The fact it was parked only yards from hers didn't mean a thing.

She stepped inside, jolting when the door slammed shut behind her. Whipping round, she took in a thick bull's neck garlanded with a spider's web tattoo. A face from the past, last seen on TV outside the Court of Appeal, confronted her.

'Hello, Jackie. Or is it Eden, now?'

'Hello, Nutter.'

They eyeballed each other for a long moment.

'Well, it's been nice chatting to you, Dave,' Eden said, her breath tight in her chest, 'but I've got to get on.'

'We both know that's not going to happen.'

Her eyes locked on his.

'Time's up,' Nutter said. 'You're going on a little journey.'

'How did you find me?'

Nutter laughed. 'Hammond can buy anyone he wants,' he said.

'You're still working for him, then?' Keep him talking; there must be a way out. Think!

'I'm loyal, me.' He jutted his chin. 'Not like you.'

Eden spread her hands. 'Just doing my job. Nothing personal.'

'I did two years in high security 'cause of you,' Nutter spat. A glob of spittle landed on Eden's cheek. She fought the urge to wipe it away.

Nutter took a step towards her and she rammed the scorching butty into his face. He hesitated only for a second, then came for her. She backed away until the edge of the desk slammed the back of her thighs. Desperately she groped behind her for anything she could use as a weapon. Her hand fastened around a pencil.

Nutter grabbed her arm and twisted it. Little Jimmy captured and tortured; Hammond's hallmarks on his body. Now it was her turn. A low moan escaped her lips.

She lunged with the pencil, aiming for Nutter's eye. He anticipated the blow and swiped her arm aside. With his other arm, he punched the side of her head. It was his left hand, and the punch fell short, but it knocked her off her feet. Winded and dazed, she had a close up of the carpet before Nutter hauled her to her feet, clamping his arm round her neck in a stranglehold.

'Fire! Fire!' was all she managed to scream before his meaty arm crushed her throat. She kicked wildly for his instep. He grunted but didn't release her. The pressure increased. She tasted blood; smelled a dark, feral odour. Black spots exploded before her eyes. As she faded, she saw what he'd left on her desk, and knew the fate that awaited her: plastic ties, a gag, and a hood.

'Eden! Eden!' Light in her eyes. She fumbled her hand to her throat, gasped, retched, and rolled on to her side, groaning.

'Where's he gone?' she croaked.

'He's there.' Aidan nodded at Nutter lying motionless on the floor.

'Is he dead?'

'No.'

'Never mind.' Her throat spasmed as she fought for breath. She coughed and struggled to sit up.

Footsteps sounded on the metal walkway and Tony burst inside. 'What the hell's going on? Eden? Are you OK? Where's the fire?'

'I'm fine, Tony. Call the police, please. I've been attacked.'

'And the ambulance,' Aidan called after him. Turning back to her, he said, 'You need checking out. He nearly killed you.'

Slowly she eased herself to her feet and looked about her. The office door was wide open. A bouquet lay outside, and one of her planters was smashed. Bulbs, flowers and compost were strewn over the carpet.

Her throat was on fire. She staggered to the kitchen unit and poured a glass of water. Impossible to swallow. She choked it back up, spitting bloody froth into the sink.

'What happened?' she whispered.

'I came to bring you these,' Aidan said, picking up the bouquet. 'I was locking the car when I heard you scream, so I ran up, and found him trying to strangle you.' He perched on the desk next to her and slipped his arm round her shoulders. 'I didn't think. I grabbed the plant pot and hit him with it.'

'Thank God you did,' Eden said. She glanced at the plastic ties, the hood, the gag. How long would Nutter have kept her here, captive, before delivering her to her executioner? She shivered and pressed closer to Aidan.

Nutter snorted and let out a groan, then crumpled back into unconsciousness.

'Who is he?' Aidan asked.

'Someone from my life before.'

Aidan said nothing, just squeezed her tight. She winced. 'Bruises from last night's fight,' she said, ruefully.

'Eden,' he began, lacing his fingers in hers. 'Is it all over now? The past?'

For now, she thought. After this escapade, sending Nutter to kill her, Hammond would be moved to a high-security prison. That'd clip his wings for a little while.

Sirens wailed close by. 'I think they might be for us,' she said, and went to meet them.

ABOUT THE AUTHOR
KIM FLEET

KIM FLEET holds an MA and a PhD in Social Anthropology from the University of St Andrews and is a Fellow of the Royal Anthropological Institute. A freelance writer, life coach and teacher, she is the author of two books, *Featherfoot* (Kindle, 2012) and *Sacred Site* (Picnic Publishing, 2009), and has had over forty short stories published in magazines in the UK and Australia, including *Woman's Weekly*, *People's Friend*, *Take a Break*, and *That's Life Fast Fiction*. She lives in Cheltenham.

Visit our website and discover thousands of
other History Press books.

www.thehistorypress.co.uk

Lightning Source UK Ltd.
Milton Keynes UK
UKOW06f1104190415

249899UK00002B/5/P